14 DAY BOOK
OVERDUE FINE
25¢ PER DAY

BURIED

Also by Ellison Cooper

Caged

BURIED

ELLISON COOPER

Minotaur Books
New York

This is a work of fiction. All of the characters, organizations, and events portrayed in this novel are either products of the author's imagination or are used fictitiously.

First published in the United States by Minotaur Books,
an imprint of St. Martin's Publishing Group

 For information, address St. Martin's Publishing Group, 120 Broadway, New York, NY 10271.

www.minotaurbooks.com

Library of Congress Cataloging-in-Publication Data

Names: Cooper, Ellison, author.
Title: Buried / Ellison Cooper.
Description: First Edition. | New York : Minotaur Books, 2019.
Identifiers: LCCN 2018055981 | ISBN 9781250173867 (hardcover) |
ISBN 9781250173881 (ebook)
Subjects: LCSH: Women detectives—Fiction. | Serial murder
investigation—Fiction. | GSAFD: Suspense fiction.
Classification: LCC PS3603.O582623 B87 2019 | DDC 813/.6—dc23
LC record available at https://lccn.loc.gov/2018055981

Our books may be purchased in bulk for promotional, educational, or business use. Please contact your local bookseller or the Macmillan Corporate and Premium Sales Department at 1-800-221-7945, extension 5442, or by email at MacmillanSpecialMarkets@macmillan.com.

First Edition: July 2019

10 9 8 7 6 5 4 3 2 1

For my son, Grayson, who teaches me something new
every day about living a life full of courage and joy

Acknowledgments

I would like to express my heartfelt thanks to everyone who helped to make *Buried* happen. While writing is a solitary endeavor, publishing a book takes a team, and there is no way *Buried* would exist without the help and support of all these people.

Thank you to my agent and goddess of calm, Amy Tannenbaum. I am so grateful for her expert guidance and advice. Thanks also to Danielle Sickles and Meg Ruley. All of the people at the Jane Rotrosen Agency are both kick-ass and kind and I appreciate everything they do.

I'm also immensely grateful for my incomparable editor, Leslie Gelbman, who wields her experience and vision with kindness and humor. Thanks also to Hector DeJean, Joe Brosnan, Allison Ziegler, Paul Hochman, Tiffany Shelton, and Kelley Ragland. Everyone at St. Martin's is a dynamo and I feel so lucky to have such an amazing team working on the Sayer series with me.

Endless thanks to Megan Coen for our long brainstorming lunches. I get to hammer out most of my best ideas talking to her, and she helps make everything so much creepier!

A special thank-you to my neighbors, Theresa Iantosca, who is the best beta reader and first editor out there, and to David Head for all of his encouragement.

Thank you also to Sarah Madwell, child-wrangler extraordinaire and social media consultant for when I can't figure out how to work that new-fangled Instagram.

Much appreciation to all the experts I spoke with, including Anna Cordova, Michael Stowe, and Amiee Placas; thank you for lending me your time and expertise!

Thank you to my sensitivity readers, who wish to remain anonymous. And I raise a glass to the entire Curbside Crew, the best neighbors in the world, who regularly let me to talk to them about serial killers.

I would like to acknowledge the incredible people who volunteer to be bone marrow donors. Organizations like Be the Match are out there helping people connect with life-saving donors every day.

Finally, thank you to my family for their endless faith in me. To my parents, Bob and Judy, who taught me to be fearless while pursuing my dreams. To my sister, Shelley, and her family, Pat, Thomas, and Rowan, for being my biggest cheerleaders. To my son, Grayson, who is always so proud of my accomplishments.

And, as always, eternal thanks to Sean, my partner and best friend. His unyielding belief in me and my writing makes all the difference.

BURIED

TURK GAP TRAIL,
SHENANDOAH NATIONAL PARK, VA

Maxwell Cho enjoyed the hushed stillness of the Shenandoah Mountains. Even his wolfish dog, Kona, sensed the need to rein in her boundless energy as she walked quietly by his side. Max took a deep breath and leaned back to stare up at the thick canopy of copper and gold foliage in the cool morning sun.

"I think we've reached peak autumn, girl." The off-duty FBI agent spoke softly, not wanting to break the spell. He'd been waiting months for a day off and could practically feel the stress melting away. He loved living in the vibrant grittiness of Washington, D.C., but he sure as hell missed the mountains sometimes.

Max was about to continue along the steep trail when Kona froze. She stood at full attention, nose working furiously in the air.

He froze as well. He knew damn well enough to trust his dog. Plus, there'd been a few bear sightings nearby.

"What is it, Kona?"

He scanned the rocky bluff rising above the treetops to the north. Along the thick woods to the east.

Nothing.

But then Kona barked. Not the deep *ruff* she was trained to use when they were on a live search, this was the sharp bark, tail straight out behind her, that she used when she scented a dead body.

Her human-cadaver alert.

"We're not working. Let's keep moving." He waved the dog onward, but Kona alerted again, refusing to budge. As an FBI Human Remains Detection K9 Team, Max and Kona specialized in finding lost people, dead or alive. And she seemed firmly convinced that they were suddenly on duty.

Max stopped and sighed. So much for a late lunch with his mom after a long hike in the mountains. She was probably already cooking a banquet just for him and there would be hell to pay if he had to cancel.

"You really smell something?"

Kona barked again and then did something Max had never seen in their four years working together—she whimpered.

Apprehension tickled the nape of his neck.

"Hold up. Let me call this in before we go off on some wild-goose chase."

Max pulled out his phone and dialed.

"Shenandoah National Park, how can I direct your call?" a woman asked with a deep Southern twang.

Max recognized the voice and paused for a long moment, rethinking his strategy. He knew practically everyone in the area, having grown up in Rockfish Gap, not twenty miles south of where he was. When he'd come back from Iraq, there was a damn good reason he joined the FBI rather than the local police force. But he couldn't let old wounds get in the way of doing his job.

"Piper, it's Max Cho."

"Max! So great to hear your voice. How've you been? You in town visiting your mom?"

"Yeah, I was planning to see her later today, but I'm actually calling to report something. I'm up here hiking near Turk Mountain and my Human Remains Detection dog just alerted."

"Aw, hell. Like one of those dogs that can smell dead people? You think there's a body up there?"

"Could be. I've never seen her false-alert, and something's definitely got her spooked. You have any missing folks in the area?"

Max held his hand up flat, signaling Kona to hold. She danced in place, desperate to hunt down whatever it was that she smelled.

"No one right now," the park ranger said.

"Okay. I'll let my dog search it out and will let you know if we find anything."

"You want me to send a ranger out to help?"

Max watched Kona. She stood rigid, so focused on the scent she could barely hold her body still. "Nah, my dog's about to come out of her skin, so I'm betting whatever it is, is close. Let me find it first so we know exactly what we've got here."

As Max spoke, Kona's hackles rose. Every alarm in Max's body went off.

"Well, why don't you at least tell me where you are so I can let someone know that they'll need to head your way soon?"

Max read his coordinates from his phone and said softly, "I'll call you when I find it."

"You be careful out there in the big bad woods," the park ranger gently teased.

Max clicked off and jumped slightly when Kona alerted again. He wondered when he'd lost the bravado of youth. Hell, he used to jump out of helicopters behind enemy lines. Here he was now, spooked by the thought of a dead body somewhere out here in the Virginia woods.

"Kona, go find!" He gave the sign, flinging his hand outward.

With a bark of excitement, Kona shot off like a black comet.

In search mode, she made sweeping arcs back and forth, using the scent cone wafting on the air to guide her. Kona led Max up a steep incline, through a field of oat grass, and into a stand of maple trees. The sun moved higher, bringing a welcome bit of warmth to the crisp fall air. The scent of dew-damp soil filled Max's nose as they moved farther and farther from the trail.

Kona's arcs began to narrow, a sure sign they were nearing their target.

They climbed a rocky bluff and emerged at the top of an overlook with a view of the entire river valley. Max slowed to take in the sight of the lazy Shenandoah River meandering among the rolling mountains blanketed in fiery red and orange.

Up ahead, Kona growled. Then, without warning, she took off at full speed, careening down into the woods below.

Max sprinted to keep up. The foliage grew thicker as they dropped in elevation. Branches whipped his face while he blindly crashed through the underbrush.

"Hey!" he called. "Kona, stop!"

For the first time ever, Kona ignored his command.

Something was seriously wrong.

Unable to see her, Max frantically chased the sound of his hundred-pound dog hurtling through the woods like she was on the devil's tail. He broke through the foliage into a clearing halfway down the mountain, where Kona ran in circles, alerting over and over. Max had never seen her act this way.

High trees shaded a large rocky area gently sloping down toward a drop-off. He moved slowly, scanning the ground for any sign of what had Kona so agitated.

"Go find!" he commanded, hoping she could narrow down her search.

Kona whimpered and sat, confused. A working dog to the core, Kona was upset that she couldn't pinpoint the location of whatever she smelled.

Max carefully made his way across the craggy clearing until he stood next to Kona, who sat on a small boulder. No sign of anything other than rocks and a few patches of low grass. Nowhere to hide a body.

"What on earth? This your first false alarm, girl?" He reached out to give her an encouraging scratch.

As he leaned forward, the ground shifted.

Though it had been years, his old training kicked in and he dove to the side. But it was too late.

In a torrent of soil and stone, the ground gave way beneath him.

Limbs flailing, Max fell into the darkness below.

He torqued his legs around just in time to slam down onto his feet. He grunted in pain, knees buckling as they took the brunt of the impact.

Max covered his head and waited as loose dirt and crumbled rock rained down on him. Far above, Kona frantically barked at the sudden disappearance of her human.

When the cascade stopped, Max called up, "I'm okay, Kona. Everything's okay."

The sound of his voice calmed the dog a little and she shifted to a steady whine. Max stood, wiping a layer of grit from his face, and tried to figure out where the hell he was. As his eyes adjusted in the dim light, he could just make out a small cavern. The round chamber was no larger than his bedroom, and the only visible opening was a long horizontal slit along the opposite wall. The hole he fell through was a good twenty feet directly above him, too far to climb.

"Looks like I just fell in a damned sinkhole," he said to no one in particular. He pulled out his phone, but no signal. "Hey, Kona," he said in a calming voice. "I'm going to try to find another way out." He squinted toward the low crack in the far wall of the cavern. He would have to lie down and scoot sideways up the narrow slot, but he thought he could see faint light filtering from the other side.

Kona still paced back and forth above him and Max worried she would jump. "You stay, Kona. Stay."

The dog huffed with disapproval but plopped down on the rim of the opening to stare down.

Max took a step forward and heard a brittle snap underfoot. For the first time, he looked down at the ground.

A flash of pale bone jutted up among the recent rockfall. Holding his breath, he crouched down to get a better look. Under the thin layer of dirt from the cave-in, bones littered the cavern floor.

"Please don't let this be a bear den," he mumbled to himself, mouth dry. But there was no smell of recent animal activity. As he scanned the bones, the hair on his neck stood up just like Kona's hackles. He lifted a rounded bone resting against his foot and turned it until he stared into the empty eye sockets of a human skull.

Stomach clenching, he picked up a long bone. Definitely human.

"Well, you sure did find us a cadaver, didn't you, Kona?" Max whispered.

With steady hands he moved aside more dirt, revealing two more human skulls and at least three more limb bones, rib bones, a clavicle. Though their flesh was long gone, Max could make out a few rotting scraps of tattered red and gold cloth.

For a brief second he feared that there was no other way out and he was about to die here.

"Don't be ridiculous," he said to himself. "Piper knows you're out here. She'll send someone to come find you when you don't check in."

The sound of his voice reined in the irrational spike of fear.

Max ran through his training—take a calm breath, assess the situation, take action.

He turned on his phone's flashlight and roved it in a wide circle. In the bright light, the jumble of bones scattered across the ground cast sharp shadows that danced along the cavern floor.

He tried to take a delicate step forward, but another bone snapped beneath his foot like a dry twig. Max swallowed and fought the chill gripping his chest.

These were definitely not lost hikers or victims of a bear mauling. Someone had murdered all of these people. Unwilling to disturb the crime scene further, he pressed his mouth into a thin line. A park ranger would be here soon and Kona would know to alert when they got close. He would be found soon enough.

"Settle, girl," he called up to Kona again. "We might be here awhile."

Kona let out a short bark, acknowledging his command.

Surrounded by the dead, Maxwell Cho crouched down to wait.

SAYER ALTAIR'S TOWN HOUSE, ALEXANDRIA, VA

FBI neuroscientist Sayer Altair woke with a start, chest constricting. The sensation of being shot sent a wave of panic through her and she reached for the gun on her bedside table.

Instead of wrapping around metal, her hand connected with something cold and wet.

She startled fully awake to the sight of her gangly three-legged dog sitting on top of her, wet nose nuzzling her for a scratch.

"Dammit, Vesper, I was trying to sleep in for a few more minutes."

The silvery beast completely ignored her, nudging her hand again, tongue lolling out with a goofy smile.

She felt a flash of annoyance, heart still pounding from the nightmare, but it was impossible to stay angry in the face of such pure silliness.

"All right, all right, you spoiled beast. What're you going to do when I go back to the field?"

In a few days she would finally be allowed back on field duty after six long months stuck behind a desk. Vesper had definitely gotten used to her being on a schedule.

At the sound of her happy voice, he flopped over onto his back and Sayer playfully rubbed his belly.

The bullet wound on her left shoulder no longer screamed with pain every time she moved her arm. Even with the wriggling dog on her lap, the scar felt like nothing more than a dull pull deep in her shoulder.

After getting over the initial shock and pain of being shot, Sayer had actually relished the downtime to work on her research. As a neurobiologist with the FBI's National Center for the Analysis of Violent Crime, she studied serial killers' brains. While completing her mandatory psych evals and endless physical therapy, Sayer had taken the chance to conclude her latest project and write up reports so she could start on the next phase of her research—interviews with and brain scans of noncriminal psychopaths. She wanted to figure out why some psychopaths became surgeons or lawyers, while others became serial killers.

During her downtime she had also tried to look into the mysterious death of her fiancé, Jake, but that hit a brick wall. All she knew was that he'd been killed in the line of duty, and that the official FBI story was a lie.

Despite excitement about the next step in her research, Sayer had missed being out with her unit heading up serial-killer investigations.

"Sayer, you up?" Adi called from the living room. Sayer started at her voice. Even though it had been a few months since Sayer had taken in the eighteen-year-old, she still sometimes forgot that she had someone living with her. "You're on TV again," Adi said with clear amusement.

"Dammit." Sayer extracted herself from underneath Vesper, pushed aside the stack of files about Jake's death, and stumbled out to the living room.

Adi Stephanopolis lay sprawled on the futon couch, twirling a fading pink curl with one hand, coffee balanced in the other. She had a massive textbook on her lap. Her lidded brown eyes hid what Sayer knew was a tempest of teenage emotions.

On the television a perky blond reporter flashed perfect white teeth.

"FBI Agent Sayer Altair might have uncovered the corruption at the FBI, but I'm not so sure she's one of the good guys."

A lantern-jawed human suit next to her nodded vigorously. "I agree, Bethany. Is Agent Altair a hero, or is she emblematic of the very culture of corruption that she exposed?"

Sayer stalked over and slammed off the TV.

"Hey!" Adi half sat up.

"Enough of that."

"But they were about to talk about you punching that reporter a million years ago." Adi gave Sayer a teasing half smile.

Adi didn't take any of their questions seriously because she knew better than anyone what Sayer had been through. And she knew that Sayer had almost died saving her life.

Six months ago, Sayer had uncovered a prolific serial killer inside the FBI. A murderer who had kidnapped Adi and shot both Sayer and her dog. Now Congress was organizing hearings and seeking scapegoats. After finding a killer in their midst, the entire FBI was being dragged through the mud and half of Quantico was shut down as an independent investigator combed through hundreds of their past cases.

Sayer grabbed her cell phone and stormed into the kitchen for coffee. She was going to call that damned reporter as soon as she was sufficiently caffeinated.

She lifted the still-warm and very empty coffeepot. With a grumble, she reached for the coffee tin and shook it.

"Did you finish the last of the coffee?" Sayer called out to Adi.

"Oops, sorry."

Sayer looked down at her empty mug and took a deep breath. She pointedly stared at Adi as she walked through the living room and out the front door. Her downstairs neighbor and Vesper's coparent, Tino de la Vega, sat outside in their shared garden. Vesper bounded down to greet his other human.

"It's my favorite creature in the world!" The stocky man with wire-rimmed glasses and a bristly mustache smiled brightly, ruffling Vesper's ears. "How are you doing this fine . . ." He trailed off at the sight of Sayer stalking down the stairs in her red flannel pajamas and wild pouf of brown curls.

"Coffee?" Sayer thrust her empty mug at Tino.

He laughed. "Well, aren't you a ray of sunshine this morning."

Sayer scowled. "The devil's spawn that I took into my home out of the kindness of my heart has just finished the last of my coffee without even mentioning that we were low. Can I murder her now or do I have to wait until I've actually had coffee?"

"Pretty sure the order is supposed to be coffee and then murder. I've got a fresh pot on."

She retreated to Tino's homey downstairs apartment of their converted colonial town house and sloshed her mug full. She carefully cradled it as she flopped down at the garden table. The crisp fall air and dewy morning light made their garden look like something straight out of a fairy tale.

Between that and the deep nutty aroma of coffee, Sayer felt slightly less murderous.

She looked across the table at her neighbor. After leaving the Army, he had become a high-powered chef. But when he realized that he was gay, Tino got a divorce and quit his job. Sayer was fairly sure he was in the middle of a full-blown midlife crisis, spending his days gardening, playing with Vesper, and reading, while casting about for something meaningful to do.

"You interviewing another wack job this morning?" Tino asked with slight disdain.

Sayer shook her head. "Not this morning, but I do have one scheduled late this evening." She was about to elaborate when her cell phone rang.

She ignored it.

"You going to get that?"

"It's just another reporter," Sayer said, hunching over her mug.

The phone stopped, but then buzzed again.

"Could be your nana," Tino said, eyebrows up. Even the ex–Army interrogator knew better than to cross Sayer's nana.

With a sigh, Sayer pulled out her phone.

"Shit, it's Holt!" She fumbled to answer. Vesper jumped up at the tension in her voice.

"Sayer," Assistant Director Janice Holt barked in her usual sharp tone. As head of the FBI's Critical Incident Response Group in charge of Quantico, Janice Holt was as no-nonsense as they came. The powerful woman gleefully lived up to her reputation as an old battle-ax.

Sayer smiled at the familiar bark. "Assistant Director Holt."

"You've got a case."

"Already? I thought I was off until next week."

"Nope, we're short-staffed as hell with all the congressional-hearing nonsense and I have a form sitting here on my desk that says you're officially field-certified. Time to get your ass back to work. One of our agents fell into a sinkhole full of human remains down in Shenandoah National Park. Looks like a possible dump site. The National Park Service called us in and I've already got an Evidence Response Team and medical examiner on the way. It'll take a while for them to exhume all the skeletal remains, but I want you to head down now and take the helm."

"Skeletons. . . . Any details on how many bodies or how long they've been there?"

"Not yet. Our agent, Maxwell Cho, is waiting for you at the south entrance to the park. He'll take you to the scene and fill you in on the way."

Sayer tried not to sound disappointed. "Cold case, you think?"

"Could be." The assistant director sighed. "Listen, I know you're itching to dive into something active, but I want you to ease back into a case where no one will be shooting at you. I'll have the data team send you the files. All eyes are on us right now, so don't fuck up." Holt hung up.

Sayer blinked at the sudden silence.

"Sounds like you're back in the field?" Tino asked, clearly not thrilled.

"Agent Altair, back in action." Sayer chugged the last of her coffee and sprinted upstairs to get dressed.

SHENANDOAH NATIONAL PARK, VA

Sayer leaned her vintage motorcycle into the turn off Highway 64 onto Skyline Drive. She rumbled a few miles up the narrow road to the entrance of Shenandoah National Park. Late morning sun shone through the fall foliage, making it look like the sky was aflame.

She rolled the Matchless Silver Hawk to a stop next to a low stone wall running alongside the ranger station and pulled off her helmet to enjoy the cool mountain air. After being cooped up in her office for so long, it felt good to be back out in the field.

A man of medium height dressed in hiking gear sat casually on the wall, a large black dog curled at his feet. "Ah, Senior Special Agent Altair, I recognize you from TV." He strode over, smiling warmly, and held out his hand. Everything from his sun-worn cheeks to his broad shoulders to his cropped black hair screamed ex-military.

Sayer gave a strained smile as they shook. Her face had been on heavy media rotation over the past few months and she was beginning to wonder if she would ever be anonymous again. The only benefit to being on TV was that at least no one was surprised anymore when the FBI agent turned out to be a thirty-something brown-skinned woman.

"And you must be the agent who found us a crime scene," Sayer said.

"I think *crashed* into a crime scene might be more accurate. I'm Max Cho, K9 Unit." The wolfish dog stood at attention at his side. "This's Kona, my Human Remains Detection dog. She should really get the credit for finding the bodies." He put a gentle hand on Kona's head. "Why don't you park your bike here? We can ride up to the scene in my truck."

The American flag flying above the ranger station whipped in a sudden gust of wind. Sayer glanced over her shoulder and was surprised to see a wall of gray clouds overtaking the clear blue sky. As she climbed into Max's truck she felt a trickle of unease at the coming storm.

"So, Assistant Director Holt said you're assigned to the D.C. office. What were you and Kona doing out here this morning?" Sayer asked as they drove farther into the mountains.

"This was supposed to be my day off. My plan was to take a nice morning hike up to Turk Mountain, then head down to Rockfish Gap to visit with my mom for the afternoon."

"So much for a day off." Sayer tried giving Kona an ear scratch that would have turned Vesper into a puddle of wiggling dog. Kona didn't move, attention forward, barrel chest rigid.

Max chuckled. "Sorry, she doesn't really do normal dog stuff. She's the most serious creature I've ever worked with."

They turned off Skyline Drive onto something that Sayer would only politely call a road, and she was rarely polite. Max kept his eyes straight ahead, expertly wrangling the steering wheel to keep the bucking truck from sliding sideways on the gravelly track. Sayer almost laughed out loud at Max and Kona's matching intense looks.

"So, you grew up around here?" she asked.

"Born and bred. I grew up in Rockfish Gap, which you just drove through on your way here."

"I drove through a town?"

Max nodded. "Exactly. It's more a barnacle on the side of the mountain than a town."

"You know of any missing people nearby who could be our victims?"

"There've been a few missing people in the park over the years, but nothing like this."

"How old could the bones be? I mean, could Kona smell ten-year-old remains? Or even older?" Sayer asked.

Max glanced fondly at his dog. "During her final qualification, Kona found a single thirty-year-old human vertebra buried two feet deep. But I've heard of dogs finding remains that are two, even three hundred years old."

"Damn, that's impressive."

They hit a bump that threw them all into the roof of the truck. Sayer rubbed her head where it bounced off the hard metal.

"Sorry. These are old mining roads. I'll ask a park ranger to send a grader up this afternoon to level out the road."

Sayer grunted approval.

Max grinned, clearly enjoying the challenge of wrestling two tons of steel as they bounced their way up the mountain.

A light rain began to fall as they pulled up next to a small phalanx of FBI SUVs, Park Service trucks, and an FBI medical examiner's van.

With a nod to the rain, Max handed Sayer a poncho and some gloves. "You probably don't want your bike jacket to get muddy."

Sayer ruefully pulled off her burgundy leather jacket and yanked the thin plastic over her T-shirt, wishing she had thought to prepare for the damn woods. Nature girl she was not. At least she had her Vibram-soled boots.

Max and Kona bounded from the truck, perfectly at home in the blustery weather. Unlike Sayer's bright green extravaganza of poncho plastic, Max's thick jacket looked cozy as could be. The dog moved at his side like an extension of his body.

With a sigh, Sayer stepped out into the cold drizzle and the poncho immediately stuck to her skin, raising goose bumps. At least the gloves Max gave her felt warm. The weight of her belt with gun and flashlight felt heavier than she remembered. Six months was a long time to be away.

"It's only a few hundred yards this way," Max called back to her with annoying enthusiasm. "The medical examiner and evidence techs are already there."

Sayer felt a pang of concern. Though most labs were open now, the actual Medical Examiner's Office at Quantico was completely shut down while the FBI was under congressional investigation, and she had no idea who they had sent. Virginia had its own ME's office, so maybe a local? The medical examiner could make or break a case, and Sayer definitely hoped she didn't get stuck with a newbie.

"So," Sayer called up to Max, "what's the surrounding area like? We close to anything?"

Max and Kona slowed so they could all walk together. "You came up Skyline Drive, which runs along the ridge of the mountains for about a hundred miles, from Rockfish Gap up to Front Royal." Max led Sayer through the thick underbrush. "Even though we're only a few hours from D.C., it's pretty wild up here. Especially farther along Skyline where you're thirty or forty miles from any of the roads that can get you down to civilization."

"Pull!" a voice shouted up ahead, interrupting Max.

Sayer's hand instinctively went to her gun at the tension in the voice. Max glanced over at her, eyebrows up. She realized she was jumpy, first-day-back jitters or something. She dropped her hand and ignored Max's look as they broke through the underbrush into a small clearing.

Four uniformed park rangers struggled with a blue tarp above a ragged hole in the ground. The rangers fought to control the tarp, which pulled open like a sail in the brisk wind.

A hulking woman in a rumpled park ranger uniform stood to the side and called out instructions. She was so big that her shoulders sloped slightly to the sides as if bending under their considerable mass. "Will, tie that off higher! Lydia, you need to pull that corner to your left!"

One of the rangers holding the tarp shouted back, "Piper, if you're not gonna help us, then just shut it!"

Looking slightly sheepish at being chastised, the park ranger turned her attention to Max and Sayer. She hurried over, rain dripping off the edges of her brown wide-brimmed hat. With rounded cheeks, freckled pale skin, slightly shaggy strawberry-blond hair, and a stocky build, she looked like a linebacker stuffed inside the body of the Gerber Baby.

The park ranger gave Max an affable wave. "Hiya, Max." She turned to Sayer. "Piper MacLaughlin, at your service." Her eyes crinkled with an easy smile. "I'll be your park liaison. You must be SSA Altair."

"Nice to meet you, Ranger MacLaughlin."

The park ranger let out a short laugh. "Please, just call me Piper."

"Nice to meet you, Piper. You two know each other?" Sayer looked back and forth between the compact FBI agent and the massive park ranger.

"Piper's a fixture here in the park. You've worked here, what, twenty years?" Max asked.

"Only sixteen," Piper said.

"Piper's been working here longer than any other ranger, so she's the old-timer."

"I just belong in these woods, is all." Piper looked up at the trees with the kind of warmth usually reserved for loved ones.

Between Piper and Max, Sayer wondered if everyone in the Virginia mountains was always so full of annoying enthusiasm. "So what can you two tell me?"

"This is a hell of a thing we've got here, isn't it?" Piper led them under the tarp as the other rangers managed to finish tying it off. "We're still setting up. Should have a few canopies erected soon. Your evidence team is already down in the cave." She pointed to the ragged-edged hole.

Sayer leaned forward to take a look and could just make out a rope ladder descending into the darkness.

Max held out an arm in front of her. "You don't want to get too close or you might trigger another cave-in."

Sayer took half a step back and eyed the rocky ground they stood on. "It feels like we're in the middle of nowhere. Not the kind of place you stumble on casually. Think it's likely that whoever dumped these bodies is from around here?"

Piper looked thoughtful for a bit. "Could be. Here, let me show you how the skeletons got in the cave in the first place." She led them toward a low ridge.

Twenty feet from the sinkhole, Piper stopped at a small rock ledge and jumped down, equipment belt clattering when she landed. "Here, you've got to come on this side to see it."

Sayer jumped down as well. At the very base of the ledge, a horizontal slit cut into the rock.

"See"—Piper shone her flashlight into the hole—"whoever dumped the bodies just slid 'em in here."

Max leaned forward and whistled. "I saw where it comes out at the bottom when I was in the cave. It's like the book return at the library, a perfect little slot to slide your murder victims into."

Sayer frowned as she looked around at nothing but rocks and trees. She pulled her string of amber worry beads from her pocket to fidget with while she contemplated the scene. Originally a gift from her father, the beads helped her focus while she thought.

"Are these kind of caves common around here?" Sayer asked.

"Oh, for sure," Piper answered with a mischievous smile. "These mountains here are a manifestation of the divine. . . ." She threw her arms wide, gesturing to everything around them.

"I'm sorry?"

"What I mean to say is, this area is holy. Get it? Holy, like divine . . . but also holey like full of holes. . . ."

Max snorted.

Sayer raised her eyebrows.

"Sorry." Piper cleared her throat. "Yeah, the whole area is karst, porous limestone with some granite outcroppings. Over time, water eats away the softer rock, which is why this whole region is full of caverns, some as big as cathedrals underground. We've got your underground rivers, underground pools, underground everything."

Sayer turned a full circle. "This entrance can't be more than thirty feet from the mining road. How many people would know about that?"

Piper shrugged. "Used to be a ton of mines along the western edge of the mountains. Most roads are overgrown now, but they aren't hard to clear. Townie kids use them to party up here, so anyone living nearby would know about 'em."

"So our killer was probably a local. And someone could've just driven the bodies up here?" Sayer looked around. "I mean, this feels pretty isolated to me."

"Yeah, it might feel isolated, but, like you said, we're just off the old road and we're only a few hundred yards from the main trail. Anyone hiking around up here could've stumbled on this cave. Plus we're close to the edge of the park, so it wouldn't be too hard to come up from the valley." She pointed down the gentle slope. "There's a few little towns about fifteen miles west of here as the crow flies."

"Okay, Piper, since you're the park liaison, why don't you notify all the local police departments what we've got here? And I'll need a map of the area, one with the old mine roads, if possible."

"I already called all the locals. In this area, word travels fast, best to stay in front of the news. And no one makes a map with all the old mine roads, but between me and a few of the other locals, we could mark up all the roads on a topographic map," Piper offered.

"Great." Sayer nodded and turned her attention back to the narrow opening, rubbing her worry beads. About three feet tall and seven feet long, it really was the perfect size for a human body.

"So, this crack leads down to the cavern?" She leaned in close. The opening gently exhaled stale, warm air.

"Yes, ma'am," Piper said. "It's a flat little chute, like one of those covered waterslides but with rock a few inches from your face. You could probably lie down and slide through, but I wouldn't recommend it."

"We're going to need someone to go down, just to make sure no more remains are caught in the chute."

Piper nodded slowly. "I can send one of our rangers down."

"Great," Sayer said again, taking a moment to absorb the whole scene. Isolated but easily accessible. Their killer probably only had to drag the bodies a few dozen feet. Any reasonably fit person could be their killer. "All right. How do I get down to my team?"

"The rope ladder from the sinkhole rim," Piper said.

Sayer tried to smile but probably grimaced instead. She tucked her beads back in her pocket as she wondered just how much climbing down some damn rope ladder was going to hurt her shoulder.

She headed back up to the sinkhole and was just about to descend into the cave when an angry voice bellowed from the woods, "Maxwell Cho!"

A lanky, red-faced man in a crisp blue police uniform stormed into the clearing. He zeroed in on Max. "Where is she?"

"Kyle"—Max held his hands up as if in surrender—"we don't know anything yet."

"I know you found human remains." The policeman pointed a finger at Max and advanced toward him, thrusting his finger in the air. "Is she here?"

Kona moved closer to Max, sensing a threat.

Sayer stepped in between Max and the angry police officer. "I'm FBI Senior Special Agent Altair. And you are?"

The slender officer was significantly taller than Sayer and he stared over her head at Max.

"Officer . . . ?" Sayer demanded his attention.

He finally looked down at Sayer, nose flaring. "I apologize. Kyle Nelson, chief of the Rockfish Gap Police." He firmly shook Sayer's offered hand, eyes burning with enough animus that Sayer almost shuddered. His long face twitched slightly, contorting his mouth into a grimace.

"Who exactly are you looking for, Chief Nelson?" she asked loudly.

He spoke with a soft Southern twang, but his voice was edged with malice. "I came to see if you all found my sister. She went missing seventeen years ago and I thought maybe . . . and then I get here to find Max Cho at the scene." Kyle spat Max's name.

Sayer turned to look at Max, who was wide-eyed, one hand still held up, the other on Kona's head to calm the dog.

"You didn't mention a missing girl," she said to Max.

Kyle Nelson snorted. "Of course he didn't."

Sayer could feel the tension crackling in the air between Max and Kyle. "Okay, I'm not sure what's going on here, but standing over our crime scene is not the place to work it out. Right now I need to secure the scene, get the evidence teams going, and then I want to hear more about this. Chief Nelson, once we've set up our home base, I'll ask you to come in and tell me everything about your sister. But for now I'm going to ask you to head back to town." She turned to Max. "We've got a bunch of park rangers standing around with nothing to do. Max, you and Piper organize a grid search of the surrounding area. Have them look for signs of recent activity, pieces of trash, anything at all. Make it a mile radius."

The local police chief took a measured breath as if fighting to control his emotions. Max dropped his hands and nodded sharply.

"All right, Agent Altair. I apologize for storming up here." Kyle bowed his head slightly. "I'll plan to come talk to you later today. In the meantime, if you'd like, I can send up an officer to help secure things."

"Offer appreciated. Let me get the lay of the land and I'll let you know when we could use some help."

Kyle bowed again, glared one more time at Max, and strode away. At the edge of the clearing, he looked back at the sinkhole. "Agent Altair, it's possible you just found my sister. . . ."

Now that his rage had drained, Sayer caught a glimpse of sorrow in his eyes. "I understand," she said.

He was asking for respect for the dead.

SHENANDOAH NATIONAL PARK, VA

Heart still beating fast from the confrontation between Max and Kyle, Sayer climbed onto the rope ladder leading down into the cavern. Just what she needed, tension between the local cops and one of her agents.

Sayer's scar pulled painfully as she lowered herself down, distracting her from the drama above. She breathed deeply, acknowledging the pain, trying to let the sensation roll away like her physical therapist suggested. Rather than roll away, the feeling balled up around her shoulder and she was clenching her teeth by the time she got to the cavern floor.

She took another deep breath and shook out her arms, trying to release the tension. She turned to assess the scene but was suddenly blinded by the floodlights. For a brief moment her only sensory input was the sound of rain muted into a distant rumble.

"Sayer," a sharp voice greeted her.

A sharp voice she recognized.

"Dana?"

A weatherworn woman in her early fifties materialized. Small as a mosquito and tough as nails, forensic anthropologist and expert medical examiner Dana Wilbanks still had the same bright green eyes and narrow smile she'd had when Sayer met her years ago. Before Sayer's fiancé, Jake, was killed, the three of them had spent countless hours together at the local pub just outside the FBI offices at Quantico.

Two little skull earrings dangled from her ears as she threw her arms wide and wrapped Sayer in a tiny bear hug.

"Holt didn't tell you I was here?"

Sayer returned her hug. Though the wiry woman only came up to Sayer's shoulders, she still had a grip. "Holt told me a medical examiner was here, but I didn't know you were back! I thought you were digging up bodies in the Congo. What are you doing here?"

The world's foremost expert on mass graves, Dana had left the FBI to join the United Nations. Last Sayer heard, she was off to the Democratic Republic of the Congo to help the UN document war crimes.

"I just got back yesterday." Dana pulled off her work gloves, revealing tiny callused hands. "I guess with all the scandal, the MEs from Quantico are stretched thin, so they called in a favor. I'm officially on loan from the UN while we unravel this mess. And wouldn't you know it, Holt couldn't even give me a day off before assigning me a case." She reached out and put a warm hand on Sayer's shoulder, a stark contrast to the chilled air. "I hear you went and got yourself shot."

"Only a little shot," Sayer said, a joke she'd repeated hundreds of times. According to the FBI psychologist, she felt the need to downplay her injuries in the hope that no one would think her abilities were diminished.

"Hey, getting shot is no small thing." Dana saw right through her ruse. "I'm glad you're okay."

Sayer nodded curtly, not wanting to discuss her injury any further. Certainly not in front of anyone else. "So, what do you have for me here?"

Dana gave her a momentary squint to see if she was really okay before turning her attention to the crime scene. "Well, my old friend, I give you . . . bones!"

"You don't say," Sayer deadpanned.

"I do say! In my expert opinion, I see lots and lots of bones."

Sayer gave her a "very funny" look and turned in a slow circle, careful not to tread beyond the small clearing around them. Dana wasn't kidding. Bones were scattered on the ground in every direction.

As with any forensic excavation, a grid of strings was laid out in perfect squares crisscrossing the entire fifteen-by-fifteen-foot cavern. Two evidence techs moved cautiously among the remains, photographing the squares one by one. A third tech sat sketching the scene.

Dana's face grew serious. "Based on the volume of bones here, assuming they're all human, I'd guess we have six or seven victims. Honestly, this is the most confusing mass grave I've ever seen. Not the largest by a long shot, but definitely the messiest. I'm talking massive ongoing disturbance to the bones."

"How so?"

"There's no stratigraphy." Dana crouched down and pulled a trowel from her back pocket. She used it to gently lift a long bone. "Usually a mass grave is dug, bodies are dumped in, and then they're covered with dirt. Even if they're in the ground for a while, you can tell which bones go together and what order the victims were deposited. But there's no rhyme or reason here." Dana pointed with the trowel. "See?"

Sayer leaned forward to see better.

"This is a femur, but it's far too long to go with the scatter of bones immediately around it. I'll have to measure when we get it to the lab, but I'd say this femur most likely belonged to a tall individual, upward of six feet. But this skull right next to it probably belonged to a petite person. And this pelvis looks like a young female, maybe early twenties. They're all jumbled together in a pile and they're all heavily damaged. It's like someone took apart a bunch of skeletons, shook them up in a bag, and dumped them down a hole. It will take us all day just to document the site."

Dana ran a frustrated hand through her cropped gray hair. "In silver-lining news, I don't see any children."

"I'll take whatever good news I can get." Sayer let the full weight of the scene sink in. As her eyes roved over the bones, she imagined all the lives cut short, all the people who didn't get the chance to grow old. Was

Kyle Nelson's sister among the dead? "What do you think that means? All the bodies were tossed in here at the same time? Were they killed and stored elsewhere, then dumped here as a pile of disarticulated bones? Or is this animal intrusion?"

"Those are all possibilities, but I won't know until I can get a better look. After we document everything today, we should be able to start exhuming the bones tomorrow. It'll be a slow process."

"Any sense how long these bones have been here?"

"Not yet. I see some degraded scraps of cloth, so I'm hoping those might help us figure out what happened here. At least give me a timeline to work with." Dana paused, clearly unhappy about something.

"What is it?" Sayer recognized uncertainty on Dana's face.

"Well, I'm not sure I should say anything at this point."

"About . . . ," Sayer prompted.

"This." She pointed the tip of her trowel to the end of a long bone. "See how the ends of the bone are smooth, almost polished?"

Sayer squinted. "If you say so."

"This is something called pot polish." Dana cringed, as though saying the words hurt.

"Okay, and what does pot polish mean?"

Dana sighed. "Pot polish is hugely controversial in the world of bones. It means that it is entirely possible that these people were cooked before they were dumped here. The bones get this kind of polish from rubbing along a pot in boiling water. It's almost always interpreted as a sign of cannibalism."

"What?" Sayer's voice rose. "Is this some kind of cannibal dump site?"

"No. That's why I hesitate to bring it up until I can take a better look. I'm not seeing any signs of butchery that you'd expect to see if someone ate these people. No cuts from flesh removal. None of the bones are crushed to get at the marrow."

"So, cooked but not eaten. . . . What the hell did we just stumble on?" Sayer asked, eyes scanning the cavern floor.

Dana remained silent.

"All right." Sayer finally felt ready to shift into active-investigation mode. "I'm going to make sure Agent Cho has the grid search going and I'll check back in half an hour or so."

Before she left, she took one last look at the bones. They were her responsibility now and she felt the weight of their former lives heavy on her as she pulled herself back out of the cave.

Once she was satisfied that Max and Piper had the grid search under way, Sayer found Dana and her evidence techs by the vehicles loading small boxes into the back of the FBI van.

"The park rangers have offered to let us use their southern station as our home base. I'm sending my team there now to set up the lab," Dana said loudly over the increasingly heavy rain. "I'd like to start pulling bones out of here by tomorrow, and we need a sterile place to put them."

"Great. I've got Max and Piper off on the area search." Sayer glanced over at Dana. "You sure you're comfortable working at the ranger station without a full lab?"

"Yeah, I was able to requisition all the mobile equipment we brought back from the Congo." Dana bounced on her feet to stay warm. "According to that big park-ranger lady, the ranger station nearby is massive and even has a small medical facility that'll be perfect for any analysis I want to do. I guess they shut the southern station down and only use the northern one, so the whole place is ours."

Sayer watched Dana's team drive away in the van. "Great, that will definitely be better than cramming into a building down in Rockfish Gap. So, did you want to take another look at the scene without your team here?" She grimaced up at the rain, tugging at her poncho, which had completely failed to keep the rain at bay.

Dana pulled a thermos from her bag and offered it to Sayer as they walked back to the sinkhole. "Coffee?"

Sayer gratefully took the thermos and swigged the warm liquid. She sighed as it took the edge off the chill. "You are a goddess."

"True. Yeah, I just like to take a look at a scene without the techs swarming it. It allows me to make sure I don't miss any contextual clues. Give me a minute to think, if you don't mind." They reached the tarp above the sinkhole and Sayer stared out into the downpour.

She knew that the medical examiner had her own process, so she waited quietly. They fell into companionable silence, listening to the sounds of the forest. Rain pattered rhythmically on the tarp above them. Squirrels rustled through the underbrush. The haunting calls of a wood thrush echoed through the damp trees.

Dana finally interrupted their communion with nature. "All right, let's head down and take a look with fresh eyes."

A faint bubbling sound filtered through the pounding rain.

"Do you hear that?" Sayer asked.

Dana tilted her head, listening. "Is that running water?"

Sayer swiveled her head, trying to figure out where it was coming from. "In the cave?" She shone her flashlight down. A shallow wash of water ran along the cave floor.

Dana joined her and grimaced at the sight of bones getting caught up in the water. She let out a low moan. "Well, that explains the pot polish."

"What?" Sayer looked around, trying to understand where the water was coming from.

"The disarticulated bones. The polished ends. There is no cooking pot, the cave is the pot. Look, the water is running down the chute and turning over the bones. This must happen every time it rains, tumbling them around the cave like a washing machine. The bones' edges get ground smooth. No wonder this grave is such a mess."

"Should we try to stop it before it turns everything over? Maybe we can divert the water. It's got to be running in from the chute."

Dana nodded and they ran out into the rain toward the chute entrance. Sayer jumped off the small rock ledge into a few inches of water pooling along the rocks. The water poured in over the top of her fancy waterproof boots, filling them to the brim.

"The ledge is acting like a funnel, running water down the chute and right into the cave!"

Dana jumped next to her. "We can just run the water off if we build a dam here."

They began scooping rocks into a semicircle in front of the chute. Once they had a pile of rocks, they rushed back and forth with armfuls of thick clay, packing it into the cracks. After working together for almost twenty minutes, they stood to admire their creation.

Water flowed off either side of the small dam.

"Looks like it will hold for now," Sayer said, scraping mud off her gloves.

She looked down at herself, coated with mud from head to toe. Her poncho hood had slipped off in their frantic work and rain trickled along her back, even down her legs. Water sloshed in her boots. Sayer looked over at Dana. Her once-red coat was streaked ashy brown. Her pants and boots were caked with wet clay. A single clod of mud dangled from her bangs.

Sayer let out a snort. Dana looked at her, surprised, but then looked down at herself. Then over at Sayer. Her eyes creased with laughter. "And I came home from the Congo for some downtime, a nice clean bed, some fancy food. . . ."

After making sure their small dam would hold, Sayer and Dana climbed down into the sodden cave through the sinkhole entrance.

A thin layer of fresh mud covered everything. Their carefully laid-out grid was in shambles. Dana's equipment was soaked.

"Dammit, what a disaster. I should've been able to predict this," Dana said as they surveyed the scene. "This kind of destruction of a grave . . . it's just . . ."

"Not your fault, Dana."

The medical examiner sighed loudly and gathered herself. "You're right." She clapped her hands with resolve. "In good news, this means that careful documentation as we exhume the bones has just become totally unimportant."

"How so?" Sayer asked.

"Well, we would normally document and carefully pull out bones one at a time, because how they relate to each other in situ could tell us a lot about how they were deposited."

"In situ, like in place?"

"Exactly. But now that I know the remains have been heavily disturbed, I know that their current position doesn't tell us anything about how they were deposited. So, really, great news," she said, clearly trying to convince herself. "It would've taken at least two or three weeks to carefully excavate a grave this size. Now we can yank them out in a day and get to work in the lab."

Sayer and Dana wandered carefully among the bones.

"Could these bones be really old? I mean, what if we've stumbled into some ancient Native American burial site or something?" Sayer asked.

"Fair question." Dana crouched down and pulled a flashlight off her utility belt. "But I think I can rule that out."

"Oh, yeah?" Sayer stopped to watch Dana, who had clearly found something.

Dana slid on a latex glove and reached out to gently touch one of the bones, as if apologizing before gingerly probing her fingers down underneath. She plucked something out, slowly pulling up a small rusted buckle; a long piece of rotting canvas followed, a few more buckles, a high collar.

An overlong sleeve swung from the bottom.

"I'm confident that there are no Native American tribes that use straitjackets in their religious ceremonies. . . ."

Sayer stared, mouth slightly agape. A straitjacket? She was about to say something when a loud *crack* made the two women look up.

The rope ladder crumpled to the cavern floor with a wet *thump*.

"Hey!" Sayer shouted up. "Max? Piper?"

A silhouette moved purposefully around the rim of the sinkhole.

"Hey! Who's up there?" Sayer called up again, trying to make out the figure shrouded in a puffy jacket.

A faint *glug glug* sound became audible over the rain as a thin stream of amber liquid splashed down from above.

The vaporous scent of gasoline sent a shock down Sayer's spine.

She shouted up again, "There're people down here!"

An empty gas can fell to the ground near them and another stream of liquid poured into the cave.

Sayer looked over at Dana. "Fire?"

Dana nodded, fear etched on her face.

Sayer thrust her finger toward the first-aid kit propped among the equipment. "Emergency blanket in there?" Without waiting for an answer, she pulled it open and began yanking everything out. Though thin, silver emergency blankets were designed to reflect heat.

The stream of liquid stopped and a second empty can clattered to the ground. A miasma of gas permeated the air. Sayer took short breaths, trying not to inhale the toxic fumes.

"Hurry! Over to the chute!" Sayer shouted as she triumphantly pulled out an emergency blanket and shook it open.

Sayer and Dana pressed together, pulling the edges of the blanket across their bodies.

Time seemed to stop.

Nothing . . . nothing . . . Sayer risked one last look up.

A flaming knot of cloth drifted down through the opening.

She pulled the edge of the blanket tight against the rock behind her. In the perfect stillness of pure panic, Sayer tucked her face down into her arm.

A sharp *whoosh* thudded as the gasoline ignited.

The air became fire. Then two deep *booms* as the gas cans exploded.

An inferno roared around them like an oncoming train, muted by the ringing in Sayer's ears.

Seconds ticked by like hours as the fireball raged.

Sayer tried to hold her breath, but her brain screamed in panic at the intense heat pressing against her. She involuntarily sucked in. Blistering pain flooded her nose and mouth, choking her.

She fought the irrational urge to throw aside the blanket and flee.

As suddenly as the fire began, the midair conflagration disappeared with a gentle *puff.*

Sayer looked up, gulping for air.

She blinked at the sight of her gloves on fire as she still clutched the edges of the emergency blanket.

Dana huddled next to her, shouting something.

"What?" She tried to speak, but her mouth felt full of cotton.

"Gloves off!" she finally heard. Something about Dana's commanding voice broke through the haze.

Time crashed back into place.

Sayer frantically pulled off her flaming gloves and threw them to the ground.

"Poncho!" Dana shouted, and Sayer immediately pulled the poncho over her head.

She tossed it aside and realized that the entire thing was smoking.

"Synthetics burn," Dana croaked.

Sayer watched the gloves and poncho melt into a smoldering puddle.

A few flames still danced along the opposite wall of the cavern, pushed back by the breeze being sucked down the chute by the oxygen-hungry fire.

As the firestorm dissipated, it left behind innumerable small fires along the floor of the cave.

Sayer took a wheezing breath. "Fire won't have any fuel once the last puddles of gas burn off."

Dana nodded, then winced, gently reaching up to touch her lobster-red cheeks. "Did I already mention that I thought I'd come back from a war zone for some nice food, a clean bed . . ."

They slowly stood and lowered the blanket. The last fires flickered out, leaving ashen heaps along the ground.

"Damn, there goes any chance of finding trace on the cloth remains." Sayer gestured to the charred straitjacket.

"Yeah," Dana agreed. "You know, I'm not one hundred percent sure, but I think someone might have just tried to kill us."

Sayer let out a shaky laugh. She tried to swallow but didn't have enough spit.

"Hey! What's going on?" a voice called down from above.

"Max? Piper?" Sayer called up, and immediately regretted it as her throat rasped painfully.

"Yeah!" Max and Piper looked down from above. "What the hell happened?"

"Someone just tried to set us on fire. Watch out. He could still be up there!"

Sayer was about to step forward when something heavy bumped against the backs of her legs.

She looked down to see a perfect set of cotton-candy-pink toenails sticking out from the bottom of the rocky chute.

SHENANDOAH NATIONAL PARK, VA

Max listened to Sayer's chest with his stethoscope. "You and Dana are lucky you were already soaking wet and covered in mud. I think that saved your asses."

Sayer nodded, still focusing on the very fresh-looking body they had just pulled from the sinkhole. The corpse lay on her side in a fetal position, wrapped in thick layers of clear plastic. The dead woman's wide eyes were barely visible over her knees pulled tight to her chest. Her arms were crossed over naked legs. Only her bare feet poked out from the bottom of the plastic, bright pink nails a cheerful contrast to her bluish toes.

Dana bustled around the body, wrapping the feet in evidence bags. Sayer could see that Dana's hands were still shaking.

Max followed Sayer's eyes. "How long you think she was in there?"

Sayer tore her eyes away and refocused on Max. "Don't know. Dana thinks it can't be more than a few days."

"A few days," Max repeated, shaking his head. "No wonder Kona was so frantic this morning. So we've got some old bones and now a new body. . . ."

"And someone who clearly doesn't want us to find them." Sayer looked down at the blisters along the backs of her knuckles and realized that her own hands were shaking as well. The last bits of adrenaline were draining from her body, leaving her weak and nauseous.

"No joke. I'm just glad Piper and I were nearby. You might've been stuck down there all night."

Sayer ran a hand along her curls and realized that the ends were singed. "Or he might have come back to finish the job," she said, feeling a wave of vertigo.

Max finished examining Sayer and stood up. "Well, you and Dana are both probably having some post-adrenaline symptoms, dry mouth, dizziness. You should eat something soon or your blood sugar will crash. You both also have some smoke inhalation and a few minor burns but nothing that needs a doctor. Just keep the blisters clean and dry."

"Lucky we have our very own doctor with us." Sayer gestured at Max's medical bag. "You were a medic with the Air Force?"

He stood up straight and saluted. "Proud former Air Force Pararescue at your service. No better field medics anywhere in the world. 'These things we do, that others may live,'" Max quoted the Pararescue motto.

Sayer was impressed. All she really knew about Pararescue was that they were the Special Operations teams, sent in to rescue injured soldiers stranded behind enemy lines.

"Hey, Agent Altair," Piper called from the entrance to the rock chute. "We've cleared away your rock dam and are about to see if there're any more bodies in the chute. You want to come watch?"

Sayer decided getting back to work was the best way to get over her wooziness. She thanked Max and hurried over to where Piper and another park ranger stood at the entrance to the chute, holding climbing gear.

Piper looked down at Sayer's blistered hands. "Really glad you're okay."

"Thanks." Sayer jumped down next to the rangers.

"Sayer, meet Tim. He's the best spelunker I know." Piper bowed at the ranger next to her.

"Thanks for doing this," Sayer said to the young man.

"Sure, happy to," he replied with a slight lisp.

Piper helped him step into a climbing harness and he moved with quick efficiency setting up a belay line.

"Let me know if you need more rope. I'll follow your lead. Call out if you find anything." Piper fed him some slack.

The young ranger clicked on his headlamp and, with a genuine smile, eased himself sideways into the crevice. Despite being fairly tall, he folded his body like it was made of taffy.

Sayer watched them work in perfect tandem, Piper clearly knowing when to pull and when to feed more rope. Sayer could see Tim's light for a few moments before it disappeared into the long narrow chute.

Unwilling to break Piper's concentration, Sayer watched in silence until a small voice echoed up, "One more here."

"One more body?" Sayer called down.

"Yes." Tim's voice sounded far away. "Almost to the bottom. It got snagged on rocks. There's something else. Some kind of . . ."

Sayer waited.

"I think it's a machete or a sword or something."

"Can you take a bunch of photos and then dislodge the body and the machete gently?"

"Okay."

Sayer squinted down into the dark chute as a series of flashes briefly illuminated the claustrophobic space.

"The body is . . . mushy," Tim called up. Then another long pause. A few moments later, the heavy sound of rocks and plastic sliding echoed upward. "The machete is really jammed in here. . . . Okay, I think I got it. They're both down in the cavern. I'll follow them down."

Sayer hurried to the rim to let Dana know they had one more body to pull up.

SOUTHERN RANGER STATION, SHENANDOAH NATIONAL PARK, VA

Sayer sat in the empty medical area of the ranger station, staring at her phone in the late afternoon light. She'd just hung up with the local police departments to let them know that they had an active killer on the loose.

Pinching her nose to ward off a headache, Sayer looked over at the small sword wrapped in an evidence bag, then over at the two full body bags lying on two stainless steel tables, then back at her phone. She didn't want to call Holt, but she knew she'd better report in soon.

She tried to ignore the vague stench of death permeating the air.

With a dread-filled sigh, she finally dialed.

"Holt," the assistant director barked on the phone. A muted cacophony of voices filled the background. "Make it fast, Sayer, I'm about to walk in to testify."

"We just found two fresh bodies in the bone cave." Sayer spit it out as quickly as possible. With Holt it was never a good idea to beat around the bush.

"Define *fresh*."

"One only a few days old. The other probably a few weeks or maybe a few months at most. We'll know more after Dana does the autopsies."

"Jesus, Sayer. What the hell did you find, some kind of murder convention? Are the bones and the new bodies related?"

"No clue." Sayer sipped cool water, hoping something would soothe her burning throat. Her blistered fingers protested where she curled them around the cup. "The proximity of the victims could point to a connection, but the new bodies were wrapped in plastic. There's no evidence of similar treatment for the skeletal remains. Those are pretty different methods of disposal."

"And I suppose you want to run both investigations."

"You know I do." Sayer let her comment hang. It had been a rough few years. After her fiancé's death, Sayer had spiraled into a dark place where she'd withdrawn from her friends and family. But breaking her last case and getting shot were like a wake-up call. Or more like a two-by-four to the back of her head. She felt more driven than ever to do what she did best, stopping killers.

Holt was silent for so long Sayer was about to press her case, but Holt finally said, "All right."

Sayer decided to push her luck even further. "Any chance this turns into a task force? Two women dead. Presumably another six or seven people murdered sometime in the past. This could be a local serial killer." She needed a team of data techs, a profiler, maybe another investigator or two.

"Not a chance. We're spread thin as ice in a Kentucky winter. The congressional committee's got half our agents testifying and the other half helping evaluate old cases. The FBI's the Wild West of law enforcement right now. I've arranged for Dana and her team to stay for the duration. Otherwise you're on your own."

"I at least need Ezra." Though he was still recovering from the blast that took both of his lower legs, Sayer knew she was going to need Ezra Coen, the best data-cruncher and computer wiz at the FBI.

"Done. I know he'll be thrilled," Holt said.

Sayer wasn't so sure, considering the fact that he had lost both his legs as a result of the last case they had worked together.

"Hang on." Someone spoke to Holt and she said, her voice muffled, "I'll be right in." Her voice returned to the phone. "All right, Sayer, meet me up at Quantico tonight at eight to fill me in. But it's your investigation. Ezra's yours for the duration. Use the locals if you need more help. Do it right." Holt hung up.

Dana came through the double swinging doors as Sayer put down her phone.

"I see you spoke with Holt." She smiled at Sayer's tight expression. Little arcs of white ointment smeared Dana's cheeks, covering a smattering of blisters. "We getting a task force?"

"Holt compared the FBI to the Wild West right now, so doesn't sound like it."

"Yeehaw," Dana said with a wry smile, whirling her hand over her head like she held a lasso. "Did you tell her about the fire?"

"I neglected to mention it. . . ." Sayer refused to give Holt any reason to pull her off these cases.

"Sayer! You know it'll be in my report."

Sayer ignored her, looking around the sterile room. "Quite the fancy setup, for a ranger station."

Dana gave her a hard stare but let it go. "Yeah, they used to run a medical facility. Closed down due to budget cuts." Dana began unpacking autopsy equipment. "It is perfect. There's the medical suite here, a main conference room next door, and a bunch of smaller offices down the hall, plus a utility room we can set up for the bones."

"What did Max say about security?" After the attack, Sayer wanted to make sure the ranger station could be secured.

"Piper already arranged for a Rockfish Gap uniform to guard the crime scene. There're only two ways into the building here. We'll keep the back door locked up and Piper is going to set up a rotation to make sure there's a park ranger sitting inside the front door twenty-four seven. With those precautions in place, Max seems confident we're safe." Dana pulled on gloves, face serious. "Now, let's figure out what happened to these victims and nail a bad guy, shall we?"

"Or bad girl . . . ," Sayer added, unwilling to assume anything. She watched Dana bustling around the bodies. "Man, I'm glad you're back."

Dana looked up, face pinched. "I wish Jake was here so we could all go out and celebrate after we close this case."

Sayer's throat closed with sudden emotion. Though her fiancé had died on the job almost four years ago, she had only recently discovered that his death wasn't what it seemed. All she knew was that someone at the FBI was lying about the undercover operation he had been running when he died. She really wanted to talk to Dana about what she'd discovered, but now wasn't the time.

"Me too," she managed to say. "Let's get these autopsies going. I've got to talk to Kyle Nelson about his missing sister at five and I'd like to see what we've got here first."

Dana called for an assistant to come help and began to unzip the first body bag. Sayer went to her side, feeling like the hunt was truly about to begin.

CONGRESSIONAL HEARING CHAMBERS, CAPITOL HILL, WASHINGTON, D.C.

FBI Assistant Director Janice Holt straightened her emerald-green pantsuit, smoothed her helmet of gray hair, and strode into the congressional hearing chambers with her battle face on. She'd hunted serial killers and stood up to international crime bosses, but this was different. Until recently, she had assumed that the men and women sitting in this room were on her side. Now she knew better.

Holt made her way to the table at the center of the chamber, where a single chair and microphone awaited. She sat down and looked up at the somber faces staring down at her like a row of clones forged of wealth and wrinkles.

"Thank you for coming again, Assistant Director Holt," the man at the center of the dais spoke.

Senator John DeWitt. Holt had gone to his goddamned wedding. She had been to his home for dinner. And now he stared with cold eyes.

"I hearby call into session day three of the Quantico Hearings."

He shifted in his seat. Good, at least he seemed uncomfortable with this farce. She fully supported an independent investigation into Quantico, but this hearing was nothing more than a politicized sham.

"Now, Janice"—he spoke her name with a familiarity that made her clench her teeth—"we would like to pick up where we left off talking about SSA Sayer Altair."

"All right, John." She said his name with only a little bit of venom.

"Very good. So, Janice, you promoted Agent Altair to senior special agent approximately six months ago, just as she began her investigation into the Cage Killings?"

"Correct." Holt tried to keep the bark from her voice and failed miserably.

"And were you aware at that time that she did not meet the official criteria for promotion?"

"One, I disagree with your assessment. You know perfectly well that she was more than qualified to receive that promotion. And two, I fail to see the problem. Agent Altair was promoted and then went on to bring down one of the most prolific serial killers in the history of the United States."

A young senator whom Holt barely recognized leaned forward and spoke into his microphone. "A serial killer who worked right under your nose, and alongside Agent Altair, for years. How is it, Janice"—he smiled, clearly aware that his using her name annoyed her—"that no one in your entire organization at Quantico suspected that you worked with, and I quote, 'one of the most prolific serial killers in the history of the United States'?"

Holt briefly imagined flipping the table and storming out of the room before forcing herself to calm down and answer the question.

SOUTHERN RANGER STATION, SHENANDOAH NATIONAL PARK, VA

Dana began the autopsy with a visual inspection of the first body. Her assistant hovered nearby, ready to help.

"We'll start with the most recent victim because her body is the most well preserved. Victim is wrapped in thick sheet plastic," Dana said into a small recorder. "She's bound in fetal position. I see what appears to be a nylon rope tied around her wrists holding her in said position. Based on visual cues alone, she appears to be a young woman, perhaps mid-twenties, with short blond hair. I'll remove the plastic now."

As Dana cut away the plastic, Piper peeked through the door. "You guys mind if I come watch?"

Sayer grunted an okay. "Just stay back."

Piper gently shut the door and tiptoed over against the back wall. "I'll be quiet as a mouse." She took off her brown park-ranger hat and held it as a sign of respect.

Dana peeled back the plastic and gently rolled the body from the gurney onto the sterile silver table so the assistant could gather the plastic into a large white bag. "Labeling the plastic and sending it to the lab for trace and fingerprint analysis," Dana said into the mic.

She paused to take a series of photographs, then rolled the victim onto her back, still hunched in fetal position. With the plastic gone, Sayer could clearly see the black rope wrapped tightly around her wrists. The gloved assistant held the woman's arms in place while Dana expertly snipped off the rope and put it into an evidence bag. Together they gently unfolded the woman's arms and legs.

"Limbs are pliable. Rigor mortis has completely passed. Based on that and the relative lack of bloat, my preliminary time of death estimate is three to three-and-a-half days ago."

Sayer focused on the victim. Her skin appeared slightly spongy. Despite the scrapes and bruises on her cheek and nose, it was clear that the woman had been pretty, with a slightly pointed chin and high cheekbones.

"Visual inspection suggests major damage to her torso and face." Dana leaned in to look at her hands. "There are also multiple defensive wounds on her arms and hands."

Sayer swallowed a few times to push down the bile rising in her throat. She pulled her worry beads from her pocket to keep her hands busy while she observed.

"The injuries to her face show no clear weapon marks, suggesting that they were likely done with something blunt, possibly bare hands. I'll admit, I expected to find defined cut marks based on the bladed weapon we found with the bodies. But no sign of any weapon marks here."

"So should we assume that the machete is associated with the bones instead of with these bodies?" Piper asked.

"I think it's a safe assumption that it's not associated with this body." Dana leaned in close to the victim's face and frowned. "I'll examine these injuries in more detail after I complete the visual inspection of the remains." She lifted a small handheld light and spoke into the recorder. "I'll now examine the body with a UV light for signs of sexual assault or other bodily fluids."

She looked over at Piper, who was still hugging the wall. "Would you kill the lights?"

Piper barely tore her eyes away from the dead woman long enough to flip the switch.

The UV light flickered on and Dana held it over the body.

Sayer's stomach lurched with horror. She stared down at the victim's body, which lit up head to toe under the UV light.

"Oh, my god," Dana whispered.

"What is that?" Piper's voice rose and she took a half step closer, clearly repulsed but also wanting to get a better look.

Hundreds of lines fluoresced like stripes along the woman's arms and legs.

Across her abdomen, in large block letters, the words *HELP US* glowed a bright blue.

"What on earth?" Sayer said.

"I've . . . never seen anything like this," Dana said.

"Is that written in blood?" Piper asked.

"No." Dana slowly slid the light along the victim's body. "Blood doesn't glow like this unless you use luminol. This is much more likely semen or saliva. Given the quantity here, I'd guess this is saliva."

"It says *HELP US* . . . ," Sayer said, heart hammering her chest. "And those marks on her ams and legs?"

"I'd say it looks like someone tried to deposit as much DNA here as possible."

"Like someone smeared saliva on her in stripes," Sayer said.

Dana swallowed hard and nodded.

Piper asked with a shaky voice, "So now what?"

Dana gestured for her assistant. "Now we swab all of this for DNA analysis. Once I'm done with our first victim, I'll swab the other victim for DNA and send the samples up to Quantico tonight. Let's follow directions and see if we can, in fact, help whoever wrote us a message on a dead woman's body."

UNKNOWN LOCATION

The faint roaring sound slowly woke Hannah Valdez. She opened her eyes. The bright light made her cringe and a relentless pounding filled her head as she slowly regained consciousness. Blinking rapidly, she felt as if someone had stuffed gauze around her eyes and into her mouth. Only after a few moments contemplating her inability to move did the sudden thought sear through her brain that she didn't know where she was. A wave of panic and confusion swept through her and she struggled to sit up. A second wave of panic peaked even higher as the name *Sam!* pierced Hannah's muddled head. The thought of her young daughter sent tingles of fear down to the tips of her toes, and the will to sit up finally overcame the thickness in her limbs.

She remembered leaving the gym, clipping her two-year-old, Sam, into her car seat . . . and then . . . what?

From her barely upright position, Hannah's eyes swept the room as she tried to orient herself. The scent of bleach burned her nose.

A roaring sound rumbled in the distance. A train? A river?

Hannah sat on a cold floor. Rough stone walls made her squint, and she could not seem to clear her mind. For a moment she was sure she was in some kind of windowless tomb, buried alive and left to die.

Then her eyes settled on a metal door. A cry escaped her lips as she struggled to one knee. Something heavy hung around her neck and she reached up to feel a bulky necklace. A thick plastic box hung against her throat, two dull prongs poking into her bare flesh.

On her hands and knees, she crawled to the door and pulled herself to her feet. She supported herself on the doorframe as the blood rushed from her head, the entire room disappearing from view. As her vision cleared she began banging on the cold metal.

"Help!" she tried to cry out. Instead of a full-throated shout, her voice came out in a husky whisper.

The sudden movement surged blood through her body, overcoming her ability to stand. Hannah's knees buckled and she vomited as she fell back into unconsciousness, her body smacking loudly on the rocky floor.

SOUTHERN RANGER STATION,
SHENANDOAH NATIONAL PARK, VA

Sayer stepped out of the makeshift autopsy suite to call her data analyst and tech wizard, Ezra, to make sure he was on board and to request a jump to the front of the line with the rapid DNA machines. The Quantico DNA lab had just reopened and they were going to need a rush on this.

She got voice mail and left Ezra a message.

After she hung up, Sayer watched the rain through the window for a long moment. The horrific implications of the writing on their victim tightened her chest with a potent combination of rage and disgust. Were there more victims out there right now being held somewhere? Or was it already too late?

Questions rumbling around her head, she glanced at the time. She still had an hour before Kyle Nelson was supposed to arrive to talk about his missing sister, so she returned to the autopsy room.

Under the harsh light, Dana had the flesh from the victim's face grasped in two clamps. She began to peel it down like a mask as she narrated, "I'm removing the flesh from the face and skull."

Piper stood in the corner looking slightly green. To her credit she hadn't fled or puked. Sayer briefly wondered why she had wanted to watch all this in the first place.

Dana paused for a long time, carefully inspecting the woman's face with the flesh removed. "You know, there are a number of breaks to her facial bones. I thought I could do this here without any scanning tech, but I really want X-rays of the bones before I go any further."

She stood up and stretched. "Let's call around and see if we can find a nearby hospital I can use. Though before we do that, let's cut the plastic off the other body and do some basic trace and DNA collection. That way we can get the initial DNA analysis started tonight, then I can finish up the autopsies in the morning after I take some X-rays."

"Sounds good," Sayer said.

Dana changed gloves and went to the next table with a sterile scalpel. She looked up at Piper. "I should warn everyone, I can make out some blistering on her skin through the plastic, which means that this body is in pretty active decay. Some of the soft tissue will be close to liquefaction."

"In other words, it's going to smell really bad," Sayer said.

Piper nodded wordlessly.

The medical examiner unzipped the body bag covering the second victim and sliced the plastic sheeting. With the plastic off, the putrescent stench of rot thickened the air. Sayer swallowed repeatedly, trying unsuccessfully to prevent the smell from coating her tongue.

Piper let out a strangled gagging sound but stood her ground.

Without the plastic holding it tightly, the woman's body slumped loosely on the table. Her greenish flesh looked much more bloated than the first victim's.

Dana spoke into her microphone. "I'm now doing initial DNA and trace gathering on Jane Doe Two. She's bloated but her skin is still intact. I'd estimate time of death between two and two-and-a-half weeks ago. Like Jane Doe One, Jane Doe Two shows extensive evidence of trauma to the face and body. I'm gathering DNA and will complete the autopsy tomorrow morning after X-ray analysis." She bustled around the body with a series of swabs, scraping under her loose fingernails. She finished by sweeping the UV light over the body.

"No sign of writing on Jane Doe Two." Dana clicked off the mic and spoke softly. "Hey, Sayer? I'll wrap them back up so we can take them down for X-rays." She looked at her watch. "I think we can get the X-rays done tonight and then I'll finish the autopsies first thing."

Sayer nodded and left the room, wanting to talk to Max before Kyle Nelson arrived.

While Dana and her assistant prepared the bodies for transport to the local hospital, Sayer went outside to find Max and Kona. She stood under the narrow overhang, staring out at the pouring rain, processing the terrible images of the dead women. Standing exposed on the side of the building, she wished she had on her ballistic vest. A few minutes after Dana and her assistant pulled away in the van, Max and Kona emerged from the woods.

"Keeping watch?" she asked.

Max nodded, shaking the rain off his jacket while Kona shook her fur. "Just walking some circuits around the grounds. Someone just tried to kill two FBI agents. I think we should all be on high alert. How's the autopsy going?"

Sayer grimaced. "Well, we found *HELP US* written on the victim in some kind of bodily fluid. Dana's taking the bodies down to the hospital to get X-rays before she cuts them open."

"Someone wrote *HELP US* on the body?" Max said, forehead creased.

"Yeah, on her stomach, someone wrote *HELP US*, probably with saliva." Sayer let the words hang in the air for a moment. "So, what's the deal with Kyle Nelson? I thought he was going to punch you out at our crime scene."

Max paled. "Yeah, sorry about that. That was about Kyle's sister . . . Cricket. I mean, Catherine Nelson, but everyone called her Cricket." He put his face down in his hands and took a long, deep breath before looking back up at Sayer. "Oh, man, this is complicated. Cricket disappeared seventeen years ago . . . and I helped her do it."

UNKNOWN LOCATION

"Wake now."

The soft voice trickled slowly into Hannah Valdez's consciousness. The stench of bleach seared her nose before the rest of her senses returned.

"Wake now."

Someone shook her and she snapped awake, memories crashing through her body like a tidal wave.

Something wet wiped her face. Hannah instinctively jerked her head back and it slammed into something hard.

Starbursts exploded.

She blinked rapidly and forced her eyes open.

"I need to clean you up," a soft voice said.

Hannah's vision slid into focus on the woman hunched over her.

Her blond hair hung in thick clumps. Cuts and bruises in varying stages of healing mottled her face and arms. Between the bruises and her sunken cheeks, Hannah couldn't tell if she was fifteen or fifty. The woman held out a damp cloth, about to wipe Hannah's face again.

Hannah remembered waking in this room. Was that minutes ago, or days? And where was Sam?

The thought of her daughter shocked her entire system with a buzzing rage unlike anything she'd ever felt. She violently grabbed the woman's wrist and got in her face, spit flying as she shouted, "Where is my daughter?"

"Shhhh." The woman looked down at the box hanging at Hannah's neck, eyes wide with fear. "He might be here. . . ."

"Where am I?" Hannah persisted.

"Just let me clean you up, please."

"Answer me!" Hannah yanked the woman forward, almost pulling her off her feet.

The woman blinked a few times and hissed, "Careful!" She gestured to her collar.

Hannah let go of the woman's wrist and felt the box the size of her fist hanging tight around her throat. Its metal prongs poked uncomfortably against her bare flesh. She realized that this woman wore a similar necklace.

The woman pressed her mouth into a thin line, eyes pleading. "Please."

Overwhelmed by the horror of everything happening, Hannah wretched as bile flooded her mouth. A thick ball of the bile dribbled down her chin.

Hannah's voice dipped low, emotion building in her chest so violently she half stood up, pushing the woman away. "Please, just tell me if you have a little girl here." She tried to keep her tone calm and even. "My daughter . . ." her voice broke, unable to complete the sentence.

The woman's eyes flickered to her face. "I don't know," she whispered. "I don't know if she's here."

The fear on her face and her injuries made Hannah want to take her in her arms and protect her. But, at the same time, she wanted to wrap her hands around the woman's neck and throttle her, force her to tell her where Sam was.

This woman clearly had a key to Hannah's door and could move about freely, but she was also obviously injured. Was she one of Hannah's captors? Or was she a victim as well?

The wildly conflicting emotions turned into a sob that broke from her mouth, body shuddering. "Sam," Hannah whispered, "my baby, please."

The corners of the woman's chapped lips twitched strangely. "Just let me clean you up."

She resumed her rote wiping, gently removing the bile from Hannah's chin.

Too weak and dizzy to act on her rage, Hannah let her.

SOUTHERN RANGER STATION, SHENANDOAH NATIONAL PARK, VA

Sayer stared at Max expectantly. "I'm going to need you to explain exactly what you mean. You helped the chief of police's sister disappear?"

He blew out a hard breath. "Well, this isn't the story I expected to be telling right now. . . ." He looked out at the rain.

Sayer tried to wait but was all out of patience. "Max?"

"Yeah, sorry. This is just . . . back in high school I had a reputation."

"As?"

"I don't know, a good guy, I guess. It started when some assholes were really hassling a girl at a party out on an old farm. They cornered her in the barn and I heard her scream. I went in and ran them off."

"Ran them off?"

"To be more precise, I punched the lights out of one of them." Max smiled at the memory. "They were seniors and I was a freshman. . . ."

"Okay, so you were seen as a safe person by the girls at your high school."

"Right," Max said, "which is probably why Cricket came to my house in the middle of the night."

"When was this?" Sayer asked.

"About four days after our high school graduation. We were in the same class but, honestly, I barely knew her. Only in that way you know someone in a small town, you know? I was about to ship off to the Air Force Academy for a summer program. I'm not sure if she had college plans or what. Like I said, we weren't exactly friends."

"But she showed up at your house in the middle of the night?"

"Covered in blood."

"Okay. . . ."

"Yeah, I know. She had a split lip, bruises around her neck where someone had clearly tried to strangle her. Her knuckles were split open and she had a major cut on her hand. She said that her dad was trying to kill her and that she had to get away."

"Her dad?"

Max squinted. Uncomfortable. "I'll admit, I was shocked, because I knew her dad. He always seemed totally nice. But I was no idiot kid. Even back then I knew how domestic abuse works."

"Abusers never do conveniently have fangs and horns," Sayer agreed.

"They're usually really good at hiding what they do behind closed doors," Max continued. "Hell, for my social studies class I'd even read a whole book I found in the library about domestic violence. It scared the crap out of me."

Sayer almost smiled at the image of an earnest eighteen-year-old Max hunched over a book about domestic violence.

"So"—Max gestured awkwardly—"I've got this scared girl hiding in my room and had no idea what to do. Two small-town kids. I couldn't send her home. My mom is great, but not at that kind of thing, you know? And after reading about how cops sometimes deal with domestic violence, I didn't know if the police would even believe her. Some teenage girl's word against her churchgoing dad's word. So we came up with a plan. . . ."

"Which was?"

"Which was to help her run away. That night. She took a shower, cleaned herself up. I stole some of my mom's clothes for her to wear and gave her four hundred bucks, which was all I had. I called a battered women's shelter up in D.C. and arranged for her to stay there that night. Then I took her to the bus station just after dawn."

Max fell silent, hand resting on Kona's back.

"I sense there's a 'but' to the story," Sayer said.

"But"—Max gave a rueful smile—"I have no idea what happened to her after I dropped her at the bus station. I called the shelter that evening to make sure she got there safely and they said she never showed. At the time I figured that she must have just wanted to put all of Rockfish Gap behind her, including me. And I thought that maybe the shelter was lying to me. For all they knew, I was the guy she was running from."

"So you don't really know what happened to her?"

"No clue. I never heard from her again, but Kyle must have known I was involved somehow, because he was convinced I did something to his sister." Max stared out at the rain for a long moment. "Kyle and his dad came out the next day and asked me a bunch of questions about that night. If I'd seen Cricket at all. I told her dad that I hadn't seen her. I mean, he had to know that she just ran away, considering he's the one that hurt her in the first place. Far as I know, no one in Rockfish Gap has seen her since. . . ."

"But Kyle obviously thinks something happened to her and that you had something to do with it. You let her family think she was dead?"

Max nodded slowly. "I mean, I guess, as far as I know, she is dead. But it's even worse than that. I left Rockfish the next day, but heard later that her mom had a stroke and died just after Cricket left. I still wonder, did Cricket's dad hurt her mom, or did her mom die of grief not knowing what happened to her daughter? It felt right at the time. I mean, Cricket was so afraid. But looking back, maybe I royally screwed up. And now her brother is chief of police. . . ."

Sayer stood silent for a long time, processing Max's story. "Bottom line is that you don't actually know what happened to her?"

"Right."

"And the local chief of police is convinced that you had something to do with his sister's disappearance."

"Also right."

"And he clearly suspects that she is dead. So much so, he was convinced that we'd just found his dead sister when he heard about these remains." Sayer let that sink in. "Okay, Kyle will be here any minute."

"You think I should tell him what really happened?" Max did not look happy.

"Unless you can think of a legitimate reason not to."

Max's confidence wilted slightly. "Does not wanting to admit that I might have really fucked up count as a legitimate reason?"

Sayer didn't even dignify the comment with an answer as they watched Kyle park his police cruiser next to the ranger station.

The police chief hunched forward as he followed Sayer and Max into the main conference room.

"Please sit, Chief Nelson." She gestured to a chair and took a seat at the head of the table. Max sat next to her, Kona at his feet.

Kyle's eyes drifted over to Max.

Max met his stare with a neutral expression.

"Chief Nelson, as a fellow law enforcement officer, you understand that we are still in the preliminary stages of our investigation here, so I'm not even sure yet if your sister will be among the remains we've found."

He tore his eyes away from Max to look at Sayer. "Of course I understand. And please, call me Kyle." He took a deep breath. "Could you let me know what you have so far? All I know is what Piper told me when she called to notify us of the presence of human remains."

Sayer slid a file folder across the table. "This is everything we have. This morning, Agent Cho fell into a sinkhole, where we found the remains of approximately six or seven skeletons that do not appear to be recently deposited."

"Any sense how old they are?" Kyle asked.

"Not yet. But, in addition to the bones, we also found two recently deposited victims, and our forensic anthropologist has begun to autopsy the recent victims."

"How recent?"

Sayer spread her hands. "Again, we don't know yet."

"Any ID?" Kyle's eyes momentarily drifted back to Max.

"Not yet. We've sent blood samples to the three-hour DNA machines up at Quantico and should have the results by morning."

Kyle nodded, mouth in a white line. Every time his eyes drifted back to Max, his long face tensed.

"We have a team documenting and removing the skeletal remains right now and will hopefully begin to process those tomorrow. As you can see, we're still trying to understand what's going on," Sayer said.

Kyle slowly leaned forward. "What's going on is that Max Cho knows something about Cricket's disappearance that he has been lying about for seventeen years."

"You're right, Kyle," Max said softly.

Kyle blinked a few times with surprise but didn't move. His balled fists pressed into the table in front of him.

"Seventeen years ago your sister came to me and told me what your dad did to her," Max said evenly. "She was beaten up, terrified. So I tried to help her escape. She was supposed to build a new life. . . ."

Kyle's blinking got more rapid, his breathing shallow. His knuckles whitened as he pressed harder and harder onto the conference table.

Max rushed on. "But I genuinely don't know what happened to her after I dropped her off at the bus station. I thought she just . . . put us all behind her. I thought I was helping her get away from your dad by lying—"

Kyle lunged toward Max. He moved so quickly that Sayer barely had time to step between the two men.

"Hey!" Sayer put a firm hand on Kyle's chest, ready to react if he struck out at either her or Max.

Kyle stopped his advance, but his body quivered, rage radiating off him like heat. She could hear Max's shallow breath just behind her.

Standing next to Max, Kona let out a rumbling growl.

No one moved for a very long moment.

Finally Kyle forced words out. "You have the nerve to admit what I've always known, that you had something to do with Cricket's disappearance. Then you accuse my father of some kind of abuse?" Kyle's voice rose to a shout so loud Sayer's ears rang. "You spew disgusting lies about my dead father not even six months after he dies? How can anyone possibly believe a word you say, you lying bastard?"

Shaking, he looked at Sayer. "You get him the hell out of my sight or I won't be responsible for what I do next."

Sayer kept a light hand on Kyle's chest but turned to Max and nodded. "Just go. I'll finish up here."

"But—" Max began.

"Go!" Kyle's voice thundered so loudly the walls vibrated.

Max held up his hands and backed out of the room. Kona followed.

Kyle remained frozen, towering over Sayer, panting with emotion as they listened to Max and Kona's footsteps retreat down the hall.

"Chief Nelson." Sayer used his title, hoping to remind him that he wasn't just an angry brother and son. It worked, and Kyle took a step back, shoulders falling slightly.

"Agent Altair, that man is a snake and a liar," he said as he moved to his chair and slowly lowered himself down. "I see he has you just as snowed as everyone else."

Kyle placed both hands flat on the table, trying to steady himself. "He pulls the same thing everywhere he goes. White-knight war hero with a heart of gold. And the ladies fall for it every time."

Sayer reined in her sharp response that she was no lady fawning over a white knight. "I just met Agent Cho this morning. Even though he works at the FBI, I promise you that I have no allegiance to anyone or anything other than the truth."

Kyle stared at Sayer, blue eyes stormy. "I apologize, but surely you'll understand if I don't take your word on that one. I've heard about your illustrious history working with killers. It's enough for me to wonder about the FBI's screening process. . . ."

Sayer bit her tongue to prevent herself from reacting to his barb. She took a measured breath, trying to remind herself that this man had lost his entire family and that he had good enough instincts to know that Max was hiding something. No wonder he was suspicious of Max, and of the FBI by extension. And the current scandal and circus on Capitol Hill wasn't helping matters. This was exactly what Assistant Director Holt was most worried about, local law enforcement no longer trusting the FBI.

"Kyle"—she purposefully switched back to his first name—"I promise I'll keep you up-to-date on things as they unfold, and I hope we can work together to figure out if your sister is involved here in any way. In that spirit, I'll grant you full access to our files." She stopped just short of inviting him to join her team. He was too emotionally involved to be of use.

They stared at each other in a small standoff before Kyle seemed to release something. "Thank you. You know, my dad was a good man. He didn't raise a hand to us. Ever. Which is why I don't believe Max's story for a second."

Sayer nodded slowly. "I would really appreciate it if you could talk me through what happened back then."

"Listen, I was fifteen when Cricket disappeared. She was eighteen and didn't exactly hang out with her baby brother. She left and my mom died. It was . . . hard on me and my dad."

"Is there anything at all you can remember about her disappearance? Anything about that night?"

Kyle closed his eyes as if pained by the thought. When he opened them, Sayer could see the boy who had lost his sister all those years ago.

"All I know is that, on that night, I lost someone I dearly loved. And no matter what Maxwell Cho claims, I'm entirely sure that he had something more to do with it."

As he stalked from the room, Sayer wondered what exactly had happened to Cricket Nelson seventeen years ago.

• • •

Sayer went outside to watch Kyle drive off in his cruiser.

Max and Kona emerged behind her as the police chief wound down the long road toward Skyline Drive.

"That went well," Sayer said. Her voice was slightly hoarse. From the fire? Or had she yelled during the confrontation between Max and Kyle? She couldn't even remember for sure.

"Yeah . . . guess I shouldn't be the liaison with the locals. . . ." Max tried for lighthearted.

"You think?" Sayer was in no mood for jokes. The adrenaline rush from Kyle's aggression shouldn't have shaken her so much. Agents went through highly stressful training to short-circuit the instinctual reaction to danger, sometimes called the goofy loop because people did and said nonsensical things. At the academy, she'd been famously calm no matter what they threw at her, but right now Sayer could feel her heart still thudding in her chest.

She looked over at Max for a very long time. The man was a veteran, a respected FBI agent, and her gut said he was a genuinely good guy. She sure as hell hoped that her gut was right and that he hadn't actually done something to Cricket Nelson. But for all she knew, he could be their killer. She hated that she even thought it, but she'd learned the hard way not to trust anyone, not even her coworkers at the FBI.

Because Kyle Nelson was right, she had worked alongside a serial killer for years and she hadn't known it. A truly skilled psychopath is virtually impossible to detect. What if Max was the same?

Max kept his eyes on the rain, face drawn. "He's not wrong, you know. I lied to him. I always assumed that she just . . . left this all behind."

"I know." Sayer watched him closely but saw only remorse. Nothing to suggest that Kyle was right about Max, but she wasn't taking anything for granted.

"Now I can't stop thinking, what if she's one of the skeletons we just found and I left her there that morning to be murdered?"

Sayer had no answer.

Max closed his eyes, clearly about to say something. Eventually he opened them and seemed to shake off whatever he was thinking. Instead he changed the subject. "Hey, Dana said we're going to stay nearby."

"Yeah, there's a hotel down the hill. I have to head back up to Quantico tonight, but I'll swing by on my way out of town and get you all set up to stay there."

"Piper said the ranger cabins are empty." Max pointed down a muddy trail.

Sayer could just make out a series of tin-roofed cabins along a small ravine.

"The rangers assigned to the park all stay at the northern station. She said we're welcome to stay in the cabins if we want."

"You think it's safe here?"

"I've checked the door locks and they meet my approval," Max said. "I actually think we'll be safer here than a hotel where we can't control the environment. I was thinking of staying with my mom, but I'll stay up here with you all."

Sayer side-eyed the cabins. *Rustic* was too kind a word for the moss-covered buildings.

"They're pretty utilitarian, but warm and dry," Max added.

"All right. That's easier, at least."

Sayer could see that Max was still distracted. She decided to try and be supportive. "Hey. We'll figure out what happened with Cricket Nelson. Let's just focus on saving whoever wrote *HELP US* on our victim right now."

Max waited for her to say more.

"That was it for my encouraging pep talk."

Max let out a joyless laugh. "So, the writing on our recent body suggests we've got more victims out there somewhere." He pointed to the thick woods surrounding the ranger station.

"I think it's a good possibility. I called the search team at Quantico and they're putting a helicopter up at first light to look for any heat signatures in the surrounding area, but this park is over three hundred square miles." Sayer glanced down at Kona. "You think we should bring in a K9 team to search around the bone cave?"

"Nah." Max ruffled the dog's fur. "Kona did a full sweep. The rain really messes with scent. If we had a concentrated area to search, it might work, but a random grid search won't give us much in this weather."

"How does that even work? Doesn't she need the scent of a specific person to follow?"

"Not really. I mean, she can do that, but dogs who trail a specific person tend to be ground-scenters. They follow the scent along a specific path at the ground level. Kona's an air-scenter, which means that she can follow any human or cadaver smell that she finds in the air."

"The smell is up in the air?" Sayer asked, genuinely curious. She'd seen tracking dogs in action but had no idea how it worked.

"Yeah, you shed thousands of cells a second. Those particles linger in what I like to think of as currents, each one with a distinct smell. There are thousands of these rivers of scent constantly flowing around everything." Max waved his hand.

"So Kona follows those currents."

"Exactly. If you were to walk down a path, you would leave a trail. As you move, it dissipates out into a cone shape behind you."

"And she finds those cones."

Max nodded. "And once she finds the scent cone, she does a zigzag pattern back and forth, finding the edges of the scent. Then she follows those edges as the cone narrows inward toward the person. Kona is one of the best air-scenters I've ever seen." His eyes shone with pride. "But the rain pulls all that down to the ground, where it pools into little eddies, making it almost impossible for her to follow over any distance."

"All right, damn." Sayer stared out at the rain. "Well, we'll have DNA results by tomorrow. Dana and her team should be back soon with the X-rays."

Max absentmindedly petted Kona, who leaned against his leg. "So the writing said *HELP US* . . . plural."

"Yeah . . ." Sayer trailed off as she glanced at the time. She still had a few minutes before she needed to head up to meet with Holt. With a sigh, she slid down against the wall and sat on the cold concrete. Max joined her. Kona lay down across his feet, sitting at attention like a sphinx.

"Does she ever relax?" Sayer asked, petting Kona's damp fur. "My dog would already be sprawled out, trolling for belly rubs."

"Never. Kona's always on duty."

Sayer looked over at Max. His eyes roved the edge of the woods, his shoulders tense, face tight with concentration. "Looks to me like Kona takes after her human."

Max let out a short laugh. "Yeah, I suppose that might be true."

"I know how that feels." Sayer pictured her spartan apartment back in Alexandria. Since taking in Adi, Sayer had tried to spruce the place up, but it was still essentially bare.

They watched the rain for a few more minutes before Sayer shifted back to the case. "What are the chances that a nonlocal knew about that cave? Especially considering how big this park is."

"We could ask around, but I've never heard of it. It's not particularly remote, but it is well hidden."

"That makes it seem more likely that our bones and our recent bodies are related. If that cave isn't common knowledge, what are the chances that two different killers decided to dump bodies in the same place?" Sayer shifted on the cold concrete. "But I guess we can't really answer that until we ID our victims and determine cause of death."

"Sounds to me like we're on hold until we get more data."

"Too many questions, not enough answers," Sayer agreed. She hated this point in an investigation. It always felt like the quiet before the storm.

"Well, when I hit walls like that, I usually eat. It's dinnertime. Would you care to join me?" Max flourished a box of granola bars from his bag. Sayer half smiled.

"I'd love to, but I've actually got to report in with Holt up at Quantico tonight, then head home to interview a psychopath."

"Wow, guess I can't compete with the assistant director of the FBI and a psychopath," he said with mock offense.

Sayer couldn't even force another partial smile, feeling no humor in the moment.

As night began to fall, she rode northeast beneath the weeping sky.

FBI HEADQUARTERS,
QUANTICO, VA

Sayer arrived at Quantico after a miserable two-hour ride. The downpour stopped just as she pulled into the parking lot.

"Really?" She looked up at the last streaks of dusk on the horizon. "The rain stops now?"

Across the training field, Assistant Director Janice Holt stood under an overhang outside the headquarters of the Behavioral Analysis Unit.

Holt raised a hand in a gruff greeting. "Let's walk and talk. I need some fresh air while there's a break in the rain." Her voice carried on the wind.

Sayer fell in beside Holt and the two women strolled in silence around the grounds of Quantico. FBI trainees jogged by in small groups. Staccato bursts of automatic gunfire in the distance competed with the rhythmic clacking of Holt's heels. At the FBI Academy, up-and-coming agents didn't let a little bad weather or the late hour get in the way of their training.

"You ready to be back in the field?" Holt finally asked.

"You know I am."

Holt nodded, stress lines pulling at the corners of her mouth.

"You want to tell me why we're not having this conversation in your office?" Sayer asked. Holt wasn't exactly the stroll-around-outside-on-a-blustery-evening type.

Holt let out a sharp laugh. She always seemed a little surprised by Sayer's bluntness. "First you tell me what the hell Agent Cho found us. Some kind of cannibalistic serial-killer dump site?"

"We're not sure. Dana doesn't actually think there are any signs of cannibalism." Sayer pulled her sodden leather jacket around her shoulders.

"Well, that's good news. I was not looking forward to the media circus on that one. So, you've got a cave full of old bones and two new bodies."

"Along with some kind of sword-type thing. And someone wrote *HELP US* on the most recent body."

Holt stopped walking and looked at Sayer. "Wrote on the body?"

"With saliva, we think. I'm about to head over to the lab to drop off a bunch of samples from the bodies and a few DNA swabs from the sword. We'll know more by tomorrow."

Holt resumed walking, so Sayer kept talking.

"I let the surrounding police departments know what we found, see if they have any missing people we should know about. We've got one lead on a girl gone missing seventeen years ago, but no concrete link to anyone yet. The park rangers have offered to let us use their station house, so Dana is doing the autopsies and bone analysis there," Sayer said.

"She can do that without a lab?"

"She's got all her mobile lab equipment from the UN. She's going to do the autopsies first and then move on to the bones. I've already asked Ezra to get on the DNA up here. We'll hit the ground running first thing tomorrow."

Sayer and Holt walked in silence for a few moments.

"You want a partner for this case?" Holt finally asked.

Since she spent so much time on her neuroscience research, Sayer wasn't assigned a regular partner.

"Is Vik free?" Sayer hadn't seen Vik Devereaux, her previous partner and dear friend, in a few days. While she'd been recovering, he had been a constant presence, always showing up with good food and good company.

"Sorry, I know you two work well together, but he just left this morning to head up a task force chasing down a child-trafficking ring out in L.A. You want me to send Andy Wagner down to help?"

"No!" Sayer definitely did not want to work with the profiler she had recently accused of murder. Falsely. "I mean, no, thanks." She tried to sound casual.

Holt chuckled. "I'm just giving you a hard time. Andy is actually working with Vik in L.A. What about Max Cho? I think his supervisor was going to pull him off the case once you're settled in but we could have him assigned to you for the duration. He seems competent and he's from there. Could be an asset."

Sayer grunted agreement. She didn't have the energy to explain all the drama between Max and Kyle. Plus, despite her reservations about Max, he did know the lay of the land.

"Call my cell tomorrow with updates," Holt said. "I've been testifying all day and I'll be up in D.C. for the rest of the week." Her mood quickly shifted from vague bemusement to Valkyrie death stare.

Sayer stopped walking and looked intently at Holt. "More congressional hearings? Oh my god, you're worried they've bugged your office! That's why we're out here."

As residing head of Quantico, Assistant Director Holt was caught up in the fallout surrounding the murderous FBI agent. Sayer was convinced that Holt was going to end up being the ultimate scapegoat, despite being a loyal agent for over thirty years.

Holt pressed her lips together. "It would seem that's how the political cookie crumbles."

"But you've dedicated your life to this place." Sayer had always hated politics, but this was beyond comprehension. Holt had spent her entire career building up Quantico.

Holt waved her hand. "Politics will always matter more than things like that. Anyway, all this scandal happened on my watch. As goes Quantico, so go I." She smiled ruefully. "I'm just glad your new case is far away enough that you'll be out of the office for the next few weeks. Definitely stay down there, because I promise you do not want to be anywhere near this clusterfuck."

SAYER'S TOWN HOUSE,
ALEXANDRIA, VA

Sayer sped from Quantico to her town house in the oppressive dark, determined to make it home by nine-thirty to conduct her latest interview with a noncriminal psychopath. Balancing research with a field investigation was always a juggling act, but she would have to make it work.

She leaped from her motorcycle and sprinted upstairs, waving at Adi, who was once again reading on the futon. "Can't talk. I've got an interview!"

Sayer plopped down at the desk next to her mattress on the floor.

While the computer whirred to life, she checked the mirror and realized that she looked half feral. Between the cave fire, endless rain, and the long motorcycle ride, the first day of this case had taken its toll. She threw on a clean button-up shirt and smoothed back her hair before opening the video-chat app.

Almost immediately her computer *pinged* an incoming call. Subject 037's scheduled evaluation session.

She quickly ushered Vesper out into the living room so he wouldn't jump on-camera, then clicked answer.

A shadowy face appeared. Sayer could just make out a masculine silhouette in an otherwise dark room.

This was her thirty-seventh interview in less than a month and many of her previous subjects seemed unconcerned with showing her their faces. They actually seemed happy to video-chat with Sayer without obscuring their identity at all. A fact that surprised her until she remembered that psychopaths are nothing if not overconfident narcissists.

Hell, when she'd sent out the e-mails and put up flyers asking people who suspected they were psychopaths to contact her for an anonymous study of psychopaths without criminal records, she half expected no one to respond. But it turned out that Washington, D.C., was full of ambitious psychopaths wanting to brag about their exploits.

But Subject 037 was different. He clearly wanted to remain anonymous, a right she granted all her interview subjects. Even though she was interviewing psychopaths who claimed to have no criminal record, she knew that didn't necessarily mean they hadn't committed any crimes.

"Good evening." She read off her script. "Thank you for taking the time to participate in this research project. You have already read the information pamphlet explaining my research. Today I'm going to administer a series of diagnostic tests for psychopathy. These tests will take approximately two hours and the results will remain confidential. Do you consent to these evaluations?"

"I do, Agent Altair," the shadowy face said with a low voice.

"I would like to record these proceedings. Do you consent to being recorded?"

"I do."

"Great." Sayer checked the box on the form in front of her and then clicked record. "I'm now recording. In addition to this evaluation, I would like to conduct at least one follow-up interview, as well as ask you to participate in a series of noninvasive brain scans. I personally guarantee your anonymity during this process and you would be welcome to obscure your face at any stage. Do you understand and consent to this as well?"

"I do, Agent Altair. Goodness, with all these I do's it's almost like we're getting married." He chuckled. "You know, maybe once this interview is over we could get to know each other in person."

Sayer looked down at her list of evaluation questions. The first question was, *Does the subject exhibit glib and superficial charm?* She stopped herself from smiling. His response was a textbook example of superficial charm, which told her that he would most likely score high on the Psychopathy Checklist she was about to administer.

"I'm afraid it would be unethical to develop a personal relationship with a study subject," Sayer said calmly. "Now, let's begin."

After questioning Subject 037 about his suburban childhood, where he had multiple brushes with the law and extensive experience torturing animals, she moved on to his current life. He was quickly shaping up to be one of the highest-scoring psychopaths she had ever interviewed, criminal or not.

"So, can you tell me what you do for a living now? Feel free to leave out potentially identifying information. Do you hold down a stable job?"

"I'm someone of substantial power in Washington. I think that's all I'll say at the moment."

"A psychopath in Washington, D.C., is not unusual."

"True, we're all power-hungry and self-centered, aren't we? You know what the most fun part of my job is? I can justify anything I do as somehow good for the American public." He laughed the same low chuckle. "But you know all that already. You grew up here."

"You did your research about me," Sayer said with a casual smile. She knew this comment was an attempt to shift the power dynamic of the interview.

"No need for research. Before he passed away, I knew your grandfather, Senator McDuff, rather well. I also know your grandmother. Sophia is still a force to be reckoned with in this city."

Sayer felt slightly sick. If he was telling the truth, this man really was a Washington insider. Someone high up the food chain. Fortunately, psychopaths were consummate liars and often exaggerated their own importance.

"I even knew your mother." He paused. "Before she died, of course. . . ."

The mention of her mother blindsided Sayer. A ball of anger tinged with sorrow rose into her throat. She swallowed it back down, keeping her face neutral. He was trying to get an emotional reaction from her, and her family history wasn't exactly secret.

"Never met your father, though," Subject 037 continued. "He was from Senegal, right? I wonder how it was for you growing up here, a little biracial girl raised by her conservative white grandparents after Mommy and Daddy were killed in a car accident. How old were you when they died? Nine?"

Sayer said calmly, "Clearly you know the answer to that question."

"Now you're wondering who I am," he said. "If I'm telling the truth about knowing them."

"Maybe." Sayer shrugged as though she didn't have a care in the world. "But I agreed not to identify any of my interview subjects. I still want to scan your brain at some point and would never violate your anonymity."

"Of course you can scan my brain, Agent Altair." He said it in a way that implied something far more than brain scans.

Ignoring the comment, Sayer said, "Let's get back to the interview questions. So you hold a steady job. What do you think is the difference between you and a criminal psychopath?"

"I know exactly where the line is."

"Which line?"

"The line I can't cross without destroying everything I've worked for."

"And that's why you don't cross it? It's a risk assessment?" This was exactly the kind of information Sayer was seeking. Researchers believe that, for every psychopath caught by police, there are twenty thousand, maybe even thirty thousand psychopaths outside prison. She wanted to understand why some psychopaths become criminals and murderers while others manage to channel their psychopathy into productive careers.

"Exactly right," Subject 037 said slowly. "I have the same . . . dark urges as everyone, but I don't act on them because I have larger goals that are more important."

Sayer scrawled in her notes that perhaps the parts of his brain that allowed for impulse control were more intact than a typical serial killer. Most criminal psychopaths felt the need for instant gratification. Subject 037's ability to delay gratification was unusual. She couldn't wait to take a look inside his skull.

"So, you can purposefully inhibit criminal behavior?"

"Exactly. I might fantasize about sneaking into your place in Alexandria and trapping you in bed, then slowly sliding my knife across your throat just for the thrill of it all. Or better yet, your young ward, what's her name, Adi? Or your nana? Or your charming neighbor, Tino? But I wouldn't bother to do that."

Sayer swallowed. She had spent a lot of time and effort setting up safeguards to protect her private information, yet this man clearly knew where she lived, knew her nicknames for her family and friends. Perhaps he hadn't been lying about who he was. Intellectually she recognized that this was a typical power play of a psychopath. He was showing her that he had knowledge about her that would frighten her. He would feed off her fear.

She smiled casually and waited for him to continue.

"What, no, *You leave Adi alone!* or demands that I stay away from your family?" he asked.

Sayer smiled, baring her teeth just a little more than necessary. "No. I understand what you're trying to do and I'm not so easy to manipulate."

Subject 037 leaned forward, and in the screen light, Sayer could just make out his sneering grin. "Ah, how wonderful! That makes it much more fun." He paused and let out a long, satisfied sigh. "To answer your question, I wouldn't kill you because I have much more exciting things to do. Killing you would be fun but isn't worth the risk."

"So, the only reason you aren't a murderer is because you have other things you'd rather do."

"That's about right. Though I never said I wasn't a murderer."

"So, are you telling me that you have murdered before?" Sayer tried to sound casual, but her stomach twisted in a knot. Something about this man was way off. She'd heard researchers talk about a skin-crawling sensation when talking to a psychopath, but this was the first time she'd truly experienced it herself.

He chuckled. "Well, I can't tell you that. Let me just say that I wield more power than you can imagine. With a word, I could make you disappear from the earth as if you never even existed."

The confidence in his voice sent a chill along Sayer's spine.

"Do you believe me?" he asked softly, almost seductively.

"I certainly believe you believe what you're saying." Sayer flattened her tone, draining it of any emotion.

He let out another laugh, this time lower. Something about the sound made every hair on her body stand up, goose bumps rising along her arms, her deeply instinctual alarms sounding a warning.

He leaned forward with another smile. Had he noticed that he'd gotten to her?

"The serial killers you study are so plebeian. Why would I waste my time killing a single woman? I shape the course of history. I declare wars and then get to look into the eyes of the widows I've created. I hold the lives of millions of people in my hands. I have entire armies and world leaders acting out my will. I wonder, where do you think the line is between murder and war?"

"And you can do that now? Start wars?" Sayer asked through her tight throat. "Not many people have that kind of power."

There was a long silence. "I'm going to decline to respond to that comment."

Sayer looked at the clock and realized that she had gone way over the two hours she had set aside.

"You know," she said as lightly as possible, "I'm afraid the time I allotted for this interview has run out. Thank you for participating. Let's talk briefly tomorrow night for a follow-up. I'll send details via the chat feature."

Without waiting for him to acknowledge her comment, Sayer disconnected the call.

Her entire body sagged and she realized that her hands were shaking.

She quickly tallied up Subject 037's score on the checklist and she stared down at the number.

Forty out of forty. Anything above thirty qualified him as a genuine psychopath, but this was the first time that she had interviewed someone with a perfect score.

Notes in hand, Sayer retreated to the kitchen. She popped open a beer and went to check on Adi before heading to bed.

In the small circle of her reading light, Adi looked up from her textbook. "Another good interview, I see."

"Well, they're psychopaths, none of them are good. But this guy's history was disturbing. Suburban childhood with middle-class, doting parents." She took a swig of beer.

"So why does that bother you?"

"Because it sounds like he had a picture-book childhood. It's hard to reconcile that with the seriously dark shit he claims to have done in his lifetime. I understand all the science of psychopathy, but I still just have a hard time understanding how someone so screwed up can come out of such a good family."

Sayer flopped down next to Adi on the futon.

"You look kind of like you're about to be sick." Adi put her book down.

"Yeah." Sayer wiggled her fingers at Vesper. He enthusiastically jumped onto her lap. She buried her hand in his silvery fur. "It's pretty disturbing sometimes."

"What part is disturbing? That they're out there, or that the ones you're interviewing now have never been caught?"

"Both." Sayer realized that she was far more shaken than usual. That he named Adi in his list of theoretical targets caused a ball of conflicting emotions—primarily anger, but also fear, because now that she'd taken Adi in, it was her job to protect the girl from harm. Adi had already been through hell in her eighteen years. Sayer wanted to protect her, give her a stable place to live while she recovered from everything. But what if taking Adi in had just put the young woman at risk?

Adi grunted understanding. Her eyes looked slightly scared, and that made Sayer's rage flare even more. Adi had almost died at the hands of a psychopath, and here she was being triggered by Sayer's research.

Sayer wrapped her arms around Adi in a fierce hug. "But then I remind myself that, for every one of them, there are a hundred people like me working to make sure they can't hurt anyone." Sayer tried to sound confident, but the pit in her stomach wouldn't unclench. Something about Subject 037 set off every alarm in her body, but she couldn't pinpoint why. What was she afraid of?

EZRA COEN'S APARTMENT, QUANTICO, VA

Data analyst Ezra Coen sat in the dark and listened to Sayer's phone message a third time.

"Hey, Ez, Holt said you're up for working on my latest case. I've sent you the files. I dropped off DNA samples from the bodies and swabs off a sword we found. Can you talk to someone at the lab and get them going on the three-hour DNA machine ASAP? Hope you're ready to get back to work. Let me know if you've got questions."

He pushed play again and looked down at his amputated legs. The ends just below the knees looked like fleshy cookie dough, puckered and lumpy. The wounds were long healed but he still had phantom pain where his calves, ankles, and feet had once been. The burning sometimes hurt so much it forced a cry from his lips. What if that happened while he was talking to someone about the investigation?

Even worse, sometimes the explosion that took his legs played in his mind, and he could never really predict when it would happen.

It was great to hear Sayer's voice, but dread also settled into his chest. It had been on the last case he worked with her that a bomb had done this to him. Once Sayer Altair got her teeth into a case, she was a juggernaut, single-minded and unstoppable. What if he couldn't keep up? What if the pain interfered with his ability to do the job? Would Sayer understand?

"Okay, Ezra," he muttered to himself, "it's go time."

He roughly pulled on his gel-lined socks and his new full-sized prosthetics. The metallic devices glinted in the bluish light from his computer screen, glowing like robotic legs. That thought at least made him smile.

"You got this," he said loudly.

He pulled himself up with his walker and tried to hurry to his car, which was outfitted specially for him. The slow *click-step-step*, *click-step-step* of his walker and stiff legs made him grit his teeth. He'd always been in a hurry and now nothing he did felt fast enough.

He drove the few miles to Quantico, repeating over and over, "You got this, Ezra. You got this."

The guard at the front gate recognized him and welcomed him back. Ezra forced a cheerful smile.

At the front door, he struggled to balance himself against his walker and fumbled the door pass from his pocket. Things that had once been mindlessly easy suddenly felt insurmountable. By the time he got to his old desk in the evidence lab, Ezra was shaking with exhaustion.

The physical therapist had told him to take it easy, but Ezra's new legs felt like the promise of freedom; he didn't want to take it easy. But he could see that learning to walk all over again was going to take some time. His eyes watered with frustration.

Rather than let himself cry, he lowered himself into the chair and phoned the DNA lab to make sure they were already on the results. Recent murders always took precedence, and once he dropped Sayer's name, he had no trouble convincing the tech to move this case to the front of the line. Although the media and Congress were questioning Sayer, people inside the Bureau knew she was the real deal.

While the samples were processed, Ezra closed his eyes to rest for a moment.

"Just a minute of rest," he murmured.

A loud *bong* on his computer jolted him awake. Heart pounding, he looked around, dazed.

"Did I just fucking fall asleep?" he said out loud, incredulous. Embarrassed.

Shaking off grogginess, he clicked on the alert. The DNA results from the bodies were back. He must've slept for hours.

He opened the file and began to read. He compared the DNA with women in the National Missing Person DNA Database.

"What the . . . ?" He opened one file and another and put them side by side. He checked the original report. Back to the comparison.

Confusion slowly transformed into horror. This case was about to take off like a bullet train. Ezra hurried to pack his things. He'd better get on the road if he wanted to get to Shenandoah National Park before dawn.

ROAD TO SHENANDOAH NATIONAL PARK, VA

Before the sun reached the horizon, Sayer made sure Tino and Adi could be on full-time Vesper duty for a few days and then packed her waterproof bag. She double-checked that the ballistic panels were properly inserted in her bulletproof vest as she slid it into the bag. She briefly touched the scar on her shoulder before carrying her gear out to her bike. Sayer rode away from her quiet Alexandria town house already missing her warm bed where she'd left her snoring dog.

Mist-heavy air beaded off her FBI rain parka as she rode back toward the Shenandoah Mountains.

Letting her mind wander, Sayer still couldn't shake the chill left from her interview with Subject 037. She jumped when her phone buzzed in her headset.

"Agent Altair," she barked into the mic.

For half a second she expected to hear Subject 037's low voice.

"Good morning!" Sophia McDuff's cheerful voice sounded overloud inside Sayer's helmet.

"Nana, are you okay?" Sayer increasingly worried about her seventy-three-year-old grandmother. The former librarian and widowed wife to

Senator Charles McDuff had been acting wild lately, going skydiving and staking out criminals.

"Honestly Sayer, why wouldn't I be okay?"

"Because it's not even seven A.M. and I worry. . . ." Sayer didn't want to admit how much last night's interview had shaken her. "What's going on? Is Adi all right?" Even though Adi was technically an adult, Sayer was still adjusting to having a young person to watch over.

"Yes, of course, Adi's fine! I'm actually over at your place with her and Tino."

"Hi, Sayer!" Tino's and Adi's voices called out in the background. Vesper barked, joining in the shouting.

"What's going on?"

"Goodness, Sayer, when did you become such a worrywart?"

Sayer let out a sharp breath. "Well, you aren't calling for no reason . . . and what're you doing over at my place so early?"

"You know I'm up by five most days. When Adi called with her news, I came right over to celebrate."

"News?" Sayer asked.

The phone jostled and Adi's voice came on. "The e-mail with my SAT scores came right after you left."

"And?" After the last few years of turmoil, Adi had fallen behind in school. She only recently took her GRE to get her high school diploma and decided to try taking the SAT just to see how she would do. If she did well she would apply for college this year. But if she bombed, Sayer knew it would hit Adi hard.

"I aced it! Like, I really aced it." The joy in Adi's voice caused a flutter in Sayer's chest—an unfamiliar sensation she vaguely recognized as happiness.

"That's great!"

Adi's words flooded in a jumble of excitement, "I mean, I might be able to get a full ride somewhere! I'm gonna apply to all the Ivies and then I guess UVA and maybe Georgetown and I don't know where else. I might need to visit some of the schools and then I'll get to pick one and

I hope I get a scholarship but even if I don't I'll work and make sure I can swing it!"

"Huzzah!" Tino called out in the background, and the whole group laughed.

Sayer smiled, imagining her motley family piled into her apartment, all joyous together.

"Well, that is really great news, Adi. I'm so proud of you!"

"Thanks, Sayer." The excitement in Adi's voice softened and Sayer realized that she must be thinking about her dead family. How proud her parents would have been. And her twin sister.

"We're all here with you," Sayer said gently. Sayer knew nothing she could say would make Adi feel better, but she wanted the young woman to know that she wasn't alone. "When I get home let's have a family meeting and plan some college visits?"

"That would be great." Adi paused. "I'm going to go message my friends, but wanted to call you first."

"Okay, Adi. I'm just so happy for you. You all should go out and celebrate."

"Nah, I want to wait until you're home. We'll do something when your case is done. So hurry up."

"Yes, ma'am."

Adi laughed. "Okay. 'Bye!"

The rumble of Sayer's Silver Hawk replaced Adi's happy voice, leaving Sayer feeling slightly melancholy. Morning fog turned into a light rain as she swung the motorcycle onto Skyline Drive. The predawn chill made her shoulder ache and she momentarily wondered if it was time to buy an actual car.

"A little cold won't kill you," she muttered.

When she finally got to the ranger station, she fervently hoped that they had a coffee machine somewhere in the building. Inside, the smell of maple syrup made her stomach clench with hunger and she realized that she'd completely forgotten to eat breakfast. Had she even eaten dinner the night before? She waved a good morning to the park ranger sitting at the desk just inside the front door and made her way to the conference room.

Max, Piper, and Dana sat around a table over plates stacked high with pancakes and bacon. A blond man sat with his back to Sayer.

"Morning, Sayer." Max called her over. Kona sat at attention next to him, watching the bacon on the table with rapt attention. "Dana and I got up early, so we decided to whip up breakfast for everyone. Oh, and your friend just got here."

He turned and Sayer gasped. "Ezra! What on earth are you doing here? I thought you would be working from Quantico." She hurried over to give him a hug.

Ezra smiled and struggled to stand from the table.

"No, no, don't get up."

"I want to." Though his hair was no longer bright blue, he had put back in all his piercings. His tongue piercing clacked lightly as he spoke. His eyebrow bar arched up as he smiled.

He grasped the walker next to him and pulled himself up. Breathing hard, he balanced himself and let go. "Ta-da!"

They hugged and Sayer stepped back to look down at his double prosthetics. "Ezra, this is amazing." She had been regularly visiting Ezra in the recovery ward. Only a month ago he had just gotten his first prosthetics, called "stubbies" because they were only a few inches tall.

He nodded, slightly pale from the effort of standing. "I graduated from the stubbies two weeks ago. I still can't move very fast, but I'm getting there."

"And Holt let you come down here?"

Ezra squinted with discomfort. "I might have called for permission after I left. But yeah, as long as I promised to keep up with my physical therapy exercises every day, she let me stay. Though I'm supposed to tell you that this isn't officially a field assignment. I'm on desk duty only."

"I thought the doctor said it would be a month or two before you progressed to full-sized prosthetics. You must be working your ass off."

"No joke, check it out. . . ." He did a little ass-shake.

Sayer rolled her eyes. It felt good to see Ezra the smart-ass emerging again.

Trembling a little from the effort, he lowered himself back down into his seat and propped one of his legs up on a chair. "And check out these babies. I've got a buddy over in the tech department helping me tweak them out. Soon I'll be running faster than you."

Sayer nodded appreciatively and sat next to Ezra, giving his shoulder a gentle squeeze. "I'm so happy you came."

Max handed Sayer a plate and a mug of coffee.

Ezra looked around the ranger station with a sigh. "And I'm happy to be out of that medical ward. I never want to see the inside of a hospital again."

"You know I understand," Sayer said as she gulped the lukewarm coffee. Her hand drifted momentarily to her shoulder scar.

The group fell into companionable silence while they ate. Sayer was itching to ask Ezra why he'd come all the way from Quantico, but she knew everyone needed a good breakfast before jumping into the day. After coffees were drained and plates cleared, Sayer turned to Ezra. "All right, tell me what you got on the DNA."

Ezra's cocky smile faded. "I found a hell of a lot. If you all can bring my equipment in from the car, I'll show you."

After they unpacked and set up what felt like a million pieces of electronic equipment in the main conference room, Ezra clicked on his computer and connected it to a small projector. Sayer, Piper, Dana, and Max crowded around the table. Always at Max's side, Kona lay down against his feet. Piper, who had looked right at home out in the woods, struggled to force her bulk into one of the small office chairs. Dana tucked her small feet under her, face alight with anticipation.

As the projector warmed up, Sayer stood in front of a whiteboard she'd asked Piper to rustle up from the supply closet.

"All right, let's get our murder board going."

"Like on TV?" Piper asked.

"Yeah, just a place to visualize what we've got on the case so far. It can help us brainstorm and allows us to share data."

Sayer wrote *Bones* on one side and *New Victims* on the other.

"Let's summarize, bones first." Sayer wrote *6–7 victims* and *straitjacket.* "Dana, can you give me a very rough estimate of how long those bones have been there?"

"You know I don't like to—"

"Rough estimate, please," Sayer pushed.

Dana nodded curtly. "Based on the level of wear to the bones, I'd say they are at least ten years old, probably more like fifteen to twenty."

"Thank you. Okay," Sayer wrote *15–20 years old* and thought for a moment. "Based on the age of the bones, I'd suggest that we set them aside for now."

"Even though they were dumped in the same location?" Piper asked.

Sayer sighed. "Yeah, we've got such a small team that I just don't think we can divide our focus. Even if the cases are related, I think there's a much better chance of finding an evidence trail from the new victims. Until we have more information on the bones, I want us to work the bodies first. We've possibly got live victims out there somewhere, and this gives us the best chance to save them." She took a deep breath, frustrated at having to make do without a task force, because Piper was right, they should be working both cases at the same time.

"Even though one of the skeletons could be Cricket Nelson?" the park ranger pressed.

"I'm not saying we won't work the case, Piper. Just that we need to focus on the recent victims first. Once Dana finishes the autopsies, she'll analyze the bones. I had Chief Nelson send over his sister's dental records, so we should be able to identify her if she's here."

The projector lit up, interrupting Piper's response. The image of two women appeared on the white wall.

Sayer recognized the narrow chin and high cheekbones of Jane Doe One. She had long waves of blond hair and pale skin, her blue eyes smiling with genuine joy. She looked carefree, happy. "You found a match for both victims?"

Ezra nodded. "Behold the results of my NMPDD search."

"Sorry I keep asking clueless questions, but the what?" Piper asked.

"The FBI's National Missing Person DNA Database. It's part of our national Combined DNA Index System. Family members of missing persons can submit their own DNA or a sample from the missing person."

Ezra pulled his chair over to his notes. "We really lucked out identifying them both. What you see here are pictures of the two victims found yesterday." He slid the cursor over the woman that Sayer recognized as Jane Doe One. "This is the victim with *HELP US* written on her body. Meet Victoria Winslow, twenty-two. She went missing from Old Dominion University in Norfolk, Virginia, on the morning of September twelfth."

Sayer took the printed photo Ezra handed her of Victoria Winslow. She taped it to the whiteboard and wrote the young woman's name and abduction date beneath her smiling image.

Ezra slid the cursor over to the second woman, a young blonde with short curly hair and a serious look on her face. "And this is Christina Jacobs. Jacobs was twenty-three, and also went missing on September twelfth, around two-thirty P.M. after leaving class at the University of Virginia."

"So our UNSUB . . ." Sayer paused. "That's 'unknown subject,' Piper."

Piper nodded a thanks for the explanation.

"Our UNSUB kidnapped Victoria Winslow, then drove three hours west and kidnapped Christina Jacobs on the same day? Then, based on time of death, they were held somewhere for over a month and then killed about two weeks apart?"

Ezra nodded. "Exactly right."

"Well, that's unusual. Okay, go on."

Ezra clicked on the next slide, displaying a photograph of a woman and child.

"Oh, no," Sayer said, voice heavy.

"Meet the woman who wrote on Victoria Winslow with her own

saliva. This"—he moused over the mother and child—"is Jillian Watts and her three-year-old daughter, Grace. They both went missing September fifteenth from Charlottesville, three days after the other two women were taken."

Sayer stared at the photo of the mother and child together. They both had blond curls sticking out from beneath sparkly party hats. Jillian Watts was smiling at the camera. She had her arms wrapped around Grace. The girl looked up at her mother with pure love on her face. Sayer's throat tightened and she momentarily hated her job with every fiber of her being.

"They both went missing? The UNSUB took a child?" Sayer asked. If their UNSUB only wanted the women, that could be very bad for Grace Watts.

"That's right."

"And the saliva writing on the body belongs to this Watts woman." Sayer let that thought sink in. "Well, she used the term *HELP US*. The use of the plural means the UNSUB either has another victim we're unaware of, or Grace is still alive. No matter what, it means that he's been holding Jillian Watts for well over a month now."

"Jesus," Max mumbled.

"I want us to assume that her use of 'us' means that the child is still alive. . . ." Sayer trailed off as she walked up to the image to get a better look.

Like the other two women, Jillian Watts was young, with wavy blond hair, blue eyes, and the same pointy chin. "I wonder if he took Grace for a reason, or if she was just in the way when he took Jillian? And why on earth hasn't local law enforcement noticed these young women missing? I mean, look at them, they could all be sisters."

Ezra frowned. "Well, they're all legal adults. It's not unheard-of for women to take off, which means none of these cases were taken all that seriously. We're just lucky they were all entered in our DNA database. The police might not have made the connection, but their families are clearly looking for them."

Sayer hated to think of the trail of devastated people she was about to create as she notified those families. "Okay, so we're going to assume that Jillian and Grace Watts are still alive out there somewhere. Give me details about their abductions."

"I'm still compiling the police reports, but it looks like all of these women went missing while running errands or after class. The various police departments are sending me what they have now, so I'll cross-check those reports next."

Sayer put the photos of the rest of the victims up on the whiteboard. "Did you try to find any connections between these women?"

Ezra let out an indignant huff. "Of course I did." He spun his chair around to grab a new stack of notes. "And I can't find one. These women are all squeaky clean and, as far as I can tell, none of their lives have ever overlapped."

"Okay, keep digging." Sayer stood next to the projected image. She hoped that Ezra could uncover some kind of connection. Completely unrelated victims were the worst-case scenario, because it meant there was no trail to follow. "So, we've got a kidnapped mother and child, and two dead women. They were all taken a little over a month ago from around Virginia. These victims are high-risk." Sayer glanced at Piper. "High-risk means that they aren't easy targets. People would clearly notice them missing. Either our UNSUB is incredibly smart or incredibly dumb."

Max leaned back in his chair. "I vote dumb; that kind is much easier to catch."

Sayer glanced at the clock. It wasn't even eight A.M. yet. "Is that all you've got, Ezra?"

Ezra clicked the image over to a DNA panel. "No, uh, this is where things get . . . concerning."

"Get concerning?" Piper said. "This all seems pretty darn concerning." She looked around the room.

"What is it?" Sayer asked as she began pacing.

"They got a DNA match to each of the samples taken from underneath the fingernails of the two beaten women."

"But that's great news." Sayer knew that the DNA from under their victims' fingernails was most certainly deposited by whoever beat them to death.

Ezra cringed slightly. "The DNA matches the missing mom, Jillian Watts."

"What?" Dana said loudly.

Sayer stopped pacing and looked at Ezra. "Jillian Watts? The woman missing with her daughter."

"The same."

"You got Jillian Watts's DNA from underneath our beaten victims' fingernails?" Sayer tried to clarify again, mind churning.

Ezra nodded. "And off the swabs taken from their knuckles."

"But wouldn't her DNA under their fingernails mean that she's the one that beat them?" Piper asked.

Sayer nodded slowly. "That would certainly be my first interpretation." She looked more closely at the photograph of Jillian Watts holding her young daughter. The young girl's eyes danced with happiness. Jillian's casual stance and comfort with Grace made her look like nothing more than a loving mother. No hint of any darkness at all. Which Sayer knew meant nothing.

"Okay . . ." Sayer tried to process. "If Jillian Watts beat the other two women, perhaps her disappearance wasn't a kidnapping but a cover-up for her own role in all this. But then why would she also write *HELP US* in saliva on one of the victims? Ezra, dig hard into the mother's background and let me know what you find. Until we know more, I want us to consider her a victim. And her daughter is certainly a victim in all this."

"On it." Ezra typed himself another note. "That's all I've got for now. The lab is working on the swabs from the sword thing next, so we should get those results soon."

"Great, thanks, Ez. Dana," Sayer said, "could you fill us in on the X-rays of our two victims?"

Dana cleared her throat. "Of course. Both women were brutally beaten. I found extensive damage to their faces, ribs, and even a broken leg. I'll need to take a closer look to confirm, but I didn't see any evidence of weapon marks on the X-rays. Based on the type of damage, my preliminary assessment is that both women were beaten to death. And based on the defensive marks on their hands and forearms, they put up quite a fight." Dana paused.

Sayer remembered that this was one of the things she loved about working with Dana. No matter how long she worked with the dead, the woman always seemed to remember the humanity of the victims.

"Given the DNA match to Jillian Watts, when I do the actual autopsy I'll see if I can figure out about how tall the killer was."

"Thank you, Dana." Sayer wrote *Beaten* on the whiteboard. "So we've got our basic MO. That's modus operandi, the method used to kill," she said to Piper.

"Don't forget arson," Max added. "He did try to set you guys on fire. Anything from that to help us track him down?"

"The evidence techs didn't find anything around the rim of the bone cave to help us track down our fire starter," Sayer said. "Plus no tire tracks coming up the mining road from the other direction, but the rain probably washed away anything of use."

She wrote *Arson* on the whiteboard. "One question: How did our UNSUB even know we were there? Max, you found the bones early in the morning, right? It wasn't even noon when someone tried to set us on fire."

"This area is pretty small. Word gets around fast when dead bodies are found," Max said. "It's not crazy to think our UNSUB could've heard through the grapevine."

"All right, yet again that sure makes it sound like we're looking for a local." Sayer stared at the whiteboard. "No matter where this UNSUB is from, the fire yesterday means we have an active killer very nearby. A killer who doesn't mind hurting law enforcement, which also means we need to be on high alert. I want everyone wearing their bulletproof vests when they're out of the immediate vicinity of the building."

She looked around the room at her strange little team, making sure everyone understood. She'd lost an agent on her previous case and had almost lost Ezra. Sayer wasn't about to let that happen again.

Satisfied that everyone was taking the threat seriously, she continued, "Okay. We've got two dead women, and a missing mother and child still out there. We need to hit the ground running. There are too many questions that we can't answer yet, so let's focus on what we can do. Dana, you finish up the autopsies to make sure we didn't miss anything, and settle cause of death. Once you finish those up, jump over to the bones. Let's see if any of our skulls match Cricket Nelson."

"Sounds good. The rest of my team is already on the way to the bone cave." Dana tapped the notes in front of her. "Now that we know stratigraphy doesn't matter, they can yank those bones out in a few hours."

"Thanks, Dana. I'll go make phone-call notifications to the victims' families," Sayer said. "While I do that, Ezra, first thing I want you to do is cross-check things like parking tickets and toll roads to see if you can tie a specific person to our abduction sites. Then dig into Jillian Watts. Is there anything that suggests a suburban mom could be our killer? Anything strange at all?"

"Easy-peasy." Ezra cracked his knuckles.

"Max, I'd like you to take a look at the files from the missing persons cases. See if you can find a pattern. Also, can you take a look at the bladed weapon we found with the bodies? See if you can identify it? Figure out where it came from. If you can't figure it out, find someone who can."

He saluted sharply.

"Piper, you get the local police canvassing area businesses with photos of our victims. Did anyone see these women or this child come through here? Can you also update Kyle Nelson? Just let the chief know where we are with everything."

The park ranger nodded solemnly, clearly taking her duty seriously.

Sayer continued, "Once I've talked to the families and have gotten some more info on our victims, I'll talk to a profiler. A forensic psychologist just down the hill at UVA heard about the murders and called me last night offering to help. Since we're spread thin at Quantico, I sent her what we've got and she's working on a preliminary profile. Let's see if we can figure out what kind of pathology is at play here. Maybe start to figure out how our UNSUB selected his victims. Once we have that information together, let's assess next steps."

With a long sigh, Sayer sat down and rolled her shoulders, trying to stop the ache radiating along her left arm. "One last question: Do we need to close down Shenandoah National Park? None of the victims were taken from the immediate area, but we need to protect the public and we've got an active killer on the loose. Piper, you're our park representative, what do you think?"

"Oof, that's a tough one. I would have to talk to the Park Service higher-ups, but the Appalachian Trail runs through the park. Closing down the trail is a big deal. Some people plan their entire lives to make the walk and . . . well, I don't know."

"All right, our victims haven't been taken from off the trail. No random hikers have been threatened or harmed. So let's keep it open for now." Sayer pondered. She didn't think there was a risk to the general public, and she hated to set off a media feeding frenzy, but she also wanted to let people know to be cautious. "Ezra, can you tell PR to release a very basic statement saying that there is an active murder investigation in the area and that people should be alert?"

"Will do."

Sayer faced the small room. These cases already felt like they were spiraling out of control. Old bones, a missing toddler, a girl gone for seventeen years, and a murderous mom? They sure as hell needed a task force.

"All right." Sayer stood. "Let's get on it. I'm going to go call the families of these women. . . ."

Ezra held up a folder. "All the victims' family info is in here. Names and numbers."

"That's why you're the best, Ezra." Sayer patted him on the back and reluctantly went to a small office to tell the families something unthinkable.

SOUTHERN RANGER STATION,
SHENANDOAH NATIONAL PARK, VA

After completing the notification calls to the victims' families, Sayer staggered out into the hall and sagged against the cool tile wall.

Doing family notifications felt like standing next to a black hole of grief that siphoned off a piece of her every time. Her heart felt battered from listening to people crumble into sobbing or shrieking, though the worst was the reverberating silence of those so broken they could no longer make a sound at all. To ward off her own grief, she stood up, shoulders back, and strode into the small office where Max was reading through the current missing persons files.

He glanced up and did a double take. "Jesus, rough notifications?"

"Eh." She waved her hand dismissively, not wanting to dwell.

"Did you talk to Jillian Watts's family? Anything to suggest that she's more than a victim here?"

"Nothing strange. Her husband was suitably upset. He seemed genuinely worried about Jillian and Grace. He's been putting up flyers, talking to anyone who will listen, searching for his wife and child. Anything here?"

"Sadly, not much here. The women all disappeared like ghosts. Winslow and Jacobs from campus and the Wattses while Jillian and Grace were out running errands. They left home and just never returned. No one saw anything, their cars were found abandoned in parking lots outside a grocery store or on campus."

"Damn. No security cameras caught anything?"

"Not as far as I can tell. I've got a few local uniforms canvassing the abduction sites to see if there's any chance of security footage."

Sayer flopped down in a chair. "I guess no one was taking their disappearances very seriously."

"I mean, there are over forty thousand women missing in the U.S. at any given time." Max lifted the small stack of files in one hand. "The locals took missing persons reports, but none of the investigations went any further."

"Did you get a chance to look at the sword we found with the bodies?" She looked over where the weapon rested on the table. Through the thick plastic evidence bag she could see that the curved blade was rusted.

"Yeah, one of the techs processed it this morning and I got to take a closer look. It's definitely not a machete. It's more like a long sword of some kind. Weirdly, I think it looks like a yataghan."

"A what?"

"It's an old Turkish sword. I only recognize it because I went through a nerdy sword stage in junior high. I took a few photos and sent them down to a professor at UVA that specializes in Ottoman history. Hopefully he can ID it."

"A Turkish sword? Well, that's definitely not what I expected. . . ." Sayer let that sink in.

Max was about to say something more when Sayer's phone buzzed in her pocket. She read the text.

"Hey, that UVA psychologist already has a profile ready."

"That was fast."

"No kidding. She said we could come by her office later to discuss her preliminary thoughts." Sayer assessed Max. She still wasn't sure what to make of his story about Cricket. He seemed like a solid agent, but she wanted to observe him in the field before she decided how much to trust him. "Why don't you come with me to hear what she has to say? I'd love a second set of ears if you think everyone is safe here without you and Kona on watch."

"Sure thing. The building is secure and we've got a ranger on watch. Going to UVA will be perfect. We can swing by and see if the historian has had a chance to look at the sword. Actually, can we just bring it with us? If he doesn't know, maybe someone else on campus can help."

"Okay, as long as it's already been processed and we keep it wrapped we can bring it along. I'll have someone run it up to Quantico later for further analysis."

He and Kona jumped up. "Great. I'll check in with the ranger on watch, and get Kona settled, then meet you at my truck."

As they left the office, Ezra's voice called from the conference room next door.

"Hey, Sayer?"

Something about Ezra's tone made Sayer and Max glance at each other with concern as they hurried to find Ezra looking even more pale than usual.

"I, uh, set up a notification alert for any missing women that fit our profile, blond and young, basically, and I just got a hit."

"Oh, no." Sayer leaned over Ezra to look at the photo on his screen. A woman with a messy blond bun and sparkling blue eyes smiled back. Other than having slightly darker skin, she looked just like the other three women.

"Meet Hannah Valdez, a UVA grad student who went missing two days ago just down the hill in Charlottesville. Police found her abandoned car with her toddler still strapped in the car seat."

"Is the kid okay?" Max asked.

"Fine. The kid's with Hannah's wife. I have the case file on its way."

"Two days ago," Sayer said. "Why are we just getting the notification now?"

“The Charlottesville department must have just uploaded the case to the missing persons database,” Ezra said.

“Two days ago is just after we think the most recent victim’s body was dumped in the cave,” Max said.

“You’re right. So, maybe Hannah Valdez is her replacement,” Sayer said, face grim. “I mean, look at her. She’s definitely our UNSUB’s type. Let’s go talk to Hannah Valdez’s wife on our way to UVA. See if we can find a lead to follow there.”

Sayer took one last look at Hannah, then over at the photo of Jillian and Grace Watts. Were the two women together somewhere? And was little Grace even still alive?

ROAD TO CHARLOTTESVILLE, VA

As Max and Sayer drove away from the ranger station toward Charlottesville, the rain shifted from heavy to downpour.

"So, we're going to talk to Hannah Valdez's wife?"

"Correct," Sayer said, staring out at the clouds. "Zoe Valdez. They've been married for"—Sayer flipped open the file—"five years. Both graduate students. Squeaky-clean records. Had Samantha two and half years ago. Maybe she can shed some light."

"Let's hope so," Max replied.

Sayer decided to change the subject and get to know more about Max. "So, you work up in D.C. Do you spend much time here in Rockfish?"

"Really only to visit my mom. She travels home to Korea a lot, but when she's here I come down about once a month. Any less than that and she starts to talk about moving up to D.C. to be closer to me." Max dramatically shook his head.

"So you knew Kyle back in high school?" Sayer was thinking of asking Kyle to officially join the investigation, but she didn't like working with so many new people. She needed to know who she could depend on.

"Yeah. Kyle was a few years behind me. All I really remember about him was how quiet he was. Oh, and he can draw."

"Draw?"

"Yeah, at lunch every day, kids would suggest to him two animals, and he would draw them while he ate. By the end of lunch period, he would have this amazing sketch. Called them mash-ups."

"Mash-ups?"

"Yeah, like if you told him a pig and a bear, he would draw them kind of stitched together. The drawings were cool, so kids would hang them in their lockers and stuff. Made him kind of popular despite being quiet. After high school he went to UVA but then moved back and joined the Rockfish Police Department after he graduated. Worked his way up to chief pretty quickly. He's known around town as kind of intense but a genuinely nice guy. Other than wanting to punch my lights out. . . ."

"What about Piper? Seems like you know her fairly well?" While Kyle seemed to wear his emotions on his sleeve, Sayer couldn't get a read on the park ranger.

Max let out a short laugh. "She's got a reputation as a kind of harmless crackpot. You know, off-the-grid-cabin-in-the-woods type. I think she prefers the company of plants to people."

"Hmm." Sayer leaned her head back against the seat and closed her eyes.

"Sometimes it feels weird to come home, you know?" Max continued. "All those childish relationships are still there, lurking beneath our adult façades. You spend time with anyone from your high school?"

Sayer thought back to her awkward days as a complete outcast in her very wealthy private school. Though her grandparents were rich, her parents had been solidly working class. After her parents died, the culture shock going from happy, blue-collar urban neighborhood to wealthy suburban enclave had been rough. She opened her eyes and let out a sharp laugh. "Not if I can help it."

"Not prom queen, I take it?"

"I was a science-obsessed black girl with dead parents. And I ended up getting a Ph.D. in neuroscience. That should tell you how popular I was."

"Sure, but you're a neuroscientist who rides a motorcycle and chases serial killers for the FBI."

Sayer waved her hand. "All that immense level of coolness came later in life."

Max laughed. "I see. . . . I actually have a question about your research, if you don't mind talking about it."

He glanced cautiously at her. Sayer recognized the look that inevitably happened with every new partner. While everyone was familiar with profilers, not many people could figure out why the FBI needed a neuroscientist.

"Sure."

"You study serial-killer brains, right?" he asked as he steered his truck along the narrow highway.

"Well, right now I'm studying psychopaths' brains. Not all killers are psychopaths, and not all psychopaths are killers. Psychopathy is really just a group of behavioral traits. They're glib, narcissistic thrill-seekers with a tendency toward pathological lying and a total lack of empathy for others. Before this project, yeah, I was scanning serial killers' brains."

"And people like that have different brains somehow?"

"They do." Sayer shifted toward Max so she could face him while they chatted. "If you give me the right kind of brain scan, I can tell you if the person is likely to be a psychopath."

"But not a killer, right?"

"Right, like I said, not all psychopaths are killers. Criminal behavior isn't necessary for a diagnosis of psychopathy."

"So, what's wrong with their brains?"

"It's complicated, but they basically have a faulty paralimbic system. There's a whole interconnected circuit in their brains that doesn't work properly, involving the insula, amygdala, anterior and posterior cingulate, orbitofrontal cortex—"

Max interrupted her. "Their orbito what?"

Sayer smiled. "Sorry, it's basically the brain system that processes emotion and controls decision making, that kind of thing."

"So, they don't make decisions like normal people?"

"More importantly, they don't process emotion the same way. I'll give you an example. Imagine you're standing at a railroad station and the tracks split in two. On one side, five people are tied to the track. On the other side, only one person is tied down. You see a train hurtling toward the people. You don't have time to untie them, but you can choose which track the train goes down. Right now the train is going to run over five people, but if you pull the lever you could direct the train to run over one person instead. Would you pull the lever?"

Max thought for a moment. "Well, of course I'd pull it. If I have no other choice, I'd rather save five people than just one."

Sayer got more animated as she spoke. "Exactly, that's what most people say, including psychopaths. But now imagine a slightly different scenario. Instead of two train tracks, imagine you're on a bridge over a single track. There are five people tied to the track up ahead and one person standing on the bridge with you. If you push that person off the bridge onto the tracks below, that person will die, but the body will also stop the train, saving the lives of the five other people. Would you push that person off?"

Max's mouth pulled back with disgust. "Yikes. I'm not sure. . . . I don't think I could."

"Exactly. To you, those two scenarios feel very different."

"Yeah, pushing a guy, well, that feels like I'm actively murdering him."

Sayer nodded, getting into the discussion. "But the calculation is the same, right? Kill one person to save five."

"I guess so. But something about pushing the guy just feels really different."

"Which shows me that you probably aren't a psychopath. Psychopaths generally see no difference between the two situations."

"So they would push the guy off the bridge?" Max asked.

"Yeah, to them the calculation is all utilitarian, one life versus five."

"That's kind of . . . monstrous."

"Is it, though?" Sayer asked.

"What do you mean?" Max glanced over at Sayer, slightly concerned. "I mean, aren't psychopaths . . . defective?"

Sayer looked out the window. This was one of the key questions she was grappling with, interviewing noncriminal psychopaths. "I think it's . . . complicated. There are undeniable benefits to having psychopaths around."

"Seriously?" Max couldn't hide his surprise.

"Well, if you needed brain surgery, what kind of person do you want doing the surgery?"

Max thought for a long moment. "I guess someone confident, well trained, calm and cool under pressure. I'm willing to bet I just described a psychopath."

"Exactly right. You want someone unfazed by emotion and very unlikely to panic no matter what might go wrong. You want someone able to make emotionless, utilitarian calculations under intense pressure. You want someone whose heart rate goes down the more stress they're under. In other words, you want a psychopath."

Max nodded. "Huh. Interesting."

"I obviously agree." Sayer smiled, letting her own enthusiasm for her research break through the stress gnawing at her gut. "There're a lot of reasons why the ability to achieve a sort of detached focus is beneficial. Or the ability to be truly fearless. Brain surgeons, bomb-squad techs, soldiers and cops, even lawyers or politicians."

"You make it sound like there're a lot of psychopaths out there."

"Some people think there might be thirty thousand psychopaths for every one in jail. They're often delusional narcissists that believe they're gods. They rarely maintain stable families and are often abusive to those around them. But they are also often at the top of their field."

"I've definitely worked with people like that." Max chuckled mirthlessly. "So, can you tell the difference between a good and a bad psycho when you look at their brains?"

"Not as far as we know, though we don't have many brain scans of what are called pro-social psychopaths, people who are clearly psychopaths but harness their skill set in a noncriminal way. That's actually what I'm researching now, trying to figure out if there are any neurological differences between a so-called good psychopath versus a bad one. Maybe if we can figure out some of the differences, we can find ways to help bad psychopaths become more . . . good, I guess."

"Very cool."

They pulled into the suburban driveway of Hannah Valdez's house, interrupting Max's next question.

Sayer crashed from excitement about her research into the harsh reality that they were about to go meet with the family of a missing woman.

The Valdez house retained that avocado-green, characterless style that was so in fashion in the seventies. Despite the outdated architecture and pouring rain, the neighborhood looked idyllic, with manicured, bright green lawns.

Sayer couldn't help but think of *The Brady Bunch*. "What did we do, warp back in time?" she asked as they both walked up to the house.

The illusion of perfection was shattered when Zoe Valdez opened the door. She stared at them with feverish eyes rimmed with crust. She wore pajama pants and a grimy T-shirt. Sayer realized that this woman had probably not changed clothes or showered since the day her wife disappeared.

"Ms. Valdez, I'm Senior Special Agent Altair with the FBI, this is Special Agent Cho. May we come in to ask you a few questions about your wife?"

She nodded, wild-eyed. "No one will tell me what's going on. Have you found Hannah?"

Sayer shook her head slightly. "No, sorry, we're just here to ask you a few questions, see if we can retrace what happened when she disappeared."

With a look of relief, Zoe Valdez croaked, "Well, thank goodness someone is finally taking this seriously. . . ." She trailed off, blinking with confusion.

"Ms. Valdez?" Sayer said loudly, snapping her out of her exhausted stupor.

She shook her head. "Of course. I'm just . . ." Her voice trailed off again, but she straightened her clothes. She suddenly seemed to realize that she was wearing dirty pajamas. "I'm sorry about . . . this. I've been too afraid that if I do anything . . . I thought I might miss a call. What if she called while I was in the shower? Plus I've got Sam. . . ." She paused in her rambling dialogue. "Wait, why is the FBI involved?"

"Ms. Valdez, if we could come in . . ." Max moved toward the door.

"Oh, sorry." She stepped aside and seemed oblivious to the water dripping from their jackets onto the floor. "Sam is taking a nap. We can talk in the kitchen."

Inside, the entire house was decorated with bright colors and unusual art. Sayer stopped to study one particularly brilliant piece with flowers, stylized deer, and starbursts.

Noticing her interest, Zoe Valdez smiled weakly. "Hannah loves to travel and she's bought something from everywhere she goes. That one's Huichol yarn art from the Sierra Madre in Mexico. That drum next to it was made somewhere in West Africa—Senegal, I think."

Sayer nodded. "My father was from Senegal." She ran her finger along the edge of the drum. "This one is called a tama. A talking drum."

"That's right!" Talking about Hannah's things brightened Zoe's whole face. In that moment Sayer dismissed her as a possible suspect in her wife's disappearance.

The moment gone, the woman's face fell again and the wrinkles of tension returned.

They settled in the kitchen, and Sayer dove right into questions. "Ms. Valdez, I know you've already told the police, but could you go over the details of the day Hannah disappeared?"

She licked her pasty lips. "I was supposed to take care of Sam that morning, but I got called in to work. Since the gym has day care, Hannah decided to go there instead of running errands. Hannah'd let her training slide while she was pregnant."

"Training?" Sayer asked.

"Yeah, she does aikido. But she wouldn't have gone to the gym if I'd taken Sam."

"You couldn't have known, Ms. Valdez." Sayer interrupted the thought, trying to keep her on track. "So she and Sam went to the gym."

"Hannah did her regular workout and they left around two o'clock. They must have made it to her car in the parking garage. She strapped Sam into her car seat, and that's it. She disappeared."

"And when did you realize she was missing?"

Zoe Valdez looked stricken. "She'd texted me before she left the gym, asked me to make dinner. When I got home around four, I put some frozen enchiladas in the oven and waited. She never came home." Her eyes wandered over to the oven.

Sayer suspected that if she opened the oven door she would find the enchiladas still on the rack.

"I tried her cell phone, figuring she was just running errands or something." Her voice began to take on a flat quality, as if she had to turn off her emotions just to be able to finish the story. "A few hours later I called her mom. Around eight I called the hospitals. It wasn't until almost nine that I called the police. They'd just found Sam and were trying to track Hannah down." She looked directly into Sayer's eyes. "Hannah's the strongest person I've ever met."

Sayer looked down at the table, trying not to take on any of Zoe's sorrow, but then she forced herself to look at her. Let her pain wash over her.

"Are you going to tell me why the FBI is here?" she said, barely above a whisper.

"All I can tell you is that we've got another ongoing investigation that could be connected to your wife's disappearance. But until we know for sure, I can't divulge any details of that case."

She hung her head but nodded. "I understand."

The sound of a small voice calling, "Mommy?" drifted from the hall.

Zoe looked toward the crying, stricken. "What am I going to do without Hannah?" She blinked back tears.

Sayer put a hand on hers. "You'll do whatever you have to, to take care of your daughter. Thank you so much for your time, Ms. Valdez. We're doing everything we can to find your wife."

"Thank you." She stood on unsteady legs. "Please let yourself out. I've got to get Sam." She hurried off down the hall. Sayer and Max looked at each other.

"That poor woman," Max whispered.

Sayer nodded, gut burning with determination to find Hannah Valdez and bring her home.

UNKNOWN LOCATION

Hannah Valdez sat on the edge of the cot, biting her cuticle until it bled. The tang of blood rolled on her tongue and she savored the coppery sharpness. The flavor felt somehow real, unlike the nightmare unfolding around her.

How could this be happening?

She'd tried to keep herself alert with word problems. She'd tried exercise. But nothing staved off the thrumming horror that was living in her chest like a parasitic animal burrowing deep into her bones.

She contemplated the room.

An unopened water bottle sat on the floor next to an empty bucket and a box of granola bars. Her stomach curled in on itself with hunger and her lips cracked at the corners from thirst, but she was afraid to eat or drink anything. She knew she would have to drink water soon or risk serious dehydration.

Avoiding the thought, she examined the room with clinical detachment. The walls were partially carved from solid rock, but parts were drywalled. The metal door was riveted to the rock wall, but there was also a vent that suggested an air circulation system of some kind. The roaring sound in the background created a steady white noise.

Was she in a cave system? An old mine? Why was she even here? Hannah couldn't seem to think straight.

But she also couldn't just sit here.

She got up to check the vent for the tenth time. The screws were coated with rubbery paint. With a new focus, Hannah was suddenly overcome by a frantic need to get out. Hands shaking, she used her fingernails to scrape away thick peels of paint from the edge of the vent. The paint curled painfully into the quick of her nails, but she ignored it and soon lost herself in the new work.

Clink.

The sound of a key in the lock almost made her scream. She couldn't bear to imagine who or what was coming for her.

She had to force herself to stop her wild scraping. Heart pounding, she scattered the small pile of paint shavings just as the door swung open.

The skeletal woman stood there in a loose cotton wrap barely one step up from a hospital gown.

"Testing time," she said in her dull monotone.

Hannah confrontationally faced the woman. "Why are you doing this?"

"Please just come."

She stepped right next to her. "I could easily overpower you and run."

The woman looked at her with such unbridled horror that Hannah backed off. The look on her face was not born of casual fear. This woman had clearly experienced a nightmare beyond imagining. It was the first time Hannah was convinced that this woman was nothing but a fellow victim.

Hannah tried not to let that fear infect her, but it seeped into her pores.

She did not want to find out what this woman was afraid of.

"He left your daughter behind. She's not here," the woman said.

"Sam is safe?" Hannah could barely say the words.

The woman nodded. "Did you . . . before you came here, did anyone get my message?" she whispered.

"Your message?"

"I had to clean them afterward. . . . I wrote a message on her body, but . . . I guess it didn't work." Her face fell. "Now please come." She held out her hand.

Unsure what else to do, Hannah took it.

CHARLOTTESVILLE, VA

Sayer's phone buzzed as they drove away from the Valdezes' house.

"Hey, Ez, you're on speaker."

"Just calling to report that Dana finished the autopsies." Ezra's voice sounded slightly tinny. "Official cause of death for our two recent victims, internal injuries caused by blunt-force trauma to their head and body. In other words, they were beaten to death, most likely by hand. No weapon marks and all of their injuries were consistent with a fight."

"Not just a beating, a fight."

"Yeah, according to Dana they fought back hard."

"Okay, so they weren't sedated. Anything else?" Sayer asked.

"Yeah." Ezra rifled through paper. "There were burn marks on both of their necks consistent with a taser or some kind of electric shock device."

"Hum, probably a way to control his victims."

"One more thing. . . ." He paused. "Both women had a broken left pinkie finger that looked wonky."

"Define *wonky,* please. . . ."

"Well, the breaks don't look defensive or offensive. Here, I'll read

Dana's note." Ezra cleared his throat. "*In both women, the phalanges of the left fourth finger bone were shattered. Injuries not consistent with offensive or defensive wounds. The injuries are consistent with a finger being smashed between two hard objects. Possible that both victims had one finger broken on purpose.*"

Sayer remained silent, processing.

"So maybe our victims were tortured?" Max said softly.

"Maybe. That's it for now," Ezra said.

"Thanks, Ez. We're going to head to UVA to find out more about the sword and get a profile, then we'll head back up to you."

Sayer hung up and gave Max a look. "What the hell is our UNSUB doing to these women?"

UNKNOWN LOCATION

The skeletal woman led Hannah Valdez through the metal door.

Hannah curled her fingers tight and the woman responded, holding her hand firmly. Their hands felt warm and papery against each other.

It was strangely comforting.

Hand in hand, they walked through a swinging wooden door out into an open area.

Hannah's mouth fell open in shock. The short hall emptied into a cavern the size of a soccer field. Sheer rock walls rose to a high arched ceiling, so high it was almost impossible to see in the spotlights that lined the cavern walls.

The roaring sound she'd heard in her room was louder here, filling the entire cavern with an echo.

Rusted industrial equipment littered the rocky ground. A single metal table and chair sat at the center of the cavern.

By far the most terrifying thing in the room was an upright metal contraption covered with thick leather straps and with a large silver blade propped out to the side. It looked like a torture device. Was she about to be strapped down? Hannah's heart started racing.

"Welcome to the pit, Hannah," a voice crackled from a loudspeaker, filling the cavern. Hannah searched for the source.

At the far end of the massive chamber, a ladder ran up to a glass-enclosed control room perched on a ledge far above. She realized that, rather than a cave, this was actually a massive pit dug down into the ground. Some kind of mine complex?

A shadowy figure stood in the control room overlooking the pit.

"Let me go, you bastard!" Hannah let her rage and fear out in a harsh shout.

"If you cooperate, this will go smoothly and you'll be back to your room in no time." The voice echoed loudly in the large chamber.

"I'm not going to cooperate with anything."

The skeletal woman painfully squeezed her hand and gave her a desperate, pleading look. Then she pulled away.

As Hannah's hand fell to her side, a shock exploded from her neck.

She let out a strangled cry as her muscles went rigid. Her jaw slammed shut. Molars cracked on impact.

Hannah toppled backward to the ground, hitting her head. She lay jerking on the floor.

As quickly as it had begun, the pain stopped.

Her muscles turned to jelly and she curled forward, groaning.

The skeletal woman hurried to her, gently stroking her hair back from her face.

"That was on four," the voice echoed down. "Your collar goes to ten. I repeat, if you cooperate, this will go smoothly and you'll be back to your room in no time."

Unable to speak, Hannah grunted a sound of agreement.

"Very good. Go sit at the table."

The woman helped Hannah up and nodded toward the table. Something in her eyes was unreadable, but Hannah couldn't think beyond the fact that she never wanted to feel that pain again.

Shaky, she sat down and almost fell from the chair.

She put her head down on the table. The metal felt cool against her forehead and she closed her eyes.

Everything jumbled in her mind like a churning ocean. This pit. The roaring sound in the background. Being held here. The strange skeletal woman. It all felt so far beyond any nightmare she could have ever imagined.

"Hannah!" the voice boomed from above.

She jolted up with a gasp.

"Don't fade on me. I'm just here to conduct my first test, then I'll be on my way."

Hannah tried to get her bearings, but when she lifted her head, the whole world tilted. She slid from the chair, barely catching herself on her hands and knees. She stayed like that, unsure if she could stand.

"Ah, I see you haven't eaten. Jillian, get her food and water," the voice commanded loudly.

The woman hurried to gather a bottle of water and a stale sandwich.

Hannah took them from her trembling hands. She drank the entire bottle and inhaled the food without wondering if they were drugged. She was well beyond such prosaic fear.

The food hit her stomach, sending it into a spasm. But she could feel her body responding. She used the table to pull herself back into the chair.

"It's time for your first trial," the voice said.

Hannah's mouth went dry at the look of pure terror on the skeletal woman's face.

The woman reluctantly left Hannah's side and disappeared into one of the side tunnels. Hannah watched the dark archway, breath held in anticipation of the next horror.

She was confused when the woman returned with a single brick.

"Just a simple trial to help you begin your transformation." The voice sounded almost gleeful. "Pretend you're Hercules."

The woman placed the brick on the table next to Hannah and stepped over to the wall. She pressed herself against the rock.

"Transformation? Trial? What's happening?" Hannah asked the woman, but she wouldn't meet her eyes.

"Now, smash your left pinkie finger with the brick or I will shoot your new friend in the head."

"What?" Hannah stood up and turned to face the figure.

"Smash your left pinkie finger or I will shoot her in the head," he repeated calmly. "I assume you'd rather not have to clean up her corpse."

"What the fuck is wrong with you?" Hannah shouted up.

A gun went off. Hannah's whole body jolted at the sound.

A chip of stone flew off only a few inches from the other woman's head.

Hannah stared up in shock.

"Do it!" the voice shouted.

She looked over at the woman, who trembled uncontrollably. Tears leaked out of the sides of her eyes.

"You have until three."

Hannah looked down at the brick.

"One."

She looked up at the woman. A small circle of urine appeared on the front of her cotton wrap.

"Two."

Hannah's own tears began to fall, but she lifted the brick. Without hesitation, she slammed it down.

A feral cry burst from her mouth as her finger exploded with pain.

The woman collapsed to the floor with relief.

Hannah swooned and leaned forward, putting her head back down on the table, unable to do anything but breathe in and out. In and out.

UNIVERSITY OF VIRGINIA
HISTORY DEPARTMENT,
CHARLOTTESVILLE, VA

Sayer shivered slightly in the cool air as she and Max made their way across the UVA campus. Maple trees lined the bustling promenade, littering the green lawn with blazing red and orange leaves. They entered the UVA History Department and wandered along the glass rotunda until they found the office of Dr. Hamza Suvari.

Max knocked and a soft voice answered, "Enter!"

A spry man in his eighties sat behind a small desk, sprigs of silver hair perched on his head like a preening bird.

"You do not appear to be students here to complain about the pop quiz on Ottoman history this morning." He smiled, wrinkles deepening.

"Dr. Suvari. I'm Agent Maxwell Cho with the FBI. I sent you an e-mail this morning about a bladed weapon we found in the course of a criminal investigation." Max held up the plastic-wrapped sword.

"Ah, yes! Come in, please sit. Can I get you some tea?"

"No, thank you," Sayer answered, not wanting to take too long. "We're on an active case right now."

Dr. Suvari frowned with disapproval but nodded. "Of course. Let me cut right to the chase then, Agent . . . ?"

“I’m sorry. Senior Special Agent Altair.”

Dr. Suvari bowed slightly. “Altair, what an auspicious name. What you have, Agent Altair, is not actually a Turkish yataghan at all, though I can see why you thought so. What you actually have is a Greek kopis. Both have short, recurved blades, but a yataghan tends to be slightly longer and more slender. Actually, the yataghan was probably an evolution from the kopis, but true yataghans weren’t even found in the Ottoman Empire until the mid-sixteenth century, when it was—”

“Dr. Suvari,” Sayer gently interrupted. She’d spent enough time with academics to recognize the beginning of a lecture.

“Of course, sorry. As I said, you have a Greek sword. A kopis has a shorter, thicker blade, though the real diagnostic difference is the hilt. Yours has a hook handle rather than a straight hilt.”

“And what would a kopis be used for?” Sayer asked.

Dr. Suvari frowned again. “In my limited knowledge about such things, I believe it was used for war, but also for butchery, including ritual sacrifice.”

Goose bumps rose along Sayer’s arms and she momentarily wished she had accepted the offer of a warm tea.

“Hang on.” He held up a finger. “Let me see if our Greek historian is in her office.”

Sayer expected him to lift the phone on his desk, but instead he belted out, “Delores!” so loudly that she jumped.

Dr. Suvari let out a mischievous grin. “Sorry, didn’t mean to startle you. She’s just in the office next door. . . .”

A middle-aged woman peeked through the doorway. “You need me, Hamza?”

“Yes, could you come take a look at this? I believe it’s a kopis, but you would have a much better idea.”

The willowy woman in a suede skirt and silk blouse hurried in, her sleek brown bob swinging as she moved.

Max held up the weapon and she took it without any form of greeting.

“You have a kopis?” She turned it over in her hand. “Where did you find this?”

"It's part of our current investigation." Sayer tried to catch her eye. "I'm with the FBI. . . ."

The Greek-history professor barely acknowledged her existence. She leaned in close, turning the short sword over in her hand.

"Sorry, Delores can be . . . focused. Dr. Delores Schneider, these are agents Altair and Cho with the FBI. They need to know anything you can tell them about this sword."

The Greek historian glanced up from her inspection. "What? Oh, yes, sorry. I've just never seen one up close like this. Can I take it out of this bag?"

"No, sorry. It hasn't been fully processed."

The historian frowned.

"So it is a kopis?" Sayer asked.

"Most definitely."

"And could you tell us what a kopis would have been used for?"

"Certainly. The word *kopis* was really just slang for "chopper" in ancient Greece. It was most often used in combat. The curved blade would allow the user to strike downward over the top of an enemy's shield. But they were also commonly used for ritual purposes. Sacrifices and such."

"Did the Greeks sacrifice humans?"

"Debatable." She continued turning the sword over in her hands. "But, in my expert opinion, yes. There's a growing consensus that they did ritually slaughter human beings."

"And what would that look like?" Sayer asked, thinking about cause of death. "A ritual sacrifice."

"A good question. Despite what you see in movies, there was a great deal of religious variation across the ancient Greek world. But the stereotypical sacrificial ritual would involve binding the victim, then decorating them in ritual vestments like ribbons or fine gowns. They would bring the victim to the altar and ritually slit their throat, possibly catching blood in a shallow basin. From there, they would often process the femur or tailbone and eat only the meat from that part, burning the rest." She squinted at the handle. "Hamza, do you have a magnifier?"

Dr. Suvari handed her his reading glasses. "Will these do?"

She grunted approval and she squinted at the handle through the thick glasses, turning the sword in the light.

"Aha! This is a real kopis."

"A real one?"

"Yes, it's possible to get a modern kopis from a speciality shop, but I think this one is genuine."

"As in an actual ancient Greek sword?"

The historian looked like a kid with a new toy. "Exactly."

"How hard would it be to buy something like this?"

"A good question. The answer all depends on how long ago it was purchased. Right now, no way you could find anything like this legally, so you would have to buy it on the black market. Did you know that the antiquities black market almost rivals drugs and guns? Billions of dollars a year. But twenty or thirty years ago, looting laws were virtually nonexistent. How else would museums have any exhibits?" She laughed at her own joke. When no one else laughed, she looked up. "Because most of what you see in museums was stolen. . . ." She paused. "Anyway, it would have been fairly easy to find something like this maybe twenty years ago."

"That's really useful—"

"You'll also probably want to know what this says," the historian interrupted Sayer, pointing to the curved handle.

"What what says?"

Dr. Schneider turned the sword, and at just the right angle, Sayer could see faint scratch marks. Unlike the fine craftsmanship of the kopis, the symbols were crudely etched into the metal. "Is that Greek?"

"Indeed. Ἔχιδνα. Ekhidna, the she-viper."

"Echidna, like the spiky little Australian animal?" Max asked.

The Greek historian looked up at Max, annoyed. She did a double-take, as if noticing him for the first time. "The animal is named after a Greek monster. Echidnas are marsupials, half mammal, half amphibian. The Greek Ekhidna was half fair maiden, half snake. The she-viper," she repeated, as if they were children.

"Okay." Sayer let that roll around in her mind. "So we've got a Greek sword and a Greek monster. What can you tell me about Ekhidna?"

"She was a drakaina of ancient Greek mythology—half serpent, half human. She was known as the mother of all monsters."

"The mother of all monsters . . . ," Sayer said.

"Here, let me quote Hesiod's *Theogony*." The historian closed her eyes as though reading from an invisible book. "*She was an unmanageable monster like nothing human nor like the immortal gods either, in a hollow cave. This was the divine and haughty Ekhidna, and half of her is a nymph with a fair face and eyes glancing, but the other half is a monstrous serpent, terrible, enormous and squirming and voracious, there in earth's secret places. For there she has her cave on the underside of a hollow rock, far from the immortal gods, and far from all mortals.*"

She opened her eyes.

"That was all a quote?" Max asked.

"Yes, a direct quote. Photographic memory comes in handy as a historian." She tilted her head and smiled at Max. Sayer realized she was trying to flirt. Poorly.

"So, Ekhidna was a monster who lived in a cave. . . ." Sayer couldn't help but think about the cave where they'd just found human remains.

"Correct. Or at least in some kind of underground lair. Various quotes also have her living off the flesh and blood of the innocent. She gave birth to quite a few famous mythological monsters—Hydra, Cerberus, and so on."

Sayer glanced at the time and realized they were due in the profiler's office. "We've got to get going, but thank you both. Could I call you if I have more questions?" Sayer said while plucking the kopis from the historian's hands.

"Of course. More than happy to help." She looked slightly forlorn. "When you're done, I would love to get another look at this. Maybe write a paper. . . ."

"Now, Delores, let the agents get back to their case," Dr. Suvari said. "Stay for tea and we can gossip about everything we just saw here."

UNIVERSITY OF VIRGINIA PSYCHOLOGY DEPARTMENT, CHARLOTTESVILLE, VA

Though the rain had stopped, a brisk wind snaked its way inside Sayer's parka as they hurried toward the UVA Psychology Department. Students passed in gaggles, heads down, hunched forward over jackets pulled tight.

"Who is this psychologist again? Don't we have plenty of profilers at Quantico?" Max asked.

"Not right now. Things with the congressional hearings are spreading everyone thin. The Behavioral Analysis Unit told me that Dr. . . ."—Sayer glanced down at her phone—"Alice Beaumont is a Stanford-trained forensic psychologist specializing in criminal psychopathy who has interviewed hundreds of psychopaths in prison. When she heard about the murders she offered to help. Apparently she came in on her day off, so let's be extra nice."

"I'm always nice. Nothing but rainbows and lollipops. . . ." Max gave her a deadpan look.

They made it to the portico in front of the main entrance just as two people rushed out the sliding glass doors.

A camera was shoved into Sayer's face, bright light forcing her to squint. Her hand instinctively went to her gun, but she stopped herself

The elderly gentleman winked conspiratorially at Sayer and Max and ushered them out. As they made their way toward the Psychology Department, Sayer decided that she wasn't entirely sure she wanted to know why they had just found a sword designed for ritual sacrifice.

from actually touching it. A young man in a suit pressed a microphone close to her mouth.

"Agent Altair, we understand that there's been a series of murders in the Shenandoah Mountains and that you're leading the investigation?"

Sayer hated the press and tried to remember all her training. Short, simple answers. Don't elaborate. Don't lie. Keep walking. "I am," she managed to squeeze out.

"And were you surprised that the FBI put you in charge of such a big case, even though you're currently under investigation in the Quantico Hearings?" The reporter pressed the mic even closer to her.

Sayer stopped walking. "What?"

He ignored her question. "Is this a task force?"

Sayer tried to decide if she should press him for information or just get the hell inside. "No." She resumed her quick pace toward the door.

"Two women are dead, a woman and child are missing, and the FBI doesn't think this warrants a task force?"

"Well, we're spread thin . . . but . . . how did you . . ."

"So the FBI's no longer able to fulfill its duty to the American people. Thank you for your comments, Agent Altair."

Before she could even try to correct him, the reporter and cameraman hurried away into the parking lot.

"Dammit," Sayer muttered under her breath.

Max waited for her just inside. "Sorry, I expected you to just keep walking so I powered ahead. Was just about to come back out."

Sayer shook her head. "No, just avoid the press at all costs. I talk to them for half a second and I screw something up."

"Everything okay?"

Sayer closed her eyes for a second. "Everything's fine. Nothing we should worry about right now."

In the lobby they scanned the directory, but Sayer was still playing over the reporter's comment about the hearings. Was she being investigated? For what? Wouldn't Holt tell her if something was going on?

"Here we go, Dr. Beaumont, third floor," Max said.

They made their way to Alice Beaumont's office and knocked.

"Come in," a woman called from behind an ornate desk. Plump and tall, Alice Beaumont wore a flowing floor-length dress that perfectly matched her slightly mussed matte-black hair. She held herself with the confidence of someone comfortable taking up space.

Between her loose dress and dyed hair, she looked more rumpled goth-mom than psychology professor.

"You must be Agent Altair." Dr. Beaumont came toward them but didn't offer her hand.

"And this is Agent Cho," Sayer said.

The psychologist glanced at Max and nodded. "Please, sit." Her dark-berry lips formed a no-nonsense line.

"Thank you so much for doing this. We've got a time-sensitive case and your expertise will really help us out." Sayer glanced around the room. A massive photograph of a snow-covered mountain dominated one wall. The rest of the wall space was covered floor-to-ceiling with books.

"I'm happy to help the FBI any way I can," Dr. Beaumont said.

Sayer tried to smile genuinely. She hated pleasantries but knew they were part of the job.

Dr. Beaumont held out a thin stack of paper. "I've written up my notes, but I have a few more questions before I finalize my preliminary profile."

"Of course." Sayer shifted in the slightly uncomfortable seat.

"It says here that there was writing on the latest victim? Have you matched the DNA to anyone?"

"Ah, sorry, I e-mailed you the latest update from our lab as soon as we got it. We've now identified both victims, and we matched the saliva writing to another missing woman. She and her child were kidnapped over a month ago."

Dr. Beaumont visibly paled, eyes crinkling with genuine sorrow. "He took a child?"

"He did." Sayer noted her confident use of the pronoun *he* to describe the UNSUB.

"So he's probably still holding them somewhere," she said softly.

"The women are all blond, early to mid-twenties, educated. They look so much alike they could be sisters. He took them from university campuses and a mall. No connection found yet between them."

Dr. Beaumont clicked on her computer. "Yes, I see the e-mail from you now." She opened the file and skimmed. "That is a high-risk victim pool. Anything else from the DNA?"

"One more thing," Sayer said. "The DNA from beneath the fingernails of our two beaten victims matches the missing mother."

Dr. Beaumont's eyes widened. "Are you interpreting that to mean . . ."

"We aren't sure how to interpret it. Obviously our first thought is that the missing mother is also our killer."

Dr. Beaumont stared down at her notes.

Sayer watched closely but couldn't interpret Dr. Beaumont's reaction. Her surface demeanor said calm professional, but Sayer sensed a tempest happening just below the surface. The involvement of a child really seemed to throw her.

"Okay." Dr. Beaumont cleared her throat. "Well, none of that actually changes my initial profile. I think you're looking for a single perpetrator. He's organized, methodical, and very good at hiding what he is."

The doctor leaned back, squeaking her office chair.

"You said *he*. Do you think this is a male UNSUB despite the DNA evidence suggesting that the killer might be the missing mom?"

"Despite the DNA, I would be genuinely shocked to find that this killer is a woman."

Sayer's gut agreed. "That makes sense, but then I'm not sure how to interpret the DNA evidence."

Dr. Beaumont held her hands open in an I-don't-know gesture. "It is confusing, but beating someone to death is very rarely a female act. Even more rare is a woman, on her own, holding other women in captivity for extended periods of time."

Sayer thought about historical female serial killers. "What about people like Delphine LaLaurie and Madame de Brinvilliers? They both held and tortured other women to death."

Dr. Beaumont let out a small sound of approval. "As you well know, there are of course examples, but they're the exception to the rule. While it is certainly possible, it's rare. As I'm also sure you know, profiling is ninety percent statistics and ten percent interpretive magic."

"Don't tell our lead profiler at Quantico; he seems to think it's all magic."

Instead of smiling, the woman deepened her frown into a stern rebuke. "I would say that you're looking for a white male, approximately thirty-five, who most likely has a steady job. Maybe a high-status job. He can blend into places like malls and universities, so he likely has above-average social skills." She cleared her throat again.

"And the victimology? Any thoughts there?"

Dr. Beaumont took a long breath, picking at the end of her sleeve. "I'll want to look at their files as soon as possible. For right now, nothing beyond the obvious. They're all educated women, very high-risk victims. These are not people you randomly grab off the street. The fact that the women are all very similar in appearance clearly means that these abductions are planned and executed with precision. He picks these women because they fit his pathological need, whatever that might be. Perhaps they all look like his mother. . . . No signs of sexual assault?"

"None," Sayer said.

"Hmm, okay. Until we have more victims and more information, I'm afraid that's all I have right now. Feel free to let me know as you gather more evidence and I can revise my profile."

"Any thoughts on the bones?" Sayer asked. She had primarily wanted a profile based on their new victims, but had also asked Dr. Beaumont to look at the skeletal remains.

"Not really. I would definitely need more information about the victims and cause of death."

"Oh, we did just find out from your colleagues in the History Department that the sword we found with the bodies is a kopis, an ancient Greek sword used for human sacrifice."

Dr. Beaumont paled slightly. "Well, that doesn't bode well. . . . I assume it's associated with the bones?"

"We don't know yet."

The psychologist nodded but seemed done talking.

"Well, Dr. Beaumont, I really appreciate you taking the time to help us with this case."

She stood and gestured to her office door. "Of course. Now, I apologize but I've got some work to get to."

"Thank you so much." Sayer paused in the doorway. "If I have more questions, can I get back in touch?"

"Of course," the doctor replied, and ushered them out.

Both lost in thought, Sayer and Max didn't say a word all the way back up to the ranger station.

CONGRESSIONAL HEARING CHAMBERS, CAPITOL HILL, WASHINGTON, D.C.

FBI Assistant Director Janice Holt settled into her chair, straightening the microphone and glass of water in front of her.

"Good afternoon, Janice," Senator DeWitt said into his microphone. "Sorry to get started so late. Shall we get back to our discussion about the fact that a serial killer was operating under your direction at Quantico?"

Holt leaned forward, composing herself. She'd lain awake the previous night thinking about exactly what she wanted to say on the record. It was time.

"Yes, John, let's go back to that. Because, while I understand a postmortem asking how we missed something so big and how we can keep it from happening again—"

"Two valid questions to which you seem to have no answer," DeWitt interrupted her.

Holt took a calming breath. "And that is because there is no answer. The reality is that we can't prevent this from happening again because there is no serial killer detection kit. I can't wave a magic wand over people and know if they are a clever psychopath intent on deceiving me.

No one can, because that's what serial killers do. They are smart and organized and, like some politicians"—she stared daggers at the row of men and women judging her—"they have no compunction about destroying the lives of innocent, hardworking people for their own ends."

"Now, Janice," DeWitt said.

"Don't 'now' me. I've answered your inane questions because I believe in the system. You know better than anyone how much I love the FBI. But it has become clear to me that these hearings are a farce. None of you wants to hear the truth. The truth doesn't look good to the electorate, and here you all are"—Holt gestured to the line of senators—"saving face for the upcoming elections."

Murmurs of disapproval swept the room.

"None of you wants to tell the public that there is no easy way to prevent this kind of horrific murder. In fact, this committee is targeting one of the few people out there who might just be able to help us stop them. Sayer Altair isn't the one you should be after here if you really want to stop those men and women from killing again. So, let me be clear on the record. I was responsible for hiring and promoting the people at Quantico. I am the one who didn't see the signs of a problem. And I am the only one who should take the blame for this fiasco. Do not attack our hardworking agents who sacrifice every day to do this job that they love."

"That's not—"

Ignoring the senator, Holt leaned in close to the microphone. "That concludes my testimony on this subject."

She stood, straightened her blazer, and walked proudly out the door.

SOUTHERN RANGER STATION, SHENANDOAH NATIONAL PARK, VA

Sayer and Max found Piper and Ezra in the main conference room. The park ranger sat hunched in her chair next to Ezra, and they were reading together from the computer screen.

They looked up as Sayer approached.

"Hey, got your message about Ekhidna and the kopis. We were just looking up some info," Ezra said.

"Those are some nasty swords," Piper added.

"Yeah, come check it out." Ezra gestured at his computer. "This is from a Tyrrhenian amphora, a kind of ancient Greek terra-cotta vase. This one shows a human sacrifice during the Trojan War."

Sayer leaned in to see the image of three soldiers holding a tightly bound woman while a fourth soldier slit her throat. Despite being a relatively primitive image, the wide-eyed look of fear on the victim's face, coupled with the soldiers' faint smiles, was unnerving. "What're the little *x*'s all over the victim's clothes?" Sayer asked, pointing to the strange design.

"They would dress their sacrificial victims up in fancy clothing. I think those are little decorative ribbons."

Sayer shifted her attention to the sword that Max put on the table. Its recurved blade was dull and corroded but she could imagine how much damage it could do when sharp. It looked exactly like the sacrificial weapon on the amphora. "So, the question is, why is there an ancient Greek sword in the bone cave and which dead bodies is it associated with?"

"And why is it inscribed with the name of an ancient Greek monster?" Max added.

"Ezra, keep digging there and see what you can find. See if you can figure out any way this connects to Greece or mythological monsters."

He pulled his chair in front of his computer, fingers poised like he was about to conduct a symphony. "You got it, ma'am."

Sayer gave Ezra a stare. He knew she didn't like being called ma'am.

"We've also got our preliminary profile from the UVA psychologist. She was very confident that our UNSUB is a lone male, but I'm not entirely convinced, especially considering Jillian Watts's DNA on our victims. Would you do a cursory look at Dr. Beaumont? Just see what her reputation is. Should I trust her profile?"

Ezra nodded without looking up from his computer, already lost in his world of information.

"Piper, any word from the local departments on their canvass?"

"Nothing so far." Piper looked very disappointed to have nothing to report. "I called Kyle." She glanced over at Max. "I wanted to let him know that Dana was starting to analyze the bones."

"Okay. Ezra, can you have one of the evidence techs run the sword up to Quantico? I think we should get them on analysis. See if they can figure out where it's from."

Ezra nodded.

"And Dana is already working on the bones?"

Ezra nodded again.

"Great. While you guys dig into ancient monsters and ritual swords, I'll go check in with her."

Sayer hurried along the hall until she found Dana in the utility room they'd set up as the bone repository.

All five tables in the large room were covered with clear plastic. Parts of a few skeletons were laid out together, but the rest of the bones were sorted by type—femurs here, rib bones there, and so on. Dana and two evidence techs were hunched over tables.

Dana looked up, eyes overlarge in thick magnifying glasses, and grunted a greeting. "Finished the autopsies, so wanted to get started on the bones."

Sayer leaned against the desk. "I got the brief overview of the autopsy results from Ezra. Anything else I need to know? Did you find anything to dispute the idea that Jillian Watts beat those women to death?"

Dana propped her glasses up on her head. "No, in fact I spent quite a while analyzing the size and power of the killer. There's a great deal of forensic data out there on force requirements to break bones and such. It's a fascinating subfield . . . using the extent and angle of the breaks to determine the height and gender of the UNSUB." Her face twisted with discomfort.

"And?"

"And, based on the damage suffered by the two women beaten to death, angles of breaks, as well as their defensive wounds, I would say that they were very likely beaten by a five-foot-six woman. Which is exactly how tall Jillian Watts is. . . ."

"Shit." Sayer wasn't sure what else to say. Could their missing mother really also be their killer? "Anything new with the bones?" She leaned in to see what Dana was examining.

Dana stood and pulled off her gloves. "Two of my team are still out at the bone cave sifting through the mud to make sure we didn't miss any small fragments, but we've managed to pull all the major bones and sort this mess into seven separate individuals. We've also already sent off samples for DNA testing. Sadly, because of the damage, I'm not sure we got workable samples."

"Still, that was fast. You all are amazing," Sayer said to Dana's techs.

Proud smiles appeared on their faces.

"They truly are. I'll update you as those results roll in, but it could take a while. Since this is being considered a cold case, we're at the back of the line. Come check this out."

Dana led Sayer over to a different table. Two charred and tattered straitjackets were laid out, surrounded by scraps of faded red and gold fabric streaked with ash and rust-colored splotches.

"You found two straitjackets total? Why is the rest of the material shredded like that?"

Dana nodded. "Two straitjackets, and this"—she gently lifted a long strip of bright red material—"isn't shredded material. I think it's rotting ribbon. Hundreds of pieces of red and gold ribbon."

"Ribbon?" Sayer leaned in. "Ezra literally just showed me an ancient Greek vase with a picture of a woman being sacrificed. The victim was bound in a heavy cloth and then decorated with ribbon. You think this is all blood?" She waved her hand over the dark splotches.

"That would be my first guess. Ancient Greek human sacrifice, eh? Well, nothing is ever boring around you, Sayer. We're lucky that most of the fabric was trapped down in the mud so the fire didn't damage it, but it is waterlogged and delicate. I sent samples up, along with the bone samples, for DNA and analysis, but I'm not optimistic." Dana led Sayer over to a table covered with bones. "In better news, despite how beat-up the bones are, my team has already managed to reconstruct quite a bit."

"That's great."

"It is, though my definition of 'quite a bit' might not be the same as yours. We have seven skulls, seven sets of pelvic bones, so it's easy to identify how many victims we have. But the next step is a lot more difficult. For example"—Dana held up a tiny finger bone—"figuring out which phalanges go with which body is a challenge."

Dana rolled her neck but then forced a smile. "Oh, and I've sent teeth off to be radiocarbon dated. We can at least figure out how long they've been in that cave."

"I thought radiocarbon dating was only for ancient bone," Sayer said. "Doesn't it have to be really old?"

"Normally that's correct, but a colleague of mine has developed a new technique based on the fact that nuclear testing sent up a ton of radiation in the 1950s. There was a spike in environmental radiation, then a steady drop after the Nuclear Test Ban Treaty, which she can apparently measure. As long as these bodies were deposited after the 1950s, she should be able to get an approximate date."

"Great." Sayer was impressed. She surveyed the bones, momentarily overwhelmed by the sheer number of dead. "Seven. At least we know how many people we need to identify. Have you had a chance to see if any of these remains matches Cricket Nelson?"

"That's what I just finished doing when you walked in. I've compared the dental records to all seven skulls and I'm confident that none of these are the remains of Cricket Nelson."

Sayer's shoulders fell a bit with relief. She had definitely not looked forward to telling Kyle Nelson that they found his sister's remains. Now she could put his mind to rest that Cricket wasn't among the dead here. Though perhaps not knowing was worse than finding her body.

"Any thoughts on cause of death yet? We did find a big old sword in the cave with them. . . ."

Dana picked up one of the skulls, absentmindedly turning it over in her hands as she spoke. "Yeah, looking for blade strikes on the bones will be tough. They got so beaten up in the cave, there's a lot of chipping and general damage which might cover cut marks or bone breaks. We're just starting to look for consistent damage that might reflect cause of death."

"And what about gender?"

Dana led Sayer over to another partial skeleton. "This one is clearly a young woman, eighteen to twenty years old. The other possibly female skeleton is in much worse shape. I'm having a hard time even determining age. Look at this." Dana held up a long bone so charred, bits of the ends were burned away. "I originally thought some of these bones took the brunt of the fire in the cave, but as we separate them out, I actually think this one skeleton had already been previously set on fire. Maybe an attempt at cremation."

"But just one skeleton?"

"Yes, and if I had to guess, I'd say it's female, but I won't be completely confident about gender until we finish sorting them. So right now I'm thinking we have five men and two women. "

"Whoa, male victims. That's a huge departure from our modern case." Sayer flopped into a chair. "So maybe these two cases really aren't connected. . . ."

Dana flopped into the chair next to her. "I dunno. That's your job." She flashed a vulpine smile at Sayer. "What I do know is that this case cries out for a beer sandwich."

"A beer sandwich?" Sayer perked up. "I have no idea what that is, but it sounds like something I want."

"Holy hell, woman, how do you do this job without a nightly beer, then shower, then another beer—a beer sandwich? Essential for survival in the Congo . . . or during cases like this."

Sayer smiled at the juxtaposition of Dana's appearance—small, older, almost pixie-like—with her frat-boy demeanor.

"I will definitely have to try that," Sayer said. "Only problem, I forgot to bring beer and I'm certainly not driving down to town in this rain."

"Ha, ha! That's why you need me." Dana jumped up and strolled over to a cooler that Sayer had assumed was some kind of equipment.

She popped open the lid. "Behold, beer for everyone. Once we're done for the day, of course." She slammed the cooler shut. "Now get out of my way so I can get back to my bones."

SAYER'S TOWN HOUSE, ALEXANDRIA, VA

Adi struggled to carry the dusty cardboard box across the apartment. Old tape began to peel away from the bottom, threatening to dump Sayer's books onto the floor. She just barely managed to thump the box down. Her fingers, still sore from assembling five bookcases, protested as she pried open the box top.

Sayer had moved into this place right after her fiancé Jake died, and she'd been living half out of boxes since then. It had seemed like a genius idea to unpack everything while Sayer was away. But that was before Adi realized that most of the boxes were full of books.

She glared down at the textbooks and sighed.

"Won't it be a nice surprise when Sayer sees all her old boxes unpacked?" Adi said out loud. "Way to go, genius."

Hearing her voice, Vesper got up from his nap on the futon and came over to investigate. Tail wagging, the silvery dog gave her a quick hand lick before settling down at her feet.

From the apartment below, Adi could just barely hear Tino singing, no doubt while cooking something delicious for dinner. Her stomach rumbled at the thought. He would be expecting her in a few hours so they could go out to the garden to eat and chat while Vesper played.

She looked around the sparsely furnished apartment, down at Vesper, to the pile of now-empty cartons and almost-full bookcases, and realized that this felt like home. The thought set off a swell of emotion that she almost shut down. Then she remembered her therapist told her that it was normal to feel out of control of her emotions once in a while. But this felt different. Unlike the fear that sometimes overwhelmed her, this was gratitude. She felt loved and cared for. She felt safe.

Adi wiped sweat away from her forehead and went back to unpacking with a renewed desire to do something nice for Sayer.

As she shelved the textbooks, she got lost in the subjects indicated by their titles. Criminology, abnormal psychology, neurophenomenology . . . whatever that was. She got to a well-worn textbook with tattered corners.

"*Rewiring the Killer Brain: The Latest Research on Neuroplasticity.*" Adi read the title out loud. Unable to resist, she flipped it open. The title page was signed.

Dear Sayer, You've checked this book out from the library so many times, I figured you should have your own copy. To the horizon together, Jake.

As Adi fanned through the pages, an envelope slid from the bottom. In the same handwriting, it read *Sayer* across the front. The envelope was still sealed. Adi wondered if she should call about the note from Jake, or just wait until Sayer got home.

SOUTHERN RANGER STATION, SHENANDOAH NATIONAL PARK, VA

Sayer stepped out of the bone room and stood in the darkened hallway of the ranger station. At the end of the hall she could just see the park ranger guarding the front door. The ranger sat with her nose in a book, oblivious to her surroundings. Something about the young woman in the midafternoon light, lost in her reading, made Sayer long for something indefinable. She seemed so at peace. So content.

Instead of dwelling on her own lack of inner peace, Sayer replayed her day so far. A killer mom. A Greek sacrificial sword. A monstrous snake beast. Beatings and fire and broken fingers. And none of that even touched the seven older skeletons, victims yet to even be identified.

Barely two-thirty on the second day of this investigation, and she felt simultaneously buried under information while also left without any clear leads.

Head buzzing, she entered the main conference room. Ezra and Piper looked up from what they were doing.

"I took a quick look into our illustrious UVA psychologist," Ezra said.

Sayer came over to the computer and looked over his shoulder. "And what did you learn about Dr. Beaumont?"

Ezra shrugged. "She was a star student, grew up in Boston. Harvard for undergrad. Moved to California for graduate school at Stanford. Distinguished research career leading to her position as a professor at UVA."

"Any sense of her reputation?"

"Well, she gets asked to speak at conferences all over the world. And she's published half a dozen books. She seems pretty darn fancy to me."

"All right, thanks, Ezra. So, Dana's autopsy suggests that whoever beat our two victims to death was the same size as Jillian Watts."

"You think she's really the UNSUB?" Piper asked. The word *UNSUB* fell awkwardly off the park ranger's lips.

"It looks increasingly possible. But we've also got a presumably good profiler suggesting this is a lone male UNSUB. I figure there are a few explanations for the discrepancy. One, Jillian Watts is working with a male partner. Or two, our profiler is dead wrong and Jillian Watts really is our sole killer. Despite my reservations, all the evidence so far says that Watts is it. Ezra, have you dug up anything new on her?"

"I've done a deep dive into her background and haven't found anything. She's studying child development at UVA. Works part-time at a coffee shop a few blocks from her house. She and her husband are active members in their church. By all accounts a great mother."

"Who's a great mother?" Max stood in the doorway holding an unwieldy stack of plastic-wrapped sandwiches. Kona stood at attention beside him. He held up a sandwich. "I know it's late for lunch, but I ran to town for some grub, figured our soldiers need fuel." He tossed one to Sayer.

She caught the sandwich. "Jillian Watts is apparently a great mom."

"Ah, our possible killer." Max passed sandwiches to Ezra and Piper.

"Possible . . . yeah." Sayer hated when the evidence didn't quite make sense. Not that mothers couldn't also be killers, but something about this just didn't fit. "Dana did an analysis of the injuries to the two women beaten to death and concluded that they are consistent with a woman the same height as Jillian Watts."

Max whistled and then took a massive bite of sandwich. "Well, that's no bueno."

"No, it's not." Sayer thought about Hannah Valdez. Was Hannah being held somewhere, about to be murdered by Jillian Watts? And where was little Grace? "Oh, and Dana says that Cricket Nelson is not a match to any of our skeletal remains."

Max fell into a chair and let out a long breath. "Well, thank god for that. So, maybe she really did just run off all those years ago. Have you told Kyle?"

"Not yet. When we're done here, I'll call the chief to let him know." Sayer walked over to the murder board and stared briefly into Grace Watts's eyes. "All right, we need to bring this little girl home." Sayer felt her heart constricting at the sight of the girl's bright smile. All she could imagine was that face contorted with fear.

"Let's review leads. What've we got?" Sayer began to pace.

No one said anything.

"Yeah, that seems about right," Sayer muttered. "Okay, no matter how much I don't want to buy it, I'm pretty damn convinced at this point that Jillian Watts beat our two victims to death. Which makes Jillian our best lead right now. Let's approach our next move based on that assumption. Why would a quiet college student, mom, and wife suddenly start killing people?

"Ezra and Piper, you two look into her associations. See if you can find anywhere Jillian could be hiding these women. Any landholdings in her family? Any ties to the mountains here? Anyone who could be her partner in all this? After that, give them a few hours for analysis, then see what Quantico comes up with on our Greek sword. I'm pretty sure it's associated with the skeletal remains instead of our modern case, but let's follow up just to be sure. They should be able to tell us how old it is, where it's from. It's unusual enough to be a potentially good lead."

Ezra's computer *pinged*. "Speaking of the sword, we've got DNA results from the swabs you sent up. Oh, there's a match." As he read off his screen his mouth fell open with surprise.

“We have a DNA match from the kopis?” Sayer asked.

“We do. There were multiple blood contributions found on the handle, but only one DNA hit.” Ezra paused. “It’s a match to Catherine ‘Cricket’ Nelson.”

“Cricket Nelson? But I thought her remains weren’t in the cave. That doesn’t make any sense.” Max’s voice rose slightly.

“Sorry, man.” Ezra leaned back away from Max’s accusatory tone.

“I’m just . . . I mean, was Kyle right? Does this mean Cricket is dead?”

Sayer held up a hand. “The only thing this tells us is that Cricket is somehow connected to one of our cases. We didn’t find her remains in the cave, so we don’t actually know if she is alive or dead at this point.”

“But, I mean, her blood is on the sword,” Max pressed. “And I will swear till the day I die that she was terrified of something the night she showed up at my house.”

“You said she had a cut on her hand that night? Maybe she came into contact with someone wielding the kopis. That would explain her blood on it. Maybe that’s what she was running from.”

“That makes sense. So maybe her blood was deposited on the sword before she ran and she really did get away,” Max said.

“Uh,” Ezra said tentatively, “I didn’t say anything earlier because I didn’t think she was connected, but now that she’s clearly connected . . . I’ll admit I’m a little worried that I can’t find any evidence of Cricket Nelson beyond that day. It’s pretty hard to totally cover your tracks and create a new identity without leaving some kind of trail. It’s like she fell off the face of the earth the morning you dropped her off.”

“How easy would it’ve been for someone to grab Cricket from the bus stop after you dropped her off?” Sayer asked.

“Easy. It’s on the edge of town, pretty far from anything. You thinking she was nabbed that morning?”

Sayer rubbed her temples. “I think it’s possible. Clearly someone attacked her the night she fled. Maybe they caught up with her that morning at the bus stop. It would explain how she disappeared so thoroughly. Though that doesn’t explain why her remains weren’t found with the others. We also can't dismiss the possibility that Cricket's blood is on the handle because she was the one wielding it."

"Wait, you think Cricket Nelson could be the murderer?" Max turned to face Sayer.

"I don't think anything yet," Sayer said firmly. "Right now we don't have any idea if Cricket Nelson is a victim or a killer."

"It's like the Schrödinger's cat of murder. . . ." Ezra smiled.

Max flashed him a dark look. "None of this is funny. Because it's starting to sound like, seventeen years ago, I either left a young woman alone at a bus stop to be kidnapped, or I helped a killer get away." Max put his head down in his hands. "Fantastic."

"Though if Cricket was kidnapped back then and her remains weren't in the cave, where has she been for the last seventeen years?" Sayer said softly.

Sayer, Max, Ezra, and Piper sat in silence for a few moments, letting that thought sink in.

"All right, well, this adds a new twist to our old case. But, assuming this sword is associated with the bones, it's just that, a cold case. We need to keep our attention on the people missing right now. Ezra and Piper, keep digging into Jillian Watts. Max and I will head down to interview her husband."

The sound of hurried footsteps from the hall interrupted Sayer.

Dana hurried in, eyes bright with excitement. "One of my techs just brought something back from the cave. You need to come see this."

Sayer, Max, Ezra, and Piper hurried after Dana into the bone room, where a small, ornately carved wooden box sat on one of the tables. Stylized flowers ran along the edges, caked with thick streaks of mud. A rusted brass latch held it closed.

"It was buried in the muck, which protected it from the fire. Considering the fact that it's been encased in mud for quite a while, it's in pretty decent shape. I thought you might want to see what we find when we open it," Dana said.

"I think it's safe to open . . . ," one of the evidence techs said.

"Let's try, but don't force it if it doesn't open easily. I'd hate to destroy anything," Sayer said.

They anxiously gathered around the table.

The gloved tech gently pulled at the latch. "It's not sliding easily, but let me . . ." He increased the pressure and it scraped open. "Got it!"

He delicately lifted the lid. Everyone in the room held their breath as the hinges creaked. A single leather-bound book sat inside. Lacy black mold grew along the walls of the box and up onto the leather binding.

"Looks like some water damage," the tech said. "Since I'm not sure how wet it is, I don't feel comfortable taking the book out of the box here. Want me to try and get a look inside before we take it up to the lab?"

Sayer grunted a yes.

The tech gently lifted the leather cover. The pages were soaked through. On the front page, it was just possible to make out a single word scrawled in looping handwriting. Sayer's breath caught.

"*Ekhidna,*" she read out loud.

"Just like on the sword," Ezra said, just above a whisper.

Sayer leaned in to closely inspect the journal. The paper was so wet that she could make out more writing bleeding through from the next page. "You think you can turn the page?"

The evidence tech grimaced. "I can try." He rubbed his hands together like he was about to perform a magic trick. With the tip of his finger he pried at the edge of the journal. "It's sticking. No way I can turn to the next page, but I think I can . . ." The journal opened somewhere in the middle.

The ink blurred along the wet page, making most of it indecipherable.

"I can make out a little bit. *A monster* . . . ," Sayer read aloud, "*will kill to protect if I have to . . . bleating like a lamb.*" She looked up at her team.

"This looks like something about *blood.*" Ezra pointed farther down the page.

"That's all I see here. Can we go to another page?" Sayer asked the tech.

He tried to pull apart another section, but the paper formed a solid clot. "Sorry, I'm pretty sure forcing these apart will destroy them. We've got equipment up at Quantico that should be able to dry this out enough to read whatever's left."

"All right," Sayer said. "While the lab works their magic, we need to stay focused. Ezra, you and Piper get back to tracking down anything you can on Jillian Watts. Max, let's go visit Jillian Watts's husband and see what we can learn about our killer mom."

ROAD TO THE WATTS HOUSE, CHARLOTTESVILLE, VA

While Max drove them down the mountain toward the Wattses' house, Sayer called Kyle and let him know that they had found Cricket's blood on the kopis but that they didn't have a match to his sister's remains.

When she hung up, Max asked, "So, did he sound relieved that at least we didn't find her remains?"

"Not really. I think finding her blood on the sword freaked him out. Sometimes not knowing what really happened is even worse."

Max grimaced. "Man, I wish I could go back in time and stay with her at that bus station, then I'd at least know she got on the bus up to the city."

Not in the mood to reassure anyone, Sayer looked out at the old houses and quaint shops sliding by. Charlottesville was a consummate university town, colonnaded brick homes wedged among bars and bookstores, all with a distinctive colonial Virginia flair. The end of apple-picking season tinged the air with the faint smell of spiced cider, making her mouth water.

"So, what's the deal with Jillian's family?" Max asked as they neared the Wattses' house.

Sayer reluctantly flipped open the file that Ezra had given her. She was already tired of thinking about frightened children and damaged families. "Jillian and her husband, Mark, have been married for four years but together since high school. They had Grace three years ago. Solid family with a good reputation. Unitarian Universalists, active in their church. Not a whiff of scandal."

"Do we tell him that we suspect his wife is beating people to death?"

"Let's play it by ear," Sayer said, dreading the thought.

Mark Watts pulled open the door, face hopeful. Though he was well dressed and composed, Sayer recognized profound stress in the tightness of his face and body.

He led Sayer and Max to a small living room. The arts-and-crafts-style house was clean and cozy. A child-sized table and a neat shelf of toys and books took up one corner of the room. Rainbow letters spelled out GRACE on the wall in an arch above the table. A bright starburst of finger paint covered a piece of paper hanging from a small easel. The art, the hand-stenciled name, and the setup of the room told Sayer all she needed to know. While it was possible to reproduce the trappings of a happy family, this kind of scene was impossible to fake. Grace Watts was a well-loved child.

The only unhappy note was the stack of flyers askew on the coffee table. They featured the same photo that Sayer had tacked to her murder board, Jillian and Grace Watts in their sparkly party hats. Above the photo, in all capital letters, the flyer screamed, *MISSING*.

After reviewing the details of the case with Mark Watts, Sayer realized she was going to have to ask the grieving man some hard questions.

"Mr. Watts, I apologize for what I'm about to ask, but did Jillian have any history we should know about?"

Mark Watts looked genuinely shocked. "Like what?"

"Psychiatric history? A history of violence?" Sayer tried to soften her words, but there was no way to avoid the harsh reality of what she was asking.

He stared incredulously at Sayer, his face transforming from sorrow to anger. "What? No! You think she's . . . what? Involved somehow?"

"I'm sorry, Mr. Watts. We're following up on every lead, and there is some evidence to suggest that Jillian and the other victims fought with each other. We're just trying to figure out what is going on."

Mark Watts looked at Sayer with pure disgust. "I don't know what you think you've found, but my wife is the most peaceful person I've ever met. She won't even let me use mousetraps, do you understand? She catches bugs and puts them outside. . . ."

"I understand," Sayer said gently. "So, you've never seen Jillian display any kind of violence or aggressions?"

Nose flaring, he stared directly into Sayer's eyes. "There is only one thing in this world that could possibly make Jillian violent. Protecting Grace."

Max gripped the steering wheel, staring straight ahead as he drove back toward the ranger station.

"We wondered if our UNSUB needed Grace for something or if the girl was just in the way," Sayer said.

"So you really think . . ." Max trailed off.

"Well, it makes sense." Sayer didn't want to say it out loud either. She cleared her throat. "I mean, mothers can be killers. I've seen that before, but there is usually some sign of previous violence or mental illness when that happens. There's nothing like that here. So, yeah, I strongly suspect Jillian Watts is being forced to kill those women to save the life of her daughter. Obviously we need more evidence to know for sure, but it's the most convincing motive I've heard so far."

"Jesus, Sayer." Max cast his eyes upward.

"You know what worries me?"

"What?"

"We just uncovered a journal associated with our old bones talking about killing to protect someone. I literally just read the words 'kill to protect' in that journal and now, less than an hour later, we hear those exact same words about our modern case. That can't be a coincidence."

Max nodded slowly, processing the idea. "Which would mean that our cases are somehow connected."

"So much for my attempt to focus only on the modern case. It's definitely not enough to convince me that the cases are connected, but I do think we need to step back and look at everything together."

"If Jillian Watts is only killing to protect Grace, then who is making it all happen? And what could that possibly have to do with Cricket or sacrificial swords and ancient Greek monsters?"

"I have no idea, but this is the first theory that's made any sense to me." Sayer felt like she'd been punched in the gut. "He's using a loved one as leverage. Our UNSUB is forcing Jillian Watts to kill other women to save her daughter's life." She was saying it out loud again just to make sure it still made sense.

As the thought seared a path of horror through her gut, Sayer's phone buzzed. A text from Holt read, *Quantico. Now.*

ROAD TO QUANTICO, VA

Sayer roared off on her Silver Hawk toward Quantico. Despite the break in the rain, thick clouds made it feel much later than five-thirty. The road was still slick with runoff. Her shoulders cramped with tension as she rode, frustrated at being called away just when they'd made such a potentially huge breakthrough.

Had they actually figured out their UNSUB's modus operandi? Using Grace as leverage to make Jillian beat the other women to death? It explained all the confusing pieces of evidence, and in Sayer's experience the most parsimonious explanation was usually true.

She imagined the UNSUB holding a gun to Grace's head. What would any mother do in that situation? How far would someone go to save the ones they love?

What horrific things had Jillian Watts done to save her daughter?

For the rest of the long ride, Sayer let those images roll around while she focused on the road in front of her.

She finally pulled up to the security gate at Quantico and managed to make small talk with the guard despite the acid burn of disgust in her gut. Sodden and wound tight, she made her way to the outdoor shooting range where Holt wanted to meet.

"Assistant Director Holt?" Sayer called out as she walked into the partially enclosed firing point.

Holt stood alone, staring down along the range. She wordlessly gestured for Sayer to join her.

"I got here as quickly as I could. Is everything okay?" Sayer looked down and realized that she was dripping water everywhere. She was about to suggest drying herself off when Holt turned. The look on her face made Sayer freeze.

In the dim gray light, Holt's lips curled in a fixed sneer. Sayer had seen Holt angry before. Hell, Sayer had seen Holt punch a hole in the wall with rage. But this look was different . . . predatory, genuinely dangerous.

"Thanks for coming so quickly," Holt growled.

Sayer thought about running. She knew it was completely irrational, that Holt wouldn't actually kill her, but her fight-or-flight instinct kicked into overdrive.

Instead of fleeing, Sayer forced herself to move next to Holt and lean against the bulletproof sidewall.

"What happened?" she managed to say calmly.

Holt took a long, deep breath. "First, tell me what's happening with your cases."

Sayer quickly explained their new theory.

Holt listened, though the predatory gleam never left her eyes. "Damn, that is horrific. So, you've got an MO, involvement of this missing girl from seventeen years ago, and a possible connection between the cases, but still no suspect and nothing else actionable?"

"That's right." Sayer swallowed hard. Being questioned directly by Holt was always uncomfortable and Sayer hated not having better news to share.

"And the skeletal remains?"

Sayer sighed. "Not much there either. There are seven victims, five male and two female, but Dana is just starting to dig into her analysis. No causes of death or IDs yet."

Holt gave a sharp nod. "All right. Sorry to be so cryptic, but it's time we have a talk about the hearings. The shit is hitting the fan and I need to bring you up to speed."

"Okay."

Holt let out another long breath and her eyes softened a little. "I'm done at the FBI. It's not official yet, but it's coming. There's some kind of power play happening that I don't fully understand."

"A power play?"

Holt somehow managed to look weary and dangerous in the same moment. "Honestly, I don't really know what kind of power play this is. I've known for a long time that something was in the works. Director Anderson never liked me, but this feels more like a leviathan lurking beneath the surface. Whether it's the director or someone even higher up the food chain, they're using the Quantico Hearings to clean house."

"Director Anderson or higher up the food chain? What does that even mean?"

"No clue. Someone in Congress, maybe. All I know is that someone is consolidating power. They know I'm not going to play along, so they're wielding these hearings like a bat to knock me out."

Sayer had so many questions she didn't know where to begin. "You've known about this for a while? How long?"

Holt paused and looked away from Sayer in a very uncharacteristic display of hesitation. "I'm not sure." She turned and stared directly into Sayer's eyes. "But I believe that Jake's death started the dominoes falling, and here we are. . . ."

Sayer's mouth fell into an O. How could her fiancé have something to do with this, four years after his death? "I don't understand. You think this has something to do with Jake?"

"I know Jake was onto something big. A few days before he died, he came to my office and asked me a bunch of cryptic questions about Director Anderson. He implied that there was something rotten somewhere in the Bureau, but he refused to tell me more. When he died . . . well, I assumed he'd stepped on someone's toes. Someone dangerous. And now I have no idea who is pulling the strings here."

Holt sighed and Sayer saw a flash of exhaustion beneath the surface. Holt was as tough as they came, but this was taking a toll. "I suspected this day might come and I pushed you as far up the ladder as I could, hoping to protect you, but you're seen as one of my agents. Which is why I think you're being taken down with me."

"Taken down. . . . Am I about to be fired?" Sayer's mouth turned pasty as she said the word *fired*. She'd come here expecting some political nonsense, but this was a whole different level of fuckery. Would she be able to finish this case? What would happen to Jillian and Grace Watts or Hannah Valdez?

"I'm afraid so, Sayer. It's not set in stone yet, but like I said, I see the writing on the proverbial wall and it's scrawled in our blood. I'll be asked to resign in the next day or two and then I suspect you will be summarily fired not long after I go. They're building an image of you as a ladder-climbing careerist in over her head and out for nothing more than power. I wanted to give you a heads-up before anything becomes official."

Sayer blinked, trying to formulate a coherent response from the wild emotions bouncing around her chest like rogue bullets.

"You know why I was pushing you so hard?" Holt asked.

Sayer looked up at her. "What?"

"Do you know why I've been pushing you up the ladder here?"

Sayer shook her head, not trusting her voice.

"Working my way up to assistant director, I had to . . . master some level of politicking. You made me see how cynical I've gotten over the years. You reminded me what the FBI is supposed to be about. Your single-mindedness is your biggest asset, but it's also what makes you dangerous, because you can't be won over with promises of power."

Sayer finally found her voice as her ricocheting emotions focused into one clear note—fury. "You're saying that someone corrupt is trying to take over the FBI and that there's nothing we can do about it?"

Holt's lips curled up at the edges. "I didn't say there's nothing we can do about it."

Sayer blinked, letting Holt's comment sink in.

"What I'm saying," Holt continued, "is that anything we do won't happen from inside the FBI."

Sayer nodded vigorously. "Good. But, before we do anything else, I'll be damned if I'm going to stop investigating this case I'm on. I won't quit until I find those missing women and that missing child, even if I have to do it on my own."

"That's exactly what I knew you'd say." Holt flashed a wolfish grin. "You hang on as long as you can while I figure out the best way to fight back. Surely they don't believe I'm just going to walk away from a place I've spent my life building. I didn't become the assistant director of the FBI by being a pushover. There are tens of thousands of good agents here and I will not let this institution be corrupted," she said, eyes raging like a tempest. "In the meantime, trust no one. Now get back to work."

Dismissed, Sayer rode back toward the Shenandoah Mountains feeling like she was preparing for a war.

SOUTHERN RANGER STATION,
SHENANDOAH NATIONAL PARK, VA

Exhausted from the long ride back, Sayer pulled off her helmet and sat outside the ranger station in the quiet. The night air felt cold and damp, teetering on the edge of more rain. The moon created a silvery glow behind thick clouds, too faint to shine light into the dark woods.

She jumped slightly when her bag buzzed.

"Oh, dammit!" With Holt's summons, she had completely forgotten that she'd scheduled the follow-up interview with Subject 037. But if she was about to be fired, did she even still have a research project? What would happen to all her data?

She hurried past the ranger at the front door to the main conference room. Ezra's computer was off and no one was around.

Sayer opened her laptop and clicked answer. The shadowy silhouette appeared.

"Ah, Sayer, I wasn't sure you'd answer." Subject 037's deep voice shook the computer speakers.

"Why is that?" She aimed for casual, but she could hear the tightness in her own voice. His familiar use of her first name didn't help.

"I'm perfectly aware of everything happening with your case and the

Quantico Hearings right now." Subject 037 leaned forward slightly, as though trying to get a better look at Sayer on his computer screen.

Sayer ignored his comment. "I do apologize, but I'm not going to be able to conduct the follow-up interview we scheduled today. Let's reschedule, and I would love to arrange a time for your brain scan as well."

He chuckled. "Of course, I understand. I was actually calling to tell you that I plan to fix this pesky little problem for you."

"I'm sorry, what?"

"As I'm sure Assistant Director Holt told you today"—he chuckled again—"it seems clear that someone is trying to get you fired."

"My career has nothing to do with you," Sayer said through her teeth.

"On the contrary," he purred, "I've been quite looking forward to this interview and I don't like that they are interfering with our time together."

Our time together? Sayer wondered if he was displaying signs of de Clérambault's syndrome—imagining a relationship with her that didn't really exist. It was a dangerous delusion to trigger in a psychopath.

"They?" She immediately regretted asking the question. "This is not something you want to get involved with," she quickly added.

"Ah, that's where you're wrong. You see, I've decided that I like talking to you. I don't take kindly to anyone interfering with something I want. And so, I'll fix this for you."

"Let me be clear. I do not want your help, with this or anything else." Sayer definitely did not want to find out how this man went about "fixing" things.

"Too late. I hope you have a restful evening, Sayer. Trust no one." He chuckled again and then disconnected the video.

Sayer sat in the dark conference room, unsure what to make of Subject 037. If he knew about the inner workings of the Quantico Hearings, he clearly was someone connected to Congress.

A deep ache of exhaustion settled into her muscles. She had to find a way to ignore the political circus and focus on this case.

Rather than dwell on everything, she went to find her team.

"Ezra?" she called.

"I'm in here." His faint voice filtered through the thin walls.

Sayer found him in the small office next door, unpacking his Go Bag onto a small cot.

"Heard you on the phone or something," he said. "Everything okay?"

"Yeah." Sayer waved him off, not wanting to explain. "You sleeping here instead of a cabin?"

"It seemed easier. Piper got me set up with a cot. I wasn't sure I would be able to, you know, make it down the muddy path to the cabins. . . ."

"Ah," Sayer said, heart aching for Ezra, whose life had changed so much. "Well, this looks comfy."

"It's fine. . . ." Ezra looked slightly wan, cheeks hollow. Being here was clearly taking a physical toll.

She tried to smile. "You doing okay?"

"Yeah. It just . . . hurts sometimes and I'm probably not resting enough. I'm going to crash soon."

"Of course. Whatever you need. And you know you can take off anytime."

"What, and leave this palatial suite! Hush, now." He gave her a real smile.

"The park rangers are bringing us dinner soon. I hear it's going to be chili. Want me to bring you some?"

Ezra shook his head. "Nah, I've got a sandwich left over from lunch. I'm going to eat, then fall sound asleep. I'll see you tomorrow."

Sayer looked at the time. Just past 10:30. He was even more wiped out than she thought.

"All right, sleep well."

She gently shut the door behind her and wondered if she should make him go home, but then decided that he was a grown man and, to be honest, she needed his help.

Mulling that over, she peeked in on Dana in the bone room.

The forensic anthropologist looked up from her computer and smiled.

"Hello! Did Holt tear you a new asshole?"

"Heh, no, just an update." Not wanting to talk about Holt and Quantico, Sayer dramatically eyed the beer cooler. "You still planning to share that? The park rangers are bringing us some chili soon for a late dinner."

"Hang on." Dana finished typing with a flourish and shut the laptop with a *click*. "One opening salvo of a beer sandwich coming right up."

She popped the caps off two bottles and slid one to Sayer.

"Cheers."

They clinked bottles and both took a long swig.

Sayer savored the crisp lager cooling her burned throat. "Thanks, Dana. I think I needed to sit down for a minute."

Dana's eyes crinkled with a smile. "Yeah, though I know you. In twenty minutes you'll be back up, pacing the room, rubbing a hole in your worry beads, obsessing over the case again. You need to learn how to relax."

Sayer let out a harsh laugh.

Dana's face grew serious. "I mean it, Sayer. If I've learned anything over the past ten years, it's that we've all got to get a life."

"Did you just tell me to get a life?" Sayer laughed again.

"You know what I mean. Our job is high pressure and we're elbow-deep in death. I think we both focus on the victims so much that we forget that we need to make sure we live our own lives sometimes." Her voice was tinged with sadness.

Sayer swallowed more beer and looked at her old friend. Dana was in her early fifties. Not old, but not young either. For some reason it had never occurred to Sayer that Dana had never married. Had no pets. No family that she knew of. Did Dana regret the decisions she had made?

Dana caught Sayer staring. "What . . . oh, you think I'm talking about myself?"

"You aren't?"

"Me? No. Holy hell, Sayer, I'm not talking about settling down or having kids. All I mean is that we've got to occasionally connect with the actual living people around us. Take some happiness from life while we're still around to enjoy it."

"Ah, thus the beer sandwich." Sayer held her bottle up for another cheers. "I think that was easier for me to do when Jake was around," she said softly.

"Of course it was. Last time we spoke, you mentioned something was off about Jake's death. . . . Do you want to talk about it?"

Sayer drained the beer, mulling over everything Holt had just implied. "You know the official story, that Jake was KIA on an undercover mission?"

"The official story? Implying that there's an unofficial story. . . ."

"Yeah. The short version is that I don't think Jake was killed in action. I at least know for sure he wasn't shot, which is what the official report said. Somehow, Jake drowned. Someone put pressure on Holt to change the autopsy result. And I can't find any information about the mission he was on. I've been looking into it and all I've got is an autopsy report showing cause of death and a stack of papers so redacted that they look like they were printed on black paper."

"What does Holt say?"

"Holt doesn't know shit other than he was onto something big within the Bureau." Sayer got up to get a second beer. "One more?" she held one up for Dana.

"Please."

Sayer slid back into her seat and handed Dana a beer.

"So wait, Holt doesn't know what really happened?"

"No, my impression is that someone higher up told her to cover up the autopsy report, but that was all she was told. She has no idea how he died. And now she thinks that whatever he was working on is connected to the Quantico Hearings."

"Holy hell. Even Holt doesn't know? You're still digging into it, though, right?"

"Of course I am, but I've been digging for months now and haven't found a single lead. Someone obviously doesn't want me to find anything. . . ." Sayer glanced over at the bones. "Oh, hey, did you hear what Max and I figured out about Jillian Watts? We think the UNSUB forced her to kill those other women by threatening Grace's life. And, based on what the journal said about killing to protect, we think the cases might be connected."

Dana looked up at the clock. "I take it back."

"You take what back?"

"I said you'd be back to obsessing over the case in twenty minutes, but you didn't even make it ten," Dana said.

"Har, har. I'm just not in the mood to talk about Jake right now. But you're right, let's try to talk about something other than the case. For a few minutes, at least."

"Hmm, let's see . . . you could talk about psychopathic brains, or I could tell you the latest on the genocide in the eastern Congo." Dana said it lightly, but Sayer could tell she was also serious. Both women understood that it was impossible to venture deep into the well of human darkness and emerge somehow undamaged, somehow still whole.

THE PIT

Hannah Valdez lay curled on the cot in her room. She cradled her smashed finger, her entire body shaking from the pain.

Tears stained her cheeks, though she made no sound. Her mind felt blank, overwhelmed by everything.

"Sam," she whispered, trying to focus on anything but here. She forced herself to picture her life before this.

Had it only been a few days? A few weeks? And already she felt so distant from her previous life. Her days doing aikido, going to class, taking care of Sam, dining with Zoe, felt like a movie she'd once watched.

She forced herself to sit up and look down at her finger. It was swollen and purple.

The pain was awful, but even worse was her shattered sense of hope. Until that moment, she had convinced herself that this was nothing more than a nightmare that would be over soon. Somehow, she had believed that this couldn't possibly be real. But now her finger was proof. Was she going to die here?

"Stop it!" Hannah said loudly. She had to take action. Do something.

But every time she moved, her finger screamed in agony, wiping her mind clear of anything but the pain.

"So fix your finger."

Hannah examined her clothing. The cotton wrap was thin and the end looked slightly tattered. With her right hand, she lifted it to her mouth and bit down. She pulled sharply and a strip of cloth tore away.

She lay the strip of cotton on her knees and gingerly placed her broken pinkie on top. Moaning, she pulled the wrapping up and over, then wound it around her pinkie and ring finger, binding them together.

Ignoring the wave of nausea, she fumblingly tied off the wrapping and pulled it tight with her teeth. The final pull sent her over the edge and she gagged. But it was done.

The finger still hurt, but she could at least move her left hand without almost passing out.

"Progress," she whispered, and lay back down to try and get some sleep. She would need it if she was going to figure out a way to get out of this place.

It felt like only a few moments after she closed her eyes that she woke to the sound of a key sliding into the lock.

SOUTHERN RANGER STATION, SHENANDOAH NATIONAL PARK, VA

Max and Piper eventually joined Sayer and Dana in the conference room and they shared the chili and beer. They discussed the new theory about Jillian, trying to find a way to use that as a lead, but came up empty-handed. By midnight they were all exhausted and Piper led them to their cabins. The rain began again as they made their way down the short muddy path.

When she got to the cabin assigned to her, Sayer dropped her overnight bag and looked around the single room with a sigh. The scent of industrial pine cleaner made her cringe. The pale green linoleum floors were scarred by years of use. A forest-green wool blanket stretched over a narrow cot in one corner. The fluorescent light flickered, creating a faint strobe effect.

The bare bathroom was nothing more than an open-stalled shower and a composting toilet.

Sayer turned on the water for a quick rinse, but changed her mind when she realized that there was no warm water. Instead she washed her blistered knuckles and simply pulled on her pajamas.

Running her hands over still-singed curls, she wandered to the door to double-check that it was locked.

Out of habit, Sayer pulled out her files on Jake. Nearly every night she combed through the files, hoping something new about her fiancé's death would jump out at her. Holt had given Sayer the original autopsy report and the name of the operation he was on, but then she'd hit a wall. No one seemed to have heard of the operation, so she didn't even know who he was with when he died.

Files in hand, she plopped on the cot and winced. It felt more like a board than a mattress. Something about the sparse cabin and the heavy rain echoed the disastrous trip she and Jake had taken to the Ozarks long ago. She closed her eyes and let herself remember.

They'd only been dating a few weeks and the idea of a trip to the mountains sounded so romantic. But the cabin they'd rented was barely one step above a lean-to, with nothing but a single lantern and an old moth-eaten mattress. They'd awkwardly fallen asleep next to each other, unsure of the boundaries of their new relationship. But when a storm rolled in, the roof acted like a catchment, creating a waterfall into the cabin's interior. After half an hour frantically trying to stop the water from pouring into the cabin, they both started laughing. Overcome by the absurdity of it all, they collapsed together, soaked, half dressed, onto the mattress. Their physical connection felt unlike anything she'd ever experienced. That was the first time it occurred to Sayer that Jake might be more than a fling.

The memory crept from a dark corner of Sayer's brain to twist the dagger of grief that permanently lived in her heart.

With that memory awakening feelings she wanted to ignore, Sayer couldn't bring herself to read the Jake files for the thousandth time. Instead, she forced herself to picture the women they had pulled from the cave. The two beaten women had died horrible deaths, but she would try to remember them alive, smiling. Was Hannah Valdez now in the same place where they had been? Was their UNSUB threatening Grace Watts? Was Jillian Watts about to kill again?

Sayer had seen plenty of horrific things, but forcing a mother to kill for her child was beyond anything she could've imagined. Sometimes Sayer wished she were a psychopath herself. How nice it must be to never worry, never feel fear, never experience that dark ache that lived inside her chest.

Instead of muting her emotions, Sayer let horrific images of trapped women churn through her mind. With the roaring sound of rain on the tin roof overhead, Sayer was about to drift off when her phone rang.

She bolted up. The display read *Nana* and she momentarily thought about ignoring it, but she'd learned the hard way that it is never a good idea to ignore Sophia McDuff. Plus it was well after midnight. Nana would never call this late without good cause.

"I'm calling for two reasons." Nana didn't even bother with a greeting.

"Uh-oh. Did I forget someone's birthday?"

"No, no, something much more important than that."

Sayer's heart skipped a beat. Was Nana sick? Or her sister? Her nephew?

"Adi will be calling you tomorrow to ask if you will legally adopt her."

"If I'll, uh . . . what?" Sayer stammered.

"This is why I called to talk to you before she does. 'I, uh, what' is not what that young woman needs to hear from you. She needs you to be her rock, her stability, while she rebuilds her life."

Adi had survived the death of her family and being kidnapped and tortured by a serial killer. She was a survivor, but Nana was right, she also needed someone to be there for her. "She needs a nana," Sayer said, exhaustion flattening her voice.

"Damn straight she needs someone like me. And it's your job to be that person now. You've got serious commitment issues, Sayer, and you need to get over that whiny crap so you can stand up and do the right thing."

"I don't have commitment issues. I was engaged. . . ." As she said it, Sayer could hear the petulance in her voice and cringed. Something about talking to her nana turned her back into a whining teenager.

"You were engaged four years ago," Nana interrupted. "Now you live half out of boxes in a barren apartment. You won't even commit to an apartment, Sayer. But you took Adi in and that's the kind of thing that you follow through on."

"I know. Whew, that just feels big. But of course I'll do it."

"The best things in life should scare you," Nana said matter-of-factly.

Sayer took a deep breath. "You're totally right. Thank you for calling me tonight so I don't act like a total jerk while I'm talking to her."

"That's what nanas are for, to weed out the jerky. On to the second thing, the hearings aren't going well."

"The hearings . . . like the closed congressional hearings about Quantico?"

"Yes, of course those hearings."

"And how, exactly, do you know what's going on in the closed Quantico Hearings?"

Nana let out a high musical laugh. "Congressional spouses stick together. Charles might be dead, but my old friends aren't." Wife of a former senator, Sophia McDuff pretended like she wasn't involved in politics, but she was still a power player behind the scenes in Washington. "Corey called me last night to warn me that someone on that committee is trying to destroy your career."

Sayer thought about everything Holt had told her. "So I've been told. It might not go well for me, Nana. Did you get any details? Any sense of who is targeting me?"

"No, just that they are on the attack. Not really sure who 'they' are, beyond Senator DeWitt, but he's so corrupt he could be bought off with a wad of used chewing gum."

"All right, thanks, Nana. I guess I need to figure out what that's all about. But not tonight. Right now I've got some people to find, including a missing little girl."

"You okay there?" Nana was worried about her back at work after being shot.

"I'm good. Just a long day. We're making progress, but right now I have no idea who to trust. Everyone keeps telling me to trust no one."

"You know that's bullshit. Trust your gut, Sayer."

"Yeah. The same gut that missed the fact that my friend and coworker was a serial killer? My gut that missed the fact that Jake's death wasn't what it seemed? That gut?"

"Oh, quit the pity party. You're the one who eventually brought down the killer inside the FBI, and you are investigating Jake's death. Which is why I say, trust your gut. Are the people you're not sure about good guys or not?"

Sayer thought about Max. "Well, one of them clearly loves his dog . . . which perhaps irrationally leads me to believe that he's a good guy despite a history of deception."

Nana laughed. "Whatever works. How about trust but verify?"

"Sounds right."

"Okay, well, it's late. My advice, trust your gut, but then just shoot anyone who looks like they're going to shoot you, okay?"

"Good advice, Nana. Shoot first."

Nana laughed again and hung up.

Sayer sat in the dark wondering who was going after her up in D.C. She'd spent her entire career trying to avoid politics, but, like Holt said, that's how the political cookie crumbles.

"Whatever," Sayer said out loud. "I just don't care."

As soon as she said it, she knew it was a lie. Sayer let everything that had happened in the past few days wash over her. Being back in the field felt . . . amazing. She hadn't even realized how much she missed it until her leave was over. For a long time, Sayer had believed she would have been equally happy pursuing an academic career, but the past few months behind a desk made it clear that wasn't true. No matter how much she loved her research, she could never work a desk full-time. She needed to be out there, on the hunt. And now maybe that was over?

Was she about to be fired from the thing that gave her life meaning?

And there was no way she could walk away from the missing women and child still out there somewhere. Saving people like them was, more than anything, why she did this.

"Nothing I can do about what's happening in D.C.," she said firmly to herself. "Focus on what you can do, which is to find those missing people."

As she drifted off, she thought about what both Holt and Subject 037 had said—trust no one.

"Fuck that," she whispered to herself. That wasn't the life she wanted to live, always looking over her shoulder. Never letting herself be vulnerable to anyone. Nana was right. If she couldn't trust her own gut, then what the hell did she have left? She knew who she could trust, and she was going to work with them to come out swinging to protect everything and everyone she loved, including the goddamned FBI. But first she had some missing people to save.

Fanning the flames of determination, she curled up on top of the scratchy wool blanket and fell into a dreamless sleep.

THE PIT

The woman summoned Hannah from the room and they held hands again as they walked together out to the pit. The skeletal woman's grip was overly firm, verging on painful. Hannah desperately tried to read the look in her eyes. Sorrow? Apology? Fear?

"Welcome to the main event," the voice crackled down through the loudspeaker as they entered the cavernous room.

Her escort squeezed one last time and then dropped her hand.

Hannah blinked. As her eyes adjusted to the bright floodlights, she gasped.

A young child was strapped into the horrifying contraption she had seen last time. Thick straps crisscrossed the child's body, holding her firmly upright. A spring-loaded metallic arm jutted off to the side with a pointed metal blade at the end. The blade hung a few inches away from the side of the child's neck like a razor-sharp piston about to fire.

The child's eyes were blank despite being strapped into the nightmarish machine. Hannah realized this was not her first time here.

Almost as terrifying was the emaciated woman. She went over to the machine and folded her hands over the child's as though in prayer.

The woman's expression looked like she was descending into a nightmare. The hollows beneath her eyes sank into deep crescents of agony. Her slack mouth moved, murmuring words that Hannah knew told a tale of abomination.

"Hannah," the voice boomed from above. "You've already met Jillian. I'd like you to meet her daughter, Grace. Jillian has already begun her transformation," he said with glee.

Hannah turned to stare up at the silhouette in the control room far above her.

"You're a monster," she said almost softly. She had never felt such a simple emotion—pure hatred.

"True. True. But so is Jillian. Tell her, Jillian. What have you done?"

The woman's eyes flickered to Hannah, tears forming at their corners. Hannah almost made a move toward the ladder. Maybe she could get to the top before he shocked her. She had never wanted to kill anyone before, but she would kill this person.

"I have my finger on the button, Hannah. . . ." The malice in his voice matched the glee. "Tell her what you've done, Jillian!" the voice shouted, so loud that both women jumped.

Jillian tried to speak but couldn't seem to make her voice work.

"Ah, she isn't feeling talkative. Let me explain."

Hannah stared at Jillian, trying to keep her face neutral. Calm.

"Don't you want to know why you're about to die, Hannah?"

Hannah's head snapped up but she remained silent. Was she about to die? Somehow the thought felt distant, held no real emotion. Something inside her had shut down.

"Of course you do. I'm here to free the monster that you've buried inside of you. No one wants to admit that it exists, but I know it lurks in the deepest part of your heart. And I'm here to free it in all of its beautiful glory."

Hannah felt a wave of nausea. This person was truly insane. "There is no monster inside me," she said, voice thick with emotion.

"I know that's what you'd like to believe. Or maybe you're not even aware of it. But it's in there. Buried beyond your consciousness. Don't take my word for it. Haven't you ever heard of the Stanford Prison Experiment? Or what about Abu Ghraib? Nazi Germany? Anywhere people are freed from the bonds of social convention and have the power to do whatever they want, they release their true nature. Beneath it all, we're monsters, and it is . . . beautiful." The voice fell low, whispering the last word.

"Jillian has already killed two other women, haven't you? She thinks she does it to save her daughter, but I've seen a glimpse of her true nature."

Jillian looked up at Hannah as though she were pleading for something.

"And, Hannah, even though you're about to die, I promise you will get to feel the pleasure of release, letting that inner monster rage for a glorious moment. Jillian, I know you can do it, my deadly little monster. I'm starting the timer now. You know what to do."

A digital clock lit up along the cavern wall. The red numbers began to count down from five minutes.

Hannah's brain spun wildly. This broken woman wouldn't actually try to kill her, would she?

Jillian ran a finger along the small girl's cheek before turning to Hannah. Her expression shifted from anguish to a fixed blankness. No one was there behind the dead eyes that now looked into hers.

There was no way this half-dead, injured woman would be able to hurt her, let alone kill her. But Jillian slowly advanced toward Hannah.

The woman lifted the same hands that had just gently touched her daughter's face and formed them into balled fists.

"It's the only way to save her," Jillian said flatly.

"No," was all Hannah managed to say as Jillian lowered her head and rushed toward her.

Hannah's training kicked in. Her body relaxed, focus collapsing until the only thing she could see was the incoming figure. Her weight settled low, ready.

Jillian expected to blitz Hannah with a direct punch.

In a sweeping motion, Hannah deflected the punch to the side. She harnessed the energy of Jillian's forward motion, shoving her to the ground.

Jillian let out a cry and stumbled to one knee. She stayed like that, breathing hard. Her breath wheezed in her chest, and Hannah wondered if the woman had a broken rib from a previous fight. Maybe more than one.

Jillian rallied, pulling herself up and making another charge. Hannah shoved her aside again. And again. And again. With every fall, Hannah could tell her attacker was in more pain. The last time, she could barely stand, her muscles quivering. A bubble of blood formed at the corner of Jillian's mouth.

"Please stop," Hannah pleaded.

Jillian finally seemed to realize that she wasn't going to be able to beat Hannah. Instead of charging again, she looked up at the timer and then into Hannah's eyes. "Please, I have to save my daughter." She stood, soul broken, begging for her daughter's life.

Less than two minutes remained.

Both women looked over at the small child strapped with a blade poised at her neck.

Jillian's emotionless calm snapped into a visceral howl of sorrow. "I don't know what to do," she sobbed.

Hannah mirrored her agony. How could she let this child die? But how could she let this woman kill her?

Face collapsed with defeat, Jillian looked up at the shadowy figure above them and shouted, "If she kills me, will you let Grace live?"

"Oh, interesting . . . ," the voice said slowly. It remained quiet for a long moment. "I'm disappointed in you, Jillian. I thought you were my champion, but I see that you're right to give up. I had no idea Hannah was such a formidable opponent."

The timer reached one minute.

Hannah stood frozen, unable to do anything but watch the scene unfold like a horror movie.

"Yes, I think that's fair," the voice finally said. "I would very much like to see Hannah's monster."

"Do you swear?" Jillian's voice broke, sounding like a frightened child. "Swear you'll let Grace go."

"I swear. Now, Hannah, the outcome is up to you. You have forty-five seconds to decide. . . . Kill Jillian and save her child's life. Or let them both die."

Jillian stumbled over to Hannah and looked up. "Please, please kill me. Please. . . ."

Hannah's mouth opened and closed, but she was unable to speak.

"You have to do it now!" Jillian grasped at her, clawed at her, took another frantic swing. "Please!"

Jillian beat at Hannah's chest, trying to drive her to act. With a yelp of desperation, she swung at Hannah one last time.

Hannah gently deflected the flailing attack. Jillian threw herself to the side and kept the momentum going. She increased her speed and, with an animalistic cry, she rammed herself into the cavern wall. Her head connected with a sickening wet thunk.

She crumpled to the floor.

Hannah stood frozen for a long moment. Time slowed into a roaring silence of horror. It was a small sound from the child that snapped her back to reality.

She ran over to Grace and tried to pull away the straps. Hannah's fingers slipped uselessly off the thick leather. She had to save this child.

"No, no, no," she moaned, tears falling.

The timer reached zero.

Hannah turned her face slightly away while tangling her hands into the girl's impossibly small fingers. She was unable to watch but also couldn't abandon the girl.

She held her breath.

Would their captor keep his word and let the girl live? Or would the blade fall?

Silence.

Nothing.

"Oh, calm down, I'm going to let Grace go." The voice rang with bemusement.

Hannah let out a hard breath of relief and looked back at the wide-eyed child. "You're going to be okay, little one. Everything is going to be okay," she tried to coo, though her throat felt ragged with emotion.

"I'm going to do so for two reasons," the voice continued. "One, because I said I would, and I keep my word. And two, I want you to know that I keep my word because I believe it will be . . . motivational. After all, you have a daughter, don't you? I have something else to take care of first, but then I think it's time for me to pay little Sam a visit."

Hannah's world tilted wildly. A choking scream caught in her throat.

"Congratulations, Hannah. You've officially become my new monster."

Unable to breathe, Hannah collapsed onto the rocky floor, the only sound a distant roar in the background as the world faded to black.

DANA'S CABIN, SHENANDOAH NATIONAL PARK, VA

Dana couldn't sleep. The incessant rain pounded on the tin roof of her cabin like someone playing a steel drum next to her head. Even worse, images of dead mothers and children invaded her mind. She had dug up many terrible things in the mass graves she'd exhumed, but the worst were always the mothers, arms still wrapped around the tiny bones of their children. How many mothers had she dug up now? How many murdered children?

For some reason she had imagined that coming back to the States to work with the FBI again would give her a reprieve from those horrors. Instead she couldn't stop thinking about Jillian Watts and her little daughter, Grace. Would she be autopsying another mother-child duo soon?

Dana tried to shake off the thought. Instead of dwelling on her worst fears, she got dressed and headed up to the ranger station. Dawn was only a few hours away; she might as well get some work done on the skeletons.

She waved at the groggy park ranger who let her in the front door and tiptoed to the bone room, making sure not to wake Ezra.

Dana carefully lifted the charred skull. Why was this skeleton burned far more than the others? Had someone tried to cremate it before depositing it in the cave? She turned the skull until she stared into the hollow eyes. "Okay my osseous friend, let's see if I can get a workable DNA sample from you."

She looked down at her notes. The attempt at cremation had damaged the DNA preservation of this skeleton. Phenol-chloroform protocol hadn't produced a viable sample. Neither had total demineralization. DNA extraction from crystal aggregates was her last chance.

Dana delicately pulled a test tube from her portable centrifuge. Hands steady, she gently pipetted distilled water over the pellet of ground bone powder she had prepared earlier.

"This has to work," she murmured to herself. She might not be able to run out into the field guns ablaze, but she could damn well do something to bring down this UNSUB.

As she rinsed the pellet one last time, she held her breath. It looked like a viable sample.

"Gotcha!" Dana said as she sealed the sample in an evidence bag to send up to Quantico.

That done, she pulled on her magnification glasses and began a detailed examination of the other skeletons. The damage done in the cave left the bones shattered, chipped, and broken, but Dana was slow and methodical, determined not to miss anything.

Her frustration grew as she moved back and forth between bones, looking for any consistent signs of damage. But then she picked up the C3 vertebra of a young female skeleton and turned it in the light.

A flash of recognition jolted Dana out of her frustration.

With her magnification glasses and bright light, she moved to the next skeleton and inspected one cervical vertebra and then the next.

"Well, hot damn!" she muttered to herself, not even noticing the soft scrape of leather in the hall behind her.

SOUTHERN RANGER STATION, SHENANDOAH NATIONAL PARK, VA

Ezra's eyes opened, though he wasn't sure why.

He stared up at the ceiling, straining to listen for any unexpected sound. Somewhere in the ranger station water dripped in a steady drumbeat onto metal. A well-worn furnace expanded with a faint *tick-tick-tick,* matching the old clock on the wall.

Nothing but the sounds of a place he wasn't used to.

At least he hadn't had one of the dreams. Sometimes the bomb played in his nightmares, tearing his legs from beneath him. But sometimes it was even worse. The dream where he was frozen in slow motion. Trapped in air like molasses, helpless as horrific things happened around him. His baby sister slaughtered before his eyes by a knife-wielding monster, or his mother smashed in a car accident, every graphic second playing out as she slammed into the steering wheel. All the while he stood there, a helpless screaming witness. He knew those nightmares were just his brain trying to process his feelings about the bomb, but logic was nowhere to be found in the middle of the night when he woke thrashing and screaming.

Okay, almost four A.M., time to sit up and do some mindfulness exercises.

Long breath in. Externalize the anxiety. Examine it objectively. . . .

Scrape.

The sound down the hall caused an explosion of fear, blurring his vision. The bizarre image of a monster roaming the building leaped unbidden to his mind.

Ezra tried to control his shaking hands, listening with every cell in his being.

A dull clacking sound?

Another scrape made him jump.

He made a fist and squeezed, trying to release the fear ricocheting around his body.

The sound started again. No mistaking it now. The unmistakable sounds of a scuffle.

Ezra fumbled for his phone and texted Sayer, *SOMEONE HERE IN BUILDING!*

Should he sneak into the hall and look? But how could he? Even if he could get his prosthetics on in time, he couldn't move quietly down the hall. Damn metal legs. Fucking walker. Tears of frustration welled. What kind of FBI agent was he?

The sound grew more confident. Someone was ransacking the bone room.

He put his phone down and decided he wasn't going to just lie there in bed waiting for Sayer to come save him.

He scooted to the edge and, using his newly strong arms, he carefully lowered himself to the floor. Half crawling, half dragging himself along the cold tile, he quietly shuffled over to the door.

Heart jackhammering, he turned the knob and slowly slid the door open. Large wet footprints puddled along the tile floor. The exaggerated shadow of a head and shoulders extended from the bone room, moving across the tile like a ghost.

Unable to think clearly, Ezra paused and took a slow breath. *Don't be an idiot. Just see if you can get a look at the guy. Just a look. ID him and break the case.*

Ezra repeated the mantra in his head. *Just a look. Just a look. Just need to see who it is.*

He propelled himself down the hall. The sensitive nerve in his right leg felt like pressing broken glass into the stump with every move forward. Every hair on his body quivered upright, senses assaulting him with too much input.

He neared the open door and braced himself to peek around the corner.

What were the chances that the killer would be looking out into the hall at the exact moment Ezra looked in? Slim. But not none. Not none.

Don't be an idiot. Just look and then retreat to your room. Hide until he's gone. Hope Sayer comes. It's all you can do.

It's all you can do.

The footsteps caught him off guard. The figure rounded the corner before Ezra could react.

A flashlight blinded him. He heard the soft leather swish of a gun sliding from its holster. The metal of a gun barrel swung up. Pointed at his head.

Bang!

Sayer shot upright, heart pounding. Was it the familiar nightmare playing in her head? The gun going off. The gasping pain in her left shoulder.

She lifted her phone to check the time and saw Ezra's text. *SOMEONE HERE IN BUILDING!*

Bang!

Another shot from the ranger station.

She flew out of bed and ran through the rain, gun already in her hand. She had no memory of even picking it up.

Sayer shouldered open the front door and flew down the hall, where she found Ezra lying on his side. A small slick of blood, black in the faint light, smeared the floor next to him like a Rorschach blob.

"Ezra!"

She ran to him, gun trained on the dark hallway.

Sayer rolled him over, eyes skittering around the room to make sure they were alone.

He blinked up at her.

She let out a moan of relief that he was alive.

"Is it clear?" she demanded.

"Yeah, he ran out the door," Ezra croaked.

"Are you shot?" She ran her hands over his chest and shoulders.

"No. No, I'm good." He panted. "He missed. Just a kick to the mouth." He reached up to his face and Sayer realized blood was pouring from a split lip.

"Jesus." Sayer collapsed on the floor next to Ezra, hand still gripping his shoulder. "Fuck," she said before she could rein in her wild emotions.

"You sure he's gone?" she asked, eyes still darting around the room.

Unable to get the words out, Ezra nodded.

Sayer practically jumped out of her skin when Max and Kona burst through the door. Max's gun swung a circuit of the entry hall.

"Someone broke in, attacked Ezra. He's okay," Sayer said with a staccato burst.

"Clear?" Max demanded, voice all business.

Sayer barked, "Clear here. He's on the run," as Max was already spinning on his heel out the door.

Kona followed, low, in hunter mode.

On autopilot, Sayer realized no one sat at the front desk. Where was the ranger on duty? *Dear god, let him be okay.* She hurried over to find him on the floor, bound and blindfolded, gagged with duct tape.

Sayer pulled the tape off quickly.

"Are you okay?"

"He tasered me," the ranger said, voice husky with fear.

Still crouching over him, Sayer pulled out her phone and called 911.

"This is FBI Agent Sayer Altair calling from the southern ranger station in Shenandoah National Park reporting shots fired. An FBI agent and park ranger both in need of immediate medical assistance. Armed suspect on the run from the ranger station. FBI Agent Maxwell Cho and his K9 are in pursuit of the suspect."

A soft moan from the bone room made Sayer's heart leap to her throat. Dana!

Rain temporarily blinded Max as he flew from the building.

He could hear Kona's huffing breath as she loped beside him.

They ran to a stand of trees, where Max crouched to take stock of his surroundings and make sure no one was waiting to take a shot at them.

Nothing but rain pelting the leaves and Kona sniffing the air.

"You have the scent?" he whispered to Kona, who responded with a low woof.

Max clenched his teeth. He had avoided fugitive training for Kona on purpose. That was how dogs got killed in action. But Kona clearly understood what was happening and she was ready to go.

He looked out into the moonless night, the dark woods like a void. He pulled out a flashlight and nodded to Kona. "Go find, girl!"

She shot off in pursuit. Max held up his flashlight and ran to keep up.

The world became nothing but a small circle of light in front of him. The only sounds were Kona's heavy breath accompanied by his boots thumping the wet ground. They hurtled through the trees. Max realized they were heading toward Black Hollow Cliff. The desire to catch this bastard burned like wildfire in his gut. When he joined the Air Force, he became a Pararescueman to save lives, but he was also trained to kill. He would take no pleasure in killing this UNSUB, but he would do it if he had to.

"Go on," he said just loud enough for Kona to hear. She knew to constantly check in to make sure he was keeping up, but now he gave her the command to ignore him and follow the scent before the rain could pull it from the air.

Understanding, she unleashed her true speed and the black dog disappeared into the darkness.

Max broke off to the side, running parallel to Kona, silent and fast.

Though he couldn't see him, Max could hear their prey up ahead crashing through the underbrush. They were almost to the cliffs. He would have nowhere to go. Cornered. Dangerous.

Max began to funnel back toward Kona, pinching the killer to a dead end at the drop-off.

Kona let out a sharp aggressive bark and Max knew she was closing in.

A guttural human sound of impact. Kona tackling their target.

A shout accompanied a gunshot.

Max cried out, not sure what emotion he was feeling.

Then nothing.

Max exploded through the underbrush to find Kona standing sentinel atop the cliff, looking down into the river raging below.

Seeing that she was alone, he rushed to her side and ran his hands over her body. "You okay, Kona?"

No signs of injury.

Max cautiously looked over the cliff's edge. Far below, the river rushed by. It was difficult to see anything in the dark and the pouring rain.

Whoever they were after had just jumped.

Kona whined.

"Dammit," Max said, returning his attention to Kona to double-check that she hadn't been shot. "Good girl, Kona. Good girl."

SOUTHERN RANGER STATION, SHENANDOAH NATIONAL PARK, VA

After seeing off the ambulance and setting the phalanx of police who showed up on an area search, Sayer came back in the front door of the ranger station, face a blank mask. Her mouth was pulled into a tight O of anger at the sight of her team sitting in the entry hall.

Dana sat on a low chair, ice pack held to her side where she had been tased. Ezra curled on one of the small sofas, ice to his swelling lips. An evidence tech held one of Ezra's hands, scraping material from under his fingernails into a bag. Soaked head to toe, Max and Kona sat on the edge of the large stone fireplace, water puddling around them on the floor.

"Okay, the park ranger is off in the ambulance. They want to keep him overnight for observation, since he briefly lost consciousness. Dana, Ezra, you both sure you don't want to go as well? I can get a ranger to drive you down."

Dana lifted her shirt and grimaced at the raw circles on her stomach. "Nah, it's just a taser burn. A lovely pairing with my blisters from the cave fire."

Ezra just shook his head.

Sayer grunted understanding. Their injuries were minor and they didn't want to miss anything. She gathered herself. Time to lead her team. "All right, the rangers and locals are sweeping below the cliffs and downriver to see if we can find any sign of our visitor. You think he jumped into the river?" she asked Max.

"Yeah, we used to do it all the time as kids. It's the only place where the river's deep enough to do that. Definitely something only a local would know." The veins on his forehead pulsed and his body moved in stiff, jerky motions. Sayer could see him struggling with his post-adrenaline letdown.

Sayer turned to Ezra and gestured to the tech still scraping under his nails. "Did you manage to scratch the attacker?"

"Did I actually get something?" Ezra asked the evidence tech, who stood up, sealing a small evidence bag.

"There's definitely some blood and skin here."

"Great, I want a ranger to drive that up to Quantico right fucking now." Sayer tried to calm her own adrenal response, but her desire to nail this UNSUB made her body shake with intensity. The bastard came after two of her own.

"How the hell did this happen?" Max asked. "I thought we had the doors locked at night."

"Exactly my question." Sayer crouched down to examine the lock on the front door. "No signs of forced entry here or at the back door."

It was only then that Sayer realized she was in her pajamas and wasn't wearing shoes. No wonder she was so damn cold.

"So did we forget to lock down for the night or did he have a key?" Max asked.

"The ranger said he locked up after he let Dana in and was reading when someone snuck up behind him." Sayer turned her attention to Ezra. His eyes were already showing signs of bruising from the hit to his face. She looked back over at Dana.

"So, he was after something in the bone room?"

Dana winced as she shifted in her seat. "I think he took the charred skeleton."

Sayer sat down across from Ezra and cradled her head in one hand, rubbing her temple. "Okay." She looked up. "I need you both to tell me exactly what happened. Dana, you first. Why were you even up here?"

"I couldn't sleep, so I thought I'd work on getting DNA from the charred skeleton. Since it was so damaged, I was having a hard time getting a good sample, but I think I got one. After that I started working on cause of death for the other skeletons and was so absorbed in what I found, I didn't even hear him coming. Next thing I know, I'm on the floor, a thousand volts jerking me around like a marionette. I was pretty out of it but saw him shove bones into a big canvas bag. Then I heard a shot and some scuffling but couldn't see what happened."

"You can tell us what you found in a bit. Did you get a description?" Sayer asked gently.

"He was wearing a mask and I was on the floor, so my perspective is messed up. He was definitely taller than me," the short woman said with dark humor. "Sorry, not much of a description."

Sayer nodded. "What about you, Ezra? What happened?"

"Something woke me up and I realized someone was here. I went out in the hall trying to get a look at him. But he came out of the room just as I got there."

"You're sure it was a him?"

"Maybe eighty percent sure? Tall, strong for sure. Wearing a mask and a puffy jacket."

"Okay. So he sees you, and then what?"

"He pulled a gun on me, flashlight in my eyes." Ezra paused, his breathing shallow.

"Take your time," Sayer said gently. Recalling an assault was often difficult. Beyond the trauma of the event, even just remembering the actual events in sequence could be difficult. The human brain often reacted by blurring the scariest details.

"Right, so I realized I couldn't run or get away, so my reaction was . . . to attack."

Max looked up from his own reverie. His wide eyes drifted down to Ezra's missing legs. "You attacked a guy pointing a gun at you?"

ale face glowing in the fluorescent lights. "I guess so.
; stupid?"
call and it worked," Sayer said firmly.
n't it . . . ?"
head of yourself. So then what? You dove at him?"
ed mystified by his own actions. "I'm not sure how,
lf at him, hard. I knocked him back and he fum-
k that first shot." He closed his eyes, remembering
step back to stay upright, then took off toward the
ı around one of his knees and held on. He swung
n't knock me off, then dragged me for a few sec-
d to point the gun at me again. So I twisted my
him down."
down," Sayer prompted, not wanting to lose the

ent off again, but I think it was an accident. I
ı again, thinking maybe I could hold him until
scrape the hell out of his leg. That's when he

out the door?"
ped until he was almost whispering.

ı. He was strong enough to drag me for a bit,
All I can say for sure is that he wasn't small."
ou should let Max stitch you up . . . unless
, which I heartily endorse. Or even if you
rest . . . ," Sayer offered.
read across his face. "I beat the fucker off.
onna help catch him." Pride rang in his
d his lip began bleeding again. "Ow," he
le. "Okay to stitches from Max, though.
. . ."
feeling scared at all. He felt victorious.

Proud. She tried to laugh at his comment but was too emotionally wr
out to make it happen.

"All right." She took a relieved breath. "Can we avoid anyone else
ing the shit out of me for the rest of the case?"

"Yes, ma'am," Max and Ezra said in unison.

A guff of laughter escaped Sayer's mouth. "All right, smart-asses.
anyone want to try to get some sleep? It's not even five A.M. and we h
long day ahead of us."

Max shook his head as he gathered his medical bag to treat Ez

"No way I'm going back to sleep," Ezra said.

"I'm wide awake," Dana agreed. "And I think I might have just f
out cause of death for the other skeletons before I was so rudely
rupted."

Shortly after they retreated to the bone room, Piper showed up,
eyed, carrying coffee and a box of donuts. "Heard all the excite
the radio. Figured everyone could use a jolt of coffee and some

Sayer nodded thanks. "We were just trying to figure out w
attacker took."

Dana spent a few moments going from table to table. "He c
the previously burned skeleton." She moved gingerly over to anot
and held up a small evidence bag triumphantly. "But he didn't
DNA sample I got."

Sayer wiped powdered sugar from her blistered hands and to
breath. "Great, at least we still have a possible ID. Let's mak
send that to DNA with the scrapings from Ezra's nails. So wha
cial about that skeleton? And why break in here to retrieve it?
serious risk."

Dana pulled out her notes and flipped through a few page
get a chance to do a full analysis of the charred skeleton, but
nitely different. It was the only one that showed signs of previo
which, like I said earlier, looks like a possible attempt at cre

"An attempt?" Piper asked.

"Yeah, a regular wood fire burns at around eight hundred fifty degrees centigrade. But to turn bone to ash, you need a fire closer to fourteen hundred degrees. That's why you need a fancy crematorium. These bones were charred but otherwise unharmed, suggesting that they were placed in a wood fire before being dropped into the cave. Let me see." Dana read through more notes. "Though they weren't damaged by that initial burning, the fire the other day did make them more brittle than the other bones, which is why that skeleton was way more damaged than the others in the cave. Which is also why it was hard for me to be sure about gender or age. Last difference, and I can't swear to this one, since I didn't have a chance to confirm, but I think the burned skull showed signs of head trauma. To be precise, it looked like someone shattered the temporal bone right here." She tapped above her own temple. "My guess would be a strike from a sharp object. Enough to suggest cause of death."

"A sharp object, like maybe a ritual sword?"

"Exactly like that."

"And you aren't seeing that with any of the other skeletons?"

"Not at all." Dana bustled over to another table and lifted a small bone. "See, this is a cervical vertebra. The vertebrae in your neck." She tapped the front of her throat. "And all of these skeletons show signs of cutting on the front of their cervical vertebrae."

"Someone slit their throats?"

"That's my current thought. I was just about to do a microanalysis of the actual cuts to see if they were made by the same blade, but all six skeletons here show a single cut to the neck. So deep the blade cut into the bone of the vertebral column."

"Whoa." Piper put down her coffee, looking a little pale. "Just like that picture of that Greek sacrifice."

Sayer nodded slowly. "There's our definitive link between these skeletons, the Greek sacrificial stuff, and the sword. Dana, once you finish your microanalysis, compare the cuts to the blade from the kopis just to make sure that's really our murder weapon. They should be sending that report soon."

"I'll do my best." Dana's phone buzzed on the table, accompanied by a cheerful polka ringtone. "Oops, sorry." She read off the screen. "Oh, more good news, the dates have been determined for our skeletons." She read out loud, "*Definitive date acquired for the seven teeth submitted.*" She looked up at Sayer. "According to the radiation levels, these bones were deposited between 1996 and 2002."

"Meaning they were deposited sometime in that range?" Sayer asked.

"No, what I mean is, the oldest skeleton was deposited in 1996, and the most recent was deposited in 2002."

"So we have a killer that was actively killing in this area for over six years?"

Dana grunted yes. "And our victims are scattered pretty evenly across those years, a little over one a year. Oh, and the cremated skeleton wasn't the first kill. It was the last."

"Whoa," Piper said, rubbing her hand along the edge of her park ranger hat. "Someone was killing people here in Rockfish Gap? How did no one notice that?"

"I'd be willing to bet the victims weren't local," Sayer said. "Let's go to the other room, I want to write this new info on the murder board."

They went back to the conference room and everyone but Sayer sat down, the intense morning already taking its toll.

Sayer wrote *1996–2002* under *Bones* on the murder board. She added *cremated skeleton 2002, head trauma.* Under that she wrote *6 victims with throats cut, ritual sacrifice?*

"So"—Sayer paced at the head of the room—"we've got cause of death and possibly the murder weapon and we know that the first of these people was murdered over twenty years ago. But what the hell does that all mean? And does all this connect to our modern case?" She paused here.

Sayer faced her team.

Ezra looked pale, but his eyes burned with a new emotion that she realized was excitement. Piper sat wide-eyed and at full attention, her rumpled park ranger uniform looking like she hadn't changed in days. Max rested his hand on Kona, who stood beside his chair looking ready for action. Dana looked pissed off, her small mouth pressed in a steely line.

"I'm still not entirely convinced the older and recent cases are connected," Max said. "All we've got to connect them is the same dump spot and a vague mention of killing to protect someone in a blurry journal. I mean, tying up and slitting the throats of people is really different than forcing Jillian Watts to kill those other women. . . ."

"Fair point. But if they aren't connected," Sayer said, "that would imply that our recent attacker is actually linked to the old case, not the new one, since he did just break in and try to take an old skeleton." She paced in front of the murder board. "Let's review what we know for sure. We know that we have Cricket's blood on the sword. Thanks to the dates, we also know that the last murder was around 2002. . . . Isn't that the same year that Cricket left?"

"It is," Ezra answered.

Sayer watched Max's reaction. He looked shocked, slightly angry, definitely upset. She pressed on. "That can't be a coincidence. How old was she when the first murders began in '96?"

"Twelve," Ezra said.

"So the murders end the same year she disappears. But the fact that she was so young when they began makes it seem unlikely that she was the killer back then," Sayer said. "Unless she had an older partner."

"What about her dad?" Dana asked. "She accused him of physical abuse. Virtually every modern mass shooter has a history of intimate-partner violence. Maybe he was the killer back then and she found out?"

Max shook his head. "Not possible. Mr. Nelson was in the reserves and was deployed for almost two years, '98 and '99, I think. I only know that because my mom used to hire him as a handyman. She didn't like the other guy she had to hire while Mr. Nelson was deployed."

"Hmm, Ezra, confirm that he really was gone during that time, but let's assume that's true. If he was away for two years of the killing, there's no way he's our guy, which brings me back to Cricket. We do have her DNA on the handle of what I assume is the murder weapon. Let's pretend she was the killer."

"You really think a twelve-year-old could've done something like that?" Piper did not look convinced.

"I've heard of children as young as eleven killing people," Sayer said. "Actually, as young as ten, now that I think about it."

"Kids as young as ten have killed people?" Piper asked.

"Yeah, look up Mary Bell, strangled two toddlers when she was ten." Sayer waved her hand, mind on the case. "I'm just playing out scenarios to see what might make sense. But you do have a point. Binding someone in a straitjacket and slitting their throats with an ancient Greek sword is pretty damn sophisticated for a twelve-year-old. So my bet is that she was either a victim or that she was working with an older partner. But the last murder and her disappearance happened at the same time. We need to know what the hell happened in 2002," Sayer said, frustrated.

Realizing everyone felt slightly defeated, she clapped her hands. "All right, let's figure out what's next. I want to know for sure if these cases are connected somehow and I think the best way to do that is to learn more about Cricket's disappearance. Max, since her DNA is on file, I assume that means the Nelsons filed a missing persons report?"

"Yeah, for sure."

"Good. While Dana keeps working on getting us an ID on the remaining skeletons, I want to look at all the old police records from 1996 through 2002." Sayer took a deep breath.

Ezra's computer *pinged*. "Well, that's weird," he muttered as he read.

"What is it?" Sayer asked.

"I just got another hit on Cricket's DNA."

"What do you mean?"

"Uh, you know how there are a ton of DNA databases out there? FBI, state police, some other medical, genealogical . . ."

"Sure." Sayer went over to Ezra's computer and read off the screen. "Donor list?"

"Yeah, so right now we have to separately search every single database. I've been experimenting with a program that crawls all the publicly accessible DNA databases out there. I've been entering the DNA we've found into my program, you know, just to see if it's working. And the blood off the handle of the sword just came back with a match to the"—Ezra squinted as he read—"*BMDD, the Bone Marrow Donor Database*. It looks like the match is to an anonymous submission to the Bone Marrow Donor list from someone offering their bone marrow."

"And that submission matches Cricket Nelson?" Sayer asked.

"Yeah, Cricket must've made the donation anonymously, but it's definitely her DNA."

"Which must mean that Cricket is still alive?" Max said, perking up a bit.

"Is that true?" Sayer said. "Can you tell when the donation was made?"

Ezra typed. "Here we go. The donation was made seven months ago and . . . whoa. It was processed just down the mountain at the University Hospital in Charlottesville!"

"Cricket's not only alive, she's nearby?" Max looked shaken. "I can't decide if I should feel relieved or pissed."

"Could the people who run the database tell us the name of the donor?" Sayer asked. "Cricket is clearly living under a pseudonym, and I would sure love to ask her a few questions."

"No way. People who volunteer to donate do so with assurances that their DNA will remain anonymous. The bone marrow folks would never violate that anonymity without a court order."

"Then let's get a court order," Sayer pressed.

"I'll get that in the works, but there's some pretty intense court cases happening right now looking at privacy rights with this kind of DNA database. A court order might not be that easy to get."

"All right, Ezra, court order or not, double down on trying to find her. She had to build a new identity somehow," Sayer said. "Max, anyone she knew back in high school you could track down?"

"She was one of those kids that was popular enough but didn't seem to have any close friends," Max said. "I think she did date some older guy for a few months. Why don't I try to find him and see if he remembers anyone?"

Sayer glanced at the DNA match on Ezra's computer screen again. "Before we do anything else, I should call Kyle and tell him what's going on." It was early but she was sure he'd want to know right away. None too happy about that thought, Sayer retreated to a small office to make the call.

Kyle answered the phone, voice thick with sleep.

"Hello?"

"Morning, Chief Nelson, it's Agent Altair. I need to fill you in on the latest."

"What time is it?"

Sayer could hear him rustling in bed.

"Sorry to wake you. It's just after six, but someone attacked us here last night, and—"

"Wait what?" Kyle's voice became sharper. "Is everyone okay?"

"Yeah, we're all fine." Sayer decided to be blunt. "But I just wanted to fill you in on the latest. We're trying to determine if our older and more recent cases are connected. We've decided that your sister's disappearance might be our best lead to figure that out."

Silence.

Sayer continued, "Right now we aren't sure if the evidence suggests that Cricket is a victim or a potential UNSUB, but, if the two sets of cases are connected, then that means they could both have something to do with your sister. . . ."

Sayer could hear Kyle breathing over the phone. He said nothing for a very long time.

"Kyle?"

"I'm sorry, I'm just trying to decide how pissed to be, but I haven't even had my morning coffee yet, so all I can muster is disbelief. First Max accuses my dad of abusing Cricket, and now you're, what? Accusing my sister of murder? I don't even know what to say."

"I understand. And I assure you we aren't assuming anything beyond the fact that she is involved. That said, we do have her DNA on the presumed murder weapon. . . ." Sayer let that hang, making it clear that this wasn't her fault.

"Is it possible your lab screwed up? I mean, I've heard about the hearings. . . ." Kyle trailed off as well.

"Fair enough. But they're under the microscope right now. There's no way her DNA match is a mistake. Which brings me to our other news." Sayer tried to soften her voice. "We also have DNA evidence suggesting that Cricket is still alive, and that she was in the area as recently as seven months ago."

Silence again.

"Kyle?" Sayer prompted.

"She's alive?" His voice sounded so hopeful.

"We think so. She apparently submitted a blood sample to some kind of bone marrow donor database. Does that mean anything to you?"

"Not at all. Sorry, I'm just having a hard time with this. I mean"—he let out a huff of disbelief—"we were the most boring American family you've ever seen. And now Cricket's all tied up in something like this. There's just no way she killed those people."

"I agree it's most unlikely, which is why we would really like to take a look at the old police report from your sister's disappearance in 2002, as well as all the police records between '96 and '02. Max said the old police records and paper copies of the local paper would all be at the county archives?"

Kyle grunted, clearly getting up. "All right, fine." He sighed. "Yeah. Until about ten years ago, they kept all the police records there. It's gone digital now, but back then it was all paper."

"I'd like to get a look at those records as soon as possible. When do they open?"

"They don't open today at all. But I've got keys," Kyle continued. "Meet me there in thirty."

He hung up.

Sayer went to gather Max for a trip down to Rockfish Gap.

ROAD TO COUNTY ARCHIVES, ROCKFISH GAP, VA

Max drove his truck off Main Street, away from the small center of Rockfish Gap and up a long driveway toward the county archives.

"The archives are way up here?" Sayer asked after they had been driving for a few miles.

"Yeah, the archives are housed in an old estate. Some rich family that used to live up above town. When they left the area, they donated their estate to be used as a county building. Now it houses the library, the local history museum, and the archives."

They finally pulled through a massive stone arch. The words AGERE PRO ALIIS were etched in the marble above the grand entry.

"*To act for others*," Max read the sign. "That's a nice family motto."

Sayer looked over at him. "You read Latin?"

He raised an eyebrow at her. "I'm much more than just a pretty face."

She rolled her eyes as they emerged from the narrow driveway into a manicured open space. A topiary of sculpted bushes stretched off to their right, while rows of perfectly tended flower beds stepped up to their left, ending at an imposing stone structure that Sayer might have even called a castle.

"Well, this's fancier than I expected," she said.

Max grunted. "Yeah, we used to come up here all the time as kids. Make out in the gardens and such."

As the rain picked up, Max pulled the truck under the large stone portico. Sayer was grateful that they wouldn't have to sprint through the rain yet again.

They sat in the car, waiting for Kyle.

"So"—Sayer watched down the driveway—"whether or not the old and new cases are connected, the old cases clearly revolve around Cricket Nelson. You said you didn't know her all that well, but what do you remember about her?"

"I actually had a crush on her in ninth grade." Max's mouth flickered up into a faint smile. "She was the only girl in my shop class and she just gave off this tough vibe. Her dad was a metalworker and did a ton of handyman work around town. He must've taught her how to use power tools, because she already knew what she was doing in shop class. She kicked our asses in the CO_2 car competition . . . won the gold trophy and all."

Max shifted to face Sayer. "But we weren't in many other classes together, and after that I mostly just saw her as a nice girl who I didn't have much in common with. I certainly never thought she seemed mentally unstable or anything. She had a reputation as a sweet, maybe slightly awkward kid. I do wonder who beat the hell out of her the night she ran."

"Assuming it was really her father, do we buy the idea that Kyle didn't know, or is he lying to us?"

"Good question. If Mr. Nelson was really beating her up that badly, how could he not know? But then again, his reaction to the idea of his dad being an abuser sure felt real," Max said.

"Agreed," Sayer said. "Just asking for your gut opinion."

"I see. You're wondering if Kyle might also be involved in this case somehow."

"The thought has occurred to me. We're talking an awful lot about his dad and his sister. A lot of serial killers manage to hide what they're doing from their families, but I can't help but wonder if that's true here. What do you think? Any red flags about Kyle?"

"Well," Max said slowly, "I honestly don't know."

"Yeah. Okay. Either way, it's best to keep him close, that way we can keep an eye on him." Sayer realized that, despite all of her concerns, she trusted Max and his opinion. That was something at least.

Moments later, Kyle Nelson rolled up in his cruiser.

The chief got out, police-issue raincoat flapping in the stiff breeze as he approached the truck. Sayer got out and waved a greeting.

"Thanks for coming so early."

He gave her a pinched nod, then eyed Max before heading to the keypad next to the front door. "Follow me," he said brusquely.

He punched a code and the solid wooden door swung open.

As they entered the shadowy mansion, Sayer felt a tingling along her spine that she couldn't explain. Not entirely sure why, she rested her hand casually on her gun.

The entry was a grand hallway with a curving staircase at the end. Kyle strode in, confident.

"County archives are on the first floor, over to the left."

He led them into a narrow hallway and pointed at doors as they passed. "Main library is that way in the ballroom and dining hall. These are the offices for librarians and local researchers. They only open once a week, so we've got the place to ourselves today. And this"—he stopped in front of a massive metal door—"is the archives."

"You've been here a lot?" Sayer asked.

Kyle nodded. "We patrol up here pretty regularly, make sure no kids are breaking in. Never opened the archives, though."

"Don't you ever have to consult old police files?" Sayer asked.

Kyle let out a gruff laugh. "Have you seen Rockfish Gap? It's not like we have cold cases or anything. Unless you count trying to figure out who stole old lady Johnson's garden gnome. Never did solve that one. . . ."

He tried a few keys until the lock clicked loudly. A cloud of dust puffed out as the door opened, making Sayer sneeze.

They stepped into a two-story room lined with shelves.

Max groaned.

"Yeah, the previous police chief used to drop off a box of files once or twice a year and the librarian, Lettie, would put them away," Kyle said. "Lettie might've had a system but she died a few years back and no one has been able to figure it out. These are land records and county files going back, I don't know, a few hundred years probably. Not exactly well organized."

"No kidding." Max stepped in farther and turned in a circle, looking up at the balcony running around the second story. "This is like a whole second library. We might be here awhile."

Sayer didn't hesitate. "Right, so we'd better get started."

Sayer began upstairs, while Max and Kyle tackled the downstairs. Row after row of musty books sent up dust that tickled the back of her throat. In one corner, a heaping pile of old newspapers threatened to swallow a row of moth-worn chairs.

"There's a huge section of reference books up here," she called down. "Nothing that looks like records."

"I've got boxes here that might have something," Max called up. "What kind of archives don't label everything?" he grumbled.

From the other side of the room Kyle's voice filtered from behind a wall of shelves. "I've got some possible records here as well."

Sayer finished her circuit of the upstairs and was about to head down the curving staircase at the back of the room when her phone buzzed.

She'd almost forgotten that Adi would be calling. It was barely seven in the morning; the young woman must have been up early fretting about this call.

"I've got to take a call," Sayer called down and then headed away from the balcony for some privacy. She faced the wall and spoke softly. "Hey, Adi."

"Hi, Sayer. How's the case going?"

"Fine, fine. How's the I'm-going-to-college celebration there?"

Adi laughed, which made Sayer smile. When she'd first moved in, Adi had been surly, angry at the world. Not that Sayer blamed her after what she'd been through. But slowly over the past few months she'd actually begun laughing occasionally. It made Sayer feel like they might both be doing something right. Now she just had to not fuck this up.

"My friends took me out for Thai food last night."

"Nice," Sayer said.

"I've also got a surprise for you when you get home. . . ."

"You do? I can't wait." Sayer didn't say more, letting Adi get to why she called.

"So, uh . . . I'm calling because I have a question for you . . . I'm . . . I mean, I've been talking to my counselor . . . about college, and then the applications, and financial aid, and I was wondering if . . ." She jumbled her words together.

"Slow down, Adi. Nana called me last night and told me what's up."

Adi blew out a hard breath. "Ha, I should've known she would do that. So, what do you think?"

"Of course, I'd love to make everything official. Nana e-mailed me this morning to let me know she's already got a lawyer in mind," Sayer said. "Nothing would make me happier."

Adi let out an emotion-laden sigh.

"Thank you. . . ."

Bang!

A gunshot exploded from below.

Bang, bang, bang!

Max and Kyle both shouted as the gunshots continued.

Their chaotic voices echoed upward.

"Get down!"

"Gun!"

Sayer's entire body went into high alert, heart roaring in her ears.

She dropped the phone and slid out her Glock as she ran in a crouch toward the edge of the balcony. She scanned the room below.

Max pressed himself against the back wall, but she couldn't see Kyle, who was directly below her.

"Down, Kyle!" Max shouted, firing toward the door. The door was just out of sight, so she couldn't see who Max was shooting at.

Another *bang* from the direction of the doorway. Kyle let out a sharp grunt. The wet sound of someone being shot sent Sayer flying down the stairs.

Kyle lay just at the bottom, crawling for cover. Blood seeped from his head onto the threadbare green carpet.

Max crouched behind a low shelf, clearly about to dash out and grab Kyle.

Max and Sayer locked eyes for a brief moment. He lifted his chin toward Kyle. She pressed herself against the wall and nodded toward the door.

Go, she mouthed as she leaned around a corner and pulled the trigger twice.

With her gunfire as cover, Max dove for Kyle and dragged him behind the nearest shelves.

Low and fast, Sayer circled toward the door, gun steady.

Footsteps echoed from the hall. The shooter was fleeing her approach.

"FBI. Freeze!" she shouted, but the shooter was off and running.

Sayer switched into pursuit mode and unleashed her full speed.

She cleared the doorway just in time to see the figure at the end of the long hallway, nothing but a blur of black clothes.

She steadied her gun, still at a sprint, and squeezed the trigger. The gun thudded in her hand with a *bang* as the figure disappeared around the corner.

Moments later, Sayer rounded the same corner.

Nothing.

Open doors lined the next hall, and Sayer moved, steady and quiet, clearing each doorway. The shooter could be lying in wait anywhere.

By the time she got to the end, she knew he was gone.

She followed the curving hall around until it emptied into the grand entryway. The front door hung wide open, wind blowing rain in across the marble floor.

"Dammit," she said, jogging outside.

Sayer ran onto the manicured lawn in the now heavy rain. Standing in the downpour, she turned, eyes roving in a circle, but the heavy rain created a gray curtain obscuring everything. The grass squished under her boots, too sodden to leave footprints she could follow. She had no idea which direction the shooter had gone.

Sayer hurried back to help Kyle and Max.

Kyle leaned against the wall. Max knelt over him, pulling off his own shirt. With his teeth, Max tore a strip off his T-shirt and tied it around Kyle's head.

"He got away," Sayer said as she crouched next to Kyle. "You okay?"

"Yeah." Kyle looked furious. "Someone shot me," he growled.

Sayer understood the reaction. When you got shot, angry was better than scared.

"He'll be okay," Max said. "Looks like a graze to his head. I've already got EMTs on the way. You get a look at the shooter?"

"No." Sayer took a deep breath to calm the fading adrenaline rush. "I think he knew where he was going. Knew the layout of the place."

Kyle's burning gaze intensified.

A faint sound drifted down from the balcony above. Sayer was about to draw her gun when she realized it was Adi's voice.

"Sayer! Sayer!"

She ran upstairs and grabbed the phone that she had dropped when the shooting began. "Adi!"

"Sayer, oh, my god, Sayer." The panic in her voice made it gravelly. "Are you okay? Were those gunshots?"

"Yeah, but I'm fine. Everyone is okay. Sorry, I just dropped the phone."

Adi sobbed into the phone. "Oh, my god, Sayer, oh, my god." She cried uncontrollably.

"Hey, hey, Adi. I'm really okay. Everything is all right."

"I just thought . . ." Adi tried to catch her breath. "I just thought that I'd lost you too."

Sayer comforted Adi as much as she could as guilt burned a hole in her gut. Was she doing the right thing, bringing Adi into this kind of life?

UNIVERSITY HOSPITAL, CHARLOTTESVILLE, VA

Max and Sayer hovered outside the emergency room while Kyle got stitched up. Max wore a boxy blue hospital shirt that pulled across his shoulders. They both pressed themselves against the wall, trying to stay out of the way of the busy staff.

The doctor finally came out, beaming. "Chief Nelson's going to be totally fine. He'll have one hell of a headache and needs to keep his stitches clean, but the bullet only grazed him. Skimmed right along his skull. He got lucky as hell. Millimeter to one side, and he'd be dead."

After the doctor left, Max took a deep breath and tugged at the awkwardly fitting shirt. "Well, that was more exciting than I expected. Though I've got to say, our UNSUB has a pretty lousy track record. First he tried and failed to set you and Dana on fire, then tried to shoot Ezra and missed, and now he barely managed to graze Kyle." Max's phone buzzed and he read the text. "I sent Piper and a Rockfish officer up to the archives. Looks like they've already finished gathering anything that could be the right police records to bring to the ranger station along with Kyle's cruiser." Max looked up at the operating-room door. "Glad he's going to be okay.

And since I sacrificed my favorite T-shirt to stop his bleeding, maybe he won't hate me quite as much."

Sayer realized that Max was rambling, the aftereffect of his second adrenaline rush of the day. She nodded, distracted, unable to stop replaying the sound of Adi's frantic sobbing on the phone. She tried to refocus on the case.

"I guess we can at least cross Kyle off our list of suspects, since our UNSUB did just try to kill him," Max said.

"Silver lining, I suppose."

Max looked up at the fluorescent lights with displeasure. "Hey, let's go out and get some air while we wait for Kyle."

As they stepped out onto the portico, a small cluster of reporters rushed toward them, calling out questions, cameras up.

"Agent Altair, will Chief Nelson live?"

"What happened at the archives?"

"Did the attacker get away?"

"When do you testify at the Quantico Hearings?"

Without a word, Sayer and Max swung around and went right back inside. The reporters clustered around the door but knew they couldn't enter the ER.

"Well, shit," Sayer said. "I should probably call Assistant Director—" As she spoke, her phone buzzed. She answered.

"Sayer!" Holt barked. "What the hell just happened down there? Is everyone okay?"

She could hear the genuine concern in Holt's voice.

"Everyone's fine."

"Who was shot?" Holt pressed.

"The Rockfish Gap police chief was just grazed. He'll be totally fine."

"So much for sending you on a case where no one is shooting at you." Holt did not sound amused. "What the hell happened?"

"We were at the archives looking for the police report for that young woman that went missing back in 2002."

"And someone just opened up on you?"

"Exactly. And they knew their way around the archives."

"Did you see him, or her?"

"No visual on our UNSUB. Our next step is to see if we can figure out what the shooter didn't want us to find in those records."

Holt grunted. "Okay, Sayer. You get this total mess of a case solved."

"We need more help," Sayer said bluntly. "We need a task force. There's a thousand threads here and not enough people to follow them out. Don't forget, there's a little girl still out there. . . ."

The phone was silent for a long time and Sayer cringed, waiting for the explosion from Holt.

Instead, Holt sighed. "I know there is. And I know you need more hands. But with everything here, we just don't have the resources right now." Her voice sounded heavy, tired. "Today might be my last day running Quantico, but I'll see if I can pull some folks from another office somewhere. In the meantime, lean on the locals for help, rein in the chaos down there."

"On it," Sayer said but realized that Holt had already hung up.

She tucked away her phone as Kyle emerged, head swathed in thick white bandages.

"Want us to drop you off at home on our way out?" Max tentatively offered.

"Like hell I'm going home. Whoever did this just tried to kill me. Let's go look through those records and see what this asshole didn't want us to find."

SOUTHERN RANGER STATION, SHENANDOAH NATIONAL PARK, VA

A cluster of media vans clogged the parking lot outside the ranger station. In the light drizzle, the reporters huddled close together under the small overhang just outside the front door. Murder, missing women and a missing child, a cave full of bones, a beleaguered FBI agent at the heart of a major scandal, and now a cop shot. It was a media heyday.

Sayer, Max, and Kyle pulled up but made no move to get out of the truck, not wanting to face another wall of reporters.

"Want me to run them off?" Max offered.

"The park is public land, we can't kick them out," Kyle said.

"Just completely ignore them and let's get inside." Sayer pushed open the truck door.

They no-commented their way through the reporters shouting questions. Scowling, Sayer slammed through the front door of the station.

Ezra greeted them just inside. He balanced against his walker and gestured at the media. "I see you've brought a few friends with you."

Sayer grunted with annoyance.

"Well, I know you're famous when you manage to bring out this many vultures before ten A.M.," he continued.

Sayer checked the time, surprised that it was still so early in the morning. After the attack on Ezra and Dana, the shooting at the archives, and their trip to the hospital, she felt like it should at least be lunchtime.

"Well, we'll have them on tape now." Ezra pointed to a small camera hanging above the entry. "One of the park rangers helped me set everything up while you were down at the archives. I've got four cameras outside and six more inside, including one in the conference room. They'll record everything that happens here. If anyone tries to break in, we'll get one hell of a good look at them."

"That's perfect, Ez." Sayer put a gentle hand on his shoulder and could feel his muscles quivering beneath her hand. He was exhausted.

"Ezra, this is Kyle Nelson, Rockfish Gap police chief. Kyle, this is Ezra Coen, FBI data wizard. Where's Dana and Piper?" Sayer said to Ezra.

"Dana's still working on the bones. Piper decided to get started on the records."

"All right, then let's join her in the conference room and get to work."

The team stopped just inside the conference room door, staring at the massive number of boxes on the table.

Piper sat hunched among the teetering stacks. "You told me to bring anything that might have the right records. . . ." She trailed off apologetically.

"No, this is great, Piper." Sayer strode to the table, ready to tackle the job. "Let's get on it."

Max didn't sit down. "You mind if I run Kona before I dive in here?" His body looked wound as tight as Kona's. "I need to make sure she gets exercise every day or she goes a little bonkers."

Sayer nodded, understanding that Max also needed to blow off some steam from the shooting. Max practically ran out of the room, Kona at his hip.

Ezra, Kyle, and Piper began pulling boxes open.

"All right, we're specifically looking for the records from 2002 so we can see Cricket's missing persons report, see if they did any investigation.

But I'd also like to look through anything from '96 to '02. Maybe someone saw something suspicious. There's got to be a reason that our friendly attacker tried to stop us from getting these files."

They dove into the boxes, working quietly together. Half an hour later Max came in, flushed from exercise and damp from the rain. He joined them without a word.

With so many bodies in the room, the temperature rose slightly, and Sayer enjoyed feeling slightly warm for the first time in days.

Absorbed in her work, Sayer jumped slightly when Ezra called out, "Aha!" He triumphantly pointed to a faded gray box. "Rockfish Gap police records." He held up a thick file.

"Great!" Sayer took the papers. "Let's see." She began skimming the faded copy of the first page. "Damn, these are from the 1950s."

"Hang on." Ezra pulled open another gray box. And then another. "Uh, yeah, all of these gray boxes look like they have police records. Oh, there's more. . . ."

They all groaned as Ezra pointed to a stack of almost twenty gray boxes.

"Wow, all right, let's divide and conquer: 1996 through 2002. Let's find 'em and start to dig through the police activity."

They finally found the missing persons report for Cricket Nelson. When Sayer flipped open the file, she let out a soft gasp at the photo of young Cricket. Her pointed chin. Wavy blond hair. Sparkling blue eyes.

"Max, Kyle, neither of you told me that our modern victims look exactly like Cricket. She could literally be one of them."

"Sorry," Max said. "To be honest, I'd almost forgotten what she looked like." He looked over Sayer's shoulder at the image. "Whoa, you aren't kidding. She looks like their doppelgänger."

"And I hadn't even seen the photos of the modern victims until just now. . . ." Kyle was clearly implying that Sayer should've brought him on board sooner.

With a sigh of annoyance, Sayer went back to Cricket's missing persons file. She read through the single-page report. Only the barest of details:

eighteen, went missing right after graduation. It was clear the officer writing the report assumed she was a newly graduated young adult who ran away.

"Dammit, nothing here," Sayer grunted and went back to the box. "So what didn't he want us to find?" Sayer turned back to the police records. Missing dogs. A domestic dispute that ended with a bottle being thrown. A child's stolen wagon. A loud noise that turned out to be mating raccoons. She began to wonder if she had led her team on a wild-goose chase. But what other lead did they have?

An hour later, Sayer put down the last file as Dana hurried into the conference room. "I've got news!"

"Please tell me you have a lead we can follow, because there's fuck all here."

"Boy, do I. Two leads, actually." Dana shook the file in her hand, making her skull earrings dance. "First, we got the DNA back from our attacker this morning. Ezra, the report's in your in-box."

"We know who attacked me?" Ezra eagerly clicked on his computer. As he read, his face contorted into an uncomfortable grimace.

"Uh . . ." He glanced up at Kyle, then over at Max. "It's a match to Kyle's sister."

"Cricket Nelson attacked us this morning?" Max leaned forward in his chair.

Ezra nodded, chin jutting with anger at the memory. "Which presumably means she's also the person who shot at you at the archives."

Kyle touched the bandage on his head as a wild range of emotions danced across his face. His expression settled into genuine shock. "You're telling me that my sister who has been missing for seventeen years just tried to kill me?"

"Okay, I'll admit, that's . . . I mean, wow." Sayer went to the murder board. Despite trying to keep an open mind, she had honestly believed that Cricket was probably a victim back in 2002. This attack changed everything. "There's no doubt about the DNA results?"

"Nope. They're a clear match. She attacked Dana and me this morning. Took the DNA sample myself." Ezra held up his hand and wiggled his fingers.

"This certainly blows the idea of Cricket-as-victim out of the water," she muttered to herself, staring at the photo of Hannah hanging next to the image of Jillian and Grace Watts. Eyes still on the smiling girl, she spoke loudly. "So, twenty-three years ago, someone starts ritually murdering people and dumping their bodies in a cave. That continues for six years until 2002, when Cricket disappeared. The murders stop the same year she ran, leaving behind a sword with her blood on it. Seventeen years later, she's back and now we have two new murders on our hands. All of which suggests that Cricket could be our UNSUB in not just the old murders, but in the new ones as well."

Kyle made a slight noise as if about to protest. He leaned forward, hand up, but then dropped his hand back onto the table, shoulders slumping.

Sayer felt bad for him. How horrific it must be to realize that his sister was most likely a serial killer. Despite Kyle's struggle, the realization that they finally had their target set off a familiar flare of excitement in Sayer's chest. She stoked it, letting it blossom into rage. Having an identity for their UNSUB gave her focus, renewed her drive to hunt.

"Dana, you said you had two things. What's the second?"

"I identified the cremated skeleton. And it's a doozy. . . ." She took a deep breath, looking over at Kyle with concern. "The last skeletonized victim was Cricket and Kyle's mother, Olivia Nelson."

Max sucked in his breath.

Kyle blinked rapidly, jaw working back and forth.

No one spoke for a very long time.

"My mother died of a stroke," Kyle finally said.

"I'm afraid that's not true," Dana said gently. "The cause of death was almost certainly a blow to the head from a sharp object."

"I thought your mom died a few days after Cricket left," Max said.

"No, she died the day Cricket left. I saw her that morning at breakfast and then went to school. She wasn't home when I got back from school. Then Cricket disappeared and my dad told me that mom was dead. I always just figured it was the stress of Cricket leaving. We had a funeral for my mom. She's buried down in Rockfish."

"Was it closed casket?" Sayer asked.

"Well, yeah. . . ."

"Which means that it's possible that her body wasn't actually in the casket at all. Which would make me suspect that your father had something to do with all this, but he was away for two years between '96 and '02, correct?"

"Yeah. You think my dad had something to do with my mom's death?" Kyle seemed confused.

"Well, we originally thought maybe he was the killer back then. . . ."

"What the hell?" Kyle's face hardened.

Sayer continued, ignoring his anger. "But that's clearly not possible. But someone did very effectively cover up your mother's murder." She walked over to stare at the murder board, body buzzing. "The question is, who?" She turned to Kyle. His entire body pulled into a taut bundle of anger. "Now that we're thinking of Cricket as a possible UNSUB, is it possible she killed your mother in some kind of scuffle and then ran? The timing would work."

"Oh, for fuck's sake." Kyle stood up so quickly his chair flew backward. He gripped the edge of the table. "I'm not going to sit here and listen to this. It's one thing to accuse my sister of murder. But killing our own mother . . . I just won't hear this bullshit." He stormed out of the conference room. Moments later they heard a car screech away.

"Should someone go after him?" Ezra asked.

"No, give him some time to cool down while we try to figure out what all of this means." Sayer began to pace, trying to piece together everything they had just learned. Was it possible that Cricket was the original murderer? Did she kill her mother for some reason and then flee? If so, who covered up Mrs. Nelson's murder?

Everyone sat lost in thought. Sayer realized they needed to refocus. "All right." She leaned against the table. "I know we all have a lot going on here. Poor Kyle is dealing with the idea that his sister is a murderer who just tried to kill him and might have killed his mother. Max, you're wondering if you helped a killer escape seventeen years ago. Ezra, hell, you're learning how to walk again. Piper, you're stuck in the middle of a criminal investigation you didn't ask for. Dana, you just got back from a war zone. And I've got a whole shitload of political crap flowing from D.C. But none of that matters. You know what does matter?" She strode over to the whiteboard. "These women and this child are what matters. We're here on the front lines with badges and guns, and test tubes and computers, working tirelessly to stand between innocent people and the evil that walks this earth. We are facing off against a monster because we believe that no one deserves to suffer. Which is why we're going to buckle down and do whatever it takes to save these people." She tapped the photos of Hannah and the Wattses. "So let's figure out what's next."

Piper's phone buzzed, interrupting Sayer.

She read the text and looked up at Sayer with wide eyes. "Ranger said someone spotted a little girl on the side of the road a few miles up Skyline Drive. She matches the description of our missing girl, Grace Watts!"

SENATOR DEWITT'S OFFICE, CAPITOL HILL, WASHINGTON, D.C.

FBI Assistant Director Janice Holt pushed open the ridiculously oversized door leading to Senator John DeWitt's inner office.

"Janice, please come in," DeWitt said from one of a pair of high-backed chairs facing an ornate fireplace.

Holt stepped around the chairs to find two silver-haired men reclining comfortably.

"Senator DeWitt, Director Anderson," she said, jowls pulling into a frown. She had not expected the FBI director to be here.

The director nodded acknowledgment of her presence but kept his eyes toward the low fire.

She stood awkwardly on the overplush carpet and they did not offer her a place to sit.

"Janice, I know you're angry that you've become a target in the hearings," the senator said softly.

"That I . . . ? Is that why you think I'm angry?"

"It's not?" DeWitt steepled his fingers, bushy eyebrows arching with curiosity.

"Well, of course I'm angry that I'm about to lose my job at a place I have worked tirelessly to turn into the best forensic lab in the country. But the entire premise of these hearings is ludicrous. It's spreading my agents thin, preventing them from doing their jobs. You and your esteemed colleagues"—she waved her hand toward the director—"clearly plan to dismantle Quantico. I'm not sure why, but I see it coming. . . ."

No one spoke for a long while. Holt listened to the sound of the crackling fire, trying not to lose her temper at these arrogant men stuffed in overpriced suits.

The director finally spoke, in his soft New England accent. "Janice." He let out an exasperated sigh that made Holt want to punch him right in his aquiline nose. "I thought for a very long time that you would be loyal to us. I thought that you loved the FBI, but now I see that's not the case."

Holt clenched her teeth. "Director Anderson, you're correct. I'm not loyal to a director, nor am I loyal to an institution. I am loyal to the principles of the FBI and I'm loyal to my fellow agents."

"Does that mean you will refuse to follow orders from your superiors?" Senator DeWitt asked.

"It means that any institution can be corrupted, Senator." Holt spat the last word. "There are good and bad people everywhere. There are good cops and bad cops. There are good agents and bad agents. Hell, there are good teachers and bad teachers. An institution like the FBI can only fulfill its duty to the public when the institution itself protects against corruption by protecting the good and weeding out the bad."

"But you swore an oath. . . ."

"To defend the Constitution from enemies, foreign and domestic." She stressed the word *and*. "So, to answer your previous question, no, I will not follow orders if I believe them to work against the very things I swore to protect."

"Janice." DeWitt shook his head slowly. "I can't tell you how sorry I am to hear that. Because we've been following Agent Altair's most recent case. . . ."

Holt said nothing.

"I heard about the local police officer shot just hours ago." The senator sighed regretfully. "Altair has cobbled together a team consisting of a park ranger, a K9 agent with limited investigative experience, a UN employee who left the FBI years ago, and a local cop with a personal connection to the case."

"And you know perfectly well that our resources are limited because you are forcing us to review thousands of cases that couldn't possibly have been compromised. You've got overseers in every lab, dragging hundreds of agents through overzealous reviews," Holt said. "You know I support a review. We need to operate aboveboard to preserve public trust. But these hearings are spurious nonsense."

DeWitt ignored her comment. "Whatever the reason for Altair's incompetence, we have concluded that it reflects poorly on you. We've also concluded that it is time for new leadership at Quantico."

"And there's the true reason we're here." Holt turned to the director. "I thought you were better than this. But I see now that this is all just a power grab so you can put your pets in charge of Quantico."

Director Anderson didn't even look up at her.

"Pets?" Senator DeWitt responded instead. "I resent the implication. I care about my country and the FBI. We have an obligation to the public. If the way this case is being run is any indication of your leadership, it's time for someone new to take the helm." He looked away from Holt's Valkyrie death stare.

"At least say it to my face," Holt growled.

The senator reluctantly looked into her eyes. "We are officially requesting your resignation."

"Fine," Holt said. "But don't for a second convince yourself that I will just walk away from the FBI."

She leaned in face-to-face with Director Anderson, who studiously stared at the fire. "I'm not someone to be trifled with, and you know it," she whispered to him.

Holt straightened and walked out without looking back.

SKYLINE DRIVE, SHENANDOAH NATIONAL PARK, VA

"Max, Piper, with me. Let's go!" Sayer said, already charging out the door. She was relieved to see that the media was gone. Last thing they needed was a camera watching whatever was about to happen.

They crammed into the cab of Max's truck and headed north along Skyline Drive.

Piper hung up after speaking with another park ranger, disgust settling on her round face. "A day hiker spotted the girl that matches the description of Grace Watts. He apparently told the ranger at the northern exit on his way out of the park."

"He saw a three-year-old alone on the side of the road in the rain, in the middle of a national park, didn't stop to check on her, and then drove all the way up to the northern entrance an hour away before notifying someone?" Sayer couldn't believe it. "We sure it's not our UNSUB?"

"Doubt it. Guy's a regular day hiker but lives up in the city. He said it wasn't raining when he saw her, and he assumed her parents were nearby . . . mentioned it to the ranger just in case."

Max grunted a sound of disgust, leaning forward to focus on the road.

"I hope for that guy's sake that we find her. If something happens to that child, I will be having a . . . conversation with him," Sayer growled, eyes scanning the steep sides of the narrow road, barely visible in the downpour. "And what the hell is the deal with this rain? How is it still raining?"

"This happens every fifteen years or so," Piper said. "There's cold air pushing a storm front up and hot air pushing it back down until the weather system gets caught against the mountains. It can stay trapped here for weeks. Apparently there was one like this back in '96."

"Yeah," Max said, "rivers crested at twenty-eight feet, flooded the whole Shenandoah valley."

Sayer grunted an annoyed acknowledgment.

"The hiker said around mile eighty-seven?" Max asked.

"Yeah." Piper nodded.

They rolled past the mile-eighty-seven marker and Max slowed the truck to a crawl.

Piper rubbed her hands on her knees, eyes skittering back and forth from one side of the road to the other.

Sayer saw a flash of something. "There!"

She jumped out of the truck before it fully stopped and scrambled down a short rocky slope. At the bottom, a ditch ran with swift-moving water. Just on the other side, a small girl lay on her side. Her eyes were closed, lips slightly purple.

Sayer's breath caught.

"Please be okay," she whispered as she crashed through the run-off, soaking herself to the waist.

She gently lifted the small child. The girl's eyes fluttered open, then shut again. Her little body shivered against Sayer.

"She's alive!" Sayer shouted, carefully crossing the ditch and clambering up the slope, where Max waited with a warm blanket, his medical kit already out.

Max wrapped the blanket over the girl and rushed to the truck, where he laid her on the seat. He expertly checked her over. "Her vitals are weak, she needs a hospital. Now!"

Sayer turned to Piper, expecting her to jump in the driver's seat. Piper stood motionless in the rain, staring across the road, face drawn into a rictus of horror.

THE PIT

Hannah woke in her room. After she experienced a moment of disorientation, the events in the pit crashed into place. The fight with Jillian. That little girl in the monstrous machine. The woman's horrific sacrifice. Now he was going after Sam!

The scream still caught in her throat finally escaped in a keening wail of pure panic.

"Sam!" she shouted.

"Sam, no no no, Sam!" Hannah slammed herself against the metal door. She had to get out. Had to stop that monster from getting her daughter.

The door was bolted, metal onto stone. No way she could break it down.

Hannah remembered the small vent. Eyes rolling white with uncontrolled fear, she attacked the thick paint like a predator, clawing frantically along the edges. Guttural sounds escaped her mouth with every gouging scrape, her frenzy increasing until she was tearing at the vent in a blur of wild motion.

She let out a feral howl when it finally came loose. Breaking fingernails, pressing with her broken finger, she pried it off the wall and stood panting in front of the small opening for a brief moment.

"Sam," she said again as she clambered up on the bed and slid her head and shoulders into the narrow vent. She managed to push her body forward until only her feet hung out of the opening. Wriggling, Hannah managed to work her arms up along the side her body. With a groan of effort, she pushed herself a few inches forward. Her elbows hit the metal vent with a *clang*.

The wild panic she had felt moments before faded into a shivering determination. The vent had to lead somewhere. It was the only possible escape.

She slid her arms up and pushed again. A few more inches. And again. And again, a few inches. After a few minutes, her arm muscles quivered, but she ignored the straining ache, rhythmically sliding up her arms, push, *clang*. Slide, push, *clang*.

Her legs were useless, dangling behind her, unable to bend enough to propel her forward. The metal slid slowly by only a few inches from her nose. Her broken finger turned from a sharp pain into something that felt almost foreign, a sensation so painful that she couldn't even tell it belonged to her own body.

As Hannah pushed deeper into the vent, the air began to feel thick and still, squeezing her chest with every breath. The light dimmed until it was nothing more than faint backscatter from some unseen source.

She recognized the signs of claustrophobia setting in, but she couldn't stop the crashing wave of panic.

Trembling, she started chanting, "Have to save Sam. Have to save Sam. Have to save Sam," in repetitive monotone with every push forward.

Slide, push, *clang*. "Have to save Sam." Slide, push, *clang*.

Hannah became lost in the repetition. Sweat tickled her face as it dripped onto the slick metal. Her arm muscles shook violently, but she pushed forward until she could see a turn ahead. She crawled forward for an hour, maybe two, maybe ten? When she finally reached the turn, she let out a cry of despair. Around the corner, the vent continued on into the darkness.

SKYLINE DRIVE,
SHENANDOAH NATIONAL PARK, VA

Sayer turned to see what Piper was staring at across the road.

A pale arm jutted from beneath a stand of low bushes next to the raging ditch.

"Max!"

Max jumped from the truck with Grace in his arms and hurried to Sayer's side.

Sayer said nothing, just pointed to the arm.

Max handed the girl to Sayer and rushed over to uncover the body of a woman. Her skin was dusky blue. The downpour had washed her clean, leaving nothing behind but cuts and bruises from head to toe. Her forehead was indented, gore showing through her cracked skull.

"Jesus." Piper turned away.

Max crouched down next to the body.

Sayer wrapped her arms tighter around the small girl, as if warding off the horror of the sight.

"Okay," she barked, trying to snap Piper out of her shock. "We need to get the girl to the hospital right away. Max, you stay here with the body. Start documenting the scene. I'll send an evidence team up ASAP."

Max let out a cry, sending Sayer's heart into her throat.

"She's alive!" he shouted. "We can't wait for paramedics!" He picked up the woman and sprinted toward the truck, eyes wild. "Her pulse is barely there, but I don't think she has long! Go, go, go!"

"You drive, Piper!" Sayer said as she climbed in with the girl.

Max climbed into the covered truck bed with the woman, wrapping her tightly in blankets and lying down next to her to share his own body heat.

Piper leaped into the driver's seat and took off as quickly as possible in the intense rain. The park ranger gripped the steering wheel with white knuckles, teeth chattering from the stress.

Sayer made a call to the hospital so they could prepare for their arrival.

Wind and rain whipped against the truck and Sayer alternated between whispering comfort to the girl in her arms and turning to watch Max in the back, hunched next to the half-dead woman. His lips moved and she suspected that she and Max were both whispering the same words. "Hang on. You're safe now. We've got you. Don't give up."

The forty-minute drive felt like it took forty hours, but they finally pulled up to the University Hospital. Two teams swarmed out of the emergency room door, one pulling the woman from the back and the other sweeping the girl from Sayer's arms.

After the doctors told them it would be a long while before either patient would be allowed visitors, Sayer, Max, and Piper made their way back to the ranger station, slightly dazed.

VENT, THE PIT

Hannah managed to pull herself around the turn in the vent but then stopped. Tears blurred her vision and she couldn't get her arms up far enough to wipe them away. She turned her head and rested against the cold metal, tears creating a warm pool against her cheek.

For the first time, it occurred to her that she might die here in the vent. Somehow that thought felt comforting. If she were dead, he wouldn't need Sam to motivate her. And she wouldn't have to endure this any longer. It would be over.

A buzzing hum filled her with a sense of peace and she closed her eyes, thinking that maybe she could just drift off to sleep and never wake up. She must have drifted out of consciousness, because she suddenly jolted awake, banging her head on the metal. The echoing sound sent a new wave of adrenaline to her limbs.

Hannah wiggled her body to see if it was even still there. Her muscles burned with bands of fire along her back and shoulders, but they still moved when she told them to.

"Sam." She purposefully whispered her daughter's name, forcing herself to picture the smiling girl. Hannah slid her arms forward. They shook wildly at the effort, but she let out a husky grunt and pushed herself forward until her elbow clanged against the vent. Slowly, painfully, she inched forward.

In the faint light, she could just make out an opening off to the side, halfway down the vent. If she could just reach the opening, maybe she could still save her daughter.

Crying from the pain in her muscles, Hannah pushed herself to the opening. She slid her arms up one more time and let out a harsh cry as she shoved as hard as she could.

Her eyes cleared the turn and she could see the end of the tunnel. A roaring sound became as loud as an oncoming train. Cool mist settled on her face. She almost cried with relief that nothing covered the end of the vent.

Hannah scooted forward just enough to get her head to the opening.

Her fingers curled over the edge. She pushed one last time and fell, arms flailing, to the ground.

A shudder of adrenaline convulsed her entire body. Pure terror had drained Hannah to the point of exhaustion beyond anything she could've imagined. Even swallowing felt like too much. Her broken finger thudded like it was being hit with a hammer over and over again.

"He's going after my daughter," she said out loud. Just saying those words kicked off a new wave of shudders along her body, but it also motivated her to keep moving.

The vent dropped her into a small, natural cavern. Light filtered in from a narrow doorway leading off to her left. A river ran along the back wall of the cavern. Hannah knew there were underground rivers in the area, but she'd never actually seen one. The river carved a sharp line in the rock of the cave floor and she hobbled over to the edge, muscles protesting with every movement. Hannah struggled with the surreal scene, standing on the banks of a swift river in a cavern underground.

She turned a slow circle and stopped at the sight of a stone table jutting from the rock wall. It was covered with a thick red velvet cloth, and her first thought was to wrap it around her shivering shoulders. But as she neared the table, she realized that there was a skeleton laid out on top of the cloth. The bones looked charred. A jagged hole collapsed the side of the skull.

Carved around the edges of the table were two words in a foreign-looking alphabet.

Hannah backed away, unwilling to touch the human remains.

A narrow doorway opened next to the table and she headed into the tunnel beyond it, which then split to the left and right.

To the left, a faded orange sign read WARNING: MINE! OPEN SHAFTS. DEAD END. *DO NOT ENTER!* Beyond that the tunnel led into pure darkness.

To the right, light leaked in around an arched door.

Holding her breath, Hannah pushed the wooden door. It swung open onto the pit.

Though her muscles quivered, her legs held firm and she managed to walk out to the middle of the massive cavern. Faint light filtered down from above.

The ladder!

She hurried over to the ladder and climbed, grunting at the pain, until she reached the metal gate extending horizontally out from the wall. A large padlock held it firmly in place. She would have to swing out away from the ladder and pull herself up around the edge of the gate with just her arms.

The ground was a dizzying thirty feet below. A fall from this height could kill her. Blinking back tears, she decided she had no choice but to try. She was so close to escape.

Hannah grasped the grate and screamed a full-throated howl as she wrapped her broken finger over the metal. She used the grate like monkey bars until she made it to the edge. Her arms shook violently, her finger stabbing agonizing daggers into her hand, but she managed to hang on. The fingers of her right hand curled over the edge and she felt something slice into her palm.

Hannah screamed in pain and barely hung on. She swung her legs back to the ladder and yanked her body back against the wall.

Panting, blood running warm from her palm, she hugged the metal ladder, tears dripping off her chin. She realized the entire edge of the grate must be lined with razors.

There was no way she could climb past it.

Without thinking, she let herself down in a barely controlled descent. Back on the rocky ground, she curled her entire body into a ball around her bleeding hand. She wanted to stay like that forever.

"No," she whispered hoarsely. "No!" she said more loudly. She would not curl up and die here.

Hannah forced herself up and made a slow circuit of the room. There was no way to climb the walls. No way out. This mine was a dead end. The ladder impossible.

"The river," she said. She knew underground rivers often meandered to the surface and back underground. Did the river here go up to the surface?

Hannah made her way back to the edge of the raging river. She was a strong swimmer, but she was injured. Her arms were exhausted. This seemed like madness. But what if he was kidnapping Sam right now? What if she could escape and stop him? She had to try. And if she died . . . well, then at least he wouldn't need Sam anymore.

Tears ran down her cheeks as she stood there shaking. She felt the collar at her neck, wondering if it was set to go off if she got too far away.

She knew the longer she stood there, the more she would second-guess her decision. If this was a way out, she had to try now before he came back. Before he could get to Sam.

"I love you, Sam," she whispered.

Taking a deep breath, Hannah jumped.

to narrow down where the UNSUB is keeping them? What about looking through records of old mines?"

"Thing is," Piper said, "there were tons of illegal mines in the mountains here. People would build a long tunnel in and then dig the mine shafts completely underground. So all you would see from outside would be a small tunnel entrance."

"Ezra?"

"I'd already been crawling through the old paperwork on the mines but most of that isn't digital," Ezra said. "I've also got calls in to a few local spelunking organizations; they love to find and climb around in old mines. But nothing so far."

"Damn, okay. Let's at least narrow down possibilities within a small radius of our two known locations. Ezra, can you make a map showing the bone cave and where the UNSUB dumped the Wattses?"

"On it."

"The UNSUB?" Kyle asked. "Does that mean you're not convinced that it's Cricket?"

"She clearly attacked us, but I'm not assuming anything. She's connected to the old cases, but not necessarily the new ones. Until we know for sure, the killer is the UNSUB to me."

Kyle just nodded, eyes down.

Sayer couldn't sit still any longer and began to pace, fingers working her worry beads.

The park ranger on watch poked her head in the conference room. "Uh, Agent Altair, there's someone here to see you."

"If it's the media, tell them I've got no comment."

"I'm pretty sure they aren't with the media."

Curious, Sayer hurried to the entry hall.

UNDERGROUND RIVER

The raging river swallowed Hannah. She just managed to swim to the middle of the torrent before being pulled violently under as the river sluiced into a narrow opening.

She got her feet pointed downriver and thought for a moment that she would be able to safely ride the current. If she could just hold her breath long enough, maybe this wouldn't be so bad.

But then a rock protrusion slammed into her side. The impact sent her spinning into the opposite wall. Her head and shoulder hit, forcing her to let out a sharp exhale of precious breath.

Hannah flailed her arms wildly, trying to avoid another impact.

Tumbling, she lost all sense of direction as she ricocheted off the cave walls. Rough rock scraped away flesh as the water bounced her back and forth.

Unable to do anything else, she curled her body into a defensive ball.

As she was battered against the walls, her lungs began to burn. They squeezed her chest as though they were imploding.

She clawed at her neck. Hannah knew that, at some point, her brain would become so starved of oxygen she would be forced to involuntarily inhale. The breaking point.

Her head exploded in a starburst of agony.

Arms and legs numb, Hannah's entire body seized. Her muscles collapsed forward and then spasmed her limbs behind her. Back arched, Hannah felt herself inhale. Water flowed down her throat. The black void filled her lungs. Reality faded into a churning cacophony of silence.

SOUTHERN RANGER STATION, SHENANDOAH NATIONAL PARK, VA

Sayer stepped into the entryway and barely had time to brace herself before the silvery dog flew at her through the air, tongue flapping to the side like a loose sail.

"Vesper!" she cried out, shocked at how excited she was to see her silly dog.

He collided with her chest and almost took her down. She laughed at his slobbering enthusiasm.

Nana, Adi, and Tino stood just inside the door, smiling broadly.

Tino held a bunch of rainbow-colored balloons.

Nana held a cake.

Adi a wrapped present.

"Happy birthday!" they all shouted.

"What?" Sayer fended off face-licks from Vesper.

"Adi wanted to come check out UVA, so we decided to come for a visit. Plus, I was confident that you forgot that today's your birthday." Nana handed the cake to Piper without a word, then gave Sayer a firm hug. She assessed the entry hall. "This will do," Nana said. She pulled a roll of streamers from her oversized purse.

"But—" Sayer began, but Nana held up her hand.

"I know, you're in the middle of a case. We will be here for exactly one hour. When is the last time you ate a meal?"

"I . . ." Sayer thought back to the small powdered donut she'd eaten around five A.M. She glanced at the time and was surprised to see that it was only two.

Nana held up her hand again. "I already know the answer. You need food and you also need to take a brief moment to enjoy your life and visit with your family." She turned to Max, Kyle, and Piper. "And you are?"

They introduced themselves and Nana nodded approvingly. "Lovely to meet you. Max, you're in charge of getting the food out of the car. Piper, you're in charge of getting a table out here in the entryway where we can all sit and have lunch and cake together. Kyle, since you're injured"—she pointed to his bandaged head—"you can decorate."

The team looked to Sayer, uncertain.

She shrugged. "When my nana says to do something, it's best to just do it." She turned to Nana. "One hour is all we can spare, for real."

While Max, Kyle, and Piper hustled off to do their assigned jobs, the new arrivals all hugged Ezra.

"Surprise." Adi smiled sheepishly at Sayer. "Sorry I didn't warn you that we were coming, but Nana . . ."

Sayer knew well enough that no one crossed Nana, even if it was just about surprise birthday parties.

Adi handed Sayer the small present with an envelope balanced on top.

"I also found this. . . . It's, um . . . I was going to surprise you and get all your old boxes unpacked and this was between the pages of one of your textbooks." Adi stumbled over her words. "The neuroplasticity one. It fell out and . . . I'm not sure who it's from, but thought it might be from Jake? I figured it's unopened, so . . . you might want it?"

Sayer turned the envelope over and felt a jolt of recognition seeing Jake's handwriting.

"Oh," was all Sayer managed to say before Tino moved in and gave her a bear hug. She gripped the present and letter as he held her by the shoulders. "Ah, *cálida*. You look terrible." He gave her a gentle smile.

Sayer tucked the letter into her pocket and swallowed the wave of emotion it triggered. That was far too much for her to process right now. Rather than dwell on that and everything else going on, she decided to just accept the loving attention of her family and friends for the moment.

When Max came back in from the car carrying a teetering stack of food, Kona alongside him, Vesper realized for the first time that there was another dog in the room. He loped over to Kona, sniffing around the serious black dog. Kona stood stock-still, letting Vesper circle her with curiosity.

After making a few circuits, Vesper playfully jumped around in front of Kona and gave her a play-bow, tail wagging with excitement.

Kona looked up at Max as though to say, *What am I supposed to do with this creature?*

Everyone laughed as Vesper pranced around Kona, trying to convince her to play.

Dana emerged from the bone room just as Piper returned carrying a folding table, and they began to set out forks and plates. Adi and Kyle hung streamers. Max and Nana laid out a feast of enchiladas and fresh ceviche. Tino got everyone some crisp limeade. Sayer decided to actually start a fire in the oversized fireplace.

Within minutes they were sitting around the table sharing a delicious meal.

"This is wonderful," Dana said to Nana.

She snorted. "Dear lord, I didn't make this. Tino's our resident chef."

Tino beamed. Adi laughed at something Ezra said. Nana and Max were deep in conversation. A warm fire roared its cheerful sound in the entry hall. For a brief moment, Sayer was overcome with emotion that felt strangely like coming home after being away. She hadn't realized how much she had been missing her family, a feeling she hadn't experienced in a very long time.

UNKNOWN LOCATION

Hannah Valdez felt herself vomiting before she was fully conscious. The acidic well of water poured from her mouth like a volcano.

The spasm rocked her body, sending arcs of pain along her back.

She realized that she was lying facedown somewhere.

Terrified she couldn't move, she tried to curl her fingers.

They closed over small rocks, cold and wet. Icy water washed over her legs, but she could feel the pitter-patter of rain against her back. Her face pressed against the ground.

Hannah realized it was raining. That she was on the bank of a river.

Outside.

She had survived.

She tried to breathe in, but another fountain of water erupted from her mouth.

Moaning, she wobbled up to her knees. An electric bolt of pain from her shoulder said she probably had broken bones somewhere.

But she was able to take a full breath in and out. In and out. She stayed like that for a long time, unable to think.

Where was she? She had to do something, but what?

Sam!

The thought kicked her brain out of its fog and she stumbled to her feet.

She swayed wildly, almost falling over, but managed to right herself.

Hannah turned in a slow circle. The swollen river roared behind her. In front of her, a gentle slope up looked relatively clear. No way she was going to try crossing the river. Up the slope it was.

All she could think was, *Have to find people. Someone to help Sam.*

Hannah managed to climb the slope and let out a cry at the top. A trail!

She didn't even stop to think about which direction to go. To the right, the trail sloped downward. Hopefully toward civilization.

People to help.

The rain obscured her vision, but Hannah stumbled along, focused only on the ground in front of her.

She walked until her already battered muscles cried in pain. Her legs shuddered beneath her but were strong enough to keep carrying her forward. Downward.

Time dilated into a meaningless sensation. Finally she thought she saw something up ahead. A building? Smoke from a chimney?

Light.

People.

What if it's him? What if this is his house?

Hannah couldn't think clearly. Was this safe? Was she walking into a trap?

Her legs almost buckled beneath her, but she careened toward the building. She had to find help.

SOUTHERN RANGER STATION, SHENANDOAH NATIONAL PARK, VA

Sayer held up a glass, about to make a toast to her friends and family, when the front door burst open.

A woman fell forward into the room, collapsing onto the tile floor, an animal cry on her lips. Her hair hung in tangled mats of mud. Blood streaked her pale skin. A chunky metal box hung around her neck, attached to a thick leather collar. Her left hand was swollen, fingers bound together with a strip of cloth.

"Max!" Sayer shouted, and Max went to get his medical gear while she rushed to the woman's side.

"Hey, hey," Sayer gently said as she reached out.

When Sayer touched the woman's shoulder she went wild, clawing at Sayer with feral terror.

Sayer pulled her arms back, not wanting to make it worse. "You're safe here," she said softly. "You're safe now."

The woman struggled to sit up, jabbering nonsense. Her eyes rolled, whites flashing like those of a dying animal. Sayer had to calm this woman down before she hurt herself or someone else. And they had to cut that thing off her neck.

Something about her face struck Sayer like a bolt of lightning. This was Hannah Valdez, their last missing woman.

"Hey. Hannah, you're okay." Sayer could read the fear in the woman's eyes. "I'm an FBI agent. We'll make sure you stay safe. No one will hurt you here."

The woman took a shuddering breath but couldn't seem to stop shaking. She curled forward over her lap, sweat slicking her face.

"She's having a panic attack," Max said as he arrived with his medical bag.

At the sight of Max, the woman recoiled, screaming. She seemed beyond reason, no longer even aware of where she was.

Max slowly backed away. "I'm making it worse. We've got to calm her down. I'm going to hand you a syringe with a sedative. Can you give it to her?"

Sayer nodded, still making gentle calming sounds to the woman.

"Vesper!" Adi hissed as the dog broke free of her grasp.

Sayer turned to see Vesper approaching and was about to block him when he got down on his belly. He inched forward toward Hannah, head bowed.

Unsure what he was doing, Sayer didn't want to make any sudden movements, so she let the dog approach.

Vesper crawled directly next to the woman and put his head gently onto her lap.

She gulped in air but looked down at Vesper. He scooted closer, pressing his body against her legs.

The woman put a hand on his head, fingers working his silvery fur. She noticed his missing leg and ran her hands along the scar cutting down his chest. She let out a low moan, but then took another shuddering breath and pressed her face down into the dog's neck.

The woman and dog sat together while she slowly calmed down. She finally seemed to realize she wasn't alone with Vesper. She looked at Sayer with pleading eyes.

Sayer cautiously reached out and put a gentle hand on the woman's shoulder. "My name is Sayer Altair. I'm an FBI agent. We've got you. You're safe now."

The woman nodded, tears streaming down her face.

"This man's name is Max Cho. He's also an FBI agent, and he's a medic. Would it be okay if he checked you out?"

The woman looked over at Max. Her hands tightened on Vesper and she managed to remain calm.

She nodded, then mouthed something. It took a few tries, but she finally found her voice.

"Sam," she croaked.

"Sam?" Reality hit Sayer like another lightning bolt. "Your daughter?"

The woman grunted an affirmative. The fear in her eyes sent a wave of horror through Sayer's body.

She was shouting on the phone before she even made it to her feet. "Get uniforms to the Valdez residence. Our killer is going after the Valdez girl!"

She hung up and strode toward the front door in full juggernaut mode.

"Max, you stay here with Hannah until the paramedics arrive and ride with her to the hospital," she barked. "Piper, I've called the Charlottesville PD, you get on the radio and tell all the surrounding police departments what's happening. I can get there more quickly on my bike. Kyle, follow me down in your cruiser as backup. Dana, keep working on IDing the skeletons. Ezra, you're coordinating everything. I'm going to make sure Sam Valdez is okay."

Sayer opened the front door and glanced back at her family before running out into the rain.

VALDEZ RESIDENCE, CHARLOTTESVILLE, VA

Sayer skidded her motorcycle to a stop in front of the Valdezes' Brady Bunch home. Two Charlottesville police cruisers idled out front, lights rolling.

One of the local cops opened the front door as she ran up the steps.

"All's quiet, Agent Altair. No sign of anything unusual."

Sayer did her own sweep of the living room despite the three other officers already there.

Zoe Valdez sat on the sofa, freshly showered and wearing clean clothes. Her face beamed with relief knowing that Hannah was alive and on her way to the hospital.

"Wait, where's Sam?" Sayer asked loudly.

"Uh, they just told us to come secure the Valdez household," the local cop said.

Sayer rounded on the police officer. "It's the girl he's after! Where is she?"

The officer opened his mouth but, seeing the murderous look on Sayer's face, didn't respond.

"She's at preschool," Zoe Valdez whispered from behind her. "Someone's after Sam?"

"You sent her to school?" Sayer shouted, unable to soften her reaction.

"I was trying to . . . ," Zoe said, voice gasping with emotion. "I thought some normalcy . . . I thought it would be good for her. No one told me Sam was in danger. School's out soon. I was just about to go pick her up and head to the hospital to see Hannah."

"Where?" Sayer shouted.

"What?" Zoe Valdez seemed slightly dazed.

"What school?" Sayer demanded.

"Jefferson Day."

"Where is it?" Sayer tried to stay calm, but she knew deep in her gut where the UNSUB was heading. She hoped it wasn't already too late.

"It's in the same building as the local elementary school. Just a few miles, up off Preston next to the campus!"

"Call it in right now!" Sayer barked at the cop. "Jefferson Elementary off Preston, possible child abduction in progress!" She sprinted toward her motorcycle, pulling out her phone.

"Ezra," she shouted, hoping the phone wouldn't fritz out in the rain, "I think our killer is going after Sam at Jefferson Day School! I've got the locals on their way, but send any resources you've got! Jefferson Day!" She jumped on her bike and peeled off, almost losing control on the slick road. She yanked the bike back in line, racing toward Sam Valdez's school.

She leaned into the downpour pelting her face and body, barely noticing that she forgot to put on her helmet. Sayer drove, frantically dialing the school, but kept getting a busy signal. She couldn't get through to warn them.

As she neared the location, she hit traffic and realized it was a line of cars waiting to pick up students at the end of the school day. They clogged the narrow road, forcing her to ride the center line for three blocks before the school came into view. Still a few blocks away, she could just make out a cluster of students under a large portico.

Cars stopped in both directions prevented her from riding any closer.

She was about to drop her bike and go the rest of the way on foot when a Charlottesville police cruiser rolled up from a side street and flashed its lights.

"You, on the motorcycle, hands where I can see them," the officer said over his loudspeaker.

Sayer contemplated going for her badge, but she didn't want to reach into her jacket. As a black woman she knew better than to freak out an already jumpy cop.

Hands shaking with frustration, she held her hands up, keeping her eyes on the school in the distance. Sayer shouted back, "I'm Senior Special Agent Altair with the FBI. I'm trying to stop a possible child abduction."

The officer approached and grunted. "Let me see your badge."

Sayer stifled the desire to just punch the cop. Swallowing her temper, she removed her badge and shoved it in his face.

"Sorry, Agent . . . Altair," he read off her ID. "We just got here and I saw you approaching the kids. Been told there's a possible abduction in progress."

"I'm the one who called it in," she said through clenched teeth as she got off her bike. "You secure the road. I'm going to find our possible target and get her somewhere safe."

The cop seemed slightly annoyed but nodded.

Kyle pulled up behind the local cop, jumped out of the cruiser, and sprinted toward Sayer.

Sayer and Kyle moved quickly up the hill. While they were still a block away from the school, a black truck pulled to the front of the line of cars. Someone tall in a puffy jacket got out, but Sayer couldn't clearly see the person's face, which was hidden by a shag of dark hair.

"Hey!" Sayer shouted as she ran.

The kids could sense something was wrong and began to murmur with uncertainty.

Sayer pulled her gun, but knew she could never use it here. Too many children nearby.

"Freeze!" she screamed, running.

Kyle pulled his gun, and for a horrible second Sayer thought he was going to try to take a shot. He sighted down the barrel but then pulled the gun up toward the sky and shouted with frustration.

The figure scooped up a small girl in its arms and jumped back into the truck. A teacher nearby shouted in protest.

Door still hanging open, the truck peeled away from the curb. It leaped up on the sidewalk and the engine gunned, forcing people to dive out of the way.

Sayer ran after the truck. Her feet slammed on the pavement as she let out a grunt of effort to catch up, but the red taillights disappeared in the distance. She tried desperately to read the license plate, but it was already too far away.

"Call it in!" she shouted down to the police officer as she ran back toward her motorcycle. "Black truck heading east on Preston! Single suspect with at least one hostage. Armed and dangerous!"

She yanked her Silver Hawk up and laid on the horn as she weaved between cars, trying to catch the fleeing truck.

Oblivious parents shouted and honked back.

"Hey, wait your turn like everyone else!"

"There're kids here, watch out!"

Sayer felt her teeth cracking, trying to stay calm, but she finally rode up on the sidewalk as well, shouting, "FBI! Get out of my fucking way!"

She finally made it to the end of the congestion, leaving behind a line of wide-eyed parents.

She opened up her motorcycle but only rode a few blocks before realizing it was futile. She saw no sign of the truck. It could have gone anywhere.

Where were the goddamned locals?

Where was anyone?

She pulled over and slammed a hand down hard on her handlebar. It sent a shock wave of pain up to her old scar.

"Fuck!" She vented her frustration at everything. Letting Sam Valdez get taken right under her nose. She had royally fucked up on this case and now innocent people were going to pay.

UNIVERSITY HOSPITAL, CHARLOTTESVILLE, VA

Sayer parked in front of the University Hospital. She snarled at the media waiting out front, not even offering a *No comment* as she marched past the cameras.

Max waited for her in the entry. "Ezra's got the manhunt coordinated with the Charlottesville police. They'll call if they find anything. They're almost done examining Hannah. She was so upset when they brought her in, they've let Vesper and the gang stay with her as support. Said we can probably question her in a few minutes."

"Fine," Sayer said with clipped finality. "I'm going to track down Jillian and Grace Watts while we wait. Want to make sure they've got protection on their doors."

She was directed to Jillian's room. Sayer showed her ID to the Charlottesville officer at Jillian's door and stepped just inside. The young woman was encircled by a tangle of wires and tubes. Her eyes were swollen shut. A thick bandage swathed her entire head. But her heartbeat was strong and steady.

"Agent Altair?" A doctor tapped her on the shoulder. "I'm Jillian's doctor." The short man bowed slightly.

"Is she going to be okay?"

He nodded, bobbing his bald head. "I actually think so. Her head injury was significant. The cold weather helped keep her stable until you found her. I wouldn't say that to her husband yet, since things could still go wrong, but in my opinion, she's going to pull through. And her daughter, Grace, is up and about, terrorizing the children's wing. Jillian's family is there with the girl if you want to speak with them."

Sayer felt a genuine smile flash across her face like a ghost. At least one thing had gone well on this absolute shit day. "That won't be necessary. They have a uniformed officer with her as well?"

"They do."

Sayer let out a long breath. "Okay. Can you reiterate that the officer should be with her at all times?"

"Of course, worry not," he said cheerfully.

Max was waiting anxiously out in the hall when Sayer emerged. "They said you can talk to Hannah now. Her room's just down this way." He hurried off with his compact speed-walk.

Sayer followed him for a moment but then stopped, unable to tamp down the tempest raging inside. The sight of Jillian Watts had pushed her over the edge. What had that woman gone through? Little Grace Watts too. And now another little girl had been kidnapped by the very same monster. Thirty feet. She could have stopped it, but she was thirty damned feet away. And now Sam was in the hands of a killer. Frustration boiled over into fury.

Unable to contain her rage any longer, Sayer let out a roar and slammed her helmet to the floor. The sharp *crack* echoed down the sterile hall.

Max stopped and looked back, calm-faced. "Sayer . . ."

The red cloud obscuring her vision faded to a dull throbbing behind her eyes. She took a shaky breath and held it for a long time until she felt back in control.

"Give me a minute," she managed to say.

Rage fading, Sayer felt her whole body sag with the weight of what she was about to do. "How can I tell that woman that, after everything she did to escape to protect her daughter . . . how can I tell her that I just let Sam be taken right in front of me . . . ?"

"Hey, whoa." Max came over and put a gentle hand on her arm. "We're going to get Sam back. To do that, all we've got to do is focus. So get your shit together and let's find that girl."

Sayer blinked. Max was right: time to focus. "I'll see if Hannah can tell us anything that will help, then let's regroup at the ranger station."

Without irony, Max saluted, then led her to Hannah's hospital room.

"Good luck in there." He held open the door, face grim.

Sayer entered, body still buzzing with emotion.

Tino sat in a chair next to Hannah, holding her hand. Hannah's other hand was splinted and wrapped against her chest. Long scrapes and the beginnings of bruises mottled her face and arms.

Vesper curled across her legs like a snoring blanket. Nana and Adi sat in chairs against the wall, eyes pinched with concern.

Hannah smiled weakly. "Is Sam okay?" she asked, swollen eyes so hopeful.

Sayer tried not to react, but her mouth contorted.

"Oh, no. . . ." Hannah read Sayer's expression. Her face buckled into a mask of anguish as she realized what it meant. "He got Sam."

Sayer nodded once, her heart breaking at the sight of Hannah collapsing in on herself.

Grief pulled the breath from Hannah's chest. Vesper noticed her distress and stirred just enough to nudge her hand. Hannah's knuckles whitened on Tino's hand, grasping for something to keep her tethered in the vortex of sorrow.

Sayer touched Hannah's shoulder and looked into her eyes. "I promise you, we will find Sam."

Hannah nodded, not breaking eye contact for a very long time. Whatever she saw in Sayer's eyes seemed to inject anger into the grief. Her eyes hardened. She nodded sharply. "How can I help?"

"I need to know everything you can remember," Sayer told her.

"He's taken Sam to the pit," Hannah said, voice husky.

"To the pit," Sayer repeated. "Start from the beginning. What happened?"

"Can Vesper and everyone stay?" Hannah's eyes watered again.

"Of course." Sayer scooted her chair closer to Tino's.

Hannah looked up. "Did you find the little girl Grace? He said he would let her go."

"You mean Grace Watts? We found her and Jillian."

"That poor woman. . . ."

"Jillian Watts might actually pull through."

Hannah looked up at Sayer, wonder in her eyes. "She's alive? But I saw her . . ."

"Just barely, but the doctors are optimistic."

Hannah sat back in bed, overwhelmed for a moment. "Oh, my god. He kept his word. He told me he would let her go. . . ."

"You keep calling your captor 'he.' Did you get a good look at whoever it was? Could you tell if it was a man or woman?"

"No, he was up in the control room, so all I could see was a shadow. And he only spoke through a loudspeaker that made him sound all . . . scratchy. I think it was a man, but I'm not sure. I'm sorry."

Sayer gave her an encouraging nod. "That's okay. Can you tell me what happened?"

Hannah grasped Tino's hand again. He patted it gently. "I'm right here. Vesper is here."

She nodded. "Sorry, I'm just feeling a little . . . I can't . . ."

"It's totally okay. Just take your time." Sayer finally managed to flash her noncommittal interview smile. She found that staying emotionally neutral during an interview with a trauma victim usually helped the victim stay calm as well. "Start at the beginning. You left the gym with Sam. . . ."

"That's right." Hannah swallowed loudly. "I put Sam in her seat, and next thing I know, I woke up in a room."

"Do you remember seeing anyone suspicious nearby right before you were abducted?"

"No." Hannah frowned.

"Can you describe the room?"

"It was rocky." Hannah shook her head, frustrated with herself. "I'm sorry, I can't seem to think straight. I mean the floor was concrete but parts of the wall were rock, like it was built inside a cave."

"Okay. . . ." Sayer prompted her to continue.

"Then Jillian came in. She looked beaten. Skinny. She . . . oh, I forgot, we both had shock collars on."

"You still had yours on when we found you," Sayer said gently.

"I did?" Hannah said, distraught. "I don't remember any of that."

"That's okay. So you woke up in this room and Jillian came in. . . ."

"She cleaned me up. I guess I . . . threw up."

"Do you think you were drugged?"

"I think so, yeah." Hannah closed her eyes for a moment. "I blacked out, and when I woke up, I had that collar on." Her voice rose with emotion and Sayer could see her spooling back up.

Tino gently patted her hand, bringing her back to the present.

"He shocked me once." Her voice flattened, as she distanced herself from the horror "Before the test. . . ."

No one said anything, letting her carry on in her own time.

"He threatened to shoot Jillian if I didn't smash my finger. So I did. I can't remember exactly what the voice said. . . ." She trailed off.

"Do you want to stop, Hannah?" Tino asked gently.

"No, of course not. It was just all a game to him. . . ." She trailed off again.

Sayer decided to change the topic.

"Can you describe where you were? You called it the pit?"

"Yeah, yeah. . . . The voice called it the pit. It was some old mine dug down into a cave system. He always stayed up in a control room above us. Did I already say that?"

Confusion was normal in trauma victim interviews. Sayer tried to keep her focused. "What makes you think it was an old mine?"

"There was rusting equipment. I think we were kept in the old offices.

There were tunnels that led down from the pit. One of them went to an underground river."

"And that's how you escaped?"

"Yes, I jumped in. After the fight with Jillian, he told me he was coming for Sam. I couldn't just . . ."

They sat in silence for a few moments.

"What happened with Jillian?"

Hannah swallowed again. "The girl was in this . . . machine. With a big knife to the side ready to puncture her neck," Hannah said in a jumble. "The voice set a timer for five minutes and then told Jillian to kill me. He kept talking about her becoming a monster. But she . . . it was awful. She . . . apologized to me."

"Hey, remember, she's going to be okay." Tino squeezed her hand.

Hannah nodded, but she began to cry in earnest. "It was so horrible. She didn't know what to do. I didn't know what to do. She tried to attack me, but I just kept throwing her off. She was so scared for her little girl." Hannah's voice broke, and a sob shook her entire body. Face contorted with anguish, she continued, "When she realized she couldn't beat me, she asked . . . she asked if he would let the girl go if I killed her."

Tino let out an involuntary gasp. Sayer managed to keep her emotions in check, but bile rose up the back of her throat.

"I refused, and she went crazy. She attacked me and I pushed her and she . . . oh, my god. She ran herself into the wall. She tried to kill herself." Hannah let out another shuddering sob. "And that's when the voice said he would let the girl go so I would know he kept his word. Because he said he was going to bring Sam there. That it was my turn to become a monster."

The woman completely broke down into uncontrollable sobs. Tino stood up so he could wrap his arms around her. Vesper curled closer against her body.

She shook, crying for a long time before she looked back up.

"And now he's got Sam down there in that machine. I'm so sorry I can't . . ."

"You're doing great. I only have a few more questions, if you can keep going."

Hannah nodded and wiped her face.

"Did he say anything else to you?" Sayer asked.

"Yeah, he told me that he was trying to prove that there's a killer in all of us. He mentioned, what was it?" Hannah closed her eyes to think. "Something about how we all have monsters buried deep inside. That they're beautiful. Something about Stanford prison and Nazis? I'm sorry, I don't remember everything."

"I think I understand. Is there anything else?"

The woman looked at Sayer with red-rimmed eyes. "Oh, wait. There was a weird stone table with a big red cloth draped over it. There was a skeleton on it. It looked all burned."

"It looked burned . . . ," Sayer repeated. Their stolen skeleton.

"There were two words carved on the table, in Greek, I think."

"In Greek?" Sayer sat up with excitement. This would be their first definitive link between the two sets of cases. "Can you remember what they looked like?"

"I think so. . . ." Hannah closed her eyes, remembering. "One word looked like capital *E* with a squiggly line at the top, then lowercase *x l o v a*, with another squiggle over the *o*."

"Adi?" Sayer looked over at the young woman sitting against the wall. "I think I know what she's describing, but could you try to write it down? I want to know if it's the same word."

Adi looked down her nose as only a teenager could. "I am Greek. . . . Does anyone have something I can write with?"

Nana pulled a pen and small notebook from her purse. Adi took them and thought for a minute. "Um, could it have looked like this?" She held up a page with Έχιδνα written on it.

"Maybe . . . I'm sorry I don't know for sure, but I think so."

"That looks right to me," Sayer said.

Adi looked vaguely confused. "She-viper? You've seen this before?" She glanced with concern at Hannah, whose eyes were fluttering. The shock and exhaustion were forcing Hannah's body to shut down.

Sayer could read the hesitation in Adi's expression. "Let's discuss it in the hall. Hannah, could you describe the second word?"

"Maybe capital *X i u a i p a*? But with some squiggles and a weird *u*. Sorry . . ." Hannah's voice faded to silence. Her eyes fluttered again.

"That's really helpful. You did a great job." Sayer got up and whispered, "Vesper and the whole gang can stay with you as long as you like. Are you feeling up for seeing your wife?"

"Yes, please . . . ," she barely managed to say as she drifted off.

Sayer stared at the sleeping woman for a long moment, then waved for Adi to follow her. She gave Nana a quick hug.

"We'll stay here until her family arrives. I think she just needs a posse making sure she's safe right now," Nana whispered.

"Thank you."

"You know we're always here." Nana squeezed Sayer's arm.

Max waited just outside the room, staring out a wall of windows at the silvery evening light. His face mirrored the threatening clouds churning low in the sky.

"How's she doing? Anything useful?"

Sayer let her shoulders sag, exhausted and on edge. "She's traumatized and beaten up, but I think she'll be okay. She was able to describe an old abandoned mine she called the pit. She didn't get a look at the UNSUB, but said she thought it was a man, though she wasn't sure."

"Which would mean that it wasn't Cricket."

"True, but I wonder if she's just assuming it was a man, because she also mentioned seeing 'she-viper' carved in Greek above an altar there."

"Hannah was held in a place associated with Ekhidna?" Max said.

"And she saw the charred skeleton that Cricket stole from the ranger station this morning." Sayer let the excitement of the hunt course through her body. "Which is our first real confirmation of a connection between the two sets of cases."

"Which also means that Cricket is most likely the UNSUB in both sets of murders!"

Adi gently shut the hospital room door behind her and looked back and forth between Max and Sayer, caught up in their excitement.

"We need to know more about the she-viper. Adi?"

"So, you've seen that somewhere before?"

"Yeah, it was carved on the handle of a kopis we found. She-viper is another name for a mythological monster named Ekhidna."

Adi let out an exasperated huff. "Of course I know who Ekhidna is. One of the original, primordial monsters, she lived in a watery cave, feasted on innocent people. The mother of all monsters. . . ."

"Hannah literally just said that her captor talked about monsters. Said something about there being a monster inside us all! What else do you know about Ehkidna?"

"Basically, she was fierce and feared." A wry smile crept across Adi's face. "Kind of reminds me of you, actually."

"I remind you of a primordial Greek monster that eats innocent people?"

Adi's dark eyes sparkled beneath her fringe of light pink bangs. "She might've been seen as a monster by Greek heroes, but she also protected her monstrous children from all kinds of attacks from vengeful gods. In other words, she was feared by all and fiercely protective, just like you."

"Ah . . ." Sayer was momentarily left speechless by what she took as a major compliment.

"I'm not sure about this second word, though." Adi looked down at the word Hannah had tried to describe. "It could be a word in Greek that means something like *chasing ghosts*. I'm not sure what the English translation would be. I'll noodle around with it, see if I can figure out something that makes sense."

Sayer looked over at her ward. Despite her own recent trauma, Adi was there, face burning with the desire to help. Sayer was momentarily awed by her strength and she had the overwhelming urge to hug the young woman. Instead, she put a gentle hand on Adi's shoulder. "Thanks for helping today. Are you doing all right?"

Adi's calm exterior faltered slightly. "Of course. I mean, I know . . ."

"Yeah." Sayer understood. If anyone could understand what Hannah was going through, it was Adi. She made a mental note to follow up later and make sure Adi wasn't just putting on a tough façade.

"I'm fine, really. Why don't I go look up Ekhidna and mess around with the second word? I'll send along anything else I dig up." Adi clearly didn't want to dwell on her own past. "I'll do that while we wait with Hannah for her wife to get here."

"That would be great. Thanks, Adi."

Adi gave her a quick hug and retreated into Hannah's room. Sayer let out a sigh.

"Your kid's pretty great," Max said.

Sayer was momentarily startled. It was the first time anyone had mistakenly called Adi her kid. But then she supposed that wasn't a mistake, since they were about to make it legal. The thought filled her with an emotion she couldn't identify. Pride, maybe, that she would forever get to be part of this amazing human being's life.

"Yeah, she is," she said. The brief glow of love for Adi was followed by a wave of sheer terror at the thought of something happening to her. For the first time, Sayer understood what Hannah must be feeling about Sam. And what Jillian Watts felt for her child.

It made Sayer wonder exactly how far she would go to protect the ones she loved. Would she even hesitate to kill in order to protect Adi? The intensity of the emotion left her gasping. She had to find Sam before it was too late. "Let's regroup back up at the station to figure out what's next."

As Sayer made her way to her motorcycle, a coal of violence burned in her chest.

SOUTHERN RANGER STATION, SHENANDOAH NATIONAL PARK, VA

Sayer stood at the head of the conference table. Kyle, Ezra, Max, and Dana sat at attention, faces drawn.

"Where's Piper?"

"There was some flooding up north," Kyle said. "She had to go help evacuate campers from a flooding campsite."

"Dammit." Sayer needed her team here. It was ridiculous that she was investigating this mess of a case without a reliable team, let alone without a task force. She closed her eyes, trying to organize her thoughts. "All right, it's almost"—she glanced at her phone, thinking it had to be almost midnight—"Jesus, it's not even seven. It's already been a long day, but let's focus. We now have evidence directly connecting these two cases. Cricket clearly broke in here this morning and stole the charred skeleton. Hannah just told me she saw a similar skeleton in the pit, plus a stone table that spelled out Ekhidna. Let's discuss the very good possibility that Cricket is not only connected to the old murders, but that she's also our current UNSUB. Kyle, did you manage to get a look at the person who took Sam?"

"I couldn't see her face. And she was a lot bigger than she used to be, but you know how you can just recognize someone by the way they move? I . . . think that was my sister."

"Thanks, Kyle. Based on that, plus the fact that Cricket broke in here and attacked us this morning, I'm fairly comfortable saying that Cricket Nelson is our primary UNSUB in both sets of cases and that we just watched her abduct Sam Valdez. . . ."

Sayer watched Kyle's reaction.

He nodded, head bowed with defeat. "I agree. I've spent the past few hours playing my life over in my head. I mean, my mom baked brownies for PTA fund-raisers and volunteered at the school library. I was really sick when I was a baby, in and out of the hospital with a bunch of surgeries, and she didn't leave my side. My dad was a metalworker who coached soccer in his spare time. Hell, Cricket liked ponies and reading. How could she be a killer? And how could she have murdered my mom?"

"So you honestly didn't see anything that made you suspect that there was something wrong with her?"

"She wasn't violent or anything like that. No delusions or signs of criminal behavior."

"And you have no idea who could've beaten her up the night she went to Max?"

"No clue. I know for sure it wasn't my dad. He just wasn't like that . . . and, hell, Cricket was his favorite. He would've done anything for her."

"Anything, including covering up a murder?" Sayer pressed.

"Sure, while we're at it let's destroy my memories of my dad too." Kyle closed his eyes, and no one spoke. "Yeah, I suppose maybe he would've," he said with his eyes still closed. He finally looked at Sayer. "My dad was sweet, but maybe a little too worried about being seen as a down-to-earth good guy. Not much could've been worse in his mind than being embarrassed by something we did. . . ."

"You think Mr. Nelson covered up the fact that Cricket killed his wife? To protect his reputation?" Max asked Sayer.

"I think it's possible. I've seen a parent covering for a child's crimes dozens of times," Sayer said. "But we're still missing something. . . ."

Ezra's computer let out a *ping*, interrupting her. He clicked the notification that popped up. "Uh . . ."

She hurried over to his computer screen to see two reporters speaking with solemn urgency on the screen. Fear clenched Sayer's gut. The reporters' faces suggested something big was happening and she really hoped someone hadn't just found the body of Sam Valdez.

"What's up?" Sayer leaned in to get a better look at the reporters on Ezra's screen.

"Uh, I've got an alert set up to track anything relating to the case, just to keep track of public knowledge. This looks like some kind of news report that tripped your name." Ezra clicked on the sound.

The reporter had a gleam of excitement in her eye. "No one seems to know where the four-minute video came from, but it's a candid view of the murder investigation currently being run by embattled FBI agent Sayer Altair."

Sayer's mouth fell open as the video jumped to a view of the ranger station entryway. On the video, her birthday party was in full swing. Nana and Adi were passing around plates piled high with enchiladas.

Sayer let out a groan when Hannah Valdez stumbled in through the front door.

On-screen, Sayer tried to get close to the wild woman and eventually let Vesper approach Hannah. Sayer crouched nearby while the woman calmed down. Eventually, Sayer put a gentle hand on Hannah's shoulder. "My name is Sayer Altair. I'm an FBI agent. We've got you. You're safe now."

The woman nodded, tears streaming down her face.

"This man's name is Max Cho. He's also an FBI agent, and he's a medic. Would it be okay if he checked you out?"

In the video, Sayer glanced up toward Max and her expression was clear on camera. Her eyes shone, verging on tears that Sayer didn't even remember.

"What the hell is this video?" Sayer growled.

The video jumped to the conference room, where Sayer stood at the head of the table during one of their meetings.

She watched herself talking to the team. "I know we all have a lot going on here. Poor Kyle is dealing with the idea that his sister is a murderer who just tried to kill him and might have killed his mother. Max, you're wondering if you helped a killer escape seventeen years ago. Ezra, hell, you're learning how to walk again. Piper, you're stuck in the middle of a criminal investigation you didn't ask for. Dana, you just got back from a war zone. And I've got a whole shitload of political crap flowing from D.C. But none of that matters. You know what does matter?" She strode over to the whiteboard. "These women and this child are what matters. We're here on the front lines with badges and guns, and test tubes and computers, working tirelessly to stand between innocent people and the evil that walks this earth. We are facing off against a monster because we believe that no one deserves to suffer. Which is why we're going to buckle down and do whatever it takes to save these people. So let's figure out what's next."

On the screen, Sayer's face burned with intensity as the video faded to black. The reporter leaned forward toward the camera. "Difficult to watch. We've identified the injured woman as Hannah Valdez, whose daughter was just kidnapped!" She pressed her lips together in an imitation of compassion despite her gleaming eyes. "We've verified that this video is real, and as you can see, Brock, it gives us a new perspective on Agent Altair."

Brock nodded solemnly. "It does indeed, Belinda. Sayer Altair has been painted as a ladder-climbing, backstabbing federal agent. But the person we see here is clearly emotionally invested in helping those poor victims. Did we get her all wrong? Is Agent Altair the hero of this story? We'll investigate and find out."

"These are from the cameras you set up, Ezra! Who the hell has access to those videos?" Sayer's voice rose loudly.

Ezra looked shell-shocked. "No one! That's an internal feed. It goes straight into my secure computer!"

"Well, unless you made that video, someone else clearly has access."

Pale, Ezra nodded, typing frantically. "Let me check something."

Sayer waited, replaying the video in her mind. It had obviously been created to portray her sympathetically.

The clacking of Ezra's keys faded into the background as a horrific thought formed in Sayer's mind. Subject 037. He'd told her he was going to fix the threat to her job. . . .

"Ezra," Sayer croaked. "I think I know who did this."

He paused and looked up. "You do?"

"Remember how I'm interviewing noncriminal psychopaths?"

"Yeah."

"Well, one of them said he was going to do something to protect my career. He's implied a few times that he is a very high-ranking government official . . . maybe even intelligence of some kind."

"Jesus, Sayer. Okay, that still doesn't mean he can access my computer." Ezra looked like he realized something. "Holy crap, hang on." He began typing again, face drawn. "Whoa." He leaned forward, staring at his screen. "Look at this. . . ."

Sayer read over his shoulder. "Pretend for a moment that I don't know what any of this means."

"See here." Ezra pointed to a chunk of code. "This is a RAT, a remote access Trojan. The only people who could pull this off on my computer would be someone from one of the other intelligence agencies. Most likely the National Security Agency." He looked up at Sayer, eyes wide. "I think someone from the NSA just hacked my computer."

Sayer reached up and tangled her fingers in her curls while taking deep breaths. "Is there anything we can do to cut off access?"

Ezra grimaced. "Maybe. . . ."

"Okay, make it happen. I've got someone I need to talk to."

Sayer stormed down to her cabin and opened her laptop. She impatiently clicked the link to video-chat.

Subject 037 immediately answered.

"I was expecting your call."

"What did you do?"

"I'm just sorry I couldn't save your boss as well, but this should prevent them from firing you. For now, at least."

Sayer's voice fell to a low rumble. "I am in the middle of a case where a child has just been kidnapped. This is interfering with my ability to do my job."

"And here I thought you would want to continue doing that job." Subject 037 sounded amused. "This should ensure that will happen."

"This is a distraction that might cost real lives. We are not pawns for you to play with."

He let out a dismissive sound. "You love this job, and someone was about to take it away from you. I did nothing but show the public who you really are. Public opinion is about to save your job so you can keep saving people like Sam Valdez."

Sayer remained silent, not sure which of the hundreds of things swirling at the tip of her tongue she should say.

"So, how is the case going?" he taunted her with his cheerful tone.

Sayer growled.

"My advice," he said, voice dropping low and serious, "take your research on psychopaths and think about everyone who has inserted themselves into your investigation. I think it will be enlightening."

"I don't need help from you."

"Ah, shame. I suppose that means you don't want to know what I know about Jake's death?"

Sayer's vision blurred with red static and she squeezed out the words, "What did you just say to me?"

"You heard me."

"Don't you play with me."

"Ah, I see I've upset you." He chuckled. "I certainly won't share what I've found, then. Let's leave it at the fact that I've saved your job. Now go catch a killer."

He disconnected.

Sayer stood in front of the laptop in the empty cabin, panting with emotion.

Her phone buzzed in her hand and she almost threw it to the floor with anger but managed to rein in the reaction.

With a shaky breath, she looked at the screen.

Holt.

Fuck.

She clicked answer but didn't trust herself to say anything.

"What the hell was that?" Holt said in her scary-calm voice.

Sayer forced words through taut lips. "Remember my interview subject who got a perfect score on the psychopathy checklist? Turns out he's most likely someone high up at the NSA. And he just decided to save my job because he likes talking to me."

Holt remained silent for a long time. Sayer could practically feel the black cloud of emotion radiating from the phone.

Finally Holt responded. "So, you're interviewing someone at the NSA who decided you're his pet FBI agent and he just did something that ran an end-run around a gang of high-ranking congressmen and FBI muckety-mucks after your job." She let out a harsh laugh. "Well, I'd say it pays to have friends in high places."

"I can't accept help from a psychopath just because he wants to toy with me."

"I'm not sure how you refuse this help. That video is already out there and on heavy rotation. My guess is that you've just become a public hero. Which means they can't shitcan you now. This is literally going to save your ass. Hell, it makes the FBI look like the good guys, which is PR we can use."

"But—"

"Nope, just accept that it's done. Things are happening here and I'll fill you in soon. In the meantime, I promise you I'll enjoy watching them swallow this horse pill." Laughing, Holt hung up.

SOUTHERN RANGER STATION,
SHENANDOAH NATIONAL PARK, VA

Between Sam's kidnapping, the video, and her conversation with Subject 037, Sayer was reeling as she made her way back up to the station.

Max, Kyle, Dana, and Ezra were waiting in the conference room with expectant, maybe slightly frightened looks on their faces.

"All right . . . let's get back to work," Sayer said as calmly as possible.

"We're just going to pretend that video didn't happen?" Dana asked.

"Nope, we're going to ignore it because we have much more important things to worry about."

"Fair point." Max cleared his throat. "I finally tracked down Cricket's old boyfriend somewhere up in Vermont. I just left a message, so hopefully he'll call me back soon. I've also put in a few calls to some old-timers around the region but nothing on an old mine yet."

Ezra's fingers flew over his keyboard. "Nothing on the pit here either. I've got a few uniforms heading to the archives to see what they can find on old mines in the region."

Max's phone buzzed, interrupting Sayer's next comment.

"Oh, it's the high school boyfriend calling me back." Max hurried out into the hall to talk to him. Sayer watched him leave, hoping that something would break soon that would give them a lead, because right now they were dead in the water and a little girl was out there in the hands of a monster.

"Dark Hollow!" Max held up his phone as he returned a few minutes later.

Sayer felt a thrill of excitement at Max's expression. "Dark Hollow?"

"Her boyfriend said she used to take him to some abandoned ranch, a place she called Dark Hollow House. But he couldn't remember where it was and I've never heard of it. Kyle?"

Kyle shook his head. Ezra was already typing, "Here it is! Dark Hollow. It's small, only a few miles from here. This could be it!"

Sayer took a long breath to clear the buzz of the hunt making her heart pound. "All right! Ezra, get a helicopter up to see if they can spot anything."

"If it's in a hollow, it'll be next to impossible to find a house from the air," Kyle said, eyes shining with excitement.

"And I probably can't find it on satellite imagery either," Ezra said.

"Can't hurt to try," Sayer said. "Max, if we've got a general vicinity to start, could Kona sniff them out?"

Max gave Kona a pat. "No promises—like I said, rain really messes up scenting. But it hasn't rained for a bit, and if anyone can do it, Kona can."

"Do we all agree this is our best lead?" Sayer looked at her team. They nodded, eyes aflame.

"All right, Ezra, notify the locals, see if they can track down any more info on this Dark Hollow House. Maybe they can get us coordinates. In the meantime, Max, vest up."

"No way I'm staying behind," Kyle said. "You're shorthanded. And maybe I can talk her down, make sure that girl gets out of this alive."

Sayer stared at the police chief and saw calm determination. Hoping she didn't regret the decision, she nodded sharply. "All right. Let's grab Kona and see if we can catch Cricket before she hurts Sam."

DARK HOLLOW,
SHENANDOAH NATIONAL PARK, VA

Sayer, Kyle, Max, and Kona made it to the entrance of Dark Hollow.

Despite her thick FBI parka and bulletproof vest, Sayer shivered in the cool air.

"You ready to get to work, girl?" Max asked as he pulled a reflective dog vest from his backpack.

At the sight of the vest, Kona danced with excitement, ears forward, tail straight.

"She knows it's time to work." Max smiled at her.

"Don't we need something that belonged to Sam or Cricket for her to smell?" Kyle asked.

"Nah," Max said. "I'm sending her on a general find. She's just looking for human presence, unless you think there's something else out here?" He swept his arm toward the woods.

Days of heavy wind and rain had stripped the trees bare. A thick mat of dead leaves carpeted the ground, already slick and rotting. Even the animals had sought shelter and the forest felt quiet, devoid of life.

"So, how does this work?" Kyle asked. "Won't she alert Cricket that we're approaching?"

"No way. I'm telling her to give a silent alert." Max tightened the vest over Kona's back and gave her a vigorous rub, clearly getting her even more excited. "Kona's an air-scenter, which is difficult in the rain . . . but she'll let me know the second she smells someone out there. She'll make sure I keep up with her, so you all just need to keep up with me."

"Won't we confuse her?" Kyle said, clearly not optimistic about Kona's chances.

Max looked at Kyle, slightly annoyed. "She already knows what we smell like. Kona knows she's looking for someone new." He stood and rolled his shoulders, psyching himself up as well. "Once she alerts, I'll have her follow the scent cone until she's almost there, then I'll pull her back with me."

Sayer and Kyle nodded.

They all clicked on their headlamps, piercing the deep blue night.

After stretching his arms, Max crouched down in front of Kona and gently held her face. He looked into her eyes and said, "All right, Kona, there's someone out there. You ready to find them?" His voice rose with excitement and Kona quivered.

Max stood and flung his arm outward, "Kona, go find!"

The black dog shot off so fast Sayer was sure they would lose her in seconds. But Kona ranged in a wide arc, sweeping back and forth, glancing back to make sure Max was with her.

Max moved forward with strong strides and Kona took his cue, staying just ahead of him. It was clear that man and dog were both in their element.

Sayer and Kyle scrambled to follow.

Heavy mist blurred Sayer's vision as they moved irrevocably forward at a steady pace. Kona and Max worked together like two parts of a machine connected by an unseen wire.

They walked for over a mile. In the moonless forest, the eerie light from their headlamps danced along the ground in front of them, collapsing their visibility. As the wind whipped the bare trees, Sayer had the momentary sensation that they were alive, stark branches waving like bony fingers above towering bodies. She imagined those poor victims being led through this horrifying place to be murdered.

Sayer shook her head, realizing that she was overtired. After another half mile she started thinking about heading back to the station. They needed to stay sharp, and hours marching through the mountains would wear them down quickly. Two more miles and she would call it.

But then Kona let out a soft *chuff* and she sat.

Max held up his hand. "Okay, she smells someone. I'm going to let her give us a direction, then we should go the rest of the way together."

Sayer nodded and Max made a flat-palmed gesture before he flung his hand out again.

"What's that?" Kyle asked.

"I told her to be quiet," Max said softly over his shoulder as they once again moved forward.

Kona began to sweep back and forth in smaller arcs and she let out another soft *chuff.*

"What a good girl!" Max whispered. He took a moment to give Kona a big scratch and lots of praise. Sayer would've sworn the dog was grinning ear to ear.

"Kona, to me."

She moved to his side, ready for action.

Max refocused on Sayer and Kyle. "The scent is coming from there." He pointed down a nearby creek. "The scent is pooling up along the ravine. The house must be down that hill somewhere."

"All right," Sayer whispered. "Max, you circle around to the right. I'll swing left. Kyle, you hang slightly behind us and head straight down. Cricket clearly knows this area well, so be ready for anything."

They all drew their weapons.

Sayer waved them forward and they moved off like ghosts.

In less than a hundred yards, a rambling ranch house came into view. Though old, it looked sturdy. The boards covering the windows were in good shape, clearly recent additions. A perfect place to hide out.

She made eye contact with Max and he gave her a sharp nod. The approach felt almost like a dance, three humans and a dog moving in perfect concert, eyes scanning, bodies taut with anticipation. The hunt honed their attention like a weapon.

Sayer crouched so low her thighs burned with the effort as they began to converge on the house. Her breath became shallow, eyes riveted on the front door. She and Max went wide, approaching from the sides.

Kyle moved low and fast, making a beeline forward. He got way out ahead of them and Sayer worried that he was too far beyond their cover.

As she prepared to hiss for him to stop, a shot exploded from one of the windows. Kyle dove to the ground as a second bullet hit the wet leaves at his feet.

Before Sayer could react, the ranch house door slammed open. In the darkness, a large woman flew across the front porch, animal sounds on her lips. Her wavy black hair formed a tangled halo around her face that knotted into a snarl.

Sayer struggled to understand why the UVA psychologist was here. Could Alice Beaumont be Cricket Nelson?

That thought vanished when a gun glinted in the woman's hands. Alice Beaumont aimed at Kyle.

Kyle tried to get his weapon up in time, but her third gunshot echoed through the trees and he curled into a ball.

Sayer swung her Glock upward.

Her training kicked in. In the same millisecond, Sayer's finger slid to the trigger, her left hand came up to cup the base of her pistol, and she squared her shoulders and sighted on Beaumont.

Keening like a feral cat, Alice Beaumont ran at Kyle. Her wild face was spotlit by his headlamp as he watched her come. She aimed her gun again as she neared Kyle, who scrambled to lift his own pistol.

Sayer heard herself shout, "Freeze!" as Beaumont's finger moved to the trigger. Only a few feet from Kyle, the woman would not miss this time.

Sayer pulled smoothly.

Bang! Bang!

Another shot went off just before hers.

Beaumont crashed to the ground, gun skittering away.

Kyle lay on his back, wide-eyed, unmoving.

Max and Kona sprinted up. Max held his gun on Beaumont as he knelt down to secure the injured woman. Blood spread across her chest, burbling from the gunshot wound. Her eyes fluttering, breath ragged.

"She's still alive," he said, his own breath quick with adrenaline.

Sayer hurried over to check on Kyle. "You okay?"

He stood slowly, brushed wet leaves off himself, and then stared over at the woman on the ground, eyes burning. "Yeah . . . I'm fine. Is she . . . ?"

Max looked up and shook his head. "It's a thoracic injury. Not good."

"Let Max take care of her. Max," Sayer barked, "you secure Beaumont. Keep her alive if you can. Kyle, you sure you're okay?"

Kyle felt the bandage still wrapped around his head. "Yeah, that was close. But not a scratch." He let out a bizarre half-hiccuping laugh.

Sayer had seen it before, mania after a close call.

Kyle just stood unmoving, staring at Alice Beaumont. Sayer knew he was trying to figure out if she was his long-lost sister. Rather than ask him in the heat of the moment, Sayer wanted to let him calm down first.

"Glad you're okay," Sayer said. "Why don't you come with me to clear the house?"

He gave Beaumont another long, unreadable look, then nodded in agreement. They cautiously approached the abandoned house, guns up. Sayer kicked open the door. Her heart leaped to her throat at the sight of a small child curled into a ball on an old mattress.

They cleared the room quickly and both rushed to the girl.

"Sam, we're with the FBI. You're safe now," Sayer said.

"Mommy?" she asked, clearly confused.

"Don't worry, sweetheart." Kyle spoke softly as he crouched down and held out his arms. "Your parents are waiting for you. Let's get you out of here, okay? I'm a police officer and I can keep you safe."

Shaky, with scared-child eyes, Sam Valdez got up and folded herself into Kyle's arms.

Sayer nodded approvingly. "Why don't you get her to the hospital? I'll stay here with Max while we wait for an ambulance for Beaumont. We'll meet you there as soon as we can."

Kyle nodded, carefully standing up while still cradling the girl. He smiled at Sayer and hurried off toward the truck.

Sayer called Ezra to get an ambulance and evidence team on their way.

After hanging up, she took a long look around the room. Two sleeping bags. A camping stove and a crate of canned food. Gallon jugs of water lining the wall. Strange.

Shaking her head, she headed out to check on Max.

"What's the damage?"

Max glanced up from Beaumont's semiconscious body. "It actually looks better than I originally thought. Clean exit wound on her shoulder so it's a through-and-through to the chest. I've got her stable and the bleeding under control but we won't know how bad it is until they can take a look inside."

Beaumont moaned and tried to say something.

"She's already lost a lot of blood," Max said. "She's got to be Cricket Nelson, right?"

"No clue. Let's worry about that once we have everyone taken care of. I'll go direct the EMTs here from the road. Stay alert."

Sayer found a nearby service road and called in her coordinates. While she waited, she replayed everything that had just happened.

Why the hell was Alice Beaumont here? There was only one possible explanation Sayer could come up with. Max was right. Alice Beaumont had to be Cricket Nelson.

Sayer just couldn't quite wrap her mind around the idea of Beaumont as Cricket, but it did have some logic. Beaumont had inserted herself into the investigation, offering to profile for them. Not unusual for a serial killer. She had also insisted in her profile that the UNSUB was a lone male, maybe to throw them off?

She pictured the woman that they'd met at UVA. Dr. Alice Beaumont had seemed so confident, professional. Her transformation from that to a seemingly feral killer rattled Sayer. Because there was no doubt she meant to kill Kyle just now.

"I should know better," she muttered to herself. What would it take for her to finally learn that psychopaths could fool even her as they shed personas like a snake shedding skin?

Maybe Subject 037 and Holt had been right when they told her to trust no one.

But something felt off.

She turned everything over in her mind.

Beaumont's wild attack on Kyle, even though she had to know there was backup nearby. That didn't fit with the cold, calculating killer who had kidnapped and held multiple women. Her attack here felt disorganized, off-kilter even. And the stuff in the house. A camping stove? Sleeping bags? Where was the pit?

"We're missing something," she said out loud.

Once the EMTs arrived and took over for Max, Sayer asked him to follow her inside the house.

"Take a minute and tell me what you see," she said.

Max turned slowly in a circle. The musty house was spartan but dry. The beams of their headlamps created streaks of light in the dust across the floor. Other than the mattress and supplies, the place was empty.

"Well, I don't see an entrance to the pit." Max wiped raindrops from his face, leaving a thin streak of Beaumont's blood across his cheek.

"Right, but what do you see?"

"A mattress. Camping supplies."

"And what does this feel like to you?"

"Remote location. Supplies. It feels like someone going to ground."

"Like a place to hide out for a while. And if it's not here, where is the pit?" Sayer asked.

"Maybe it's nearby?"

"Okay, but then why bring Sam here to hide out instead of going straight to the pit?"

"Yeah, I see what you mean. Though I can come up with a couple of pretty horrific reasons she would bring the girl here alone."

"Sure, but there's no evidence of any sexual assault on any of our victims." Sayer pulled out her phone. "I think we need to talk to that girl. I'll ride to the hospital in the ambulance with Beaumont. You stay and get the evidence team started, then I want you to run an area search. See if the entrance to the pit is nearby. Ezra is sending a Rockfish Gap uniform this way to help. Call me once everything's in motion here."

UNIVERSITY HOSPITAL, CHARLOTTESVILLE, VA

Sayer made sure they had an officer watching Alice Beaumont as the doctors wheeled her away to surgery, then she hurried to the hospital's front desk.

"FBI Agent Altair." She flashed her badge. "I'm looking for Sam Valdez."

The nurse looked up over thick reading glasses. "Who's that, now?"

"Samantha Valdez. Small girl, two years old, should've just come in not too long ago with a Rockfish Gap policeman. . . ."

"I'm sorry, we've got a Hannah Valdez here, but no one named Sam Valdez has been admitted. Maybe go down to emergency triage?"

An unsettling hum of fear tickled Sayer's spine as she hurried down to the ER.

"Nope, no kids've come in here in the past few hours. You sure they came to this hospital?" The triage nurse seemed vaguely annoyed, unwilling to even glance up from her computer screen.

"Would you call around and see if she's checked in somewhere else?" Sayer asked.

The triage nurse finally looked up. "Oh, hey, you're that agent from the news! I'm happy to call around. Give me one minute."

Sayer sighed at her reaction, assuming that was about to happen a hell of a lot more often.

While the nurse called around, Sayer paced the waiting room. She tried calling Kyle's cell phone but got no answer.

Was Kyle in an accident on the way down the mountain? But they would've seen him on their way down. What if Beaumont really did have a partner and he had gotten to Kyle and Sam?

The longer she waited, the more sure she was that something was seriously wrong.

She dialed Ezra. "Ez, Kyle Nelson hasn't shown up at the ER with Sam Valdez."

"What? Where are they?"

"Not here." The nurse waved Sayer over. "Hang on." She went to the triage desk.

"There's no Sam Valdez at any of the area hospitals. No two-year-old girls admitted recently at all."

"Thanks." Sayer got back on the phone. "You hear that, Ezra?"

"I did. So where did they go? Hang on, let me patch in to the local dispatch and see if there were any reported accidents in the last hour."

Sayer listened to computer keys clacking away.

"Nope, nothing reported. I'll send a few cruisers up from Charlottesville to check any possible routes just in case."

"All right, Ezra, thanks." She clicked off and called Max at Dark Hollow to fill him in.

"Want me to come down to the hospital?" Max asked. "I've got the evidence-recovery team and area search all set up here."

"No, I'm going to check in with Beaumont's doctor and then I'll meet you up at the ranger station."

"All right, Sayer. You have any clue what's going on? You think maybe Beaumont has a partner that got to them?"

"I don't know, but we're sure going to find out." Sayer hung up and went to find Beaumont's doctor. After a quick update, she paused at the hospital exit. The rain had picked back up and she was about to be, yet again, soaked to the bone. Ignoring the cold water trickling in around the edges of her hood, she ran across the parking lot to the cruiser waiting to take her up to the ranger station.

This was the second damn time she'd lost Sam Valdez in a single day. This whole case was really starting to piss her off.

SOUTHERN RANGER STATION, SHENANDOAH NATIONAL PARK, VA

Max, Ezra, and Dana all looked slightly pale when Sayer stomped into the conference room.

"Still no word on Kyle and Sam?" she asked.

"Not a peep," Ezra said. "Locals are canvassing the area."

"I left the evidence team and a Rockfish Gap officer poking around up in Dark Hollow," Max said. "Nothing so far. What's the word on Beaumont's injuries?"

"You were right, a single through-and-through that nicked her lung but missed everything vital." Sayer sat down and rubbed her temples. "Whatever magic you did out there saved her life. She's in surgery now and looks like she'll survive."

"Did they say when she might be conscious enough to talk to us? 'Cause I'd like to ask her a few questions," Max said darkly.

"Hard to tell. Once they have her stable she might be able to talk. They'll call if there's any change." Sayer let out a long breath. "So, let's tackle the obvious question first. Is Alice Beaumont Cricket Nelson? Max, you're the only one that knew her here. What do you think? Could Beaumont be Cricket?"

"I don't know. Maybe? I mean, I sat in her office not ten feet from her while she gave us her profile. How could I not recognize her?"

"Well, Beaumont did just try to kill Kyle right in front of us. And we think Cricket Nelson is our UNSUB, so . . . unless Cricket Nelson and Alice Beaumont are working together . . ."

Max closed his eyes. "Cricket was kind of twiggy and had blond hair. But she was tall just like Alice Beaumont. Add fifty pounds and black hair dye . . . yeah, she could be."

"People can change a lot in seventeen years," Sayer said.

"And I missed it. . . ." Max rubbed the stubble just starting to show on his chin.

"Oh, I know how to find out. Give me half a second. . . ." Ezra began typing away. "Ta-da!" He pointed to his computer. "I ran Beaumont and Cricket through our facial comparison program and I can definitively say that, yes, Alice Beaumont and Cricket Nelson are in fact the same person."

Sayer walked over to Ezra's computer, which showed the old photo of Cricket from her missing persons file in a side-by-side comparison to Alice Beaumont's official UVA photograph.

"See how the proportions are exactly the same? With black hair and some extra weight, she looks really different, but there's no doubt about it."

"So we finally know where Cricket went all those years ago," Sayer said.

"She must've fabricated a new identity and gone off to college under her new name. Sorry I missed it, Sayer." Ezra looked like he might tear up.

"What? Don't beat yourself up, Ez. We all miss stuff sometimes. Hell, I let Beaumont grab Sam Valdez right in front of me, and Max didn't even realize he was sitting in the same room as Cricket Nelson."

"Uh, thanks," Max said.

"What I mean is, we need to focus on what's next. Now that we know our psychology professor is in fact Cricket, the second big question is, where the hell are Kyle and Sam?"

"Could Cricket have a partner?" Max asked. "Maybe her partner grabbed them on the way down the mountain? Hannah did think it was a man while she was down in the pit."

"What about Kyle? Is it possible he was working with his sister all along?" Dana asked.

"I don't think so. Kyle did get shot in the head," Sayer said.

"Yeah, true," Max said. "If that was a diversion, well, you don't try to throw off suspicion by shooting your partner in the head. That shot could've easily shattered his skull. Anyway, I saw the look on her face up there in Dark Hollow. She sure as hell meant to kill Kyle."

"Uhhh, Sayer," Ezra said. "As much as I hate to say it out loud, I haven't heard from Piper in a while."

"Kyle said she was called away to deal with some campsite evacuation up north." Even as Sayer said the words, her stomach dropped. "There was no flooding, was there?"

"Hang on, I can access the park rangers' assignments. If she was called out for something, it'll be in here." He quickly read, and then gave Sayer an apologetic look. "There's some flooding reported in the park, but no campsite needing evacuation. . . . I haven't heard a peep from her since your birthday party."

"Jesus," Max muttered. "Piper? Really?"

Sayer leaned back in her chair, staring at the ceiling and letting the possibility of Piper as Cricket's partner sink in. She pictured the hulking ranger rushing to the bone cave right after someone tried to set them on fire. Her coming in with donuts right after Ezra and Dana were attacked in the night.

"All right." She sat back up. "Let's not jump to any conclusions, but I think we need to accept the possibility that Piper is working with Cricket. Why else would she lie about the flooding?"

Ezra, Max, and Dana looked at each other.

"But she's so . . . I mean . . . Piper likes plants," Ezra finally said.

Sayer rubbed her left shoulder. Steel bands crept from her scar along her back and neck. Anger tipped from fiery into pure fatigue and she couldn't even muster disbelief at the idea that the rumpled park ranger was partnered with a serial killer. "True, but we all know that serial killers are good at hiding who they are. Something has obviously happened to Kyle and Sam. If it's not a partner, what else could have happened? Ezra, dig into Piper's past. See if there's anything to suggest she's involved."

"Already on it," Ezra said.

Sayer leaned forward and put her forehead on the table. It was almost midnight and they had been going since four that morning. Maybe it was time for them to take a break. Try to get some sleep.

Before she could continue the thought, Sayer's phone buzzed. She read the incoming text.

"It's local 911 dispatch. I guess word's gotten around Rockfish Gap that Kyle is missing. A neighbor just called saying that they saw someone enter his house not too long ago. Let's go check it out. Ezra, while we head down to Kyle Nelson's house, you dig into Piper. See if she owns land near the park, I don't know. Anything that can lead us to her. Dana, you keep trying to ID the rest of the skeletons. Maybe their ID will help us somehow." Sayer rubbed her eyes, which were burning with exhaustion. "All I care about right now is finding that little girl. Let's make it happen."

ROAD TO THE NELSON HOUSE, ROCKFISH GAP, VA

While Max drove them toward Kyle's house, Sayer called every law enforcement department in a fifty-mile radius to fill them in on Piper's potential involvement.

She hung up and scowled out at the incessant rain.

"Who would be at the Nelson place?" Max asked.

"No clue. Maybe Piper wasn't sure where else to go and took Kyle and Sam there after she kidnapped them? We do have this whole side of the mountains crawling with law enforcement. I've got a few uniforms from the Albemarle County Sheriff's Department meeting us there just in case. That's the county sheriff, so they don't have any connection to the Nelsons or Piper. Until I know what the hell is going on here, I don't want any locals involved. I've also got an evidence team on their way from Quantico. If Piper was here, they need to scour this house top to bottom."

Max stared straight ahead, jaw clenched. "They scrambled a team in the middle of the night? I thought we were short-staffed right now."

"I can be persuasive when I want," Sayer growled.

Much to her surprise, Kona nosed Sayer in response to her growling in a gesture of support.

"You bringing Kona in with us?" Sayer asked.

"Nah, closed spaces like that mean she can't really follow scent. Whoever is in there, no way I want to risk her getting caught in the crossfire. She can stay in the car."

When they pulled up, five Albemarle Sheriff's Department officers were already waiting outside a squat house, hunched against the drizzle. Low clouds hung in the sky above them.

Sayer gathered everyone without ceremony. "Two of you go around back. You three"—she pointed to three sheriff's officers—"enter with us from the front to clear the house. We're going in hot. We have no clue who is here, but remember that there's the possibility of hostages. If you see any sign of anyone, back the hell out and get me."

Sayer stared up at the dark house. Despite the carved wooden sign that read HOME SWEET HOME in the front window, Sayer had the unshakable feeling that this place was off somehow.

"So, Kyle lives at his parents' old house?" She spoke quietly.

"Uh-hmm." Max unsnapped his holster. "He moved to an apartment down in Charlottesville while he went to UVA, but when he joined the police force here he moved back in with his dad."

Sayer waved the two officers around the back of the house. She took a deep breath, trying to calm the murderous rage burning at her core. She needed to find Sam Valdez and she said a silent prayer to no one in particular that the girl would be here. With one more calming breath, she drew her gun and gave Max a sharp nod.

He nodded back.

Max surged forward onto the porch, kicking the door just below the lock.

The wood splintered and he shoved the door inward and backed away. Sayer led everyone in like a pack of wolves on the hunt. They swarmed together, low and smooth, guns at the ready.

"Clear down!" Max shouted, loud enough for everyone to hear.

They climbed the stairs and broke off into each room.

Sayer felt slight disappointment at the chorus of *clears* from the sheriff's deputies. She hadn't really expected Kyle and Sam to be here, but she'd still held a flicker of hope that they could find Sam to just end this all now.

She entered the master bedroom and swept her gun in a circuit. She pulled open the closet. Pulled aside the shower curtain.

"Clear upstairs!" she shouted.

The alert status shifted down a notch and Sayer let herself take a real look at the house.

Orange shag carpet. Avocado-green counters in the master bath. Small fiberglass shower with a thin ring of black mildew around the drain.

"Place hasn't been touched in decades," Max said as he entered the master bedroom.

"No joke. It looks like all of Mr. Nelson's stuff is still in here. I guess Kyle stayed in his old room?"

Sayer peeked into what she assumed was Kyle's bedroom.

"My god, look at this." She pulled on gloves and then picked up an old baseball mitt off the small dresser. "It looks like he hasn't changed his room either. That's a little weird."

She took in the wall of drawings over the twin bed. The pencil sketches all featured strangely contorted animals stitched together like Frankenstein's monster. Max had been right, Kyle was quite the artist.

"These're kind of creepy."

"Yeah, those are the mash-ups I mentioned. The kids at school loved them."

Sayer's eye caught on a stack of letters. She carefully unfolded one and read it out loud.

"*Dear Mom, I still miss you so much. I wish I could talk to you about what's happening here. Classes are going well this semester though I wish I'd taken biology. . . .*" She looked at the date. "He wrote letters to his dead mother . . . while he was in college."

"Yikes, that's pretty sad." Max rifled through the drawers. He held up a soldering iron and a tangle of wires. "Nothing here but regular kid stuff. I'll grab Kona to do a sweep around the house," he said, then headed back downstairs.

As the adrenaline of their entry wore off a bit, a musty, rotting smell permeated Sayer's senses. Despite the trappings of a cozy family home, a deep current of unease ran beneath the surface of this house.

She made a small circuit of the upstairs, rifling through all the typical hiding places.

OUTSIDE THE NELSON HOUSE, ROCKFISH GAP, VA

While Sayer looked around upstairs, Max headed out to the truck to grab Kona. Might as well let her do a sweep, see if she alerted on anything.

At the sight of Max approaching the truck, Kona's tail thumped loudly on the seat, sending up a cloud of dust.

"Hey, girl, you ready to do a quick search?" Her ears came forward, tail thumping more quickly.

Max would swear her mouth fell open in a canine smile every time she was on duty.

He pulled on her work harness and led her to the porch. The front door hung open and the sheriff's deputies milled around inside, checking for evidence of recent activity.

Without giving her a direction, Max said, "Go find, Kona!" letting her decide where to start.

The dog raised her head, nose working the air. She looked sharply left and let out a low *woof*, jumping off the porch. Max followed her as she made a beeline around the side of the house toward a small wooden shed out back.

A deputy had cleared the shed, but Max put his hand on his gun as they approached the squat building.

Kona let out another sharp alert and Max unsnapped his holster again as he gently swung open the old door. He couldn't tell if she was giving her cadaver alert or her live alert.

The hinges swung smoothly open and Kona charged forward, tail straight out behind her. She vanished into the darkness of the shed while Kyle fumbled for a light switch.

He finally found one and the florescent lights flickered to life. Kona nosed along the base of the back wall. The small space was cramped with old wooden shelving and a sawdust-covered worktable piled high with power tools. A reciprocating saw. Piles of scrap metal. Soldering iron. Reels of electrical wiring.

Max turned his attention to the back wall. An old metal shelving unit sat mostly empty, covered with a thin layer of dust.

"What do you smell, Kona?"

He crouched down, shining his flashlight along the base of the wall behind the shelving unit.

A thick crack ran along the edge.

Heart pounding, Max stood and pulled aside the shelving unit.

"My god," he muttered to himself.

SOUTHERN RANGER STATION, SHENANDOAH NATIONAL PARK, VA

Ezra sat at his computer trying to decide which file to open first. Quantico had just sent him the text fragments they were able to pull from the Ekhidna journal Dana's team had found in the cave. But he also had all the files he had gathered about Alice Beaumont née Cricket Nelson.

"What's our first priority? Finding Sam," he said to himself. "So focus on Beaumont first."

He began poring over Alice Beaumont's history. With every file he opened, he felt slightly more sick to his stomach. Now that he knew Beaumont was Cricket Nelson, Beaumont's childhood history looked flimsy as hell.

How had he missed the red flags? What if he really wasn't ready to be back at work? What if he would never be able to do his job well again?

Shaking off that thought, he pulled up the records that the university had sent over. He asked UVA for everything they had on Beaumont and he was sure as hell not going to miss anything this time. He clicked on the link to her calendar, where he could look at everything she had planned over the past few months. Ezra scanned her schedule until he came to the last entry.

He stared at the time and date, mouth dry.

"This can't be right."

"Any word?" Dana's voice behind him made Ezra jump. "Whoa, sorry to startle you. Is everyone okay?"

Ezra let out a short breath. "Yeah. No sign of Piper or anyone down at the Nelson house. They're looking around a bit before they head back."

"Glad everyone is safe." Dana sat down next to Ezra. "So why do you look like someone just pissed in your cornflakes?"

"I just can't believe I missed Beaumont's fake background. I mean, that's my damn job. If I'd seen that she was really Cricket, maybe Sam would be home safe right now."

"Hey." Dana put her hand on Ezra's shoulder. "You can't take on that kind of thing. We're all doing our best here, and none of us are perfect."

"What if I'm not able to do my job anymore?" Ezra's voice cracked. He gestured at his legs.

"If I'm not mistaken, your work was pivotal in solving the last case you and Sayer worked together."

"Yeah, but . . . I don't know." Ezra pointed to his computer. "I've just found a discrepancy in Beaumont's schedule. I can't tell if I'm losing it, because this doesn't make any sense."

"Let me take a look."

"Last entry," Ezra said. "See the time?"

Dana read with wide eyes. "Well, shit. There's got to be a logical explanation for this. Let's figure it out together."

UPSTAIRS, THE NELSON HOUSE, ROCKFISH GAP, VA

Sayer saved Cricket's childhood room for last in her inspection of the Nelson house. Rainbow sheets. Wall of posters from pop stars Sayer vaguely remembered. Coldplay. Gorillaz. Death Cab for Cutie. But no trophies or photos of Cricket with her friends. It felt almost like a staged version of a normal teenager's room.

She stood in the middle, trying to reconcile everything here with what she knew about Cricket Nelson the kidnapper and killer. How had this seemingly normal young woman turned into a murderer?

Sayer's phone buzzed with a text from Adi. She read the text, unable to ignore the fact that she was surrounded by the detritus of Cricket Nelson's when she was the same age as Adi.

Made it home.

Hannah was sleeping when we left. Think she'll be okay but hope you find Sam.

Didn't find much more on Ekhidna. Mother of all monsters. Ekhidna's kids: Cerberus, the Hydra, the Sphinx, Chimera, the Gorgon, Scylla, and some others I've never heard of.

Still not sure what the second word Hannah saw was. Mirage is my best guess.

That's it so far. Will keep digging. Xoxo.

A faint smile flickered on Sayer's lips.

"Uh, Sayer," Max called up. "We've got something out back."

The tone of Max's voice swept away the smile. Sayer hurried outside to the shed, where she found Max crouching in front of an open half door set into the back wall. "Look what Kona found. It was hidden behind these shelves. Doesn't look like anyone has gone in here in years. I would've never even noticed it if Kona hadn't alerted."

"See anything inside?"

"Yeah, there's stairs down. . . ."

Sayer sighed. After her last case, she hated subterranean spaces with a burning passion.

"I'll check it out." She pulled her gun and flashlight from her belt and practically crawled through the door to cautiously make her way down the narrow stairs. They went on much longer than she expected, finally dumping her into a small room. Bare concrete floor and tall cinder-block walls made the space feel like an oubliette, one of the old medieval pit dungeons only accessible from a hole at the top.

"It's clear. Come on down," she called up to Max as she holstered her gun.

While he climbed carefully down, Sayer turned slowly. The flashlight danced along the raw cinder blocks until she came to a plywood door covered with peeling blue paint.

"Well, this has a lovely little torture-chamber vibe, doesn't it?" Max said lightly, but Sayer could hear the disgust in his voice.

"Check it out." She played the flashlight over a small desk in the corner. The wall above the desk was cluttered with photos and index cards taped to a large map. Then she focused the beam on the blue door.

A window at the top might have allowed someone to peek through to whatever was on the other side, but it was covered with grime.

She raised her chin toward the door for Max to approach first. He swung it open as Sayer stepped forward.

They both stopped short, instinctively not wanting to enter the horrifying room revealed by Sayer's flashlight. Scratches marred the walls of the small chamber. A rumpled straitjacket lay in one corner. A rusted chain was bolted to the wall. At the end, an ankle shackle lay open on the damp floor above a small drain.

Steeling herself, Sayer entered the room, hunching over to make sure her hair didn't touch the low ceiling. She crouched next to the rotting straitjacket to get a better look.

"This straitjacket's just like the ones we found in the bone cave."

"Uh-hmm," Max said, throat tight.

Sayer and Max both knew exactly what that shackle and straitjacket meant. This was no innocent storage space. A human being had once been held here.

They spoke in hushed tones, out of reverence for the people who had suffered in this room. Sayer did one more sweep of the small dungeon before retreating back out to the main chamber.

She straightened up, grateful to be out of the cramped space. She reluctantly approached the desk in the corner and shone her flashlight on the fading map. "This is a map of the entire Appalachian Trail."

Six blurry photos of hikers were pinned up around the old map. They were candids, the subjects clearly unaware that they were being photographed. A young woman with dreadlocks and tattered hiking gear. A middle-aged man decked out in a fancy jacket and expensive backpack. An elderly man with steel-gray hair and mirrored sunglasses. Beneath each photo, a small index card had a name and date.

"Six pictures . . . all hikers, it looks like," Sayer said.

"You think these are our skeletons?" Max leaned in get a better look. "Lucinda Washington, December fourteenth, 1997."

"Timothy O'Doyle, July ninth, 2000," Sayer read another, and then looked at the map. Colored pins marked locations along the Appalachian Trail as far north as Pennsylvania and all the way south to Georgia. "I

bet we'll be able to match our six skeletons to hikers that went missing along the trail. Look how widely distributed they are. No wonder no one connected them."

Max looked around the chamber. "How could Kyle not know about this? I mean, I guess the entrance was pretty well hidden, but still."

Sayer didn't answer, processing everything.

"I have no idea, but let's get the evidence team down here." Sayer took a few photos of the map with her phone and was ready to get the hell out.

Back up the stairs, rain fell in a steady rhythm on the roof of the shed. Sayer gratefully stepped out into the cold downpour, letting it wash away the fetor of death.

SOUTHERN RANGER STATION, SHENANDOAH NATIONAL PARK, VA

Back in the conference room, Sayer stood at the head of the table, mind spinning in high gear.

Max paced next to the table, clearly too riled up to sit. Unlike Sayer's broad-ranging pace, Max walked in a tight arc around Kona, who sat watching him closely. "There's no way a twelve-year-old girl built that dungeon beneath the shed."

Like Kona, Dana and Ezra watched Max pace.

"Uh, Sayer," Ezra said tentatively. "I don't mean to add to the confusion, but I think there might be a problem with our DNA results."

Sayer felt slightly sick at the look on Ezra's face. What else could possibly go wrong on this case?

"As in a we-fucked-up-somehow problem?" she asked.

"Maybe."

Sayer closed her eyes. A DNA mistake from the Quantico lab right now could cost dozens of agents their jobs. "What did we get wrong?"

"Not so much wrong as impossible," Ezra said.

"Explain, please," Sayer said curtly.

Ezra handed her a sheet of paper. "I got Beaumont's schedule from the university. Turns out that she volunteers regularly at the Children's Hospital down at UVA"

"Okay. . . ." Sayer glanced down at the list of dates and times. "These are in the middle of the night."

"Yeah, apparently she volunteered to sit with kids in recovery at the cancer ward. You know, the parents get exhausted after a few days of around-the-clock with a kid after a major surgery. But they want someone there full-time. Nurses can't just sit with one patient, so Beaumont would take over and basically just be there for the kid in case the kid needs anything or gets scared."

"That doesn't exactly sound like the kind of thing a serial killer would do," Max said.

"No kidding. But it does jibe with the fact that she offered to be a bone marrow donor. What matters here, check out her last visit." Ezra tapped the page in Sayer's hand.

She read to the bottom. "Two to five A.M. . . . wait, that's . . ."

"Yeah. . . ." Ezra trailed off.

"That's the same time she was here attacking you and Dana," Sayer continued. "We know she was here because we got her DNA from underneath your fingernails." She looked over at Ezra. "That was, what, four or four-thirty in the morning?"

"Yeah, something like that."

"Okay." Sayer shrugged. "So this schedule is just wrong. Maybe she just didn't go in this morning?" She looked at Ezra and Dana, who both had their mouths pressed into white lines.

Sayer's stomach flip-flopped. "Only it isn't wrong, is it?"

"I called the head nurse on duty. She brought Alice Beaumont a coffee around four and they spoke for over twenty minutes. There's no way she could've made it up here, tasered the park ranger, tasered Dana, and attacked me by four-thirty."

Sayer reached for the table to lean against, exhaustion and confusion knocking her off-kilter. "But we know for sure that Beaumont is Cricket, and we got Cricket's DNA off a sample that you scraped off her as she attacked you. Literally her blood and skin."

"We're sure it's real blood?" Max asked.

"Yes, dammit. They double-check that now," Sayer said.

"So, maybe someone planted her blood to frame her?" Max offered.

"How? There's no way they could've counted on planting blood under Ezra's nails. If you want to frame Beaumont, why not plant it somewhere less risky? That just doesn't make sense. Hang on."

Sayer dialed the hospital. "I need someone to confirm signs of an existing injury on Alice Beaumont. She should have scratch marks along one of her lower legs."

The doctor put her on hold for a long moment before returning. "Sorry, Agent Altair, we're not seeing any leg scratches on Alice Beaumont."

Sayer hung up with a sick knot in her stomach.

They were missing something big. And Sam was still out there somewhere.

"Okay, time to brainstorm our way out of this. We know based on facial recognition that Alice Beaumont is Cricket Nelson. We know based on DNA evidence from Ezra's nails that Cricket Nelson was here this morning attacking Ezra. And now we have an eyewitness that places her somewhere else at the same time. How is it possible that her DNA was here, but she wasn't?" Sayer asked.

No one said anything.

"Fuck," Sayer said. "Any ideas?"

"No, but I also got a report from Quantico," Ezra said. "They were able to lift some stuff from the journal Dana's team found in the cave. I was so busy following up on the whole DNA thing I haven't had a chance to look that over yet. Maybe there's something there?"

"Fine, lets see what it says," Sayer snapped.

"Okay, let me see. Looks like most of the ink was too blurred, so they were only able to lift some snippets from the journal. The first fragment they found is just a date. *February 1987.*" Ezra looked up, calculating in his head. "That's when Kyle was born."

He looked back down at the snippets from the journal. "What the hell," he whispered as he began to read.

UNIVERSITY HOSPITAL,
CHARLOTTESVILLE, VA

Hannah Valdez sat wide awake in her hospital bed. Fear held her in its grip. All she could think of was Sam down in the pit. Was her daughter terrified? Was she crying out for her mommy and wondering why Mommy wasn't there?

The hospital was quiet except for soft voices and shuffling feet occasionally moving down the hallway past her room. Zoe had agreed to go home and get a few hours of sleep with Hannah's promise that she would do the same, but Hannah knew she would never be able to fall asleep.

She looked down at her wife's cell phone in her hand. Zoe had left it in case she wanted to play a silly game to take her mind off everything. But that was a ridiculous thought. How could she ignore the dread consuming her? Her daughter had been kidnapped by a monster.

Hannah jumped when the old-fashioned phone on her bedside table chirped with a brisk ring.

Something about the ringing made her heart skip a beat.

The phone chirped again.

Hannah lifted the receiver. "Hello?"

"Are you alone, Hannah?"

She recognized the voice from the pit.

"Yes," she hissed. "What have you done with Sam?"

She looked at the closed door. Two uniformed officers sat just outside. Should she get them?

"Don't even think about telling anyone I'm on the phone . . . or Sam will die. Do you understand?"

"Yes," Hannah managed to say softly despite her need to scream. "I understand."

"Good. You know that I keep my promises, correct?"

"I do."

"Very good. Then you have a choice. You can stay there, in which case I will kill Sam now. Or you can come back to the pit and finish what you started. If you come with me, there's at least a chance you can save her. . . ."

Tears pressed from her eyes as Hannah whispered, "What do you want me to do?"

SOUTHERN RANGER STATION,
SHENANDOAH NATIONAL PARK, VA

"Okay, here's the first journal entry." Ezra read aloud, "*There's something wrong with him but no one will tell me what it is. My body is buzzing with some strange power! Perhaps I should just storm the hospital and take Kyle home. . . .*"

"Didn't Kyle say that he was in and out of the hospital as an infant?" Max asked.

"He did. And if this journal was written by his mom, that would make Mrs. Nelson our Ekhidna," Sayer said. "Keep going, Ez."

"Yeah. Listen to this. *He's recovering* . . . some stuff too blurry to read . . . *they want to hurt him. . . . I'm his mother. I know what he needs. They are just jealous and want to keep his special power for themselves. If I have to kill to protect* . . . That's it for that entry." Ezra scrolled down.

"She thought Kyle had some kind of special power and that people were trying to hurt him?" Max asked. "That sounds pretty delusional to me."

"Maybe postpartum psychosis?" Dana asked. "I mean, paranoia, self-aggrandizing delusions . . ."

"Sure sounds like it could be. Keep going, Ezra."

"Okay, it skips way ahead to 1989. *I've figured out how to fool them. I can wear my maiden mask, convince everyone that I am nothing but a meek housewife. They can never know how powerful we are or they will come to kill us all.*"

"Holy shit," Max said. "So, she decided to pretend to be some kind of perfect housewife . . . which explains why my impression of her was PTA mom."

"Right," Sayer said. "Ekhidna was half serpent but also half fair maiden. So she was pretending to be exactly that."

"That entry is two years after Kyle was born. Could postpartum psychosis last that long?" Ezra asked.

Dana shrugged. "Not on its own, but, untreated, it could definitely trigger a larger psychotic episode. Especially in someone with a history of psychosis."

"Since she was murdered, I didn't seriously consider the idea that Mrs. Nelson could be our original killer. Ezra, do we have any background on her?"

"Give me a sec." His hands flew. "Uh, let me see . . . Abigail Nelson went to college at the University of Florida. Here we go! While there, she was temporarily remanded to a mental health facility for her own protection. I don't know what the details are, but she was released a week later and there's no other record of anything else. Oh! She was a classics major . . . with a focus on Greek mythology. And she spent a semester in Greece!"

"Which is why her psychotic delusions would've taken on the form of Ekhidna," Sayer said.

"And the trip to Greece is probably where she got the kopis," Dana added.

"So," Sayer said, "her son is sick and she is suffering from postpartum psychosis. She becomes convinced people are trying to hurt him and that it's her job to protect Kyle. Okay. . . ."

"Where is Mr. Nelson during all this?" Max asked.

"I imagine he had no idea how far off the rails she was. She even said she was wearing her maiden mask. Maybe she managed to fool Kyle and his dad along with everyone else. Or maybe, as long as she was putting up a good front, he didn't really care?"

Ezra let out a disgusted sound. "You think he let his poor wife spiral into psychosis rather than get her help?"

"Who knows?"

"Ugh, okay, the next entry has a date in 1996. The beginning of the sentence is illegible something . . . *has angered them and they are punishing us with this flood. If the people here realize that he's to blame, they will want to kill him. We are all in danger now. . . . Sacrifice to appease. . . .*"

"Hey, Max, remember how Piper mentioned a flood in '96?" Sayer asked.

"Yeah, the whole valley flooded."

"Sounds like that might have been the trigger for the first murder. She thought it was caused by angry gods or something and that she needed to make a sacrifice to appease them. . . . Keep going."

"Only two readable fragments left." Ezra continued to read, ". . . *mask is so effective, he suspected nothing when I asked for help back at my car. He saw me as nothing more than a middle-aged housewife with car trouble. The taser worked well to subdue him. I'll put him in the shed until he's weak with hunger. Getting him to the pit for the ritual should be easy.*"

Dana looked slightly sick. "That is horrific. But this sure sounds like confirmation that she was the original killer."

Sayer let out a grunt of agreement.

"Last entry." Ezra swallowed hard. "*How beautiful he was, bleating like a lamb as I bound him. He wriggled and bucked but was too weak to escape. The blade was so sharp it easily slid across his throat. The blood felt so warm I had to take a drink straight from his neck. So full of power. Cricket cried and fought the feeding, but I convinced her. . . .*" Ezra looked up at the team. "That's all the lab could get from the journal."

"Jesus Mother Mary," Max whispered.

"Wow," Ezra said. "She made Cricket watch her murder someone and then forced her to drink his blood?"

They all stared at the computer as though the words on the screen were leaking evil into the room.

Finally Max spoke up. "That's messed up and all, but knowing that Mrs. Nelson was the original killer doesn't help us explain how Cricket's DNA showed up here while she was at the hospital. Or what the hell Piper has to do with any of this. Or where Kyle and Sam are now."

Sayer closed her eyes. Max was right.

She let her thoughts unfurl, and an idea began to form along the edges of her mind. Just a faint glimmer of a thought, like an amorphous blob on the periphery of her consciousness.

"You all need to give me a minute to think." She began pacing, rubbing her thumb against her worry beads, unable to hold her body still. Thoughts buzzed along her limbs, up her neck, crackling inside her skull like an electric current.

Max opened his mouth to say something but stopped himself, giving Sayer some space to think.

Feeling penned in by the small conference room, she went out into the hall so she could take long fast strides all the way to the entry and back.

She thought about the nightmarish implications of the journal.

Subject 037 suggesting she apply her own research on successful psychopaths to everyone who inserted themselves into the investigation.

The DNA results placing Cricket in two places at once.

Cricket, all grown up, donating her blood to a bone marrow transplant list and volunteering at the Children's Hospital cancer ward.

Kyle horribly sick as an infant.

His mash-up drawings.

Mrs. Nelson convinced she was Ekhidna, mother of monsters.

The list of Ekhidna's children that Adi had just sent.

Adi translating the second word on the stone table as *mirage.*

As she paced, a dark certainty blossomed in Sayer's gut like a wraith.

UNIVERSITY HOSPITAL, CHARLOTTESVILLE, VA

Hannah Valdez stared down at the phone, unable to process everything.

Sneak out? Return to the pit?

Should she call Sayer?

But they had no idea where Sam even was. And doing that could get Sam killed.

She got up from the hospital bed with a groan. Her broken finger was set in a splint. Her shoulder was held against her body in a sling, her sliced palm wrapped with clean gauze.

Hannah could feel nonc of those injuries as she stood beside her bed. She was beyond simple pain.

She had no choice.

She quietly shoved pillows into a body shape and pulled the covers over the mound.

He'd said to make sure no one followed.

How to get past the two officers at her door?

Hannah walked over to the window. Second story. But she had seen a fire ladder stored in a cabinet in the bathroom.

Not giving herself time to think, she scrawled Zoe a quick note and then tucked the cell phone into the band of her underwear.

As quietly as she could, she slid open the window and lowered the clunky ladder.

With breath held, Hannah lowered herself down in the light rain.

SOUTHERN RANGER STATION, SHENANDOAH NATIONAL PARK, VA

Sayer made three more circuits pacing along the hallway before she strode back to the head of the table. Max, Ezra, and Dana waited with anxious expressions.

She looked back, heart pounding. "Chimera," she half whispered.

"What?" Ezra said.

"When Hannah was in the pit, she saw two words carved around the stone table there. One said Ekhidna. The second one Adi translated as mirage. But *mirage* can also be translated as chimera."

"Like the Greek monster with a lion head, goat body, and serpent tail?" Max asked.

"Exactly, though chimera can actually be used to describe any creature with parts from multiple animals."

Max leaned back in his chair, confusion on his face. "Just like Kyle's mash-up drawings as a kid. Those were all chimeras?"

"Exactly right. And that explains how Cricket's blood could show up somewhere she wasn't. . . ."

"Of course!" Dana said.

"I'm sorry, I don't understand." Ezra looked back and forth between Sayer and Dana.

"I think Kyle Nelson is a chimera." As Sayer said it out loud she became even more certain.

"You think Kyle is a mythological monster?" Ezra said gently.

"No." Sayer shot him a look. "I think he's what's called a genetic chimera."

"Back up, please. A genetic chimera?" Max asked.

Sayer fidgeted with her worry beads to calm her excitement. "We like to imagine that our DNA is stable and unique to each individual. But in reality, a significant percentage of the population is what's called a genetic chimera."

"Right, I've heard of that. It's when a single person has two different sets of genes," Max said.

"Exactly. Some people become genetic chimeras in the womb, but mothers also absorb DNA from their infant in utero, and there are medical procedures that can cause a person's DNA to mix. For example, after a bone marrow transplant, the host's DNA is often completely replaced by the donor's DNA."

"So the person who got the bone marrow transplant will change their actual DNA?" Max asked.

"Yes. It's also possible that a person can end up having different parts of their body display completely different DNA. A chimera's blood and skin can have one set of DNA while their organs and saliva might have an entirely different genetic code." Dana bounced on her feet with excitement.

"There's a really famous case of a woman who took a DNA test for a paternity lawsuit," Sayer said. "The results showed that the woman wasn't actually the mother of her three children. But of course she knew that was impossible, since she had physically given birth to them. She was charged with fraud and it wasn't until they did an actual DNA test of her uterus that they realized she was a genetic chimera. So her blood wasn't a DNA match to her own children. But her uterus did match, because her uterus was made up of entirely different cells."

"Other than him drawing chimeras as a kid, what makes you think Kyle is a genetic chimera?" Ezra asked.

"We know Kyle was very sick as a child. His mother's delusions about being Ekhidna began while he was in the hospital. We've also got evidence that Cricket has some kind of connection to a bone marrow transplant since she's on the donor list. One of the signs of a successful marrow transplant is the host becoming a full-blood chimera. Which means that the host's blood cells are completely replaced by the donor's DNA. They use that exact terminology in hospitals. If Kyle needed a bone marrow transplant, the doctors would have all wanted Kyle to become a chimera. And I'll give you one guess which Greek monster was Ekhidna's child. . . ."

"Chimera! So that's what triggered her delusion that she was Chimera's mother," Max said.

"And, when someone becomes a blood chimera after a bone marrow transplant, their blood would give a positive DNA match to whoever donated the bone marrow," Dana said.

"Exactly!" Sayer continued, "And the most common bone marrow donor match is a full sibling. . . ."

"So, if Kyle needed a bone marrow transplant, Cricket would've been the most likely donor," Max said, finishing her thought.

"Exactly," Sayer repeated. "And if Kyle got a bone marrow transplant from Cricket . . ." Sayer let that comment hang.

"Then, if we tested Kyle's blood, the DNA would come back as a match to Cricket?" Ezra asked. "That is wild!"

"And I'm guessing his skin would also match Cricket's DNA. Which explains how her DNA showed up under your nails. It wasn't Cricket who attacked us, it was Kyle," Max said, voice rising.

"I think he must've broken in to take his mom's skeleton back," Sayer said.

"Hang on," Ezra said. "Kyle's a law enforcement officer. We've got his DNA on file."

"From a cheek swab." Dana flashed her narrow pixie smile. "Unlike blood, DNA in saliva can remain the host's original DNA. His saliva matches his own DNA, his blood and skin matches Cricket's."

Sayer could feel all of the strands of evidence twining together into a coherent picture. She closed her eyes, letting the pieces fall into place. The image finally clarified and Sayer could see how everything fit together. "Kyle is our UNSUB. And has been all along."

"Uh, then who tried to kill Kyle at the archives? Obviously he didn't shoot himself," Ezra said.

"We've been assuming that our attackers were the same person, but I think it was actually Cricket who shot Kyle—"

"To stop him," Ezra said, realization dawning.

"And she took Sam to protect her from Kyle!" Max practically shouted. Kona jumped up at the excitement in Max's voice.

"Exactly. Max, remember we even said that the Dark Hollow House looked like a place to hide out. I think she was trying to protect the girl."

Max half stood up. "And that explains why Kyle was running like a bat out of hell ahead of us up at Dark Hollow. He knew that Cricket, Beaumont, whatever, would tell us about him. He had to get there first to shut her up. He ran up ahead to kill her—she just got the drop on him first."

Sayer slapped the table, unable to rein in her excitement. "Yes!" Finally all the pieces fit together in a way that made sense. "In 1987, infant Kyle got horribly ill and needed a bone marrow transplant. Cricket was the donor. Abigail Nelson was suffering from postpartum psychosis and heard the doctors repeatedly talking about Kyle as a chimera. Her psychosis developed into an elaborate delusion and she became convinced in 1996 she had to sacrifice people to protect her monstrous child. I'm betting she involved both of them. Mrs. Nelson is our original UNSUB."

Sayer took a deep breath and continued. "Then, in 2002, Cricket did something that caused a confrontation with her mother. Maybe she threatened to turn her in. There was a struggle, Cricket killed her own mother, then ran to Max to help her escape. She came back and has been trying to stop Kyle all this time. Hell, she even fed us the perfect profile, describing Kyle to a tee."

Max groaned, face pale.

"What's wrong, Max?"

"Cricket was trying to protect Sam. And I shot her. . . ." Max leaned forward, grasping his head. "I shot a woman trying to protect a little girl from a serial killer."

The reality of what he said crashed onto Sayer. She looked up, shaking. "Max, I handed that little girl off to a killer. I literally asked Kyle to take her to the hospital. And he smiled and walked away with a two-year-old girl who is probably now down in the pit about to be tortured and killed. We've got to find the pit before it's too late."

Dana spoke up. "One thing I don't understand. Why wouldn't Cricket, I mean Beaumont . . . why wouldn't she just tell you it was Kyle? She had to know his DNA would match hers. Why try to stop him on her own rather than just telling us what happened?"

Sayer's phone buzzed and she read the text. "How about I ask her? Alice Beaumont is out of surgery. She wants to talk."

CHARLOTTESVILLE, VA

Hannah Valdez wandered down Fifth Street, shivering in her soaked hospital gown. She stuck to the shadows, cursing herself for not thinking to put on some clothes. It was obvious something was wrong with her, wandering the streets in the thin cotton shift. She didn't want to arouse any suspicions.

She made it to the corner where the voice had told her to wait.

Looking along the empty road, Hannah retreated against a building so she could remain out of sight.

She pulled out Zoe's cell phone. Surely it would occur to him to check her for a phone.

With weak hands, she cracked the silvery casing and plucked out the GPS microchip connected to the small battery.

Headlights turned down the road and approached slowly. Before they got too close, Hannah swallowed the GPS and battery, wires and all, choking it down her dry throat.

As the car rolled to a stop, her heart seized. A police cruiser. No! Had someone noticed her missing?

But then the window rolled down and Hannah knew it was him. The man inside smiled, but it was not the concerned smile of a police officer. It was a gleeful look that made her stomach quail with fear.

"So glad you came," he said conversationally. "Although we already know each other, let me formally introduce myself. I'm Kyle Nelson, police chief, and resident monster of Rockfish Gap." He got out, his body stringy like a gangly marionette. With warm hands, he patted her down and then opened the car door like a gentleman on a date.

"Get in, Hannah. It's time to go save Sam."

"Did Kyle get the girl?" she asked.

"Yes, he did." Sayer struggled with conflicting emotions. If Beaumont had just told her everything, Sam would be safe at home. But at least this woman had tried to intervene and protect the girl, even if it failed miserably.

"I'm so sorry. I thought I could protect her. . . . You have no idea what he's capable of."

Sayer bit back a harsh comment and tried to remember what this woman must have gone through as a child. "Is that why you tried to kill him at the archives?" she managed to say.

Beaumont nodded, a wet sound rattling in her chest as she inhaled.

Sayer didn't respond. There would be plenty of time to determine what price Alice Beaumont should pay for her silence about Kyle. For now, Sayer needed information.

"Can you tell us where he's keeping her?"

Beaumont took a wheezing breath. "No, I'm sorry. My mother never trusted me when she took us to the mine. She made me wear a blindfold. I know it's in the southern end of the park, but I have no clue where."

"Damn. Okay, I need you to tell me everything."

Alice Beaumont closed her eyes and nodded almost imperceptibly. "I guess it's finally time to stop hiding." She looked at Sayer. "Obviously you've already figured out that I used to be Cricket. What else do you know?"

"I've read parts of your mother's journal. I need you to explain what happened back then."

"After Kyle was born, he became very ill."

"Some kind of blood cancer?"

"How did you know that?"

"We've figured out that you must have been his bone marrow donor when he got sick," Sayer said.

"That's right." Beaumont's voice trembled slightly. "While he was recovering in the hospital after the transplant, our mom . . . became very ill. All the doctors talking about chimerism set off an elaborate delusion. If Kyle was a chimera, then she had to be Ekhidna." Beaumont's face

UNIVERSITY HOSPITAL, CHARLOTTESVILLE, VA

As Sayer wound her way through the hospital, she battled with guilt and anger. Kyle had taken Sam right in front of her. She had let him walk away. She had missed that he was their UNSUB all along.

Sayer pushed into Alice Beaumont's room so hard the door banged against the back wall.

A nurse fussing over Beaumont jumped at the loud sound. "Oh! You can't be in here."

Sayer held up her badge. "FBI. Beaumont wanted to talk to me."

"Oh." The nurse looked closely at the badge. "All right. I guess you can stay, but she'll tire out fast, so don't push it." The nurse hurried off like Sayer might bite her. Sayer realized she must look dangerous.

She loudly scraped a chair across the floor next to the bed. "So, do I call you Alice Beaumont or Cricket Nelson?" she said sharply.

Beaumont cast her eyes down with shame. "Alice, please. I'm not Cricket Nelson anymore. Haven't been for a long, long time," she said with a raspy voice.

With Beaumont's face slack, and without the deep berry lipstick and flowing dress, Sayer could finally see Cricket Nelson in her eyes.

pulled into a disgusted grimace. "I know now that she had a history of deep psychosis. She needed help."

"She became convinced she was the mother of a monster," Sayer said.

Beaumont nodded.

"In her journal, it sounds like she became convinced that people were out to get Kyle?"

"She thought we were constantly in danger. The idea that she was some kind of Greek monster fed her delusions of persecution. Mom started to believe that we were all monsters and that it was her job to protect us from vengeful gods angry that we were still alive. Though the delusion changed. Sometimes it was angry gods, sometimes it was people afraid of our power."

"So basically she thought people were after you?"

"Yeah. Doctors, teachers, even my dad. She thought they were all avatars of gods, or acting out the will of the gods. I don't know. Like I said, her delusions weren't exactly coherent. My dad knew that she wasn't stable, but he had no idea what she was really up to. He wouldn't let her get any help, which is why she lost it after the floods in '96."

"She thought the floods were sent to hurt Kyle?" Sayer asked.

"I guess so. She made us sacrifice goats a few times, but the flood convinced her that wasn't enough to appease the angry gods. That was the first time she brought home a person." Beaumont looked away, shame and sorrow showing.

"I read the journal entry. She kept him beneath the shed until he was weak and then led him to the old mine?"

Beaumont let out a strangled sound of agreement. "She called the mine 'the pit.' Once she had him there, she tied him up and slit his throat in front of me and Kyle. Mom was . . . in full-blown psychosis. She drank his blood and then made us drink as well." Her voice broke. She sat in silence, breathing heavily.

Sayer waited for her to continue.

"After she killed the first victim, the flooding receded. She was convinced that it worked. After that, about once a year she would just show up at home with a new victim. She kept them hidden from Dad, and Kyle and I would go on with our lives, to school and church, pretending that there wasn't someone slowly starving to death beneath our shed. I just shut down, but Kyle . . . he loved it. He couldn't take his eyes off Mom as she slit their throats. The look on his face, it was pure adoration. Like there was nothing more beautiful in the world than watching her while she killed those people to protect him."

She looked up at Sayer. "I was twelve when she started killing. I knew what she was doing was wrong. But Kyle was only nine. She told us he was a monster, and he was young enough to believe her." Alice Beaumont paused to rub away tears. "I'm sorry, I know I have no right to cry. I watched those people die."

"You were a child being horrifically abused by your own mother."

"Logically I know that." Beaumont sniffed. "I mean, it's why I became a psychologist. I know all about the effects of trauma, and how psychopathy and psychosis work. But I saw those people die right in front of me and I didn't do anything to stop her."

"If I'm guessing right, you did eventually do something to stop her. . . . We know one of the skeletons we found was your mother. And we suspect she was killed right before you ran away."

Beaumont stared down at the IV line snaking into her arm. "You're right," she whispered without looking at Sayer.

Sayer waited.

"I got into Harvard, did you know that? That's what finally convinced me to leave. I told her I wanted to go and she forbade it. I was . . . furious. I knew then that she would never let me leave, so I told her I was going to turn her in." Beaumont's story began to come out in a staccato fashion now. "She attacked me. We fought. She had the kopis and I grabbed it from her, and . . . I pushed her so hard she fell and hit her head. Kyle was so furious, I knew I had to get away from him. I knew he would kill me for what I'd done. I took her away from him." She looked up at Sayer as though asking for forgiveness.

"And that's when you ran to Max and made up the story about your dad?"

Beaumont nodded. "I knew Max would help me get away. I blamed my dad so Max wouldn't want to go to the cops."

"And then Kyle and your dad covered up your mom's death?"

"They must have. The worst part is that I still loved her. She was just sick and thought she was protecting us. Maybe if I had gotten her some help . . ."

"You were a child."

"True. And my father forbade it. He didn't know that she was killing people, but he knew she was sick and he was more worried about his reputation than anything else." Alice Beaumont fell silent, lost in thought. "You know why everyone called me Cricket?" she finally asked.

"No."

"My mom came up with it. She said that, by not embracing what she was doing, I was destined to go through life small, meek, living in a cage just like a cricket. She wanted me to revel in it and transform into a monster along with her and Kyle. I became convinced that she was right. Though it backfired on her. She thought the idea would encourage me to join them, but instead I decided that, by staying small and quiet, I could somehow contain the monster I was sure lived inside me."

"That was how you tried to fight her." Sayer understood.

"It was. But I eventually realized that me being quiet, starving myself to stay as small as possible, wasn't what I needed. It took a lot of therapy, but I realized that I control who I am and what I do, not some evil creature buried in my subconscious." She looked up at Sayer, tears gone. "That's why I picked Beaumont as my new name."

"Beautiful mountain," Sayer translated.

"Beautiful mountain," she repeated. "That's why I have that huge photo of Mount Olympus in my office. Instead of a small, scared little Cricket, I wanted to revel in my size and strength. I wanted to become a mountain, unmovable. And I did. I'm a professor. I love my job. I love my life. I never thought I could be happy, but I . . . am. I came back to Virginia to keep an eye on Kyle but ended up building myself a real life here."

"Why do you think Kyle started killing again after all that time?" Sayer asked.

"Our dad's death. I think just him being alive must've kept Kyle in line."

"And he died not long ago."

"Yeah. That must've triggered Kyle. And when he started killing"—her voice cracked—"I convinced myself that it was my job to deal with him. I just didn't have any faith that you would catch him. Or, if you did, I thought he would get off. He's a cop and I know how the system works. Plus, I . . . don't trust people very easily." She grimaced ruefully. "Legacy of my own past. If I couldn't even rely on my own parents, who else can I count on? But if I'd just told you . . . those poor women . . . that little girl . . ."

Sayer had no reassuring words for her.

"I was monitoring the police radio to make sure you didn't find any more bodies. When I heard that he was after Sam," Beaumont continued, "I knew I had to save her. I couldn't let another little girl go through that. . . ."

"Do you have any clue why he would still want Sam even though her mother escaped?"

"No clue."

Sayer tried to keep her face neutral despite her frustration. "Is there anything you can tell us that could help us find him? Anything you can remember about the location of the mine?"

Beaumont closed her eyes. "The only thing I can really remember is that the entrance is under a rocky overhang just beyond a big chestnut tree. She would take off my blindfold just outside the cave and I would always see it. But I can't imagine how that helps you."

Thinking once more about Piper, Sayer said, "One last question. Do you think Kyle would team up with someone, as partners?"

"I doubt it. Kyle would want to work alone."

Sayer got up, a dark knot tightening her gut. If Piper wasn't Kyle's partner, then where was she? "Thank you for talking to me. Please call if you think of anything that might be useful."

"Will you tell that girl's family that I'm sorry?" Beaumont asked quietly.

Sayer nodded and left without comment. She stopped by Hannah Valdez's room on her way out, but the officers at her door said Hannah was probably asleep. She decided not to disturb the poor woman. Plus she sure didn't want to explain that they'd actually found Sam, and that Sayer had literally handed the girl to the killer.

Sayer headed back to the ranger station, heart aching for the things that young Alice Beaumont had gone through, and for the things that Sam Valdez might be going through right now.

SOUTHERN RANGER STATION, SHENANDOAH NATIONAL PARK, VA

Back at the ranger station, Sayer recounted her interview with Alice Beaumont to Max, Ezra, and Dana. Despite everything they knew, they still had no clue why Kyle took Sam or how to find the pit.

After an hour of futile churning over possible leads, Sayer took a moment to assess her team. Max and Dana were clear-eyed, but Ezra was pale, shoulders sunken. She glanced up at the clock.

"Whoa, it's almost three A.M.!" She realized that no one had eaten since Nana had brought them lunch. "I know we all want to work until we find Sam, but we need food and at least a few hours of rest. We're no good to anybody overtired and underfed."

"I can go heat up the leftover chili," Max offered.

"I'm fine with a granola bar." Ezra held up a new box.

"Me too," she said, grabbing one. "I just want to scarf something and get some shut-eye." Sayer tugged on her annoyingly damp jacket and said good night, looking one last time at the photo of Sam tacked to the murder board.

Back in the cabin, she sat on the hard cot and ate the granola bar like penance for letting Kyle walk away with Sam. She glanced over at the wrapped present Adi had brought for her birthday. The cheerful blue and white wrapping paper screamed *Happy Birthday!* making her want to shred it into a thousand pieces.

Sayer tried to clear her mind, but all she could picture was Sam, her trusting eyes as she curled herself into Kyle's arms. And then Kyle's face as he walked away with the girl—his lip-curled smile. At the time, Sayer had taken it as a smile of satisfaction at saving the girl. But now she knew it was a grin of victory. He knew he'd won and was walking away with his prize.

Realizing she would just stare at the ceiling if she tried to sleep, Sayer grabbed Jake's letter and Adi's present. She wrapped herself in the wool blanket and retreated to the cabin's narrow front porch.

Rain ran off the edge of the tin roof, creating a sheet of gray water obscuring the woods beyond. She cleared away a few sticky cobwebs from a rough-hewn rocking chair and curled into the worn seat, tucking the blanket around her feet. She lightly tapped her gun, just making sure it was still there, before letting go of some of the tightly held emotion balled in her chest. Sam's trusting eyes. Kyle's grin. Sam's eyes . . . Kyle . . . Sam . . .

Sayer eyed the objects on her lap. The envelope that Adi found was brittle with age. Across the front Jake had written *Sayer* in his compact handwriting. Next to the pale letter, Adi's vibrant birthday gift felt like a colorized object in a black-and-white photo. Across the top, Adi had scrawled *Sayer* in the looping scrawl of a young woman.

Which one should she open first? The link to Jake, the past she was trying to move on from? Or the gift from Adi, part of the new life she was trying to build?

Without overthinking her choice, Sayer tore open the envelope and pulled out a single piece of paper. Seeing the short note in Jake's handwriting sent a familiar flash of grief through her body.

In the dim light, she read the note.

Sayer,

If you're reading this then the worst has happened. I'm sorry I didn't tell you what's been going on but anything I say even now might put you in too much danger.

Sayer grunted her disapproval.

I know that will piss you off. I strongly suspect you will realize that my death is not what it seems. I'm asking you not to dig into whatever happened to me. Because I know you are stubborn as an ox and will completely ignore this request, my advice is to trust Holt and no one else.

She let out a breathy laugh. Jake knew she would never walk away from this.

I'm so sorry not to be there with you. Be careful and, no matter what you might learn or hear, never doubt that I love you with all my heart.

Eyes on the horizon, my love.

Jake

A tear dripped off Sayer's chin onto the paper and she wiped it away, not wanting to ruin Jake's last communication. She dried her cheeks and reread the letter, this time focusing on his warning. *No matter what you might learn?* That sounded almost paranoid. What was Jake into before he died?

Something about the letter triggered a spark of excitement. The thrill of the hunt was a far more comfortable emotion than grief.

Stoking that feeling, Sayer refolded the letter and lifted Adi's present, tearing away the wrapping paper to reveal a small photo album. On the cover it read *This Is Us*.

She flipped it open to a photo of her and Adi. Sayer recognized it from the dog park where they'd been taking Vesper. The two women had their arms casually around each other. Adi had her head thrown back with laughter, while Sayer flashed a wry grin that suggested she was up to no good. The next four pages were photos of Sayer, Adi, Tino, and Vesper, with occasional appearances by Nana and Sayer's sister and nephew.

All of them smiling and laughing.

The back half of the book was empty.

Sayer unfolded the note stuck between the pages.

Thank you for taking me in and becoming my family. Can't wait to fill the rest of this book together. All my love, Adi.

Sayer gently closed the album and looked at the cover. "This is us," she whispered, throat tight with emotion.

Adi was trying to remind her that their pasts didn't define who they were now. That their strange little family, cobbled together through trauma and violence, could still have a joyous life to come. She thought about all the damaged lives in this case, the Wattses, Hannah and Sam, Alice Beaumont. They were all survivors of horror, but she had to believe that they could do more than just survive.

"Hey, you awake?" Max's voice made Sayer jump.

"What? Yeah." She quickly tucked the photo album and letter into the blanket.

"Mind if I join you? I brought an extra bowl of chili just in case." Max and Kona stepped through the curtain of rain. Max hunched over two bowls. "I brought Ez a bowl too. Turned out he was hungry."

Sayer took the offered chili. "Thanks." She cleared her throat, trying to rid her voice of emotion. "That granola bar sucked."

"Figured we could all use a hot meal. I remember from my Pararescue days, this is the point when the team needs some basic self-care just to keep things moving forward."

He sat down on the porch floor and leaned against the cabin. Kona slid next to him with a heavy sigh.

The warm chili thawed the core of Sayer's body. They ate in silence until their bowls were empty.

Max put his down with a heavy sigh to match Kona's.

"So," Max finally said, "do you think Kyle Nelson is a killer because of what his mom did?"

Sayer put her bowl down in Max's and curled back into the rocking chair. "I think it's complicated."

"No way I'm sleeping right now. Which means I've got plenty of time, if you're willing to share your thoughts."

Sayer nodded, her mind still replaying the moment when Kyle walked away with Sam. "Yeah, I may never sleep again if we don't save that little girl."

"Hey, as someone who just spent the last few days wondering if the girl I helped run away was in fact a serial killer, let me tell you how fun it is to beat yourself up over past mistakes. . . ."

Sayer gave him a look.

"Honest question: How could you have known it was Kyle?" Max asked.

"I should've seen it. I should be able to spot these assholes."

"You think that's how it really works? You study psychopaths and develop some magical psycho-sense?"

Sayer was about to snap at Max but then let out a hard breath. "No, of course that's not how it works. I mean, I spot psychopathic traits in people all the time, but when someone is trying to hide them, they can be really hard to see."

"Exactly. Which brings me back to my question. Is there something wrong with the Nelson genes? Something to do with being a chimera? Or did his mom teach him how to kill?"

"It's got nothing to do with him being a chimera. Chimerism can cause health problems, but it doesn't make people violent or dangerous. With killers like Kyle, no one really knows what goes wrong or when. But they do have different brains. Remember how I told you that their entire paralimbic system is faulty? That means that they just don't feel a normal range of emotions. I once asked a study subject to name the emotions he saw in photographs. When we got to the photo of a terrified woman, he correctly identified her emotion as fear. When I asked how he knew, he said he recognized the look from the faces of the women he was about to kill."

"Jesus, Sayer, that's some nightmare fuel."

"Yeah. Anyway, as far as I can tell, their brains start out slightly faulty from birth, but not everyone with an underdeveloped paralimbic system becomes a serial killer. But if you put a kid with impaired emotional systems in a bad environment, then you've got a perfect storm for a killer like Kyle Nelson."

"So his brain was probably messed up from the get-go, and then his mom exposed him to some horrific things, triggering the worst-case scenario."

"Exactly."

"So, is it incurable? I mean, if their brains are damaged, is that it?"

Sayer stretched her legs and shifted to a new position. "Not entirely. There are a few juvenile facilities working with psychopathic kids. They've had amazing success. Basically they're retraining their brains by rewarding desirable behaviors. The kids who go through those programs are way less likely to commit another violent crime."

"That's hopeful. . . . Is that what your research is about?"

"Ultimately, yeah."

Max smiled wistfully. "But then you'd be out of a job."

"A hell of a good reason to be out of work. . . ." Sayer trailed off, mind shifting to Holt and the fact that she still might be losing her job, though for a much less happy reason. Subject 037 might have saved Sayer's job for now, but things were far from over.

"Hannah mentioned some Stanford prison thing. And Nazis. You seemed to know what she meant."

"I think so. In the early seventies a Stanford psychology professor ran an experiment on undergrads. He took a bunch of typical Stanford students and split them randomly into two groups—prisoners and guards. The prisoners were kept in a mock prison in the basement of one of the buildings, but the guards worked shifts just like in a real prison."

"I vaguely remember this from psychology class. The guards went crazy abusing the prisoners, right?" Max asked.

"Yeah. They quickly became abusive toward the prisoners, even though they knew the prisoners were other students. The whole experiment was supposed to last two weeks, but things got so abusive they had to stop it after only a few days."

"I get it—just like the Nazis where average Germans participated in the slaughter of millions."

"Exactly. Both examples show how easy it is to turn people into . . . well, monsters," Sayer said.

"Do you really believe that?" Max asked. "I mean, those examples sure make it seem like there might just be a monster buried inside all of us."

"I do think that, given the right situation, people can do some terrible things," Sayer said slowly. "The Holocaust is evidence enough of that. But we know now that the Stanford Prison Experiment wasn't quite as clear-cut as we once believed. It looks like the guards might have been coached to be abusive. And the idea that we are all monsters deep down completely ignores one thing."

"What's that?"

"The Righteous Among the Nations."

"The what?"

"The Righteous, they're people who risked their own lives and the lives of their families to protect others from the Nazis."

"Ah," Max said, "like Schindler?"

"Exactly, though he's just the most famous. There were tens of thousands of people who risked everything to save the lives of others. While I think many of us certainly have the capacity for evil, I also think we have the capacity for heroism."

Sayer looked over at her fellow FBI agent. He stared out at the rain, eyes clear, expression calm, but his jaw muscle bulged with involuntary tension. Kona curled against him with her head on his lap. Mind still on Jake's letter, she thought about the nights they had sat out under the stars, talking, making love. She thought about the life she had once imagined building with him.

But then she thought about Adi's gift and the new life she was building. Very different from the one she had imagined before, but a happy life nonetheless. It's what Jake would've wanted for her.

Was all that about to end? What would she do if Sam Valdez didn't make it? What would happen if she were fired from the FBI?

"Hey." Max put a hand on her arm. "You okay?"

Sayer snapped out of her reverie. "What? Yeah. Just a little lost in my own head. I should try to get some actual sleep."

Max slowly got up and stretched. "Yeah, I hear you. Sleep well, Sayer. Tomorrow we'll catch Kyle and save Sam." He doffed an imaginary hat. With Kona at his side, he disappeared into the night.

Back inside, Sayer pawed through her small bag of clothes and found everything musty and damp. The cold invaded her bones, making her injured shoulder ache. Grumbling, she crawled onto the hard cot and closed her eyes, willing away the image of Kyle's smirk.

She tried to do the deep breathing her physical therapist had suggested but just couldn't find any damn inner peace.

SOUTHERN RANGER STATION, SHENANDOAH NATIONAL PARK, VA

Ezra stared at the map in the blue light of his computer screen. There had to be some way to track the location of the pit, but he just couldn't make his brain work. His entire body quivered with exhaustion, but he wasn't about to take a break. The second he stopped working he knew he would fall asleep and no telling how long he would be out. He could not let that happen when there was a little girl out there depending on him.

Maybe if he hadn't missed that Alice Beaumont was really Cricket Nelson, they could have protected the girl. He owed it to Sam to not screw up again.

Eyes swimming, he contemplated another mug of coffee but knew that would just make him more jumpy. Instead, he looked down at his legs. He'd taken off the prosthetics while he was reading. Without overthinking what he was about to do, he reached down and pressed against one of the nerves. It felt like a shard of glass sliding into his flesh.

He let out a sharp cry, but the pain faded as quickly as it came. Adrenaline flooded his system and he nodded, satisfied that he wouldn't drift off anytime soon.

"There's got to be a way to find that pit," he muttered. "Come on, brain, think."

Ezra glanced back over at Sayer's notes from her interviews with Hannah Valdez and Alice Beaumont in the hospital. "The pit," he said to himself. "Stuff about Stanford prison and Nazis. An overhang and a chestnut tree . . ." An idea occurred to him.

His vision clear with excitement, he let his fingers fly over the keyboard.

SAYER'S CABIN,
SHENANDOAH NATIONAL PARK, VA

Sayer's phone buzzed against her chest and she bolted upright, almost knocking it to the floor.

She fumbled it to her face and squinted at the screen. Four-thirty A.M. Unknown number.

"Agent Altair," she mumbled, still half asleep.

"Sorry to wake you, Agent Altair, but, uh, this is Officer Teegan with the Charlottesville Police. Uh, Hannah Valdez is gone, ma'am."

"What?" Sayer said, struggling to kick her brain in gear.

"Hannah Valdez, she's gone missing. We just noticed because, well, we thought she was asleep. . . ."

"When did you notice her gone?" Her voice fell low with menace.

"Uh, not five minutes ago. But she's been gone awhile, we think."

"I thought you had someone on her door." Sayer was already up reaching for her boots.

"We did."

"So how did he get her?"

"That's just it. He didn't. She left a note for her wife, said the killer called her and that she had to go back to the pit to save Sam. She put some pillows in the bed to make it look like her, then she climbed out the window."

Sayer was stunned into silence for a long moment, awed by Hannah's bravery. She knew perfectly well what horrors awaited her, yet she went anyway to save her daughter.

And now she knew why Kyle needed Sam.

"You have officers out scouring the grounds and surrounding area? She can't have gone far," Sayer barked.

"Yes, ma'am. It also looks like she took her wife's phone. We're working on a trace now."

"Send everything you have to me. Now!"

Sayer texted her team and then ran up to the ranger station.

Dana, Max, and Kona made it to the conference room less than a minute after Sayer. Ezra was already awake at his computer.

"Kyle lured Hannah back to the pit with Sam," Sayer said as soon as they gathered.

"Oh, no. . . ." Dana's hands went to her mouth. "Why didn't she call us?"

"It looks like Kyle threatened to kill Sam if she called anyone. The only good news is that she took a cell phone with her. Ezra, I'm forwarding you the info on the phone. Start a trace."

"On it!" Ezra leaned into his keyboard with intense focus. "All right, there's no signal from the phone. But I can track where it went. . . . Okay, here we go. I can see her leaving the hospital. She went south on Fifth and then stopped for a while at this mall here." He tapped his screen. "Then she's on the move again, clearly in a car. Out of Charlottesville and up toward the park. There's no road on my map, but it looks like she's moving up the mountain, probably a mining road. Not even fifteen miles straight up from Charlottesville . . . and . . . signal gone. She must've gotten out of range. There are tons of dead zones up here." Ezra turned his screen so they could all see.

"Where were they heading?" Sayer asked.

"It went dead right before they hit Wildcat Ridge," Ezra said. "And looks like there's cell service not too far beyond that area, so I'm guessing they stopped somewhere near the ridge."

"Wildcat Ridge," Max said. "Damn, that's a huge area. Ten or fifteen square miles at least."

"Hang on, I've got an idea." Ezra typed quickly, eyes aglow. He pulled up a second map and looked back and forth between the two. "Ta-da!" he pointed to a spot on the second map.

"What's that?" Sayer came around to look at the spot.

"Remember how Beaumont mentioned a chestnut tree just outside the pit?"

"I do. . . ."

"American chestnuts are endangered and there was a project a few years back that documented every large chestnut tree in the park." A Cheshire-cat grin spread across Ezra's face.

"How on earth do you know that?" Max asked.

Ezra shrugged. "I like trees, and Piper was actually telling me—"

Sayer waved her hand, not caring how he knew. "So you're saying you know where all the big chestnut trees are on Wildcat Ridge?"

Ezra's grin spread, pulling on his stitched lip, but he didn't seem to notice. "Not all the trees. The one tree. . . . I was actually just looking up their maps to see if I could figure out which tree Beaumont saw. I wasn't able to narrow it down before, but now that we know it's on Wildcat Ridge . . ." He clicked a pin on the map. "The entrance to the pit has to be near here."

A tingle of anticipation ran along Sayer's spine as she felt the familiar jolt of certainty that they were closing in.

"You are a freaking genius!" She gave Ezra a hug and pulled out her phone. "Send me the coordinates. I'm going to scramble the troops to meet us out there ASAP. Max, we leave in two minutes."

She hurried back to her cabin to prepare to confront Kyle Nelson and save Hannah and Sam Valdez.

THE PIT

Hannah Valdez paced the small room, clawing at the collar around her throat. "Let me see my daughter, you bastard!" she shouted again.

Nothing.

Kyle must have left after he locked her in this room.

She should've just gone to Sayer. But she had to do something to get her daughter away from this madman.

"Oh, Haaaannah," Kyle's voice filtered through the door. "I'm so glad you agreed to come back. How impolite to leave when you still have a job to do."

"I came with you. Just let me see Sam," she said with sad finality. Hannah knew he would probably never let her leave this place alive. She was slightly surprised that the thought of dying didn't really scare her, but her heart twisted at the thought of not being there for Sam, not getting to watch her little girl grow up. She just had to keep Sam alive until Sayer could find her.

Kyle pushed the door open and stepped in. "Aw, poor Hannah looks like she's about to cry." His eyes burned with intensity. "Did you really think I would let you get away? Now I have you right back where you should be."

Hannah closed her eyes and found a small, hollow spot deep inside. She retreated to that emotionless space where she could detach from everything happening around her. With flat affect, she stared back at Kyle. He could do whatever he wanted to her as long as Sam was safe.

Kyle reached for her arm and she tried not to flinch but couldn't stop her involuntary recoil.

He leaned in until his nose almost brushed hers. "You're going to kill for me. I get to watch you transform, that moment when you tear away the mask you wear. Good mother, fine young woman . . . all gone. Nothing but the beautiful moment when you take another life to protect your child."

Kyle's voice fell low, breath shallow with lurid excitement. His eyes glowed with pleasure.

Hannah pulled on every inner reserve she had in order to face him calmly. She stared back into his eyes. "I'm only sorry that it won't be you I kill."

They glared at each other, nose to nose, for a long time. Kyle eventually stepped back and broke into a smile. "Well done." He seemed pleased that she was willing to face off with him. "More proof that you've got the heart of a killer. See, I'm helping you get in touch with your true nature, Hannah. There's a monster lurking just beneath the surface." He ran a finger along her cheek. "I'm helping all of you."

Hannah let out a bitter laugh. "You think kidnapping women and children, shocking them with collars, forcing women to murder other women, is helping us? You're delusional."

"Never call me that!" He slapped Hannah hard enough to snap her head to the side.

"You might eventually kill me, but Sayer knows who you are. She won't let you get away with this," Hannah said.

Kyle laughed. "Sayer and the FBI are idiots. You should've seen the show I put on. Sayer got to see angry Kyle." His brow pulled into a furrow, eyes stormy. "Angry Kyle was so mad at Max Cho for hurting his sister. Or what about poor sorrowful Kyle"—his eyes went soft and wet, mouth pulled into a frown—"wondering what horrors befell his beloved family? Or how about friendly police-chief Kyle?" Kyle's shoulders fell, mouth forming a relaxed smile. "That's my favorite mask to wear. My mother was right: create the perfect mask and you can get away with anything."

Hannah felt a wave of disgust at Kyle's display of false emotion.

"And those absolute fools were completely convinced that the killer was my sister." He chuckled. "I had no clue she was even back, but it worked out perfectly." Kyle cocked his head to the side "I will say, you and Cricket both managed to surprise me. I didn't expect you to escape. And I certainly didn't expect Cricket to show up and try to stop me. I thought she was long gone, but instead she was right there waiting for me. She even almost managed to kill me. You know"—Kyle smiled, baring his teeth—"you look just like her back then. Just like Mother, too."

His expression shifted from fond remembrance to burning darkness. "And now you and Cricket have both learned that no one wins against me. You might have a monster buried inside you, but I am the original monster." He spread his arms wide. "And here you are, right where I want you."

Kyle turned to go. He paused and looked back over his shoulder. "Enough chitchat. I've got to go get little Sam strapped in my lovely machine. I think we're about to find out exactly what kind of monster you have inside."

Her bravado fell away, and the image of Sam in that nightmare machine left Hannah completely unable to breathe.

WILDCAT RIDGE, SHENANDOAH NATIONAL PARK, VA

The wind howled against the truck as Sayer and Max drove toward Wildcat Ridge. They crawled along an old mining road in the predawn light. Sheets of rain outpaced the frantic windshield wipers, making it impossible to see very far beyond the hood.

"Is Kona going to be able to do anything in this storm?" Sayer asked.

"We'll see. I'm hoping the entrance is really close to that tree."

Sayer looked at the plastic-wrapped topographic map Ezra had prepared for her. He had marked the tree with a red *X*.

She tapped the map. "We're almost here. The road should curve to the left and dead-end. From there we've got about a quarter mile upslope until we reach the tree."

"Okay, I'll start Kona just south of the tree and we can see how it goes." Max did not look optimistic.

They trudged up the rocky slope, Max checking his compass to make sure they were on the right trajectory, until they reached the tree.

"SWAT won't be here for another thirty minutes," Sayer said. "Let's get Kona going on a search while we wait."

Miserable in the torrential downpour, Max just nodded at her.

He held up Kona's fluorescent orange work vest. "You ready to go to work, girl?" He tried to sound enthusiastic but Sayer could hear the weariness in his tone.

Kona did a little half-step dance back and barked, seemingly immune to the storm. At least one of them was ready for this.

Max got Kona in her vest. "Go find, Kona!" He flung out a hand and Kona moved forward.

Unlike the last time, the dog seemed tentative. As she made sweeping arcs, her body was slumped, her tail hanging low, ears back. She glanced at Max and he gestured her forward, clearly worried.

Sayer and Max followed her slowly westward along the slope, as far apart as they could get while still able to see each other in the storm.

After a few minutes, Kona stopped and turned in a circle. Max crouched down next to her and she whimpered.

"You can't find any scent at all, can you, girl?" He gave her an affectionate scratch. "You're such a good girl, Kona. It's not your fault. Good girl!" Max whipped up an enthusiastic smile for his dog.

He stood and looked at Sayer expectantly.

They had to be close, but now what?

THE PIT

Hannah's calm fled and her entire body began trembling with the knowledge of what was about to happen. Who would this man ask her to kill? Would she be able to do it?

Overwhelmed, Hannah's body clenched, and she rocked forward, vomiting.

As she retched, the door swung open and Kyle towered over her.

He looked down at the vomit on the ground and tsked. "Poor Hannah, maybe not so tough after all. Don't worry. I'm going to fix that for you. Come see."

Hannah moved like a zombie, barely aware of her own feet carrying her toward the pit. She didn't want to go, but she had to see her daughter.

They stepped out into the pit and she squinted against the floodlights overhead. Her eyes skittered around the room until she found Sam strapped to the machine. Hannah couldn't process the sight of her own precious child strapped to the nightmarish device. The pointed blade hung just a few inches to the side of Sam's neck.

Sam's eyes were glossy, showing no recognition of her own mother. Her mouth hung open in a stupor.

"What's wrong with her?" Hannah asked softly, too scared even to move.

Kyle waved a hand. "I gave her a mild sedative so she wouldn't distract you. She'll be fine. You can go see."

Hannah rushed over to Sam. She pressed her hands to her mouth to prevent a strangled moan from escaping her lips. She ran her hands over the girl's body, making sure she wasn't hurt.

"Mommy's here, sweetheart. I've got you. I won't let anything happen to you." Hannah couldn't stop the tears rolling from her eyes.

"Hannah, I'd like you to meet Piper, your first sacrifice," Kyle said.

Hannah had been so focused on Sam that she hadn't even noticed the large woman lying on the floor. She was bound in a straitjacket, her legs wrapped with black rope.

"Hello, Hannah," Piper said, with sad eyes. "You probably don't remember me from the ranger station, but I was there when you escaped. Don't worry. Sayer is on her way and I want you to do whatever you have to, to save your little girl."

Hannah opened and closed her mouth, unable to speak. How could she possibly hurt this woman?

"Aw, well, isn't that sweet?" Kyle spat the word *sweet* as he removed a small remote from his pocket.

Piper stared at Hannah. "I mean it. Always remember that I forgive you for whatever happens here. You do what you have to. Save Sam, for me. . . ." Her voice cracked with emotion.

Smiling, Kyle tapped something on the keypad. "Enough. It's time we begin. The rules are simple. Hannah, you have five minutes to kill Piper and I'll let Sam live. Fail, and Sam dies. You don't even have to fight. I have Piper all tied up, so it should be an easy kill."

Eyes gleaming with excitement, Kyle pushed a button on the remote and a clock appeared on the wall.

WILDCAT RIDGE,
SHENANDOAH NATIONAL PARK, VA

Sayer turned in a slow circle. The entrance to the pit had to be nearby. Beaumont said beyond the big tree. . . . She looked back toward the chestnut tree. They had moved almost parallel along the slope, with Kona searching.

"Hey, if I said something is beyond that rock, what would you assume?" She pointed to a rock nearby.

Max wiped rain from his face. "I guess I'd assume it was up there." He pointed up the slope.

"Yeah, in Beaumont's description, she specifically said an overhang just 'beyond' the tree. Which sort of implies upslope, right? Let's go back to the tree and head uphill from there. Unless you've got another idea?"

Max looked down at Kona. Her eyes were alert but her ears drooped. "Nah, Kona's getting nothing here. That's a good idea."

They tromped back along the muddy slope to the tree. Sayer contemplated the steep rise to the north.

"All right, let's do it. Should we send Kona on a search again?"

"Yeah, can't hurt." Max gently cupped the black dog's face. "All right, girl, let's get back to work."

Her tail wagged slightly and her ears came forward.

Max stood and flung his hand up the slope. "Go find, Kona!"

Once again she took off in a zigzagging arc back and forth.

The steep slope meant slow progress and Sayer tucked her head forward, resigned to another long walk.

Bark!

Kona's entire body stiffened with her alert, nose high in the air.

"Good girl, go find!" Max urged her on.

They surged forward.

Sayer rested her hand on her gun just for the feel of it under her fingers. She strongly suspected this wasn't going to end without a fight.

Kona paused and tacked sharply to the left toward a rocky outcropping.

"She's on the direct scent now. We've got him." Max's hand drifted to his gun.

They were close.

Kona circled around a jutting granite outcropping as it curved along the slope toward a steep drop-off. At the top of the cliff, she bowed down and pointed her nose to the ground twenty feet below.

Sayer leaned forward over the cliff's edge and realized they were on the top of a shallow overhang. Hidden at the back of the rocky niche was a massive tunnel. Two trucks wide, the entrance was carved into a perfect arch. The remnants of a footpath ran down the slope. Signs of recent disturbance along the path convinced Sayer that they were in the right place.

She tried not to imagine Sam already strapped into the machine, blade to her neck.

"Good girl!" Max said, barely above a whisper. He petted Kona, who had a happy grin on her canine face.

"All right," Sayer said. "I go in first. You and Kona follow at a distance. I have no idea what to expect in there and I want us prepared for the worst, including traps or explosives. Backup will be here soon, but we can't wait. He could be killing Sam or Hannah right now."

"Got it." Max patted his hip. "To me, Kona." She moved to her spot next to him, clearly thrilled that they were on the hunt together.

Sayer used her satellite phone to send Ezra their coordinates and they made their way down to the entrance.

She gave Max one last nod, pulled her gun, and moved smoothly into the tunnel.

Just a few feet in, Sayer felt as though she had entered an alternate reality. The sudden quiet from the storm raging ten feet behind her felt otherworldly. She threw back her hood, nose assaulted by the earthy musk of stale air.

As she advanced, voices echoed along the passage. Someone was talking up ahead. The sound of the roaring underground river grew louder, replacing the eerie silence of the entry as she moved steadily forward. The tunnel continued straight for twenty feet and then opened onto the pit. Sayer could make out the top of a ladder from the control room along the rim.

She cautiously approached the edge and looked down.

Forty feet below her, Kyle stood at the base of the ladder, back to her. Sam Valdez was strapped into the machine. Hannah stood next to the girl, whispering something in Sam's ear.

Piper was bound on the floor. The sight of the park ranger in a straitjacket made Sayer's teeth crack. Kyle must have kidnapped her sometime right after the birthday party.

Sayer moved around to the top of the ladder, trying to figure out how to get down quickly enough to stop Kyle. A metal gate hung horizontally across the ladder. She would either have to open the gate and descend so quietly he couldn't hear her, or she would have to do something from above.

She heard Kona's chuffing breath behind her and Sayer gestured for Max and Kona to join her.

Sayer pointed to the ladder and mouthed, *Ideas?*

Max shook his head.

This was a tactical nightmare.

Below them, Kyle tapped the keypad on a remote he held, and tall red numbers began to count down on the wall.

Sayer and Max looked at each other.

"I'm going down. Cover me," Sayer whispered in Max's ear, and grudgingly holstered her gun before lowering herself onto the ladder. Max moved to the edge, gun trained on Kyle down in the pit.

Hannah let out an animal cry of anguish that made Sayer shudder. "No, Sam. No. . . ." Hannah tried to pull away the straps across the girl's body.

Sayer was almost directly above Kyle and she hoped the roaring river would cover any sounds of her descent. She moved as cautiously as she could while lowering herself down. She reached the gate and grabbed the handle, cringing as she pulled.

Kyle's attention was riveted on Hannah trying to pry Sam from the machine. "I made sure my machine could withstand any attempt to remove the child," he said, eyes gleaming. "The benefit of a dad who teaches you how to use power tools. But go ahead, waste your time trying. . . ."

The clock was already at four and a half minutes.

The gate opened without a sound and Sayer let out a soft breath of relief. She glanced down.

Hannah clearly realized that she couldn't get Sam out of the machine, and she turned on Kyle. She hunched low, about to attack.

Kyle took a few steps forward and waved the remote. "Don't even think about it. The only way to turn it off is to enter the right code. And I'll only do that after you kill Piper. It's the only way to stop the machine."

Sayer used his distraction to move quickly downward.

At her sudden movement, the ladder shifted, sending a cascade of rocks to the ground.

Kyle spun around, eyes wild.

"Sayer," he growled.

She let go of the ladder, dropping the rest of the way. She pulled her gun before Kyle could move.

"Freeze, Kyle. Drop the remote. Hands on your head."

Kyle stared at Sayer, eyes bulging with rage. "You . . ." He glanced up. "And Max. Of course."

"Turn it off," Sayer said evenly.

He panted, holding the remote for a long moment before a smile spread across his face. "You could shoot me and take the remote"—he held it up for her to see the keypad—"but, as I was just explaining to Hannah, it takes a code to turn off the machine. And I will never tell you what it is."

His toothy smirk sent a flash of red across Sayer's vision. But she glanced over at Sam. The girl was only half conscious, her head lolling forward, the blade just a few inches from her neck.

"Please," Hannah said to Sayer. "Please save her."

Sayer kept her voice steady despite her desire to shoot Kyle right between the eyes. "Hannah isn't going to kill anyone for you, Kyle. Your game is over. Why don't you let the girl go and at your sentencing I'll tell the judge you cooperated?"

"At my sentencing?" Kyle laughed with a harsh sound. "There isn't going to be any such thing." He looked back and forth between Sayer and Hannah. With a manic laugh, he tossed the remote up into the air between him and Sayer.

As Hannah scrambled to catch the remote that could free her daughter, Kyle sprinted toward the tunnel at the back of the pit.

With Hannah in the way, Sayer couldn't take a shot.

Kyle disappeared into the darkness.

"Is that a way out?" Sayer asked Hannah.

The woman looked up, cradling the remote. She opened her mouth, but no sound came out.

"Can he get out that way?" Sayer demanded loudly.

"I don't think so," Hannah said. "Unless he goes in the river."

Max was already sliding down the ladder, Kona wrapped around his shoulders.

"Can Kona scent in there?" Sayer called to him.

He shook his head. "Too enclosed. Scent will be everywhere."

"Okay, you save Sam, I'm going after Kyle!" Sayer shouted, running toward the dark tunnel at full speed.

THE PIT

Hannah stared at Max across the pit, remote in her hands like a bomb about to go off.

"Please, do something!"

Max glanced over at Piper. "You okay?"

Piper nodded. "Get the girl."

Max let his training take over—calm breath, assess the situation, take action.

He took one long, deep breath and sprinted to the machine holding Sam.

Assess the situation.

Only three and a half minutes left.

He tried to understand the gears, the mess of twisted wire, the pistons. The series of straps firmly secured across the small girl's body with slim padlocks. The metal arm poised off to the side. The four-inch blade at the end of the arm, short and slender, well chosen for its horrifying job.

Hannah stepped next to him, her breath ragged.

Kona stood at attention to his side, ready for a command.

Take action.

"Okay," Max said, "I'm going to get Sam out of here the old-fashioned way."

Hannah nodded, eyes darting with pure panic.

Max put a firm hand on Hannah's shoulder. "Hey. We'll figure this out."

Her eyes flitted over to his and she nodded vaguely.

He turned his attention back to the machine.

The wires were enclosed in thick tubing. He tried to pull them from the side, but they were secure.

Next idea.

He ran his hands along the leather straps. If he could just get them off.

Max worked his fingers beneath a strap and pulled. It held firm.

The jostling seemed to rouse Sam, and the girl looked up at him with glassy eyes. "Mommy?" she asked.

"No, sweetheart," Max said, while probing and pulling at the contraption. "My name is Max and I'm going to get you out of here."

"Hey, Mommy's here," Hannah said. "I'm right here."

Sam nodded and tears leaked from her eyes, but she didn't make a sound.

Her silence drove a dagger through Max's heart.

Two and a half minutes left.

While Hannah continued whispering comforting words to Sam, she worked her fingers bloody pulling on the straps, but to no avail.

Max got more aggressive, bracing his leg against the side of the machine to get better leverage. He tried bending the arm holding the blade. Nothing. Move on to the next option.

He circled around back and found an electronics box. Maybe if he pulled out the wiring or a computer chip?

He tried to pry open the thick black box, but it was solid metal.

Maybe he could shoot it? No, the metal would just deflect the bullet somewhere.

Less than two minutes.

He kicked at the box at an angle, desperate to remove the cover. Max felt a bone in his foot snap but tried again, crying out with the effort.

That wasn't working. Next option.

He crouched down. If he could topple the whole machine? No. Too dangerous for Sam.

Max felt his own panic rising and took another deep breath. Ignoring his heart pounding in his ears, he let his mind free-associate. All he had to do was keep the blade from her neck. Maybe he could get the blade out?

He tore off his shirt and wrapped his hand, then grasped the blade. He felt the sharp edges slicing into his palm, but the blade held firm.

Thirty seconds.

Something solid to put between her neck and the blade?

Max desperately turned and looked. A large rock? A piece of flat metal? Anything he could use to stop the blade.

There was nothing.

"Sam!" Hannah screamed.

Ten seconds.

With a shout of fury, Max attacked the machine, wrenching at the metal arm holding the blade. He torqued his muscles until he felt them practically tear from the bone.

Kona barked ferociously in support.

Hannah howled, tearing her hands as she flailed at the straps holding her daughter. She propped herself against the machine, pulling up on the arm to stop the blade.

Nothing.

Five . . . four . . . three . . .

"Jesus Mother Mary." Max instinctively crossed himself, knowing what he was going to have to do.

. . . two . . . one . . .

With no other option, he thrust his arm between Sam and the blade.

The blade released.

It slammed into his bicep.

A savage cry escaped his lips as his arm exploded with pain.

Hannah began screaming at the blood sluicing to the floor. "Sam!

Sam!" She frantically wiped away at the girl's neck, trying to see how far the blade was penetrating.

Unable to focus because of the pain, Max slid his other hand along his arm. He pressed his fingers next to Sam's neck. Her skin was barely broken by the tip of the blade protruding from the back of his bicep. He let his hand roam to the entry wound. He thought the knife had not sliced an artery, but he couldn't quite tell.

His vision began to tilt slightly.

"Sam'll be okay. Could you use my belt to tourniquet my arm at the shoulder, please?" he managed to say before he lost consciousness completely.

THE MINE TUNNELS

The roar of the river became deafening as Sayer entered the dark tunnel. She realized that a torrent of water was flowing along the entire tunnel floor, turning the tunnel into a watercourse.

The underground river must have jumped its banks and was beginning to flood the mine. No way Kyle could use the river as an escape route.

The uneven floor angled sharply down and Sayer took a few steps into the water. Though shallow, the current was swift and threatened to pull her feet out from beneath her.

She shone her flashlight down the long rocky shaft. A faded orange sign read WARNING: MINE! OPEN SHAFTS. DEAD END. *DO NOT ENTER!*

Rotting mine tracks lined the ground. In the distance, the tunnel branched in five directions.

Determined to catch Kyle, she strode into the powerful rush of water. She hurried forward, bracing her feet against the tracks to keep her balance. At the five-way junction, she searched for any sign of him. Water flooded all five branches. She turned off her light but saw no telltale glow from any of the tunnels.

When she turned her light back on, she noticed a faint streak of mud about elbow height along the far right tunnel.

She swiped the mud. It felt fresh.

Breath shallow with the hunt, Sayer hurried to the right.

The tunnel narrowed into a chute barely wide enough for her to move through without brushing against the uneven walls. The torrent of floodwater intensified in the narrow space. Sayer hunched over her gun and flashlight to prevent herself from smacking her head against the low ceiling. She pushed onward for almost a minute and then stopped, clicking off her light again.

Up ahead she could just make out the faint glow of another light.

Kyle.

With renewed determination, she sloshed forward through the knee-deep water, but then paused.

If she were Kyle, what would she do?

If there truly was no exit down here, she would try to lure a pursuer in the wrong direction.

Sayer froze. The mud streak, the light up ahead. It was too easy.

She listened in the inky darkness. Between the rushing water and her own heart pounding in her ears, it was too loud. Kyle could walk right next to her and she would never hear him coming.

She stood perfectly still for a long moment, increasingly certain that Kyle wasn't up ahead. But then where was he?

He would circle back to the only exit. Which meant he would be heading back to the pit.

Light still off, she turned to creep back up the tunnel toward the main branch. After bumping her head a few times, she holstered her gun so she could use that hand to feel her way forward.

The back of her neck prickled as she imagined Kyle sneaking up behind her. She strained to hear anything above the rushing water, which was now thigh deep.

The water was rising.

In the perfect dark, a beam momentarily glowed back toward the junction.

She was right! He must have lured her down this branch, then circled back around in a connecting tunnel. Was he circling around to catch her off guard, or was he planning to run back toward the pit?

Either way, she had to stop him.

In the black void, she fumbled along the uneven tunnel floor, the flow of water threatening her balance, flashlight off but still gripped in her slick hand. She wanted to turn on the light just to get her bearings, but she couldn't risk letting Kyle know where she was.

A shiver shook her body and she realized that her teeth were chattering, the cold and wet wrapping her in a deadly embrace.

Unable to tell if her eyes were open or closed, she felt a shift in the air. She must have emerged from the narrow branch tunnel.

Now where was Kyle?

A light clicked on.

Sayer gasped at the appearance of Kyle not ten feet away.

His wide eyes suggested that he was just as surprised to encounter Sayer.

He clicked off the light.

In the sudden dark, Sayer turned to face the afterimage of Kyle that still burned in her eyes.

She heard him rushing toward her and she tried to shuffle sideways, moving from the spot he expected her to be. The water slowed her down and Kyle slammed into her shoulder, spinning her around. Her old gunshot wound exploded with agony.

Sayer crashed into the wall. She clicked on her flashlight just as Kyle made another diving attack.

He connected with her chest and they both toppled.

Sayer's head went underwater. The flashlight slipped from her hand, its beam careening wildly as it washed down the tunnel.

Sayer scrambled along the gravelly floor, but the current caught her body.

Dazed, she wrapped a hand around Kyle's shirt as the rushing water pulled her deeper into the mine.

She dragged him with her and they tumbled together, caught in the rolling crash of water.

Unable to keep hold of him, Sayer lost her grip. His body hit something and he screamed in pain.

Churning water replaced air and Sayer wondered if they were both going to drown. She fought to stand up, but she couldn't keep her head above the current.

Then the tunnel widened, dumping them both into a long chamber.

Sayer managed to stand in the waist-deep water that swirled around her. Her flashlight had gotten caught somewhere below the surface and was casting an eerie mud-brown glow.

The water funneled toward the back of the chamber, where it disappeared straight down in a churning torrent.

A mine shaft.

Kyle's face broke the surface, eyes rolling with panic, mouth gasping like a dying fish, and then went back under. She could see him struggling against the current pulling him toward the shaft.

He washed past a large rock and managed to wrap his arm over the muddy surface. With a moan of agony, he partially pulled himself against the rock.

Sayer pulled out her gun. It had been more than five minutes. Max would have already saved Sam. Kyle's code didn't matter anymore.

Fury pulsed in her chest as she pictured Jillian and Grace Watts. What that woman had done for her child. She pictured Hannah stumbling into the ranger station, wild with fear for her daughter. And now Sam strapped in that machine. If Sayer shot Kyle, he would just wash away and never hurt anyone ever again.

He slowly looked up at her, a well of darkness in his eyes.

At the sight of her gun, he smiled.

"Do I get to see the monster beneath your mask, Sayer?" His manic eyes flashed with pleasure. "You look just like Mama right now. That look on her face in the moment she slit their throats. The primal beast buried deep inside, free for just a moment. Can't you feel how much you want to kill me?"

Sayer stared at him, her gun hand trembling. Because he was right, she did want to kill Kyle. But his smile sent a chill shuddering through her body.

She paused for a very long moment before lowering her gun. "There is no mask, Kyle."

He growled. "Lies to the end. Why is it so hard to admit that you want to watch me die?"

Sayer holstered her gun and waded toward him. "You're right, part of me wants to shoot you, but I don't actually want to watch you die. What I really want is to watch you rot in jail for the rest of your life."

Kyle snorted with disgust.

As she reached out to grab him, he let out a sharp grunt, thrusting his hand toward her.

She felt his fingers scrambling against her waist for her gun. Instinct took over. She slammed her elbow down onto his wrist and heard a sharp snap.

Kyle recoiled, losing his grip on the rock.

Sayer flung out her hand to catch him, but the current sucked him under.

She swung her arms in wide arcs underwater but found nothing to grab hold of.

Kyle resurfaced just above the burbling mine shaft. As he reached the sucking vortex, he let out a wild howl. For a moment, he flailed against the current, before disappearing into the churning water.

Shaking, Sayer stared down at her empty hands.

UNIVERSITY HOSPITAL, CHARLOTTESVILLE, VA

Sayer stood in the doorway watching Hannah and Sam Valdez sleeping together in the hospital bed, arms wrapped around each other. Vesper slept curled at their feet. Zoe Valdez stood watch over them, eyes riveted on her family like she had never seen anything so beautiful in her life.

Tiptoeing backward, Sayer slid the door shut. She retreated to the hall, taking a brief moment to appreciate the fact that her clothes were completely dry for the first time in four days.

Tino sat just outside, nose in a book.

"Vesper okay in there?" He closed the book and stood.

"Yeah, he's asleep already. Thanks for bringing him down. Hannah really wanted to see him again. I think he makes her feel safe."

"Of course." Tino rubbed his bristly mustache. "I've actually been meaning to talk to you about Vesper. . . . You know how I've been looking for something meaningful to do with my days?"

"I do. . . ."

"After all this"—he gestured at the hospital atmosphere around him—"I've been thinking about signing Vesper up for therapy-dog classes. With my own psychology training from the Army, I would already qualify as a victim advocate. I think this is what Vesper and I should be doing. Helping victims of violent crime." He looked at Sayer, warm brown eyes glowing. "What do you think?"

"Tino, I think that's an amazing idea."

He rested his hand on his slightly round belly. "Good. As Vesper's co-parent I figured I should check with you first. I'll let Vesper stay for a few hours, then I'll gather him and head home. See you for dinner?"

Adi and Nana were waiting for her at home with papers to start the adoption process. Once the papers were signed, they were planning a massive celebration meal. Sayer was looking very forward to having a beer or three.

"Of course. See you soon." She gave Tino a quick hug.

With that cheerful thought, she navigated up to the room where Max sat in bed, his arm and shoulder swathed in white bandages. Only out of surgery a few hours ago, he already looked bright-eyed and rosy-cheeked.

Sayer held up the box of breakfast tacos that Tino had brought from the city.

"Yay, the goods have finally arrived!" Max cheered.

The massive black dog curled across his lap looked up protectively. Kona eyed Sayer. Her tail thumped once in greeting, and then she immediately fell back to sleep.

Ezra sat in his wheelchair by Max's bed. "Yay, tacos!" He rolled over to intercept Sayer.

She swooped past him. "These are Max's—he can share them or not."

Dana scooted her chair closer to the bed. "Of course he'll share them . . . with the people who all have guns. . . ."

Sayer placed the box on Max's lap and sat on the edge of the bed next to Kona.

Max exaggeratedly rubbed his chin with the hand of his good arm. "Hmm, let me think. . . . I suppose I could—"

They all grabbed for the tacos before he finished the sentence.

Ezra groaned as he chewed. "Holy crap, these are good."

"So," Sayer said with her mouth full, "what's the latest?" She pointed to Max's arm.

He grimaced. "Mostly muscle damage. They're optimistic it will heal cleanly, but we'll have to wait and see how functional everything is."

"Fortunately for you, you've got two experts here who can tell you all about being on medical leave." Dana pointed at Sayer and Ezra.

"How's Piper doing?" Max asked.

"She's doing great. Sounds like Kyle tasered her right after my party. Poor thing was tied up in Kyle's trunk for hours. But she wouldn't even let the doctors keep her for observation. She's already back out in the park helping process the pit."

Max smiled. "She does love that park. Any sign of Kyle?"

Sayer nodded, mouth full. After swallowing she said, "The divers already found Kyle's body trapped at the end of one of the tunnels."

Max grunted a sound of approval and they all sat quietly contemplating Kyle's demise.

"Oh, hey, Alice Beaumont's doctor, or Cricket Nelson's doctor . . . whatever you want to call her . . . says she's going to recover fully," Sayer said gently.

Max let out a long breath of relief. "I think she's Alice Beaumont now."

"I think so too," Dana agreed. "Oh, I just heard this morning that the lab used the photos you found of those hikers to positively identify all six skeletons. Sounds like they each were hiking the trail solo and just disappeared. At least now we got their families some closure." She looked thoughtful. "So, two children raised by a serial killer. One went on to become a forensic psychologist studying psychopaths, and the other went on to become a killer in his own right."

"You think they'll charge Beaumont with everything she did?" Max asked. "Killing her own mom. Shooting at Kyle and kidnapping Sam. And what about Jillian Watts? She did beat two women to death."

"I would hope that no prosecutor would want to touch either of those cases."

"Rightfully so," Dana said. "The abuses they suffered . . ."

"You think Kyle really believed all that stuff about everyone hiding a monster inside them?" Ezra asked.

Sayer thought about Kyle's last words to her in the mine. "Yeah, even at the very end he believed it. I mean, he saw his own mother killing those people."

"And that's what he was doing, right? He wanted to watch Jillian and Hannah kill someone?" Ezra asked.

"Yeah. He must have gotten a thrill watching his mother kill those people when he was a kid. Over time, that became a compulsion. Something he hungered for. He was trying to re-create that moment, watching a mother as she killed another person to protect her child."

The room fell silent.

"Jillian Watts woke up from her coma. Her doctors are hopeful," Sayer said, changing the topic. She was done thinking about the Nelsons for a while.

"That's great news," Max said. "I celebrate with another taco!" He grabbed one and took a huge bite.

"Hannah and Sam are doing great," Sayer added.

"Physically, at least," Ezra said.

"Yeah, physically," Sayer agreed. Just like the Wattses, Hannah and Sam had a lot of therapy ahead.

"But we did it," Max said, looking down at his arm. "We got everyone home alive."

"We did," Sayer said softly.

"Huzzah," Dana said, reaching for the last taco.

Ezra playfully swatted her hand away as Max swooped in and stole it from them both.

They laughed, and Sayer watched with a smile on her face but also with a heavy heart. She trusted and even loved these people. Despite the fact that her job was safe for now, being close to her was still career suicide, and Sayer did not want to bring these people down with her.

With that thought, she patted Kona with finality.

"Sorry to break up the party, but I have to get going. One of my subjects had a brain scan this morning and the results should be ready soon."

"This from the NSA guy who sent out the video?" Ezra asked.

"Yeah," Sayer said. "As you can imagine, I'd like to get his results as soon as possible."

With that excuse, she said a quick goodbye and was about to stand up when Max gently touched her arm.

"Hey, Sayer?"

She paused.

"You know none of us give a damn about politics."

"What do you mean?"

"You're not exactly a subtle-emotion ninja." Max smiled. "We can tell that you're worried about the fallout from that news video. The video might've been engineered to save your job, but Ezra, Dana, and I know that it showed everyone the real you. Don't stay away from us on our behalf. You're one hell of an FBI agent and we've got your back no matter what's happening on Capitol Hill."

Sayer felt sideswiped by emotion. She looked over at Ezra and Dana, who were both nodding.

Her throat closed with a rush of feeling she couldn't identify—gratitude, relief, a closeness to her friends that she couldn't describe. All emotions she wasn't entirely sure how to handle.

She briskly stood, clearing her throat to ward off the tears that threatened to fall.

"Well, thanks, guys," she said gruffly. "I'll see you soon, then." She fled the room. As she hurried away, her flustered emotions settled down and Sayer realized that what she was feeling was actually happiness.

Her phone buzzed as she made her way through the hospital waiting room and she answered it with a smile, expecting it to be Nana and Adi.

"Agent Altair," she said almost cheerfully.

"Ah, Sayer . . ." Subject 037's voice shattered the easy warmth in her chest.

She stopped walking, frozen by the glee in his voice.

"Turn on the TV. Looks like everything is about to change. Just know I'll also have your back no matter what." He laughed and hung up.

With his words echoing Max's, Sayer hurried over to the television in the empty waiting room and snapped it on.

Assistant Director Holt's face appeared. She looked solemn, gray hair like a battle helmet as she stood on a low dais in front of a cluster of microphones.

"After over thirty years at the FBI, I've concluded that it's time for me to step down as assistant director." Holt tried to smile, but Sayer could see the anger in her expression.

"I'm stepping down so that I can spend more time with my family and to pursue a new career outside of the FBI." Holt paused, clearly struggling to maintain her blank smile. "I look forward to watching Quantico and the hardworking agents of the FBI continue to protect and serve this great nation. Thank you." Holt abruptly stepped away from the camera, leaving Sayer feeling sick. Jake's letter told her to trust no one but Holt, and now Holt was gone.

Sayer thought about her team laughing together back in the hospital room. She thought about her family eagerly awaiting her arrival at home. She thought about Jake's warning and how much she still had to learn about his death. Subject 037 was right: everything was about to change. And for the first time in a long while, Sayer felt like she had something to lose.